S0-AGF-650

JUGGERNAUT

BY HEINRICH MULLER

ZEBRA BOOKS
KENSINGTON PUBLISHING CORP.

ZEBRA BOOKS

are published by

KENSINGTON PUBLISHING CORP.
475 Park Avenue South
New York, N.Y. 10016

Printed in the United States of America

Dedication

This book is dedicated to four Kameraden who returned from the savage fire storm of the eastern front. Youth lost in the mind-numbing hell of total war.

Frederick Schmidt .... Pak
Willi Debrueker .... Panzer Manner
Richard Oberquell .... Rollbahn Supply
Willi Klinge .... Grenadier

And to the memory of Pyotr Nikolayevich Krasnov, commander of a Cossack unit, and his fellow Cossacks who fought against the might of Stalin, for a free motherland.

Frost paints the landscape with a cruel, heavy hand. Cold knifes like a crushing vice of steel. Dreaded Russian long night. Curse of the shivering Landser. Temperature has fallen dramatically. Stout pine trees sigh and crack. From deep within the very bowels of Mother Russia, age-old demons seem to rise up chuckling, muttering upon the harsh biting wind. Metal snaps with ease. Men and youth slip into oblivion, protesting cries mocking in the darkness. Death haunts with its insane crackling mantle of frost, skipping, dancing in the trenches, kissing the many limbs of frozen black.

Horror, dear child. As none you would imagine. You would kill for the warmth and glow of a fire. Kill and kill again. Do not judge me in your age of plenty. Unless you have known the wrath of mighty Mother Russia. A youth coming of age in the dreaded Russian long night.

And to Margreta Klima, my lifelong companion.

Chapter 1
Nyet Millosti

"Nein. Nein. Helf mir."

Four small laughing Mongolians had caught the wounded Grenadier. Scuttle away with a badly shattered knee cap. The pitiful chase is over quickly. Mocking and taunting him, they twist his arms up behind his back. Viciously pull at his hair, exposing his throat. One stands above him playing with a curved dagger, grinning sheepishly.

"Nein. Hilfe Kameraden."

Eyes that thought they had seen the worst of the brutal fighting on the savage Eastern Front turn away. They were there at the bloody slaughter of Kiev. The living hell that was Konotop. Weary, utterly exhausted, facing countless fresh onslaughts. Line upon line of shouting Siberian hordes. Isolated islands of grey green, against the swirling, overwhelming, charging mass of brown and khaki. That was war in the East. These vile atrocities. Degrading daily torture. It is too much for even the most battle-hardened veterans.

"Germanski kaputt. Kaputt. Kaputt."

Each word brings another slash at the throat. Again and again. Blood-chilling screams. Sobbing. A low animalistic whimpering. Giggling dementedly the yellow slant-eyed face dances about, smearing itself

7

in the torrent of youthful blood. A death ritual from bygone times. Vengeance from the dry wastes of Kazakstan.

For Fuehrer, Folk and Fatherland.

"I swear to you, Adolf Hitler, as Fuehrer and Reich Chancellor, loyalty and bravery, I vow to you, and those you have named to command me, obedience unto death. So help me *Gott*."

With banners flying, fine words at a marching-out parade. But on the Eastern Front. The grim reality. Mutilation. Genocide. Death to one's *Kameraden*. Many times it would strike without glory.

Sieg Heil. Heil Hitler. Blond youth your life is over. Prepare to die like a hero.

Ten youthful-looking riflemen of S.S. Das Reich are drawn up in a line. Their helmets with the dashing S.S. runes are lying flattened in the snow. No more are they among the arrogant goose-stepping ranks of the master race. Laughing, jostling one another, sneering at the peoples of a defeated race. Dirt. Subhumans. Slavic filth, that in Kiev, the capital of the Ukraine, they had knocked aside and trampled underfoot. Kiev, where in the sunshine of late September 1941 they had walked arm in arm with Blitzmadels, young conquerers spitting at passers-by.

Now they were prisoners of the Russian Red Army. Once-proud uniforms ripped and torn to shreds. They had the clear-cut eyes of youth. Now that defiant flame had been smothered. Faces were battered, blotched and bruised, with running and congealed blood. Cossacks from across the Don had toyed with them upon capture, before moving off in double file behind the long columns of T.34s pushing on towards Orel.

Another troop of Cossacks had taken them over,

weeding them out from the shuffling ranks of Wehrmacht prisoners at sabre point. Their number had been twelve, two had been cut down by sabres under the pretense of trying to escape. One still lay moaning in the bloodied snow. His right leg twitched. His hands pawing at the icy slush. A T.34 changed course. A cry of *"Urah Stalin,"* coming from the turret. The hands pounded the snow in a futile gesture as the thrashing tracks swallowed him. The helmet spun before them in a flurry of snow. It came to a stop. The dead eyes bulging wide with terror, staring accusingly.

"Germanski kaputt!" A burly Cossack kicked at the gruesome remains, his coloured robe swirling about his knees.

"Yob tvoymat," Sergi Vlasava spat at the S.S. riflemen, cursing and cracking his long cruel Nagayka whip.

Germanskis. Field-grey-uniformed Waffen S.S. Monsters of the Fascist legions. Devil serpents who gave no quarter. His drunken hate-filled eyes blazed at the frightened youthful figures. Death the quick death. Explosive bullet to the brain. Such an end would be too merciful for them. Partisan. He had fought with the People's Militia in the deep forests. Much he had seen. Horror. Terror. Whole villages that were now no more. Rubble, scorched earth, it was all that was left upon the face of Little Mother Russia. The new age had dawned. No longer would the Cossacks drive the herds to new grazing lands over the steppes. Now they were all consumed in the Motherland war.

Unteroffizier Schmidt glanced around at the remains of his platoon. Muller had a few facial cuts, but he was otherwise intact. Big blustering Schultz was already beginning to curse and swear. Maybe his concussion was wearing off. Heyer, already he was talking of trying to escape from the Ivans. Hansen, the jokes had not begun to pour out, but he looked all right. Steggeman, he was more quiet than usual, but once he got over the traumatic effect of being taken prisoner, he would come around. The Bado-wicker Boys, Griecebeck, Suckau and Fricke, farm boys, they were bearing up remarkably well. That only left Klima. The *Auslander,* the *Ami* from Seattle. He had barely returned to the platoon from hospital in Warsaw. Given a few more days the concussion would wear off.

The retreat from the village of Livny had been sheer hell. Bombarded by their own heavy Wehrmacht artillery. A higher command effort at trying to plug the gap. The hordes of Siberians proved unstoppable. The first ranging shells had fallen among the Grenadiers. Many lost their lives. Those that did remain were captured, suffering badly from concussion.

Many others died of their wounds along the way.

"Ich hatte einen Kameraden.

Einen besseren gab es nicht.

Er lag vor meinen Fuessen.

Als waeres ein Stuek von mir."

The choking words rose from a German burial party.

"Once I had a comrade.

You could not have a better one.

He lay in front of me.

As though he were part of me."

Harsh command words in Russian. Rifle butts. Cossacks' whips drove the burial party back into the throng of Wehrmacht prisoners.

Sergi Vlasava swayed over to the S.S. riflemen.

"Mein lieber Gott. They're for the chopping block," whispered Heyer. His ears still rang with the

10

after effects of concussion.

"Ivan spares none of the S.S. shits." Schultz shook his head. He was still seeing double, his vision frayed and blurred.

"Donna wetter. Here it comes," Muller nudged Schmidt.

Livid, the blood drained from his face, Sergi Vlasava prodded one of the riflemen with his Nagayka.

"Chort Germanski. Yob tvoymat." His lips curled with hatred.

"Nein." The teenager's eyes went wide with fear, his hands going protectively to his face.

The savage stunning blow sent him reeling in the snow.

"Peasants of village killed. Vlasava family. No more village. No more my people."

He stomped the cringing rifleman with his high boots. Kicked viciously at the face. The snow turned red with blood.

"No get Sergi, he live." He took a gulp at his vodka bottle.

Burping aloud as the vodka slurped down his beard. He watched as the eighteen-year-old was helped to his feet by two other riflemen.

"You die." He held the vodka bottle out to the assembled throng of prisoners, his head going back in a long drunken laugh.

Suddenly his expression changed. His eyes mere narrow slits.

"Slow like people of Kolkhos. Village of steppe where ancestors born. Little people crying for *papushka* and *mamushka*." He choked upon the broken German words, tears pouring down his face.

"No more village." The bottle went to his mouth.

"Steppe quiet. No song. No more spring dance. No children—gather yellow flower of steppe. Fire.

Black earth. My village dead.''

The long cruel-looking Nagayka was curled in the snow at his feet. With a flick of his right wrist it hurtled through the air, curling about the hated S.S. faces. They groveled at his feet. Cringing, they tried to crawl away. It drew blood. Maddened fear-crazed howling rose from them. Still the whip sought them out. When his arm grew tired, he walked among them, sobbing, kicking at their bloodied bodies.

With three other partisans he had hidden, watching from the shadows of the forest. They had no ammunition left after an all-out attack on the Rollbahn. The carefully laid ambush upon the Wehrmacht supply trucks had gone wrong. As soon as the partisans opened fire, tracked armored troop-carrying vehicles had wheeled away from the convoy. Into the woods they roared, double-mounted spandaus taking a devastating toll. Only three partisans survived from the group of over sixty. Captured and wounded comrades were given typical S.S. treatment. A bullet behind the right ear. Their bodies left upon the track. A grim reminder for others.

The reprisal action quickly followed the chase. The village was surrounded at first light. Helpless they could only watch in horror. The peasants were driven from the warmth of their *isbas*, into the grey mists of a chilly dawn. Bent old men. Young and old women. The children, some no more than bundles in their weeping mothers' arms.

His family. The Vlasavas. His wife and three children. Grandfather Rozhko and his Babushka. His comrades had to hold him down. Gag him.

Beyond the village, in the few acres set aside for private peasant cultivation, two large Waffen S.S. trucks came to a skidding halt. The tarpaulins on the trucks parted. Machine gunners hunched over their

12

spandaus set about their deadly work.

Babushka was the first to fall. Rozhko by her side. Always smiling Sabina. The children. Bewildered, terror-stricken. Running. They went down in the second hail of echoing fire.

Two old men and a young boy ran at the back of the trucks. Bloodied hands clawed at the S.S. jackboots. Grinning troopers knocked them down, pulling them away. Struggling, screaming cries of vengeance, they were saved until the very last. Their turn finally came. An officer shot them each in the stomach. Still they cursed and swore vengeance. Their pleas to Little Mother Russia echoing out shrilly over the lonely steppes.

From yawns of slumber to the field of mass murder, it was all over within the half-hour. Only several village cats were seen to slink away, hair standing on end, escaping from the Germanski carnage.

Ten wiry Asiatic soldiers marched up, under the watchful eyes of Russian lieuteant Anatoli Tsarurov.

"Firing squad," murmured Hansen.

"Shoot them down in cold blood," someone else gasped.

"The Lord's day of reckoning. That's what it is. The grim reapers have arrived," whispered Heyer.

"No trial. Just shot out of hand." Klima could not believe his own eyes.

Lieuteant Anatoli Tsarurov raised his arms turning to the Wehrmacht prisoners.

"We kill S.S. Each S.S. captured will die. In the Motherland all sick animals are shot. S.S. are men of devil. Kill children. For them life is finished."

He signalled towards the Asiatic soldiers. One after the other, their long bayonets fixed, they came to the present position. They were muttering and nodding to one another, openly talking excitedly in their ranks.

13

Anatoli Tsarurov was watching Sergi Vlasava. All that remained for him was the war, and the vengeance that he could wreak upon the Germanski. Everything else he had lost. Tormented by that dreadful dawn upon the steppes. He thought of his own Siberian village, Kultuk, nestling upon the western shores of beautiful Lake Baikal. The tales of the old fishermen. Yes, he was happy that his own village was very far from the front. One day he would return.

Commissar Isaak Tychuk had reminded his unit before the battle of Ilya Ehrenburg's famous speech.

"Kill. Kill. Kill. It is all the Germanski nation understands. Siberian bayonets to the fore. Forward. Cut the vipers down. None shall live. Cover the steppes with their blood. Let none of the invaders leave our land alive."

An Asiatic soldier was tugging at his overcoat.

"*Nyet millosti*. No mercy."

"*Nyet.*"

He raised his right arm. All eyes were upon him. Then he dropped it.

"Eee—hh."

Ten gleaming bayonets lunged forward as one. The S.S. riflemen screamed, falling groaning into the snow. Rifles rose again and again, stabbing and bludgeoning the life out of them. The cries of agony went on for five minutes. Gibbering amongst themselves the Asiatics gathered about the torn stomach of a young rifleman who was crying the loudest. Calling for his sister Hilda in far-off Hanover. His mother, the blood bubbling and frothing about his mouth. One after the other the long bayonets fall. Stomach. Shoulder. Thigh. Face. The cries are stifled. Only the twitching is left, beating out their tattoos of death, upon the ever widening pool of blood in the snow.

Another column of prisoners is being herded back from the front. Three black-uniformed panzer men from an elite regiment are dragged and prodded out from the ranks.

"Germanski S.S." shouts the drunken Sergi Vlasava.

"Nein. Nein," Heyer breaks from the ranks shouting in Russian.

"Panzer men. Like your T.34 crews."

A pounding from rifle butts sends him sprawling.

"S.S. S.S." chorus the Asiatics.

"Nyet millosti," they look at Anatoli Tsarurov, shaking their rifles.

"Nyet millosti," he shakes his fist.

Ten rifles crack. The panzer men pitch backwards into the snow. Shot at point-blank range their faces disintegrate. Blood, brains, bone fragments spit out over the horrified Wehrmacht prisoners. The day of Russian revenge had arrived.

Shock. Terror. Unspeakable horror. There are those who go insane. Raving mad. Gibbering idiots within the space of hours. Bestial barbarity, it is beyond comprehension. Cossacks strutting amongst the ranks. Drawn sabres still dripping blood. Cackling cries of triumph. Laughter that will haunt for years. Asiatics. Mongolians, smiling before they put yet another man or boy to death. Sworn vengeance to the victor. A devil's orgy of flowing blood. Kiev, Kremenchug, Gluchov, Kromy and Karachev. Places. Towns and villages. A collection of huts. Lice-ridden. The spitting rage and fury of battle. Where brothers, fathers and sons died. Comrades. Last words lost. Billowing choking palls of smoke. Words drowned by the staccato bursts of nearby Maxim machine gun fire.

Home villages. No more would they gather in the

pleasant warmth of the dying summer sun. Smoking, sipping vodka, telling of the days when Little Mother Russia shuddered. When she was pillaged and plundered by the Germanski legions. Bones littering the endless rolling steppes, bleaching white. The ploughing of the sunflower fields would help to rekindle those harsh memories in the years to come.

A new victim is pounced upon. Bewilderment etches at the face. Not fear of the unknown. The dread of what is now commonplace. Pitiful screams. A lone wailing. Long drawn out. Gut-curdling, turning the mouth dry. Mockingly they chant in unison. *Eins. Zwei. Drei*. The blood-reddened sabre falls. Sickening crunch of sharpened steel against flesh. Two older men sag, fainting. The grisly head rolls away. Nauseating. The throng of Wehrmacht prisoners gasp and reel with horror. That December day is one no man or boy will ever forget.

Eyes downcast. Straight ahead. To catch the drunken eyes of a vodka-soaked Cossack, retaliation is instant. No look of defiance is tolerated. Death. Decapitation. Disembowelment. No one is spared.

There is stumbling in the ranks. Confusion. Like a living beast the throng sways. There is no possible escape. Another selection. A cowering victim marked for death. Many Cossack eyes are upon him. He cannot scuttle free. No longer do the legs of *Kameraden* move aside. That gnarled weather-beaten hand from the East lunges for the tunic collar.

"Stoi."

Peals of drunken Russian laughter ring out.

"Heinie. Fritz."

More laughter. Taunting. The vodka bottle passes between them.

"Du komm," almost reassuringly.

"Germanski komm. Komm."

They pat him on the back.

"Nein. Nein. I'm not S.S."

The victim tries to struggle free.

"Kameraden. Hilfe."

Many strong hands are clutching at him. Bearded faces leering down. Now their smiles have gone. Only raw hatred shows. Sneers freeze on the grimacing brown faces.

He had stood so tall and resplendent in his Grenadier's uniform. A proud member of the rifle battalions attached to the panzer units. Walking the crowded Am-Sande on Saturday night, the main thoroughfare of Luneburg. Yes, proud. Like any young soldier the world over looking for the company of women. The Honky Tonk, that dive off the road near the church. What times were had there. The Rosencrug, where hold Herman would always chalk up a few beers on the slate. And always in the East the mighty Blitzkrieg was forging ahead.

Off to the river banks of the Illmenau. Where you would make love on the grassy banks to the catcalls of jealous railwaymen busily shunting the vast munition trains. Or Kur-park where the old women clicked their tongues as you came walking out of the bushes. Staggering back to the *Kaserne* before curfew. The penetrating eyes of the guard Feldwebel. Bull-necked, every inch the base bully. Stiff, pompous, a sentinel of the glorious Third Reich. A Reich the Fuehrer had predicted would last a thousand years.

"Los. Still gestanden."

His highly polished jackboots twinkle under the harsh glare of the *Kaserne* lamplight.

"Hero with the *Frauleins.* Been to the *Stadt,* hey."

The set face is contorted with deep disgust. For Feldwebel there is only the front. The constant need for replacements. Eight weeks to turn young boys into steel-hardened men.

"Had some?" He smiles cruelly.

"Tante Anna's was it? Under age." The face tightens going stern.

"Dipped your weapon. Think you are a Grenadier. Pockets undone. Juno in your hand. *Ja,* I can see it. Think I'm blind. Disgrace to the uniform of the Third Reich."

Hands clasped firmly behind his back he circles the offender.

"As for punishment drill. Round the square in double-quick time. *Ab-marsch. Marsch. Marsch.*"

The feet pound the hard tarmac. Healed blisters reopen.

That face. Annelise. *Donna wetter,* she is so beautiful. Annelise from the Alt-Stadt. My Annelise. How can one ever forget. Long flowing dark hair. Haunting laughing eyes of a tormenting gypsy. Love. A true love. Not purely sexual. Not a passing *Soldaten* affair. He treasured every moment with her.

"*Los. Schnell.* The *Ost* Front is waiting for you, *Kameraden.*"

Sweat sticks the tunic to one's back. Surges between the shoulder blades. Trickles with an itch between the buttocks. One fast tour of the vast tree-lined square. Peering eyes from the huge barrack blocks. Catcalls. Hacking laughter. The often repeated nightly ritual. Here they are trained for the Eastern Front, or drop dead of complete exhaustion in their tracks. If you were a teenager in uniform, there was no way back. All roads led to the front.

The Feldwebel is waiting under the light. He has

turned out the guard. They stand briskly at attention, mausers at their sides.

"Out of breath, Grenadier."

Is it a hint of sympathy. Surely not.

"*J-jawohl,* Herr Feldwebel."

Crabs. Shit, and jumping lice. The man was admitting defeat. A member of the Wehrmacht in the uniform of the Fuehrer.

"Round you go again you pimp's arsehole. No stamina. My platoon can outdistance a Panzer mark 2 at full throttle. A fit Grenadier can dip his wick, and still run five miles in record time. *Los. Los. Marsch.* Soon you will be a comrade of the Eastern Front. Die a hero's death for Fuehrer, Folk and Fatherland. But you must be fit, no slacking. What more could a Grenadier ask for."

"*Davay. Davay.*"

"*Chort, Germanski.*"

A hideous laugh. Foul vodka-smelling spittle hangs in the Cossack's beard. A prod of the sabre draws blood from the buttocks. A headlong sprawl into the snow and slush. High boots. Two pairs of leather. One of dull felt. A stunning sabre blow glances off the helmet. Lights dance, reeling before his eyes.

The leather boots kick at the stomach. Spittle cascades over him as another boot smashes his shoulder and head.

Please God, let it be over quick. Again the boots find their targets, this time to the groin and face. Blood runs into his mouth. He can feel the eyes swelling.

Annelise. Visualize her. It is all there is. Think of her. The hair so dark and vibrant. Face, the fragility and beauty of everlasting exquisite Dresden china. No wandering, giggling gypsy of the Heide could

19

compare. To be married on the first leave from the front. The baby. Her stomach held the love child. Such a lovely serene mother. The firm breasts were starting to swell. Love. The joy of lovemaking. Breathless dream from the *Arabian Nights*. Cold nights. Chill of winter. Her room smelling with fumes from the coal heater. Annelise. Smiling face of the Madonna. Awakening with a tempting smile. A juno. Talk. The future. Secure job at the abattoir. Good prospects Herr Meyer had promised. Once the violent drums of war had faded. Reach out. She is within grasp. Reach out. Touch the silken shining hair.

The sabre fell. An awesome crunch.

Lights. Blue. Green. Stabbing yellow. Artillery. Annelise. Cold. Damp. Darkness. Vomit.

The head spun away. The Cossacks standing nearby jumped back in alarm. The face was set in a soft smile.

"S.S. S.S.," chortled the Asiatics.

They frolic in the snow kicking the gruesome remains like a football.

"Understand, Germanski. *Tovaritch*. Ancestors talk to Sergi in sleep. Mother Russia must be avenged. Our little brothers must not be forgotten."

Sergi Vlasava came close to falling over. Heyer held him. He turned to one side and was sick.

A day later it was Sergi Vlasava who commanded the *scheissehaus* detail. Klima had stood watching the little Siberians running into the *stolovaya,* the large Kolkhos barn. Very few came out. The walls echoed with drunken cries of laughter. Frequent clapping of hands. The tortured squeals of women. Women in agonizing pain. German women.

"Filthy barstards."

"Field brothel," chided Schultz.

"Got five marks. I'll apply for membership. Shit, it's exclusive to the Ivans."

"Spoils of war," mocked Heyer.

"We can't do fuck all about it."

"Donna wetter. The swines."

"Back to the road," ordered Schmidt.

"You want to finish the war at the edge of the Rollbahn. Your throat cut."

Lieutenant Anatoli Tsarurov noticed the commotion. Unshouldering his submachine gun, he strode over.

"You like see Germanski women serve victorious Red Army."

Schmidt nodded to them.

"Los. Back to the road. *Schnell."*

"Stoi."

The submachine gun clicked, stopping them in icy silence.

No race on earth are like those of the Slavic nations. In orgies of drunkeness. The heavy intoxicating atmosphere of victory. Revenge. Cruel, wicked. Barbarity knows no bounds.

"Germanski, *komm."*

The barrel of the submachine gun was rammed hard against Klima's ribs.

Nicht ich. Nicht ich. Over and over again those words had formed in his mind, as it had with countless others. Now it was too late. The old values. Traditions of old Europe. Cast-iron discipline of the Wehrmacht. It was like walking a tightrope. A nightmare without end. Hate. Brutality. Acts of wanton destruction. They were everyday occurrences. Man was little more than an animal. No, that was far too simple. On the Eastern Front he was a devilish monster.

He was torn between two societies. Germany as his

21

place of birth. And America where his parents had taken him as a youngster. A man lost floundering in a war that he could not understand.

Seattle was very far away. A light beckoning from another world. The aircraft factory where he used to work. Elk Valley, a few hours ride by truck from Cranbrook, B.C., Canada. Where he used to hunt deer as a youth. He wondered if he would ever see the snow-clad Rockies again.

Lieutenant Anatoli Tsarurov pushed him into the *stolovaya*. Two Siberians tied him to a main supporting beam.

"For Kiev, Germanski. Where streets ran red with blood of our women. You watch, Herr *soldat*. You watch."

Slowly his eyes grew accustomed to the light thrown by the spluttering oil lanterns.

Six very young *Blitzmadels* were pegged out upon the dirt floor, their arms and legs wide. Their torn uniforms were tossed to one side, nothing but a pile of useless discarded rags. Naked and sobbing hysterically they twisted from side to side. A Siberian ranted at them. Seconds later he reappeared driving the pegs deeper into the dirt floor.

Margreta Stein had been used by thirty Siberian riflemen. They had come near to choking her, as they poured the vodka into her throat. Vile. Sexual practices that she had never associated with man. Never again would she delight in the large shopping areas of Cologne or Hamburg. Or go to Berlin with her sister-in-law gaping in wonder at the high-fashion dress shops. No, this was to be her end. The filthy dirt floor of a *stolovaya,* in the wild steppes of Russia. When she sobbed they had complained that she was too much used. Cossacks had urinated upon her and laughed.

They told her to fight. The act of creation was to be enjoyed. Like the breaking of a much spirited horse. Only now the fight had gone. Germanski woman. Was she so different from the plucky Cossack pony. No fight, the ride was too tame. For a man. A Cossack. Such a man he needed the fight. The struggle to take what was rightfully his. Cossacks had always fought against the elements. Mother Russia was hard. Fight was needed to survive upon the steppes. It was a part of life. A pony with no spirit was not worth owning.

Klima watched as other Siberians came through the door in droves. They would stand, just looking. Then the excited scramble began. Snowcapes were thrown off. Weapons left lying in the dirt. Trousers hanging below their knees they set upon them. Pure white Germanski flesh. Firm breasts. Slim silken thighs. To them they were like goddesses and they meant to have their fill.

Teeth sank into naked breasts. Nipples disappeared in a slur of blood. Some cut at the ropes, turning them over. As the *Blitzmadels* screamed and pommelled the floor with their fists, they assailed them from the buttocks. Teeth gnashing, they slobbered at their necks.

Legs still anchored to pegs, the *Blitzmadels* thrashed about. Tearing at their bonds, fingernails bleeding. When it seemed over, the giggling hulk moving away from them. A respite. The door would burst open letting in the chill winter wind.

Other vodka-smelling Siberians bore down upon them. The terrifying ordeal started all over again.

Heyer pulled with all his force against the wire tying him to the beam. Kicked out at a Siberian who stood before him, his vodka bottle raised to his lips.

"*Du Ruski dreck kerl*. Russian filthy bum."

His words brought a chorus of laughter from those eagerly waiting their turns.

A swarthy Siberian grinned sheepishly, straightening up. His right bloodied hand going to his trousers buttons. He motioned towards Klima, nodding at Anatoli Tsarurov.

"*Nyet millosti.*" He wiped the blood from his face with the back of his sleeve.

"*Nyet millosti, tovaritch.*"

"*Da.*"

They beat Klima senseless. His bruised body sagged hanging by the wire on the beam. He was vaguely aware of the *Blitzmadels'* bodies being dragged before his eyes. The door opening, the howling wind blowing in a flurry of snow. The frail white bodies being thrown outside into the snow. Many eyes had been gouged out. Heads battered by rifle butts. The last two. The heads hung on a few sinews of flesh. Their throats had been cut from ear to ear.

Chapter 2
RUSSIAN REVENGE

The whole vast, varied complex of the mighty Red Army passed before their eyes. The second surging mass of Russian troops. Many came on foot trudging down the road in disorderly fashion. So different from the earlier marching advancing columns of Wehrmacht troops.

"I remember it as clear as the snot upon me face," Hansen muttered.

"Adolf it was. Eating a carrot he was. On account of his being a vegetarian. He'd just told Uncle Himmler off for feeding his dog Blondie with a fat black sausage from the Rhine. Heinie, he says, Ivan's on his last legs. One more push for Moscow and it's all over."

"A last push. Another effort. Runts. We freeze our bollocks off before Moscow. And all he can do is scratch his arse." Schultz spat into the snow.

Hansen continued.

"Heinie, he says. The Germanic master race must have pure thoughts. Nothing like a bit of starvation. Make my Wehrmacht fast before Moscow. A fast clears the mind. No bread. No meat. No food. Coffee, every morning at eleven o'clock. They can break the fast when Moscow is taken. After the grand victory parade."

Schultz swung around facing Hansen.

"Is that what he said?"

"It was in *Ost Front*."

"You making fun of me, little friend?"

"*Nein*. Winter clothes, he said. Don't issue them before Moscow. Don't I stand out on the steps of the Reich Chancellery, every morning, doing my physical jerks, in me vest and pants. Waving to the char women going to work scrubbing the offices. If I can take a bit of cold. Bit of the frost about the balls. So can my gallant Wehrmacht."

"Where did you read that?"

"Oh I didn't read that. My Tante Lottie buys carrots for him on the Hamburg black market, she told me."

"Time I kicked your arse again, little friend."

Before he could catch Hansen he had fallen back in the ranks behind Muller and Schmidt.

Other Russians came down the Rollbahn in lorries and trucks, transport of every description. Stern-faced Cossacks in double file. On seeing the German P.O.W.s they drew their sabres, shouting "Urah Stalin!" Even low troikas on wooden and steel runners. Armed troops from every corner of Russia. Warriors from the farthest most desolate regions of Asia Minor, looking like a massive reincarnation of the savage hordes of Genghis Khan. A group of tartars trotted by, bloodied German heads dangling from their waist bands.

"Heathens. Liquidate them. Our panzers will soon roll east in a gigantic counteroffensive. The Wehrmacht will round the slant-eyed *Untermensch* up by the thousands. The Fuehrer is always right. Sheenies. Subhuman filth. We should wipe them from the face of the earth."

At first no one took any notice of the Nazi Obergefreiter. He ranted and raved. Then not to be outdone he broke into a popular S.S. marching song.

"Jewish blood shall flow."

The words clear and distinct in spite of the Russian procession on the Rollbahn.

26

"*Donna wetter.* Your sort make me sick," gasped Muller in disgust. "Have you not seen enough brutality? Still you ache for more. You snivelling Hitlerite bastard."

"Report. Report," the Obergefreiter turned full of hissing fury.

"We all supported Hitler in the thirties, even you. Everyone was for him. Our blessed Fuehrer and National Socialist party dragged us out of the thirties. Deutschland became the strongest country in the world. When the Wehrmacht marches nations tremble. After the big push starts. When we are rescued I'll have you on report. We'll see what you have to say then. You ungrateful shit. Malicious gossip. Willfully spreading a defeatist attitude. I'll see you in front of a head hunters' firing squad. Tell me, you Zionist pig. Are you sure you are not half-Jewish? Moscow will fall, you mark my words. Guderian's panzers will be at the walls of the Kremlin."

"*Aschloch. Dumkopf.* We burnt the panzers," quipped Steggeman.

"Where will we get the panzers for your Kremlin push? No petrol. Iced-up engines. We burnt them by the hundreds."

"Prize party cunt. He had his head down so much he didn't see a thing. Hansen, my little friend. Take a note from uncle Schultzy. This prize turkey goes to the top of my list. I'll deal with him with pleasure, once the concussion wears off."

Schultz began to ball his huge gloved fists, smashing his right fist into his open left hand. Hopping from one leg to the other he began doing his famous victory dance.

"Take his crap. We're all bound for the wastes of Siberia. Kick his balls in, Schultzy. Make a tobacco pouch out of his bag. It's party disciples like him that got us into this mess. *Lebensraum*. Breathing space for Greater Germany. I would sooner have stayed at home.''

Heyer spat at the Obergefreiter, catching him in the face. He waved his arms like an Italian opera singer.

''I'll have your name and number. You are still a serving member of the glorious Wehrmacht. You took the oath. It's sacred, you know that. National Socialist doctrine clearly states . . .''

''Balls to your party doctrine. All politicians should be castrated at birth. Like religion they promise everything in the hereafter. There is a need to tighten our belts. We've heard all the crap before.''

''Hitler or Himmler they don't give a damn.''

''He thinks more of his lice-ridden dog Blondie than he does of us.''

''He's in Berlin snug and warm, tossing himself off. The vegetarian twit.''

''You tell him Hansen.''

''Does it by numbers, he does. To the tune of *Deutschland, Deutschland Über Alles*. Right in front of a statue of the Kaiser. Maid caught him at it one day. She told him make him go blind, it would. Funny you know. He'd noticed a bit of a twitch at the end of his moustache. He put it down to his piles. Not having had a bore job for over nine months. Now this Tante Augustine, that was the char lady's name. Being very patriotic, like our friend here. She made a suggestion, seeing as it was in the interest of National Socialism. She finished picking her nose. And dabbed on a bit of fresh powder. I mean Adolf's like royalty, see. And I mean the old Kaiser was staring down at her as well. She gives her knickers a hitch. The elastic was from Japan, and it was Heinrich Himmler who told her the right leg needed a new string. On account of she kept losing the black market carrots—when she ran across

28

the ballroom. I mean there was Adolf giving out decorations to some S.S. And she was dropping them in gobs all over the place. Well . . ."

"*Schweinhund!*"

If the Obergefreiter had a machine gun he would have pressed the trigger. Erasing forever the leering smiles upon their faces.

"I forbid you to talk in this manner about our illustrious Fuehrer. Our leader. From the teeming millions of unemployed. The uncertainties that we faced in the thirties. We have become united. We will conquer the world."

"*Sei ruhig*. Shut up," barked Schmidt.

"You'll have the Ivans picking more victims."

Later the front of the column was winding its way into a spread-out *kolkhos*. The unmistakable aroma of burnt bacon wafted to them upon the wind. Their last hard-tack rations had long ago been shared out. The very smell of food can drive a man crazy after going days without it.

"Ruski propaganda could be right."

"Remember those leaflets. Food they said. All you can eat. Just throw your weapons away and walk over to us."

"Two rashers of bacon, just slightly burnt. Crisp as mother used to make it. It mustn't crumble. Just melt in your mouth. As many eggs as you can eat. Maybe plump Ruski women with long thigh boots serving it. Blouses bulging, nipples sticking out, all proud. It's the Ruski cold that does it. Some of them have nipples like ice cubes. Ukrainian lollies. Remember the first time."

A smile passed between Muller and Schmidt. Hansen was back in fine form. Back to normal.

"Ukrainian pieces. Nothing like them. In their twenties. Four months pregnant. Nicely swollen all over. Not fat mind you, but just nice. Go like rattle-snakes they does. Bare bums bobbing away. Fit to beat a jack rabbit. There was some that said they were Stalin's new secret weapon. Wear the Wehrmacht out before it reached Moscow. What do you say, Schultzy?''

''Shit being used to the finer things of life. You know I like them when they specialize. Take my couple in Kiev. I taught them tricks that would curl your hair. Pity they had to go to the ravine meat grinder. Tongues like moths around a *kaserne* lamp light. Of course Schultzy being an expert teacher. And what with the knocked-off Polish liquor being so cheap.''

A sinister column of black smoke was rising be-tween two *isba*s. It rose lazily drifting away over the thatched roofs. As they marched closer they heard the first terrifying screams. The sound had a dreadful familiarity about it. In the line. A turret hatch open, smoke belching out.

''Burnt bacon. The swine Tsarurov. He's burning them alive.''

The words passed quickly down the column.

They thought Russia had no more horror to offer. The front. Endless hours of fierce hand-to-hand fighting, with knives and entrenching tools. The first atrocities of Russian revenge when they were cap-tured. They had much to learn. In victory then, as now, the Russians have many forms of barbarity.

Lieutenant Anatoli Tsarurov was standing near the *isba* watching the spectacle. The blackened remains of two infantry Hauptmans were chained to iron posts. Laughing Mongolians were feeding the fire raging beneath them. Their uniforms had long since burnt away. The whites of their eyes were rolling. White teeth gleaming through swollen blistered lips. Flesh sizzled and spat at the fire. The aroma wafted to them once again. The mouths opened. Agonized choking screams came from low in their stomachs. The bodies seemed strangely shrunk. Red sinews showing through the burnt black at knees and elbows. Minute blue flames danced, seeming to rush at each new bursting aperture in the flesh.

Three younger men broke away. They could not stand the sight any longer. Waiting Russians knocked them to the ground with their rifle butts. Cocked automatic weapons were levelled at them. As the angry murmuring rose from the ranks, a sharp whistle blew. Asiatic soldiers ran from nearby *isba*s, rifles and long bayonets thrust out before them.

Anatoli Tsarurov was talking to Sergi Vlasava.

"The woods beyond Karachev. My brother Yuri was burnt alive there at the stake. Leader of partisans. Transferred from the Red Army. S.S. butchers killed him. Is it not fitting that I should take my revenge, little brother?"

"*Nyet millosti, tovaritch*. Death must come slow. Our steppes must hear. Mother Russia must hear their cries. Our land has known much suffering. Germanski he must be taught a lesson. None must leave our land alive." He kicked at the timbers the Mongols had collected.

"The fire devils are hungry. They have been waiting long for this day. May I feed them, *gospodin leytenant?*"

"*Da*, Sergi. Your need is as great as mine. Feed the flames."

"The Vlasavas. My little ones," he began to weep.

Anatoli Tsarurov passed him the vodka.

"Think only of revenge, my brave Sergi. Revenge. Revenge."

Two older Landser broke from the ranks, charging towards the fire.

A Mongol smiled, slowly raising his short submachine gun.

"*Nyet.*" Anatoli Tsarurov beckoned to them.

"*Nyet.* Tie them up. Do not kill. They must watch. I want them to remember for all time."

The two Landser were tied to the *isba* fence.

"*Marsch. Marsch.*"

Mounted Cossacks charged into the ranks, flaying left and right with their whips.

"B-bacon. I-I'll never eat it again."

A lieutenant was vomiting, retching. He staggered to the side of the road, his head lowered. He leaned against the *isba* wall, his body bucking.

"Inhuman swine. Monsters from the dark ages."

He missed his holding on the *isba* wall. Regained it. Then his whole body shook in convulsive jerks.

"*Mein Gott noch mal.*"

"*Heya. Heya. Davay.*"

They heard the squeak of leather harness. Pounding of hoofbeats. Slush and ice chips splattered over them.

"*Heya.*"

The lips parted in the bearded face. He roared with laughter. The pony reared on its hind legs. He checked the prancing with a flick of his heels. The sabre whirled high above his head.

"*Urah* Stalin."

The cry was taken up by other Cossacks.

"Stalin."

"Stalin."

Those nearby recoiled and gasped in horror.

The head skidded along the white *isba* wall. Blood gushed from the torn neck in a wild torrent. It ran down the wall in huge rivulets.

"*Heya. Heya.*"

He spurred his pony on, bending low in the saddle. The head came clear atop his sabre, blood running to the hilt. Eyes wide. Mouth fixed grotesquely. The tongue hung long below the chin, as though still frantically gasping for air.

"He . . . he was only being sick," whispered Steggeman.

"No one leaves the ranks," hissed Schmidt.

"I . . . I need to piss." Hansen felt faint, hands grabbed him.

"Do it in your trousers. That goes for all of you. They'll kill at the slightest excuse."

A padre. A Landser padre ran out of the ranks. He reached Anatoli Tsarurov before anyone could stop him. In fluent Russian he began to argue.

"This is a denial of all basic human rights, Lieutenant Tsarurov. Beastiality. Barbarous treatment. I demand to see your commissar."

"*Voina plenny*, Germanski man of God. You are a prisoner of war. You have no authority here," snapped Lieutenant Anatoli Tsarurov.

"Where were you when Russian villages were put to the torch? Our mothers and daughters raped. Did you complain then?"

The padre straightened up, pushing the searching hands of the Mongolians aside. But the deft fingers had found and taken his pocket watch. One of them held it to his ear. Showed the treasure to his comrades. They did a dance of glee. Other fingers were trying to pull his badges off.

"No one in the 45th Infantry Division committed atrocities. You have my word on that."

"Your word as a Prussian warmonger."

"I come from Hanover, Herr lieutenant."

Another Mongolian was fumbling at his tunic

pocket. His hand came clear clutching a silver cigarette case. A lighter with a crest upon it. He stuffed four cigarettes into his mouth, lighting them. Another Mongol made a lunge, grabbing his hat. He put it back to front upon his head and began to do a jig. The others clapped shouting encouragement.

A Mongol was tugging insistently at Sergi Vlasava's sleeve.

"*Tovaritch*. The little brothers want to play with the Germanski God man."

The padre made towards Anatoli Tsarurov.

"Lieutenant. You have not heard a word I've said."

Anatoli Tsarurov's thoughts were back in the forests of Karachev. Coming across the burnt remains of his brother Yuri. Shrunk. The size of a small child. Weeping peasant women had gathered about him. Yuri had not uttered one word. An S.S. Hauptsturmfuehrer had cut out his tongue, feeding it to the village dogs. Sliced his ears off. Then he lit the fire.

Two Mongolians were trying to pull the padre's boots off.

"No need. No need," they laughed in broken German.

"Besides being barbaric. Has the Red Army no discipline?"

He tried once more to push the grinning faces away.

"The little brothers, *tovaritch*," urged Sergi Vlasava.

"Take him away. All Germanskis shake head. No Nazi. Hate Hitler. Not know. There were the cries of our tortured people. Children on Germanski bayonets. Raping of our women. You look other way. Why did you go to war . . . Germanski God man?"

"I have always . . ."

Anatoli Tsarurov waved his arm.

"Give him to our little brothers the Mongolians."

Struggle as he might. The leering grinning faces closed about him. A dagger appeared from a waist band. With much laughing and snickering his trousers were lowered. The Mongols excitement became more intense. Excruciating pain tore at his loins. His body shot up in an arc. A clammy hot wetness flooded down his thighs.

When he came to they were gibbering and giggling. Trying to stuff something into his mouth. He had been nailed with arms and legs spread to an *isba* door. They grabbed him roughly by the hair. For a fleeting moment he saw the Wehrmacht prisoners passing before his eyes.

One of them jerked his head to one side. His body was becoming light. A strange numbness seeping over him. A cold like he had never known before was pressing down upon him. A dagger was thrust against his cheek, moving slowly upwards towards his eyes. There was a smell to the blood. The stale vodka upon the Mongolians' breath. A hand. Again they were trying to thrust something down his throat.

"Eee . . . hh. Eee . . . hh."

Several grimacing faces danced before him. Evil heathen yellow faces from the depths of Asia. Another face. Six cigarettes thrust between the lips. Puff. Puff. Puff. The glowing ends came nearer. He could feel the heat upon his face. It was the very last thing that he saw.

Chapter 3
ONE FOR THE CHOPPING BLOCK
INTERROGATION

N.K.V.D. Major Mikhail Kholminov was toying with the short whip lying before him upon the table, in the interrogation *isba*. He prided himself that he had never struck a Germanski prisoner. There was no need to. The mere presence of the blood stained whip was enough.

"So, Gefreiter Franz Hildenheim. You drove a Fascist panzer."

"*Ja.* I was called up to join the Wehrmacht.'

"Oh, but in Mother Russia, Gefreiter Hildenheim, our youth volunteer to serve in the great Motherland war. You did not volunteer."

"*Nein, herr kamandir.*"

"You were a member of the Hitler *Jugend.*"

"*Nein.*"

"Come now Gefreiter." He passed him a lighted cigarette.

"Our Russian youth join the komsomol. You fascists have your Hitler *Jugend.* Is same. Capitalist dictatorship they forced you to join, *ja.*"

"*Ja.* I was a member of the Hitler *Jugend.* But it was only like the Boy Scouts. We went away for summer camps. We sang songs around the bonfire."

"Songs from your Horst Wessel."

"*Ja.* Like Boy Scouts."

"*Da*. Was Hitler *Jugend* member." The N.K.V.D. major made a note.

"And you served with the 17th Panzer Corp. Captured at Oserki. Fine place. I know it well."

"We were in action against T.34s. We lost a track."

"You like T.34. Is good panzer."

For the first time Gefreiter Franz Hildenheim relaxed a little.

"*Ja*. It is a good panzer. Broad tracks—it can go anywhere."

"Our Russian winter is hard. No, Gefreiter."

"*Ja*, Herr Kamandir. We had no winter clothing."

"Is bitter, no? Snow. Wind. Metal freeze, stick to hand."

"*Ja*. But we stripped the dead for jackets. Siberians they . . ."

"So. War is war. A soldier must live. What dead soldier needs jacket," the N.K.V.D. major smiled. But his eyes remained hard. Hard as ice.

"You go now."

"No more questions, Herr Kamandir?"

"*Nyet*. Is enough, Gefreiter."

The N.K.V.D. trooper came forward taking the prisoner by the arm, leading him away. At the door he looked back at the major.

"*Germanski sabaka*. Dog," he smiled.

"*Nix karosch*. No good." The major drew the forefinger of his right hand across his throat.

Fascist pigs. They had invaded the Motherland. In the first two weeks of war half a million Russians had died. None should leave little Mother Russia alive.

A single shot rang out. No cry. No screa. A bullet in the back leaves no time for such niceties.

Klima was thrown back into the *stolovaya* later that night. Cut, bruised about the face. He was still bleeding. Some memories stay with a man for the rest of his life. *Blitzmadels*, screaming, tearing at their hair, trying to crawl away from their Siberian tormentors. The first girl being brutally slain. Others watching, hysterical, knowing their turn was yet to come. Fighting for their lives. Fingernails tearing and clawing at the hated leering faces. Retreat to a corner, drunken mocking laughter echoing high into the rafter beams.

"*Komm. Frau komm.*" Fearful words that would torment a continent in years to come.

Slow, very slow eye-gouging. A specialty created by the Russian partisans. Mutilations of an unimaginable and despicable nature. All performed on the still living and breathing body. No part of the delicate female form was left untouched.

They cleaned Klima up. With the help of vodka he came around. Heyer had made the vodka trade with Sergi Vlasava, for part of his chest collection.

Speaking through swollen lips matted with congealed blood he told his horrible story.

"Cocksucking bastards."

"Speak German."

"It—it was a nightmare. I was tied to a beam. Once, just once, while it was going on. I had the sudden urge to shout aloud: *Americanski—Americanski*. That was when they started to work on their eyes. Crushing heads. Slitting throats. I kept quiet. I knew where I belonged."

Those listening began to swear and curse. One day they would take their revenge. No Russian would be spared. The Siberians. They would be made to suffer the most. A body torn open by Russian artillery fire can be understood. A fight to the death in hand-to-hand combat. A casualty of the front. The *Soldatens* war. Multilations. Wanton. Vile. Against women. It would not be the last time. For the front-line veteran they were hard to comprehend. On the Eastern Front it was total all-out war. Bitter. Barbaric. With no holds barred.

"*Donner wetter*. Worse than the S.S."

"Muller's right. I've had enough. When do we escape?"

Heyer scowled finishing the last of the *kapusta*. The first food in five days. One mess tin of barley soup split between four men. As always, whether at the front or in captivity, it was divided into equal parts. Wehrmacht discipline remained, even under the most bizarre of circumstances.

"These Ruski runts are so drunk we could walk all over them. Shit, I'd kill them with my bare hands and enjoy every minute of it. Can't wait too long, I might get out of practise."

Schultz took the *machorka* from Schmidt. It was rolled in a piece of the Russian newspaper *Red Star*. *Isvestia* never burnt properly.

"I want everyone fully recovered from concussion first. Then and only then will we strike."

"Keep marching like this and we'll be far beyond the fucking Urals in Siberia."

Heyer was hungrily licking the last of the *kapusta* from his mess tin. There was always a tendency to keep the tongue going. The mess tin was empty, but the musty smell was still there. If you were starving, that meant food.

"Heyer, I'll choose the time and place. We might be prisoners, but I am still in charge of this platoon."

Schmidt knew he would have difficulty holding them. Too many atrocities had taken place on the march. It affected some more than others. A few men went into a prolonged stupor. Hours later they would not admit that the latest torture had taken place. Like a prisoner about to be shot who right until the very last minutes clings to the thought of a pardon. How many went to the gas chambers of Auschwitz denying their very existence until it was too late? Hope eternal. Man clings to it until the very last moment before death. Those of the platoon were different. Escape. Revenge. It was all that kept them going.

"Wait much longer and I'll be a walking zebra man. Fuck it. I'd sooner go down fighting. I'll not walk calmly to my hole in the ground like a Jude. Not while my name's Heyer."

That started Muller off.

"Have the Jews ever had any other option? What can they do with all their families about them? Man is at his most vulnerable then. They must be taken into consideration. Did the Holy Roman Catholic Pope come to their aid? Britain, that so-called seat of democracy? How many western countries offered to take them before war broke out? Not many that I can remember."

"Britain had its Nazi blackshirts. Seen it on a newsreel, I did. Run by Mosely. Those British fascists would have put all their Jews in camps, just like our Adolf. Used Buckingham Palace for a Landser brothel. They'd have been queueing all down the Mall back to Trafalgar Square. Five marks a throw. Ten for a county lady with a title—because they go to posh Swiss finishing schools."

"Hitler and the party always hated the Jews, right from the early days," added Schmidt.

"Juden. You defend the lice-ridden swine. The sworn enemies of the Third Reich."

Again it was the Nazi Obergefreiter.

"Zionist pigs. World-scheming filth. The cause of all the Fatherland's troubles in the thirties. World monopolies. Juden moneylenders. Holding honest decent German folk to ransom. The hook-noses got fatter and richer while we starved on the dole queues. They are getting their just desserts.''

"Turn the gramaphone off. This bastard will go on all night," laughed Hansen.

"Peasant women and children. We've seen them now in both Poland and Russia. Living in huts with no floors. What do they know about moneylending. World monopolies.''

Not to be outdone, the Obergefreiter continued.

"Scum. Slavish shit. National Socialism must stop the pigs from breeding. See them in their village hovels. They are like rats. Remember it was the rats that brought the bubonic plague to Europe. They spring up everywhere. At one time I thought there would be no stopping them. Then our beloved Fuehrer came to power. This is what the war is all about. *Untermensch*. Slavs. Polacks. Frenchies. Dutch. Danish. Norwegians. All their society is rotten with *Juden*. All from the same mold. It is Greater Germany's destiny. One day we will rule the world. Then and only then will the earth be fully cleansed of the *Untermensch* cancer.''

His eyes were bright, almost glowing. He looked around expecting immediate approval.

"Not my world. You jumped-up Nazi *Arschloch*.''

Schultz was busy cracking his knuckles. They knew what was coming.

"In our strive to achieve our ends, we dare not falter. There will be many unpleasant tasks ahead. We must steel our stomachs. Only the strong will survive. Brace our shoulders. Square our backs to the glorious future of the Third Reich. Read *Mein Kampf*, I cannot choose words eloquent enough to match those of the Fuehrer.''

"Muller asked a question, friend.''

"*Ja?*" he looked at Schultz with the quizzical eye of the lecturing teacher.

"*Ja.* What about the women and children?"

Schultz was making a great show of slowly coming to his feet.

"Dachau. Auschwitz. The ravines of Kiev. Are they the National Socialist answer to everything?"

"*Ja.* Juden. Half-Juden. Enemies of the state. Each conquered country must—"

Schultz lashed out with his right boot. It caught the Obergefreiter between the legs. He doubled, going low in midsentence, face wincing with pain. Schultz was upon him. His huge fists flew in a flurry of movement. Seconds later the Obergefreiter was in a heap on the dirt floor, unconscious.

"Cross his name from the list, Hansen, little friend. Now for the *coup de grace*. The good old Bienebuttel chop."

He had the head and shoulders wedged under his left arm. His right spread over the face, ready to snap the neck.

Schmdit, Heyer and Muller pulled him off.

"I told you to stop drawing attention to yourself," ranted Schmidt.

"You heard what he said." Schultz pulled a hurtful long face.

"Right, Nazi runt. Dying for the chopping block he was."

They had trouble getting the Obergefreiter from him. Just as they pulled him clear, Schultz's head went in with a grinding bone-splitting crunch. A bloodied gash appeared over the Obergefreiter's right eye.

"*Los.* Get back," snapped Schmidt.

"Had to put me mark on him. I did. Get him later I will." Schmidt was smiling, rubbing his head.

"Schultz, any more trouble from you and—"

"Balls, he's mine. Can I play with him when he recovers?"

"Keep your distance and that's an order, Schultz."

"Did I ever tell you? When I used to clean my pig sties out on the farm, if I came across a rat I had orders to kill it. Scheisse, the Obergefreiter's a rat. Why can't I lay him out? It's not right. It's Schmidt says this. Schmidt says that. Fuck it, I'm getting a bus. I'm going home. I've had enough of this war." He slunk away into the *stolovaya* shadows.

Hansen followed him.

"I've been wondering, Schultzy. We need to make a price list for our St. Paulia after the war. I mean some services should cost more than the others."

Schultz cuffed him in the ear.

"Can't you see they've hurt my feelings? I'm probably the most sensitive Grenadier here. And you go bothering me with boardroom matters."

Schultz kicked him in the rear drawing curses from those sitting in the nearby straw.

"You *Germanski*s are funny," he told Heyer.

"Fight all peoples. Comrade with comrade. Sergi no understand. For Sergi there is only war. Germanskis . . . you fight about everything."

Heyer answered in Russian.

"*Tovaritch*. It has always been the Germanski way."

"You lose. Little Mother Russia has many peoples."

"*Da, tovaritch*. It will take a long time. Germanski is stubborn. He does not give up easily."

Sergi Vlasava retraced his steps back to the supporting beam, bringing an oil lantern back with him.

"Sometimes, *tovaritch* Heyer, when we have little talks, you talk like a man from my village."

He fixed the lantern above their heads, sitting down amongst them.

"You fight for wrong cause. Flames of communism will one day set the world afire. No one can put it out. We of the Red Star. The masses of people. The proletariat. Masses of the world. Russia has fired the signal. It is we who shall inherit the world. Capitalism will rot and fade away.

He fumbled in his deep pockets. Out came a full bottle of vodka. He took a mouthful. Then handed it to Heyer. His submachine gun held before him on his chest. All eyes were on the vodka. He laughed, waving a warning finger at them.

"Good *Soldats*. Or many Germanski die."

He threw his arm around Heyer in a crushing bear hug.

"We comrades. Drink vodka."

Heyer looked at him for approval then passed the vodka to Schultz.

"You give, *tovaritch*. All foot *Soldats* comrades Sergi Vlasava. Drink. Drink. Like much thristy Cossacks from dusty steppe."

Suddenly he lurched forward his head going drunkenly between his knees, sobbing like a small child.

"*Ja bolshoi swinja. Ja bolshoi swinja*," he cried.

It took them completely by surprise.

"Thank the Cossack gentleman for the drop of vodká. But what is he crying about now? Does he want it back?" Schultz wiped his mouth licking his lips.

Heyer hesitated for a moment.

"He . . . he keeps saying he is a big pig."

Schultz and Hansen doubled with laughter.

"They're all pigs, care of uncle Joseph Stalin. I'll clear the deck when we get the word. Nothing Schultzy likes better than cracking *Ruski* skulls."

"*Ja bolshoi swinja*."

Heyer tried to comfort him. Both had lost their

44

families in the war. And somehow over the last few days they had drawn closer together. Like orphans of war tossed together upon the same beach.

So Heyer tried to comfort him.

"Sergi. *Tovaritch*. Why a big pig."

Sniffing, he wiped the tears with the sleeve of his padded jacket, staring Heyer straight in the eye.

"I make love. Once. Twice. Your *Soldat* women. I Sergi very drunk. Think of village. No had women for long time. Siberians kill. I see. I am big pig." He went into another fit of sobbing.

"What's he saying?" asked Hansen.

"Come on, tell us," insisted Steggeman.

"He—he says fuck the war."

"I'll drink to that."

Hansen grabbed the bottle and took his pull. Then passed it to the Badowicker boys.

"*Bolshoi swinja*," Griecebeck pushed Suckau in mock fight, grabbing for the vodka bottle.

Four little Siberians came away from the shadows of the walls, unshouldering their rifles.

Sergi Vlasava sprang to his feet, his submachine gun waving.

"*Nyet*, little brothers." His gloved fingers moved at the working parts.

"No touch Germanski."

The larger of them pulled a face, spitting at the floor. They walked away muttering to themselves.

When the vodka was finished, two Siberians took Sergi Vlasava to his *isba* to sleep it off.

It was Fricke, one of the Badowicker boys, who worked out that it was Christmas morning. Starved husky voices rose in song.

"*Stille Nacht. Heilige Nacht. Alles schlaeft. Einsam wacht.*"

45

Voices cracked with emotion as thoughts of those other Christmases came flooding back. Carol singers shuffling along in the snow in the back streets of Hamburg. Singing under the bright street lamps in Berlin. The *Kinder* on Christmas Eve. Presents at the foot of the Tannenbaum. Joy. Spirit of Christmas, that somehow in the Fatherland is so different.

Older men could still think of the times when there were no swastikas. Brownshirts. Or black-uniformed S.S. storm troopers. When Christmas was but a simple tree. Warmth of the fire. Happy red-cheeked laughing children.

"*Frohes Fest. Frohe Weihnachten.*"

Close the eyes and you could hear the tinkle of glasses.

Scenes of the nativity, glistening by the candlelight in the windows.

The large *stolovaya* doors burst open. Submachine gun fire cut at the air. Those nearest fell in a tangled mass of arms and legs. Froze, not daring to move. None were hit.

In the glow of the lanterns at the door they could make out the tall figure of Lieutenant Anatoli Tsarurov.

"No singing," he shouted in broken German.

"More noise and I give something to laugh about. Hand grenades. It is not for us to forget the treatment of Red Army prisoners by the Wehrmacht at the Darnitsa camp, outside Kiev."

In the grim silence that followed only one voice could be heard.

"And a fucking merry Christmas to you," growled Heyer.

"*Stoi.*"

A Cossack high boot pounded his head into the foul smelling straw.

46

Chapter 4
THE N.K.V.D. MOSCOW DECREE

N.K.V.D. Major Mikhail Kholminov sat at the long table in the *isba* picking his teeth. The pork that his men had liberated from a neighboring village had gone down well. The old village *babushka* had sworn at his men when they led their prize away. Sabotaging the work of the state. They had beaten her with their whips. Brother Stalin was right. Enemies of the people. They had to be dealt with on the spot. He burped aloud, taking up his vodka glass.

On his left sat Andri Isakouski, a big bearded partisan leader. On *his* left Red Army Lieutenant Anatoli Tsarurov.

"*Tovaritch*. It is on the direct orders of Generalissimo Stalin. Police Minister Beria also wants a full report. An example has to be made. This village of K—forgive me. As far as Moscow is concerned. This slur. This blot on our glorious history. This collection of huts no longer exists."

Anatoli Tsarurov shifted uneasily. He was never happy working with the N.K.V.D. Too many brave lives had been lost under their directives at the front. His unit could never exploit a tactical advance. Each move had to be checked out with the commissar. When finally they did attack Germanski had regrouped. His troops found themselves advancing onto well-fortified positions.

"*Da*. We understand, *gospodin* major." He erased the telltale spelling from his notepaper.

Andri Isakouski spat across the table to the dirt floor. He too had partaken of the liberated pork. His stomach was rumbling. He broke wind.

"In the forests of Karachev. We partisans know how to react on these occasions, major."

"*Da*, Andri. We know of your work in Moscow. It does not go unnoticed. Justice is swift in the forests of your area. The peasants here must be taught a lasting lesson."

"Partisans. We make peasants talk." He roared with laughter, pushing away from the table, his head going back making him look all the more fearsome.

"Your ways, Andri Isakouski, are very often copied by the Germanski S.S."

"*Tovaritch* Tsarurov. S.S. taught the partisans. Have you forgotten the way they signed the peace treaties? They invaded the Motherland in the dead of night. Fascist capitalist thieves." Once again he spat across the table; this time it hit the wall.

"Was it not your brother Yuri that they burned at the stake?"

"*Da*, Yuri died under Germanski torture."

His head was no more than the size of a Ukrainian apple at harvest. Like the two Hauptmann's. Long after the fire had burnt down they were still moaning. *Da*, he knew how Yuri must have suffered. He had taken his revenge. Terrible. Horrific. As was his right.

Andri Isakouski thumped the table.

"Brother Tsarurov. Do not talk to me of war. The partisan fights in the forest. On our native steppes. It is not like the fighting of the Red Army at the front. For us the front is everywhere. It is the partisan who sees the villages, after the S.S. have left. Our hate

48

burns in the gut. We cannot rest. Our families are forever in the battle zone. Our people. We have seen many hanging in the trees. Our wives, children and old folk. The suckling babies snatched from their mothers' breasts. Heads squashed by Germanski jackboots. My own son I have seen. His arms and legs broken. Left to freeze in the snow field.''

Major Mikhail Kholminov coughed, shuffling his papers.

''Now, now, *tovaritch*. The war is one against the Fascists. You both represent two fronts of the Motherland. That is why Moscow in all its wisdom has decreed that you should both sit at my side.''

Andri Isakouski scowled at Anatoli Tsarurov. Siberians. Their villages were far from the front, beyond the great Ural Mountains. What did they know of fighting the war on their own *kolkhos*. Ten hostages shot for one German soldier. One hundred for one officer.

The *isba* door opened. Spitting and struggling Natasha Petrov was dragged in by two small smiling Mongolians. Her hands were tied securely behind her back. They threw her to the floor, like a sack of grain. They came to attention. Eyes fixed on the large portrait reproduction of Stalin, hanging on the wall behind the N.K.V.D. major's head.

''*Pyos*,'' she cursed spitting at them.

Her eyes were blazing. Full of fury and hatred. She tried to droop her shoulders, in an effort to straighten her simple torn peasant blouse. To no avail. The upright thrust of her right breast remained showing. It was scratched, bloodied and bruised. The Mongols still smiled without taking their eyes from their beloved Stalin. In the *isba* next door they had both tried to rape her. Natasha had fought like an enraged village cat. Fiercely proud. She was from the wide steppes

49

across the Volga. Her people were of a hardy race. Wildly strong. Independent. They could not subdue her. In the end they forced her down upon her knees. Pushed her head to one of the Mongol's filthy loins. Vengeance was hers. When they thought she was submitting, her mouth opened wide contacting flesh.

"*Pomoshch. Medics!*" the Mongol had screamed with pain.

Blood had oozed from his torn thigh. He had rolled on the dirt floor. Like a stuck pig. She smiled to herself. He would be too frightened to report for medical care. The N.K.V.D. unit was a large one. The commissars would ask too many questions.

Untreated, within days the smell would be noticeable. Gangrene would set in. Pus would turn the leg yellow, green and the death-smelling black. Left too long no Red Army doctor would be able to save him.

The leg would have to be amputated. Or he would take her teeth marks to his grave.

"Natasha Petrov."

Major Mikhail Kholminov liked what he saw. A woman from the Volga. Spirited fire that could make a strong man weak. It was in the eyes. In the defiant toss of the head. Long black hair. High jutting breasts. Rounded fullness of her thighs. A classical young Russian beauty. In the full flush of her life. Not a day over twenty-four years of age.

"Natasha Petrov. You are accused of fraternizing with the Germanski. It is known that you slept with him. In the *isba* of your mother. You brought shame to your mother's *isba*. Your *kolkhos*. You have defamed the name of Little Mother Russia."

Andri Isakouski put down his vodka glass.

"*Prasstitutka*. Prostitute. What have you to say? You droppings of a steppe whore. You are not of this village."

"*Gospodin leytenant.*"

Their eyes met.

Anatoli Tsarurov nodded.

"You must answer, little *gosposha*. Little lady."

The partisan leader threw his glass against the wall.

"*Gosposha* he calls her. Lady. She is to be despised. Not honored in the Russian of the Czar's time. Where are you from, *prasstitutka?*"

"Where else but from the virgin womb of my mother. You bearded goat from Karachev. In the October Revolution my mother hung from the stirrup of a Volga Cossack. If he were here now he would cut out your devil hood and feed it to the village dogs!" Her fierce eyes were dancing.

"*Nyet.* In my Cossack village they would give it to the pigs. We honor our ponies and dogs."

She strained at the barbed wire holding her hands. She spat and kicked out at the partisan leader. The Mongols restrained her.

"*Stoi.* You stand before a court of the N.K.V.D.!" Major Mikhail Kholminov shook his fist at her.

"The N.K.V.D. is not interested in your questionable ancestry. Moscow has directed that we get at the truth. They want to know what happened in this village." He sat down.

"Start from when the Germanski came."

The Mongols were given permission to beat her. One held her by the hair. The other beat her savagely. Then the partisan leader forced vodka into her.

She told them in detail of the retreating Red Army. And enjoyed the taste of her words. An army that melted before the might of the storming Germanskis. The panzers that came to the village. The

51

Grenadiers in their half-tracks, some clustered on the backs of the panzers. Harsh winter as it settled upon the village. How the Germanski slept in the *isbas*. How the Grenadiers relieved each other, at the bunkers and trenches on the far side of the village.

She did not defile the name of Manfred, the tall blond-haired panzer driver from Bielefeld, with whom she had fallen in love. Or tell of the way the *Soldats* had fed the villagers. She knew it would not go down well with the N.K.V.D. major. Or the partisan leader. It was bands such as his that had stripped the peasant larders of food. Before the Germanski came they had been forced to eat their dogs.

Only the forward elements of the Wehrmacht were billeted at the village. Their officers had supervised the feeding of the children. Soldats gave them chocolates and sweets. Unheard of luxuries. They had been kind to the villagers. Was it any wonder they had returned such generosity? They were people of the land. Simple people. But they were also human.

She had fallen in love. Manfred. The tall Germanski. It was not planned. She did not lust for a man. It happened. Like a flower blooming upon the spring steppes. A mushroom appearing after summer rain. She knew he was an enemy of the people. A fascist. She had cried herself to sleep at nights. War had come to the village. Love, it has no boundary, no frontier. It happened suddenly. They grabbed at each passing fleeting moment. As though it was to be their very last.

"*Ich liebe dich, Natasha.*"

The cat at the stove had looked up at those strange guttural words. She knew what they meant.

"*Ya lyublyu.* I love you," she had answered hoping he would understand.

52

"Germanski whore. Did you willingly open your legs to the fascists?"

Andri Isakouski glared at her. Spittle trickled down his beard. His face was livid, a vein standing out upon his temple.

She thought back to the long nights about the stove. Holding hands. It was as though they were not of this world. As though there was no harsh dividing line of hatred. Germanski. Ruski. They were young. In a world that was not of their making. In love. Was that such a crime? Answerable to the state. To faceless people in Moscow. Because they were on opposing sides.

"Answer Germanski whore. Did you take the fascists to your bed?"

"I loved a soldat. A boy soldier. He loved me too. We were only human. Moscow does not own my body."

Her fate was sealed. Both the partisan leader and the N.K.V.D. major had made their marks upon the papers before them.

"Vote."

"Tsarurov."

"She is young. She—"

"Guilty or not guilty of sharing her bed with Germanski."

"*Nyet*. She—"

"Andri."

"*Da*. Guilty. A slut. A whore."

"The deciding vote is mine. *Da*, brazen hussy. She admitted her guilt. Take her away."

The Mongolians manhandled her out of the *isba*. Once again they were smiling. After more beating, the fire would be gone from her. She would be theirs. To do with as they wanted.

Major Mikhail Kholminov added a note on his

report for Moscow.

"In the morning she will be handed over to your men for punishment, Andri."

"*Da, gospodin* major."

He smiled with satisfaction. First the liberated pork. And now the woman Natasha to play with. His men would be pleased. He was beginning to enjoy being associated with the N.K.V.D.

Anatoli Tsarurov was having different thoughts. Natasha was the same age as Tatyana, his wife. Or Krystyna, his sister. All three of them had been in the Komsomol together. The communist youth organization. The party to them was far greater than any religion. Greater than life itself. But the punishment of the village. He choked upon his thoughts, grabbing for his vodka. This was not the Little Mother Russia that he was fighting for.

"Bring in Igor Lutchenko."

There was still fight left in the old man as he was pushed roughly through the door by the armed guards. Bald-headed, he was dressed in sheepskins. The wrinkled face of a man over seventy. A face with the story of Mother Russia written all over it. A face that had known many hardships. Thick calloused hands that had been used to the toil of the land.

"*Gospodin leytenant.*" He squared his shoulders looking at Anatoli Tsarurov.

"I am Igor Lutchenko. I served in the Revolution. I was in the regiment of Guards. I fought on the streets of Leningrad against the White Army."

Major Mikhail Kholminov consulted his file.

"You Igor Lutchenko are accused of helping the fascist invaders. You gave them a bed at your *isba*. We have been informed that you welcomed them. Served them potato wine every night from last year's harvest."

Igor's tired old eyes flitted from one judge to the other. They came to rest upon Anatoli Tsarurov. A soldier of the front line. A veteran. Like an officer in the regiment of Guards. He would listen. He must be a true comrade. The others. The N.K.V.D. major. He was only interested in his own self-importance. His standing with Moscow. Many such men had he seen in his lifetime. A political officer. Making misery for his fellow man. How he hated the epaulettes. The partisan leader. He watched the sickly smile form upon the bearded face. One day they would be both Heroes of the Soviet Union. With an apartment in Moscow. And a big house with Asian servants in the woods. This partisan. His kind treated the villagers like dirt. They took what they wanted. Food. Provisions. Women. If any man protested, he was shot down in cold blood. All for the good of little Mother Russia. They did not listen to reason. They gloried in the fear that they could spread. Devils of war. Many such men had he seen in the revolution. They had an appetite for blood. Terror. Law unto themselves.

"I did not welcome the fascist invader. It is not the way of the Lutchenko family. We have always served the state. Our Motherland. A Germanski Hauptmann told me his men would live in my *isba*. What could I, an old man, do to stop them? They numbered hundreds. Many panzers. Machine guns. Was I to fight them with my bare hands? I was a soldier in the October Revolution. If I had been a younger man I would have gone to the forests. Fought with the partisans. I—"

Andri Isakouski exploded, spitting with the rush of words.

"We do not take old goats. Reactionary pigs. Only men with stout hearts survive in the forests. Men brave enough to fall for Mother Russia. Men who do not skulk and hide when they see the grey of Germanski.''

"The N.K.V.D. are only interested in this village. Moscow must have its full report. As an ex-comrade of the Guards, one who fought the street barricades, you have been chosen to help us.''

Major Mikhail Kholminov tried a new tactic, even smiling.

"Come now, brother. *Tovaritch*. You served little Mother Russia in the glory of the Great Revolution. The time has come to serve her once again.''

Igor told them of the Red Army drive for recruits. The Germanski were pushing hard for Moscow. Already they were at Krasnaya Polyan. Some said they could see the spires, a little more than fourteen miles from the walls of the Kremlin. All men of military age were taken. With them went many boys little more than fourteen years of age. He persuaded his grandsons to join the Communist Party before the Red Army took them away. The comment drew a sigh of approval from the major and he made the appropriate note in his papers.

Igor was no old fool. He knew that with his grandsons being party members. If they were wounded, killed or captured, word would get to the village through the commissars. For a soldier who was not a party member. Many to this day still wait, not knowing of their fate.

The men and boys had gone off in the big Red Army trucks. They fought at Yeletz and Yefremov. The last had fallen at Bogorodisk. It often happened. They had been thrown straight into the fighting without any training.

"So, the fascists came to your village, Igor Lutchenko. Upstanding hero of the October Revolution.

Did you run to meet them with a club? The brave Guardsman who had proved himself in 1917.''

"I was stabling the *kolkhos* horses."

With the help of the small boys he had done just that. It was his duty. He was in charge of the *kolkhos* horses. The bursts of approaching machine gun fire had startled them. Many had stampeded, running loose among the *isbas*. In the end the women had to help in stabling them.

"When the invader was drawing near, our brave Guardsman stabled the horses. The same horses that were slaughtered days later to feed the fascist Grenadiers. Already the viper in the October hero's breast was beginning to turn its head. When partisans want ponies. Hero refused to give them up. He said they were property of the state. The *kolkhos*. Only the commissar who was in Moscow could release them. This venomous traitor. Friend of the fascists—"

"*Tovaritch*, you are putting words into his mouth," shouted Anatoli Tsarurov.

"Igor Lutchenko fought in the ranks of the Guards. An elite division. Have you no respect for a brother in arms? One who has served little Mother Russia? He was one of the fathers of our revolution. He—"

"I have no respect for traitors. Lice. They should be put to death for their misdeeds. Police Minister Beria has stated that we must ferret out these pigs. Run them to the ground."

Major Mikhail Kholminov looked up from his documents.

"Enough. Did you give the fascists shelter in your *isba*?"

"*Da*. I could not stop them."

"Did you give them potato wine?"

"*Da*. They were kind. They feed the children."

"Did you Igor Lutchenko ever lift a finger against the Germanski? Did you go out in the night and sabotage his panzers? Steal the breech blocks from his machine guns? Organize others to help in setting fire to his petrol supply?"

"*Nyet*. The *Soldats* were everywhere. I am but one old man. They were young men. Strong."

Major Mikhail Kholminov had made his mark in the documents that would soon be bound for Moscow. He looked up, a smile spreading over his face.

"*Da*, guilty. No need for vote."

He waved at the Mongol guards.

"Take the traitor away."

The guards prodded at him with their bayonets. The old man's eyes went to Lieutenant Anatoli Tsarurov.

"Is this the reward I get for serving the Motherland? Manning the barricades? Is this how Moscow looks after comrades who have served little Mother Russia?"

One of the Mongols began to beat at him with his rifle butt.

"Men, boys. The lifeblood of our village. Thrown into battle with no training. Our women accused of treason. Germanski," blood trickled from his mouth as he cursed.

"He is a saint compared to the N.K.V.D."

"You dare to besmirch the name of the N.K.V.D. protector of the nation."

Major Mikhail Kholminov ran around the long table, unholsteri ngs nagan pistol. Left. Right. The black barrel whipped at the face. He stood back, breathless, spittle running down his chin.

"When our backs are turned pigs like you betray us."

Ever smiling the Mongols held the bleeding face steady this time. He took off his gloves beating at the old man with his fist. Face. Eyes. Nose. Mouth. No longer was it recognizable as the face of a human being. A gory red mess, pulsing blood.

"Holy Mother of Kazan," he spat broken teeth, cursing.

"May your bones rot upon the steppes. Your soul . . ."

The bloodied rifle butts knocked him senseless.

Major Mikhail Kholminov went back to the table, wiping blood from his tunic.

He took the glass of vodka from the grinning partisan.

"Call Andrushka Koslva. Alina Akimenko."

"*Tovaritch*, my men will look after the fascist pig."

"*Da*, Andri. He must not die quickly. Brother Stalin wishes a slow death."

"The wish of Moscow is always my command."

The two weeping women were shoved and prodded into the isbah. They had been repeatedly raped by the Mongols. Dazed, they staggered falling into a heap before the long table. Their gaily colored peasant dresses ripped and torn. Nakedness showed through. Both were young, in their early thirties. Their menfolk had been killed at Bogorodisk. The commissar had informed them personally under protest, filling them full of vodka, taking sexual liberties. They dared not refuse. The word of the commissar was law.

"Andrushka. Alina. Such pretty names. This is a sorry day for your village. Your men fought bravely, falling for the Mother Russia. You. Your *kolkhos*. Your children . . ."

At the mention of their children their weeping rose

59

to a feverish pitch.

"This war with the fascist invader has made you suffer much. Tell us what happened when the Germanski came. Take your time. This is a democratic hearing. The N.K.V.D. wants only the truth.

Both Andrushka and Alina knew what he was referring to. The uniformed figures appeared to them, like figures of the steppe mists. Shock. The tragic loss of their husbands. The vile brutality of the Mongols. Their children snatched from them, the words finally came. Slow, stuttering. Through swollen lips. They spoke softly as if in a dream. A horrid dream.

Major Mikhail Kholminov leaned forward, striking them with his whip.

"Speak up little ones. You have nothing to fear except for the truth. The N.K.V.D. is a just judge."

Neither of them knew where their children were. They arrested them within days of the Red Army retaking.

Andrushka had been breast-feeding her baby in front. Little four-year-old Roman had been playing with the kittens. They had pulled her baby from her. Throwing it out into the snow. She knew that now it must be dead. Nothing could survive the thirty below zero frost. First her husband, now her suckling. The Mongols had beaten and raped her. None would listen to pleas for mercy. The had not the feelings of other men. Kazakstan. One stood above her giggling, holding Roman, while others took turns in raping her.

"White Russian woman good," he had lisped.

"Much pretty mother no man got. Motherland loose. Mongol he come make many new babies."

Two of them had fought with knifes wanting her. Other savage Mongols had bestially raped Alina,

60

while young boys looked on. They had tried to fight the beats. They were all under the age of ten. Her tormentors were sitting cross-legged upon the floor. Keeping them away with long bayonets. To them it was a game. As each boy rushed, they stopped him with a bayonet at the throat. Each *isba* shook with their drunken peals of laughter. When it was the fourth time, another of the monsters upon her She was struggling. Nikoli was leading his brothers through. Close to hysteria she saw them take Mushka the cat with them.XThey would go to Dyáda Rozhko. Uncle Rozhko. He would give to them. He would know what to do. Had he not taught them to ride in days of summer. They tore at her breasts, yellow hands squeezing. A fight. She felt the hot foul breath of one leaning over her slobbering excitedly. Clawing hands.. When she realized his intentions she kicked one and the other ofher arms and legs. A rifle butt hit her in the head.

The shooting was over. Only the odd sporadic shot came from below the birch wood where old Igor watered the horses in summer. Black smoke was filtering over a gulley. Two T.34s had been dug in there. Several exhausted Red Army soldiers had run back through the village.

"Germanski come!" They ran on looking fearfully over their shoulders.

The women had put on their brightest headscarves. They had gone out to meet the panzers and Grenadiers. They took the bread that was made only hours before with their last remaining flour. The salt. They greeted the invader not as an enemy. But as a friend. It was a tradition in the villages from the times of the Czar. They were without their menfolk. The older folk. The children. They had to be protected. Surely no man would fire upon helpless women bearing gifts. In war they had to find a way so that the children would survive.

The panzers belching exhaust smoke had ground to a halt. Battle-hardened Grenadiers looked on in amazement. It had happened before. It was always a sight that moved the hardest among them. Especially when the children appeared, running down the track. Many had not eaten for days.

"*Khleb. Khleb.* Bread."

A wailing pitiful sound rose from the children. Tiny hands tugged at their greatcoats.

"*Soldat. Khleb.*"

They gave them chocolates. Sweets. The remains of hard-tack rations. Frozen bits of sausage that they had secreted away in their deep greatcoat pockets. They shouldered their weapons. Many took children in their arms. The Blitzkreig was almost forgotten. The starved pinched little faces smiled. The village was not bombarded.

Food and provisions that were stripped from the village by the partisans were replenished. The villagers had plenty to eat. It was rumored that the order came from high up in the Germanski command. It did. From General Heinz Guderian. After a few days, with full stomachs, the color began to return to the children's faces. Had the women been so wrong?

"You met the fascist invaders with traditional bread and salt. Have you not forgotten the capitalist ways of the Czar? The Germanski stayed under your roofs. The order from Stalin was to destroy the *isbas*. Expose the enemy to our cruel Russian winter. Give him no rest."

Major Mikhail Kholminov made his mark in their papers. Police Minister Beria had foresight and vision. He had said no mercy should be shown.

Mother Russia was fighting for her survival. None should be spared.

"Andrushka Koslova. Alina Akimenko. By your own words you are guilty of high treason. No longer are you worthy of looking after the sons and daughters of little Mother Russia. It is their minds that you would poison."

"What has happened to my children . . ."

"Has the N.K.V.D. no mercy. Does Russian blood not run in your veins."

"Take them away," shouted Major Mikhail Kholminov.

"They are of my womb," Alina Akimenko bit one of the guards.

"They are my flesh. My blood. Suckled from my breast. The state has no right. . . ."

"Take the whores away," he barked hitting the table with his whip.

Lieutenant Anatoli Tsarurov bit his lips. Now the mothers were also guilty. They had tried to protect their children. What mother would not? The wrath of Stalin and Beria would be felt in many villages. The Motherland war was taking a turn that would soon sicken him.

"*Vodka, tovaritch.*"

Major Mikhail Kholminov was smiling, eating sunflower seeds and passing the vodka bottle.

"You are quiet, *tovaritch* Tsarurov. Is anything wrong?"

"*Nyet, gospodin* major."

"He has not the belly for total war," laughed Andri Isakouski.

"War is war. It must be fought unto the death. Traitors weeded out. Kill. Kill. Kill. None must escape alive. That is how the war should be fought. Like partisan in forest."

Andri Isakouski burped aloud. Passing wind, the foul aroma rising away from him.

"This we do in the name of communism. Will this happen to all the villages recaptured from the Germanski?"

"*Da*, if the N.K.V.D. desires it. It is Moscow's wish. Stalin's orders."

"Acts of treason and treachery must be avenged."

"Soon, *tovaritch* I fear there will be no villages left."

"Thirteen- and fourteen-year-old boys. They fight gallantly at the front. It is an honor to serve little Mother Russia."

Anatoli Tsarurov ran to the door. He was violently sick.

"Many of our brave sisters are serving in T.34s."

"*Da*, Andri. Their hate is as great as ours."

The women. Children. Old people. Remains of what was once a thriving *kolkhos*. All would be punished. It was more than Anatoli Tsarurov could bear. His revenge had been terrible upon the captured Germanski. For the horrifying death of his brother Yuri. He had sanctioned the brutality of the Cossacks under his command. It was their war with the fascists. But this senseless punishment of harmless villagers. That he could not understand. This kind of total war he wanted no part of.

"I say to you, *gospodin* major, the N.K.V.D. and partisans should run war. Red Army has no belly for Motherland war."

Andri Isakouski roared with laughter. The sound of his spitting came once again.

"*Da*, Andri. It is so. The N.K.V.D. has its duty. If Moscow decrees, village must be slaughtered. It must be done without question. It is all for the glory of Mother Russia. Who dares question Moscow in its wisdom."

"Other villagers, *gospodin* major."

"Tomorrow the village will be burnt to the ground. That order is direct from brother Stalin. No stone must be left standing. The N.K.V.D. will transport the remaining villagers to a camp in Siberia."

"Everything, *tovaritch*."

"Granary will remain. And cemetery. It must be remembered for all time. The ancestors of these people are not guilty of any crime against the state. Their tombstones will remain standing. The rubble of the village will remain forever. A curse on their black deeds. None must ever forget."

Anatoli Tsarurov walked slowly back to his men. From beside a raging bonfire a group of Siberians were singing. The soulful dirge was coming to an end. A lone, fine baritone voice held the sentence clear upon the crisp night air.

"For Russia is my homeland."

He joined them. They greeted him by clapping him about the shoulders. Someone thrust a nearly full vodka bottle into his hands.

"*Urah Stalin. Urah Stalin!*"

Voices rose in the many victory toasts.

"*Urah Stalin. Urah Stalin!*"

An automatic weapon barked, firing off a whole magazine. Rifles joined in stabbing at the dark night.

He threw the vodka bottle into the flames, sending up a shower of sparks.

"*Yob tvoymat.* Go home and fuck your mother," he cursed aloud.

They wheeled in fright. Drunken eyes staring at him. Then he walked off into the night. Alone with his troubled thoughts. Tomorrow there would be no village. Was it so different from his own Siberian village of Kultuk? Would the women there, proud

65

Russian mothers, not protect their young? Their old folk? N.K.V.D. In his youth he thought they were the protectors of the proletariat. Now he was not so sure, with the bearded partisans of Karachev. Were they not like the Germanski S.S.? Did they not also leave villages in flames? Tear children away and transport them to another land?

Chapter 5
S. S. EINSATZGRUPPEN

For three days the Wehrmacht prisoners were shut up inside a *stolovaya* without food or water. As each misty dawn filtered through the cracks in the walls, around them were the stiffened corpses of *Kameraden* who had died in the night. Frostbite. Gangrene. Others who would easily have recovered with a little medical attention. Pneumonia. Bronchitis. Severe lung infections. Hacking coughs that only eased with the final approach of death.

Many talked through the long night. Others rambled incoherently. Lives were relived. Last moments with loved ones. Unless you have known the depraved conditions of Russian captivity, how can you hope to understand. The scuffling. A mound of rotting straw moving. Crawling to the lantern light. Weeping from long-dried eyes. Photos, browning at the edges. Trying to focus upon those left behind. Wives. Children. Parents. Girlfriends. Last conversations. Lost conversations.

"Come home soon, Horst."

The windy railway station. The tramp of soldiers running to the railway carriages. A wisp of a song from drunken lips. You would hear it again at Novosil. At Yeletz. It would haunt forever. To the farthest corners of the earth. Coming from the lips of a twenty-two-year-old Grenadier. One who was insane. No legs. Shot away beneath the knees. Sang until he died. Insane. But your older brother went like a hero. Why did he not cry and scream like the others. Beat at the snow. Cry out with his rage. Hold hands. Why must the older brother always be brave.

Doors slamming. Whistles blowing. Head hunters growling threats. Wives, sweethearts, mothers . . . as one hugging their men. Refusing to let them go.

"*Los. Macht schnell.* The Eastern Front is waiting. *Zehn minuten* to train leaving."

"Make sure Rudiger takes his medicine. You know he has a weak chest."

"*Gott*, Horst. Look after yourself. Heavy socks are in your pack. Mutti put *Leberwurst* in as well."

The cough tearing at the lungs. The sound is now different. Fire at the throat. Burning. The eyes cannot take in the photos. Rudiger will be all right. He has his medicine. Ingrid. She will look after him. Bad lungs. It's in the family. Fight for breath. Heart is pounding. In the head. *Gott. Verdammt noch mal.* This cannot be. Home. Keep thinking of it. Wolfsbuettel. Family.

"*Nein. Nein. Liebchen Ingrid.*"

There is a hand at his brow.

"Hang on Horst. Fight it."

Another voice.

"Put some more straw about him."

"He must be kept warm."

"The train at Bahnsteig I is about to leave. All aboard. Close the doors," the head hunters plate on his chest dances.

He can feel the motion. Hear the release of steam. See it coming up from below the track. Hear the squeak of the wheels. They are moving. There is a clatter of field combat boots upon the hard platform. The door is thrown open. A grinning young Feldwebel of the Gross Deutschland has just made it.

68

"Fuck the popovs. Anyone want a slug of schnapps?"

"Back to the filth. The shit."

"Moscow this time."

"Adolf reckons before Christmas."

The last-thrown kiss. Ingrid cannot keep up with the train. She's waving a handkerchief. Holding Rudiger. Her face is lost. Telegraph poles race by. No, he can still see her face. Blonde hair blowing.

"*Ja* Ingrid. I will return."

A quieter voice.

"Pulse is weakening."

"Fever . . . keep him covered."

Silence.

"He . . . he's gone."

"Take his dog tags . . . paybook."

The metal is bent, one-half broken off.

Hunger drove men insane. They would attack a guard. Death was certain. A release from further torment, atrocity and starvation. With sadistic humor the Mongols stacked the dead about the walls. They had to be counted twice daily. Even in Soviet Russia there must be order.

The body can go without food for long periods of time. It must be sustained with liquid, otherwise it will perish. Back in the line, manning bunkers and trenches, urine had its use. It brought soothing relief. When the biting winter winds tore at the hands, cheeks and neck. When knots of ice formed at the beard, deforming the mouth. Chilblains, the wide cracks oozing blood. Badly frostbitten hands. Now not a drop was wasted. Each man drank his own. It burnt the gullet with its acid reaction. When you overcame the first revulsion, it satisfied the thirst tearing at the throat. For a few precious moments it also gave warmth. Man and boy had to survive. On the Eastern Front it developed into a fine art.

Talk was of the stark horrors of the Russian concentration camps. Infamous hell holes, deep in the wastes of far-off Siberia. Virgin forests where only the wolves and bears roamed free. Where generation upon generation of Russian peasants had been transported, beginning from the earlier times of the Czars. Novosibirst, Kolma and Chila. And other camps that would only be remembered as a set of numbers. Where prisoners both male and female toiled from dawn to dusk under the cruel whip of the N.K.V.D. German concentration camps would horrify the world. Russia has been at it much longer.

Each morning the ritual was the same. Stripping the dead who had died in the night. There could be a vitamin biscuit in that deep pocket. Tobacco dust in the lining, enough to roll another *machorka* to share. Boots. Heavy socks, presents from that last leave. Someone could use them on the long march.

"*Donnee wetter*. You are nothing but ghouls," hissed Muller.

"Before they are cold you are on them like a pack of rats."

Schultz and Heyer were having trouble pulling the boots off a Feldwebel. It seemed the last blood eruption from his stomach wound had long ago congealed about his lips and beard. The eyes open and glassy.

"He won't be needing them anymore," laughed Schultz.

"If we don't need them we can always trade them for a pinch of *machorka*. Been called to his resting place, he has. Must have been called real sudden. Look he's not even shit himself." Heyer crossed himself mockingly like a Catholic priest.

"Swine. Next I suppose you will be pulling their

70

gold teeth," spat Muller.

"Shit, that's a good idea, Heyer. We could make a fortune here."

"There'll be no teeth pulling while I'm in charge," barked Schmidt.

"You are Grenadiers. Not S. S."

"Muller. I've seen you strip the dead before. So don't get so fucking high and mighty with us. It's survival of the fittest now, remember."

Leaning back, two hands on each boot, they pulled them free.

"Felt-lined. Shit that'll fetch a swag of *machorka*."

"Can't go to heaven in big boots. The Lord has Daniel on the door. Makes you scrub your feet like the Moslems. . . ."

Hansen chuckled.

"Got a meter, he has. All them with crabs and lice go to the end of the queue. You'll never get in Schultz. Didn't you have a dose at Cracow. . . ."

They jumped back in alarm. The Feldwebel moved, sitting bolt upright, his eyes rolling. The blood-caked lips parted. The terror-filled high-pitched screams tore at their nerves. The musty nauseating smell of fresh pus and gangrene welled up. Whole strips of reddened and black flesh had torn away with the boots. Bare bone showed from knee to ankle.

Insanely he hunched forward, pounding his fists upon the dirt floor. The screaming grew in intensity, eyes staring straight ahead.

"He . . . he was dead."

"Wasn't breathing."

Schultz and Heyer backed off from the accusing eyes.

"Savage," someone mumbled coughing.

"Swine can't wait until he's dead."

"Give him something. Shut him up," Fricke was staring horrified at the bared bone.

"Silence him," ranted a dying Luftwaffe man.

"He'll bring the guards." His words ended with a choking cough.

"*Schweinhunds*. Got your bags for the gold teeth."

The color had drained from Schultz's face. He was trembling uncontrollably.

"Honest. We thought he'd gone. . . ."

"I'll silence him."

Heyer made towards the screaming Feldwebel. Others stopped him.

"Give him morphine. . . ."

"The last was used last night."

The *stolovaya* doors were thrown open. The foul stench stopped the Mongols one meter inside the door. They came inside pulling faces and holding their noses.

"Germanski stink," one of them uttered in broken German.

"Germanski *kaputt*," confirmed the other.

The youngest, who looked no more than fourteen years of age, waved the P.O.W.'s back, striking at some with his rifle butt. Then, smiling in that infuriating way, they began to beat the Feldwebel to death.

Burying his face in his hands Schultz slumped to the floor. His whole frame was trembling violently, as though he was about to go into convulsions. Muller and Heyer went to him. For several moments no one spoke.

The Mongols wiped their rifle butts off with straw, rubbing it into the face of the dying Luftwaffe man. The doors were slammed closed. They went out laughing hysterically like young girls.

"The boots?" asked Fricke quietly.

Schmidt nodded to him.

"Clean them up, you'll be needing them soon."

Fricke picked them up gingerly. Suckau and Griecebeck helped him to pull the black dead flesh away. Now they only needed another pair for the Badowicker boys.

"Robbing the dead. Have you no respect for your *Kameraden?* It is against all military order and discipline."

The Nazi Obergefreiter had sat down among them. He looked sternly at Unteroffizier Schmidt.

"You are in charge of this unruly mob. Offenses of this nature are punishable by death. That's a standing order."

"*Verdammt noch mal.* Leave it," snapped Schmidt.

"They . . . they thought he was dead."

"Of course I blame the generals. The Wehrmacht High Command. France, Belgium and Holland went to their heads. No preparations. No winter clothing. They thought this campaign would be over before the bad weather set in. The Fuehrer should have their heads."

Not again. Wearily they turned towards him.

"The Luftwaffe had winter clothing. And some Waffen S.S. units."

"*Aschloch.* Whole companies died of frostbite. Most of us still had our summer issue. Paper from *Ost Front* inside our boots."

Schultz shrugged Muller and Heyer away from him. He settled down by his old arch enemy.

"Mr. poxy-know-it-all. Only padded clothing we got was from dead Siberians."

"We had adequate clothing in the S.S. Einsatzgruppe."

Those nearest reeled in shock as though they had been stung. One of the more infamous units of the Waffen S.S. Specialists in murder and mayhem.

"You were with the Waffen S.S."

"I had the honour of serving with Totenkopf."

"The concentration camp guards." Muller's lips curled in disgust.

"*Jawohl*. I transferred to the Leibstandarte S.S. Adolf Hitler. The elite of the elite."

He was positively beaming. Watching for their reaction. He had fooled the Ivans. But why should he not reveal himself to these *Kameraden*. Maybe they would take heart from his example. Get some of the discipline back. They needed it. The Waffen S.S. always had to lead the way.

"Pick of the gallant Waffen S.S. units. We spearheaded most of the big advances into Russia."

His eyes were shifting as he announced, "Without us the Wehrmacht would not have got away from the starting line."

Schultz was fully recovered. Shit, there was I ready to put him on the chopping block when he was only a Nazi Obergefreiter of the Landser. Now he tells us he was in the S.S. And an Einsatzgruppe at that. A right hero of the Third Reich. Play my cards right and Schmidt will serve him to me on a silver platter. None of them had any time for the S.S. They had seen too much.

"Just think. We in the Wehrmacht just came along for the ride. Always wanted to see Moscow under snow. Pay a visit to Lenin's Tomb, to further my ignorant education. Hear all the old romantic Ivan songs. We couldn't afford a gramophone at our place. My old man was drunk too much. So ignorant I was. A farm laborer. Until Heinrich's S.S. decided to lead the way."

"*Sieg Heil* for the S.S. Our saviors in Russia," laughed Heyer.

Hansen jumped up, putting a wisp of straw in between his upper lip and nose. He strutted back and forth, hands clasped firmly behind his back.

"I stood on the British Channel, looking across at the cliffs of Dover. There are those who said to me, if you want it, why don't you take it, Adolf. But they reckoned without my secret service. My *Geheim Polizei*. Them carrots that they grow in Essex and Kent. No good. Look at the Englander—he has no backbone. Horse shit, that's the cause. They feed their carrots with horse shit. No, I had other game in mind. The Ukraine. There they piss on them. Gives them a bright red color. My doctor said I needed more bulk and protein on account of my piles. So I chose the Ukraine, the fruitbowl of Russia. Got rid of my twitch it has. Even Mussolini remarked on his last visit. Never fart now when I shoot my right arm up in salute. That's why Chamberlain went back home to England looking so sorry for himself. Run out of carrots, I did. Poor man, no wonder he faded into history."

"One day you will pay for your filthy remarks about our Fuehrer."

"Where? With you in Siberia. Because that's where we are all going."

"*Nein*, facts speak for themselves," continued the S.S. man.

"Name any battle and I'll name the S.S. unit that lead the charge."

"Give this hero his Iron Cross with oak leaves," fumed Heyer.

"More battle honors have been won by the Leibstandarte than any other S.S. Division in Russia."

"Jew-baiting bastard. You served in an Einsatz-gruppe. Murder squads. Heinrich Himmler's golden boys."

The S.S. man was warming to his subject.

"Someone had to clear the popov partisans from behind the lines."

"Your lot were specialists at killing unarmed men, women and children."

"At Uman the popovs used women, young girls and boys against us. They can kill just as good as the popov in uniform. Stab you in the back."

He began to smile, the memory of those times clearing.

"They can die just as easily, as well."

Schultz had heard just about enough. Many of the S.S. had proved that they were just as much the enemy as the Ivans. He made a grab for the S.S. man. Schmidt stopped him.

"Let him hang himself," he whispered.

"Why wait until after the war to even the score."

Schmidt's face was set hard. Rock hard. Like the time they had stood before the gibbet in Zuchow looking up at the body of a butchered Grenadier, hung by the henchmen of S.S. Hauptsturmfuehrer Sachs. Or Hendricksen, another Grenadier who had come into their clutches.

Schultz's face creased into a smile.

"Hard men, these gallant S.S. Hand-picked. Everyone a hero. No slackers in their lot. *Sieg Heil* the S.S. Storm troopers of Greater Germany. Where would the Wehrmacht be without them?"

Heyer caught the mood, after Schultz nudged him.

"*Deutschland erwache.* Germany awake. S.S. to the fore. The East must be cleansed of Jewish blood."

Muller looked over at Heyer shaking his fist. Then

Schmidt said something quietly to him and his face changed.

"The story of why Adolf took to drinking blood is a very complicated one. Was on account of how he could not get a *Stangenfieber*. A hard-on. Well, I mean that surgeon from Vienna had made a botch job on his piles. Seems he used a new cat-gut sewing technique. Sewed a part of his lower anatomy to his leg, he did. Couldn't face a woman because he couldn't straighten up. How could nature take its course. I mean imagine if you was Eva Braun leading him around by the nose. How would . . ."

Schultz cracked him playfully in the head.

"Quiet, little friend. We'll have more tales from Pushkin later."

The S.S. man's mind went back to the massive Leibstandarte barracks at Licterfelde. Each recruit had to be able to prove that he was racially pure. Father. Grandparents. Back into antiquity. There must not be the slightest taint of Jewish blood. The slightest sniff. Even suspicion, and he was thrown out of the ranks. Each trooper in those heady days had to be the ideal of Germanic manhood.

How the young eager *fräuleins* had gone for the uniform. When he first walked out with the proud S.S. runes on his collar he had to fight them off. Everyone made way for them. If they saw a girl they fancied, they moved in. Other men just stood aside. There was nothing the young *Fräuleins* would not do. Any wish of the new supermen was their command. But one had to watch the black uniform. It had to remain impeccable.

There had been talk of a breeding program. It was to be organized through *Kraft durch Freude*. Strength through joy. Men of the master race would be suitably paired with qualified young *Fräuleins*.

There were rumors that special holiday retreats had been set up in the valleys of Bavaria.

"Give me some of that strength through joy," laughed Hansen.

"Bavaria, you say. Of course, a Grenadier would have to have more than one throw. I mean he'd have to be sure that he potted her properly."

"Would they be women that specialize?" Schultz wanted to know.

"I know about the breeding bit. And I'm all for furthering the Third Reich. But do they really know how to work a Grenadier up? Could be tricky after you've been on the Reeperbahn, after a few beers."

As the tough, rigorous training progressed, many fell from the ranks. Live ammunition was used on maneuvers. Slightest hesitation under fire was frowned upon. An order was an order. A show of fear. A sudden attack of bad nerves. All reactions were noted down by harsh, brutal instructors. If they did not meet the exacting high standards, dismissal was instant. Leibstandarte wanted only first-class specimens of German manhood. Second-best was good enough for the Wehrmacht. But not the elite of the Waffen S.S. They wanted men whose loyalty was unquestionable under the most intense fire. Deaths occurred daily during the mock war games. Route marching. Double marching in quick time. Endurance tests that never seemed to come to an end. Short rest intervals. A sharp whistle. Up.

"*Vorwaerts.*"

Dry throats. Covered in dust. Muscles aching, seeming about to burst. Singing at the top of their lungs. To fight for the Fatherland you must be able to sing.

"*Annemarie scheiden tut weh, heut muss ich fort, fort von diesem ort.*"

The steeled crunch of jackboots against the hard-surfaced road. Sing. Sing. Sing.

"Annemarie, parting hurts. Today I must go. Go from this place."

The mauser cuts at the shoulder blade. The sore has not healed. It is blood running, not sweat. To become hard the new recruit to the Waffen S.S. must suffer. Suffer. Suffer. Suffer.

"Links, zwei, drei, vier."

Stones crack under the feet. Aching blistered feet.

"Left, two, three, four."

Is it thirty kilometers? No that was yesterday. Today, brave heroes, it is thirty-five. Full pack. Combat gear. Pity those with the spandaus.

Near complete exhaustion they would return to the barracks. Throat, it is a dry nagging ball stuck to the back of the neck. Water trough. They were dying to get at them. Sweat is swimming down their backs. The flying standard comes into view. Instructors run down the ranks. Backs straighten. Heads are forced back.

"Los. Singen. Singen."

Mausers and spandaus have become unbearably heavy.

"Soldaten Kameraden. Nimm das Madel, nimm das Madel bei der Hand."

Was that someone falling in the outside rank? The clatter of a Spandau as it hit the road.

"Soldier comrade. Take that girl, take that girl by the hand."

Sweat blurs the vision. It streams down the forehead from the tight rim of the steel helmet. Each footfall feels as though it must be the last. Still the instructors rave and shout.

"Lauter! Louder!"

Several officers take the salute. An S.S.

Standartenfuehrer standing behind the others is picking his nose.

Dismissed. The mad scramble to the barrack rooms. Packs thrown off. Circulation restored. Belts released. The sheer leisure of lying full length upon the back. Draw the breath deeply into the lungs. The pounding heart will slow. Give it time. Breathe deeply, it helps.

A new command. Echoing down the white marbled corridors.

"*Raus mit euren Waffen*. Outside with your weapons."

The shoulders have swollen. It is cutting to put the pack on.

"*Drei minuten. Schnell.*"

The bladder is full. But it's too late now.

Fresh grinning instructors await them at the bottom of the stairs. Panzer training. Panzer attack. Panzer defense. Alarm. Slit trenches that have to be dug within minutes. He who falters falls. Reaction must be instantaneous. A blur of steel. Short entrenching tools race, digging feverishly at the earth. Already the long broad line of Panzer Mark-Twos is advancing upon them, machine guns spitting death. If the head is not drawn down properly. Squashed against the side of the trench. Ripped off as the thrashing tracks swirl by. More casualties.

Out. Out. Don't hide in the trench. Attack. No hesitation. Wait for it. Wait for it. Four meters. *Gut.* Now. Two bounds and you are up against the turret ring. Place the practice mine. Simple. All it needed was guts. Nerves of steel. Ride the panzer motion. Don't fight it. Ride it. Dive off the side and roll clear. More casualties. Didn't jump far enough. Straight under the tracks of a Mark-Two. Lost lives. The Waffen S.S. only wants the best. Superhuman efforts. Supermen of the Fatherland. Only the very fittest will survive. What matter the others. Wastage. They are not worthy to serve in the ranks of Leibstandarte S.S. Adolf Hitler.

He regarded his posting to an Einsatzgruppe as a great honor, the culmination of his service in the S.S. First he had been with the Totenkopf, a guard at Dachau concentration camp. His adolescence. How he had admired them when he was a member of the Hitler Jugend. The enemies of the Third Reich had to be punished. The state could no longer afford opposition. He had gone about his duties with youthful zeal, beating many unfortunate victims to death. Jews. Communists. The dregs of the earth. They had to be liquidated. There would be no room for them in the new state. The dawning of the master race. Who cared about them. They were subhuman. Nothing but scum. They had to be stamped out. It was at Dachau that he had been promoted to S.S. *Sturman*. The first rung in his climb to power.

With Leibstandarte he took part in the invasion of Poland. Crazy Poles had attacked with cavalry. They were annihilated. Bloody massacre. In places they crowded the roads in with the streaming hordes of refugees. They died to the last man. Poland proved to be much easier than the maneuvers in the Fatherland.

When hostilitie started with Russia he had become an S.S. Unterscharfuehrer. After several months he was to head a small unit of the Einsatzgruppe. The East had to be Germanized. The plans had been drawn up months before by Heinrich Himmler. Lands had to be cleared, areas policed. True Germanic stock would be moving in. The new settlers for the East. Troublemakers and Jews. There was no place for them. They had to make way for the new Germanic order.

Vast tracts of land were captured under the blitz-krieg attacks of the Wehrmacht. Order and discipline had to be maintained. It was the German way. The first task was all too simple. Hitler's commissar order. All commissars were to be shot on capture. No need to send them on to the camps. They would die in the hands of the Einsatzgruppe.

He made them dig their own graves. Large graves three meters by five. At times he even weeded out Jews among the captured. How could they hide with their distinctive features. Some protested their innocence. Dropped trousers proved them right or wrong. The hole was two meters deep. He made them run into the hole five at a time. His men shot them from the high bank. Order. Each hole had to be fully utilized. He made the next victims straighten the dead into lines. Then they in turn would stand back against the wall of the hole and be shot by bursts of submachine gun fire. The holes were filled in by locally recruited women. When the hole was filled he would make an announcement to the women. A reward for information leading to the capture of any Jew or commissar.

Jew hunting was a sport they all enjoyed. The whole population of a suspected village would be lined up. Everyone was forced to attend the parade. They got many long hairs that way. Those who did try to hide away were forced out of the *isbas* at bayonet point, those who were brave enough trying to escape. Made a sudden dash for freedom and were gunned down. No mercy was shown. Men, women, children . . . if they were running they were shot down.

In Poland he had helped to herd the Jews into ghettos. From the villages around Warsaw the long forlorn columns had trudged towards the city. They were allowed to take along all they could pack in one hour. He saw no need for such niceties in Russia. Transports. The tedious escort duty. Huge distances to travel. The problem had to be solved right on the spot.

"All yids take one pace forward," came the guttural command.

No one moved. There were obviously Jews among them. Any fool could see that.

The interpreter went up and down the assembled crowd of villagers. As he drew close to them the crowd seemed to sway. He tried a different approach.

"All Juden are to be relocated. Resettled. There will be other farms that you will help to work. You have many skills. The Germanski is quick to realize this."

Several longhairs were pushed out of the crowd by their smiling neighbors.

"The days of the Russian collective is over. Besides helping to work the new farms, each peasant will be given a few acres of his own. He can work it with his family and make extra money. You will have your own stock. Pigs. Cows. Chickens. The day of the collective quota has gone forever. From this day forward, communism is dead."

He threw some chocolate bars amongst a group of children. They snatched them up hungrily. He patted one upon the head in a fatherly fashion.

"You have suffered much under the Red Star. You have been under the heel of the political commissar for too long. The new order has arrived. There will be food for everyone. No longer will you watch your children starve. While in Moscow brother Stalin gets fatter. All on the fruits of your labor, brothers."

Some villagers laughed at the mention of brother Stalin. A younger man put his left hand to the inside of his right elbow. The right arm coming up. The Russian equivalent of "he can get fucked."

The interpreter's eyes hardened. None of the villagers noticed it. They were too eagerly taking in the glowing words. No more starvation. Land for everyone. An end to the collectives and their brutal task masters. The village Soviet. No longer would he raid their larders. The cunning fat pig. Stealing their eggs. Their honey. Their prize pork. Under Germanski all peasants would be equal. What a day they were living. Freedom would return to the village. They must make a village dance. Was this not a day to remember.

"All Juden take one pace forward. *Marsch*."

Over one hundred and fifty Jews stepped forward.

"Good," the interpreter smiled, giving the children more chocolate.

"Marisha," said an old man to his daughter who was fussing with her two young children.

"Did you ever hear such a fine speech. *Das ist schmalzig*. That is good."

"*Papushka*. Have you not heard what they did to the Jews of Cherikov?"

"All talk, Marisha. You should not listen to such gossip."

"Commissar Pavel Alexandrovich Dzerzhinski told me."

"That fat louse. He steals our chickens and you talk of him. These fine Germanski officers. Look at the way they dress. Have you seen such uniforms as these? My great *papushka* came from Cologne. They have houses of brick there. Hard metalled roads with street lamps. Civilization as you would not dream of, my daughter."

"I am frightened *papushka*. They have many guns."

Other villagers were even smiling. They waved goodbye to their neighbors. Slowly the column marched off up the long dusty village street. They came to the tall barns, the front of the column turning right.

"The house of the Jew family Bernstein is mine," announced a thin peasant woman to those around her.

"Germanski will punish you."

"*Nyet*. And who will tell him of this deed? You Aleni Cherny, with your son in the Komsomol? Or you Nadia Kasatkin sister-in-law of our fine commissar Dzerzhinski? Mouths you will keep shut. When Germanski leaves, you will help me move."

Machine gun fire sounded. Heavy Spandaus. Shouting. Screaming. Unearthly wailing. Submachine gun fire. Two small children were running back up the street. They were virtually torn apart by automatic fire. The howling continued. The cry of death. Bestial like animals in pain. It went on for several minutes. Then luger pistol shots. Neck shots.

The interpreter was congratulated by the Unterscharfuehrer. They shook hands, grinning.

"Ever think of writing short stories, Brenner? You win them over every time. Never fail. What did you do before the war?"

"I worked for the Karstadt selling clothes, Herr Unterscharfuehrer."

"And before that, dear Brenner."

"Slaughterman at a pig abattoir, Herr Unterscharfuehrer."

"From one lot of swine to another." He slapped him upon the back laughing.

"*Los*. The speech. Then we move out."

85

"A curfew is to be imposed upon this area. In the morning Wehrmacht trucks will arrive. You will have all your pigs and cattle ready for loading at first light. Any infringement of this order is punishable by death."

"*Tovaritch*. Germanski *Soldat*. You say. . . ."

The *staross*. The village mayor stepped out of the throng.

"I *staross* of village. Peasants will starve. . . ."

"Hang him." The Unterscharfuehrer slapped his riding crop against his jackboot.

"Ten others as well. It will show the partisans that we mean business."

"Officer. You say villagers no starve. New *Germanski* order. Times change. . . ."

"Times have changed, Herr *staross*. Your hanging will herald the change." He laughed aloud as the S.S. troopers dragged the old man towards the stout tree.

"Ten others. Men in between the age of fourteen and seventy. Anyone capable of carrying a rifle. Better to see them hanging than meet them in the forest. Much easier."

The Einsatzgruppe action came to an end. The S.S. climbed aboard their half-tracks. As they made wide U-turns roaring out of the village in a cloud of rising dust, voices were raised in song.

"*Die fahne hoch.*
Die reihen fest geschlossen.
S.A. marschiert in unseren reihen mit."

Their work for Greater Germany had been completed in record time. Another *kolkhos* cleared of Jewish scum and troublemakers. As the half-tracks sped on, they were all looking forward to the evening's entertainment. They had two large German Alsation dogs, specialists in deflowering young girls.

This very night they would be using them on three Russian searchlight girls. There would be beer and schnapps. A young Ukrainian girl for each member of the Einsatzgruppe.

The evening promised to be a memorable one. The Eastern Front was bearable. You just had to mix pleasure with work. It made life easier. Worth living. In war there were many opportunities, you just had to make the most of it.

The entertainment was short-lived. They had gone into General Guderian's sector to steal some commissars. It was S.S. Sturmbannfuehrer Melkes' fault. He wanted to put one across on the general. It was rumored that his men were not carrying out the commissar *befehl*. He had never liked working too close to the front. Those were not their orders. He was captured after Livny was bypassed by a strong Siberian unit.

He had seen what happened to S.S. men captured by the popovs earlier in the summer. Four of them caught out on a patrol had their heads cut off. The heads were hanging at the entrance to a cemetery when an S.S. unit captured it. The bodies were lashed to a fence. Or what remained of the bloody torsos. It was the excited buzzing of thousands of flies that they heard first. The severed limbs were lined up on the ground. Like Spandau barrels prior to inspection, each arm and leg spaced at an equal distance apart.

On capture he was wearing the uniform of a Landser Obergefreiter. And his dog tags. The man was dizzy from concussion. He never really knew what was happening. He was dead before he could figure out the exploring hands. A shot between the eyes.

"You changed your uniform to avoid being recognized."

"*Jawohl*. You saw what they did to those S.S. riflemen. Savage."

Heyer grinned knowingly.

"But I thought Herr Himmler's boys were proud until the very end."

Schultz poked the Unterscharfuehrer upon the chest.

"You swore to Adolf you'd go down in a blaze of glory. That's what it was all about. For Fuehrer, Folk and Fatherland. I've heard your mob singing about it for years."

They stared at him with narrowed hate-filled eyes. The woman killer. Child killer. Only too proud to tell his own story. As he spoke he had taken their continued silence as natural consent for his Einsatz-gruppe's action. Had they not remarked with the re-settlement deceit used upon the Jews? Brenner's story to them. Agreed with him that he should become a creative writer. The big one Schultz, he had said it.

"Some writer he'd make. Better than our Pushkin Hansen here."

And Heyer, the one with the staring eyes. Talked about hanging the eleven villagers.

"Noose over the neck. The half-track drives away. No shit to clear up. Just jump in the half-track. Home James."

And Hansen—had he not questioned him about the Einsatzgruppe's Ukrainian mistresses?

"Got me little memento, I have." He had shown him his lucky charm.

The matchbox from around his neck with hairs in it.

"Nothing like a good Ukrainian bit. Mind you I've heard those Mongol pieces know a trick or two."

He was becoming uncomfortable under their steady gaze.

"Why should I die? I am still a young man."

His eyes searched their faces. The hate was there for him to read.

Heyer and Schultz grabbed him by the arms.

"For you the glorious *Krieg* is over."

"Every war has its sacrifices. For you the Lord has decreed that we take an eye for an eye."

He struggled. Schultz's iron grip held him firm.

"I will escape and rejoin my unit."

"Neck shooting innocent villagers," Muller struck him in the face.

"It is the Fuehrer's wish. Reichsfuehrer S.S. Henrich Himmler laid the plans. Greater Germany needs *lebensraum*. It is the need of the nation."

They dragged him into the shadows near the wall.

"I am German. One of you. A brother in arms. Your *Kamerad*."

The silence was stifling.

Schultz spat at him, giving his arm a further twist.

"Is he one of us?"

"*Nein*," came the reply from the Badowicker boys.

"Kill him. Kill the swine."

"I am an S.S. Unterscharfuehrer. Your superior. One of the Reich's chosen few. In 1935 . . ."

"Do you see an S.S. Unterscharfuehrer, Heyer?"

"*Nein*. I see a Landser Obergefreiter about to shit himself."

They would kill him with the same ease that they popped lice, delousing themselves. There were undoubtedly brave men in the Waffen S.S. Their many bones buried in Russia testify to that. But there were also the sadist inhuman brutes. Delighting in torture. Atrocities. They would only meet their match in the roving bands of ivan partisans. Both had one thing in common. The horror of all-out war. Where not even children were spared. Terror barbaric and inhuman. They revelled in it. It was all that they lived for. The Eastern Front gave them a chance to display their skills. They leaped to the occasion. The carnage that followed will never be forgotten.

"Unteroffizier, I beg you. It is your duty to restrain them."

Suddenly he broke free, going for the *stolovaya* door.

"Stegge. Get him."

Steggeman and Fricke caught him. He was fighting for his life. He knocked Fricke down. He had no intention of leaving this world without a fight. The Waffen S.S. The Leibstandarte. They did not go down without a fight. Fight to the last man. The last bullet. Invincible. The elite of the elite. A battalion could hold back a division of *popovs*. Then turn them and send them running. Courage. Bravery. Nerves like Krupp steel.

"Bring him back here. I'll break his neck," cried Schultz.

"The Lord says he's mine." Heyer made for the door.

Suddenly the door was thrown open.

"*Kapusta,* Germanski. *Kapusta.*"

Six Mongolians stood there with the steaming cauldrons of barley soup. It always had to be eaten quickly or it soon became solid ice. The Mongols were all drunk. They stood looking at the three Wehrmacht soldiers who had now straightened up.

"Steggeman. Fricke. Back here," rasped Schmidt.

The big Mongolian sergeant smiled, unshouldering his submachine gun.

"Germanski no want *kapusta*. No want eat."

"Germanski *kaputt*," giggled another.

Steggeman and Fricke tried to walk away.

"*Stoi*," the sergeant stopped them with the snout of his weapon.

"You want steal *kapusta*. No share with comrade."

"*Nein* I . . ."

"You go door. You no like Mongol. Want kill guard."

He was tapping Steggeman upon the chest, emphasizing each word.

"You like Ruski winter. You outside."

He nodded to two Mongol soldiers. They smiled knowingly. Then they pushed the three Wehrmacht prisoners outside into the cold.

"*Kapusta*," he roared.

"Mongols kind. Mongol give food to Germanski. You like."

Three shots rang out. No one moved towards the soup. Three more shots.

"*Komm,* Germanski. *Komm*."

There was the sound of mess tins as the first shuffled forward into line. It was happening every day. Many had got used to it. Only a few knew the victims. With regularity and death becoming commonplace, it no longer shocked some. Only food mattered. Survival.

"I tell Mongols kind people," the sergeant roared with laughter.

They had to hold Heyer back. It took three to hold Schultz.

"Rush them. We'll get them before they get us."

"Schmidt, we can't just take it. It'll be our turn next."

Steggeman, Fricke and the S.S. Unterscharfuehrer were pushed back through the doorway at bayonet point.

The Mongols roared with laughter. They kept slapping one another upon the backs. Pantomiming what the Wehrmacht prisoners had thought happened outside.

"I no say Mongols kind peoples," laughed the Mongol sergeant ladling out the first of the *kapusta*.

"Comrade no dead," he waved the wooden ladle.

"You look, Germanski. He walk."

The vodka bottle passed between the Mongols. One put a dash into the steaming soup, making the others double once again with childish laughter.

The S.S. Unterscharfuehrer hesitated. Now they were all enemies. The drunken Mongols. The scowling faces of the other Wehrmacht prisoners. There was no escape anywhere. He stayed too long by the door.

The Mongol sergeant's eyes lowered to his furlined boots.

"Germanski *Soldat* no need boots. Off," he growled.

"I give much food. *Kapusta* for boots. Off."

He tried to run into the mass of prisoners but they caught him, pulling him back to the doorway. They knocked him down with rifle butts. The boots came clear. He began to whimper, crawling away. Two silver badges fell into the straw.

A Mongol picked them up. The sergeant dropped the ladle.

"Eee—hhh."

The badges passed from hand to hand.

He had hidden his papers under the rubble. But he could not bring himself to throw away the S.S. runes. They had meant so much to him. After years of unemployment he had volunteered for the S.S. Donning the uniform had made him a man. A man of power to be reckoned with. He was proud of serving the Third Reich. Adolf Hitler was the savior. Why should he be ashamed. He had been doing his duty. Soon the mighty forces of the Wehrmacht would regroup. They would storm forward. Nothing would stop them.

Someone had brought Sergi Vlasava to the *stolovaya*. Other Cossacks handled the S.S. runes.

"Shit. We won't get him now," grumbled Schultz.

"The Lord works in many mysterious and wonderful ways," laughed Heyer.

"Why don't they hit him."

"The Cossacks will make mincemeat of him."

"They're saving him for something special."

"I was a member of Léibstandarte. You subhumans mean nothing to me.

Without uttering a word the Cossacks stripped the S.S. Unterscharfuehrer. He screamed as they prodded him at saber point out into the swirling snow. Hansen went through his discarded clothes.

"What a prize pounce."

In the S.S. man's clothes they found two sausages and a pack of *machorka*. A *kandra*, a Siberian battle knife, was found in the lining of his greatcoat.

"The patriotic shit. Holding out on us," muttered Schultz.

Heyer hid the knife in his tunic. The frozen sausages were divided equally among them.

"Did you think they'd shoot us?" laughed Steggeman nervously.

"Nah. You don't fool us," added Schultz.

"How come? You heard the shots."

"Didn't hear your rear end explode, that's what," came from Hansen.

"Won't you ever forget that blockhouse?"

Steggeman laughed with them. It had happened again. His legs were swimming in the filth. But then everyone smelled vile.

"When we get to Kolma the first thing I'm going to do is have a nice bath."

They settled back among the straw.

Outside the door the S.S. man screamed and cursed at his Cossack tormentors. In his voice there was still the defiance for which his S.S. division was well known.

"Our Unterscharfuehrer shit sings well."

Muller pulled a face and spat into the straw.

"He's had enough practice listening to hundreds of his victims."

Heyer rolled a *machorka*.

"Heinrich would be proud. Steam his glasses up. Issue a special order of the day."

"Don't like the high notes. Got a Jewish flavor, they have."

"No Annemarie, is it."

"You ever tried singing with your mouth full?"

A Luftwaffe man vomited into the straw.

Schultz grabbed Steggeman, sniffing at him.

"You holding out on us Steggeman?"

"*Nein*. What do you mean?"

"Smells like pork. Cutlets, sausages flowing on pork fat."

"Black bread soaked in the dripping," added Hansen.

"Muck coffee . . . made with lashings of evaporated milk."

"*Mein lieber Gott*. Promise I'll take a bath when we get to the Kolma prison camp."

"You won't be going to any prison camp. Any of you," Schmidt announced.

"We break out."

"When . . ."

"*Donna wetter*."

"The door. The Mongols forgot to pull the bar down."

"Can I take a crack at that slant-eyed Mongol sergeant? Cheated me with the *kapusta*, he did. Spat in it. No manners. And don't forget he also stole my Unterscharfuehrer. Swine."

"He's yours, Schultz."

"Who said there was no St. Nicholas."

"Now we go to sleep in turns. Like in the line. We break out a few hours before dawn. By then most of the guards will be in a drunken sleep."

They settled down. Schmidt and Heyer took the first watch.

Schmidt had changed his mind. The incident with Fricke and Steggeman had done it. To the Mongols, in fact to most of the ivans, the life of a Wehrmacht *Soldat* was cheap. They could so easily have lost their lives. He shuddered at the thought. Schultz and Heyer could have so easily have followed them. To wait for another opportunity meant he could very well be waiting alone.

"You lead the attack Heyer."

"I'll take them. It'll be a pleasure."

The screams of the S.S. Scharfuehrer were now more of a whining sound. The Cossacks did not mark his body. None called for the taking of his manhood. Little Mother Russia wanted him whole. No Cossack raised his voice suggesting disembowelment, or beheading. None wanted to brand him with the irons or tear him limb from limb. Lieutenant Anatoli Tsarurov had ordered that the torturing was over. Not one hair would be touched upon a Germanski prisoner. No more blood should flow.

No blood did flow. He was not marked. But his cries of terror went on for what seemed hours. They put his feet into a water trough. Then poured hot

95

water in. Held him while it cooled. Then froze solid. Naked, turning blue, they left him anchored in the frozen water trough. An offering in vengeance for ever hungry little Mother Russia.

Chapter 6
RUSSIA IS MY HOMELAND

The villagers were standing before their *isbas* in family groups. The exodus was about to begin. A sharp Russian command and they formed into a long column. A herd. Vicious guard dogs strained at their leashes. Brutal N.K.V.D. guards cracked their long whips. The head of the column started forward. Many had sacks over their shoulders, small cardboard boxes under their arms. Enough food to last them a few days. It would soon run out. For most of them the journey to prolonged captivity would take many weeks.

For days on end the railway transports would be forced to wait in sidings, letting the long trains through from the Ural Mountains. Trains loaded with artillery pieces. Flat decks full of T.34s. Industries, whole factories had been dismantled and moved, lathe by lathe, to beyond the Urals. No dead would be thrown out into the snow. The N.K.V.D. body count had to remain constant. Most would travel on to Siberia and be interred there. Had not brother Stalin decreed that the whole village would be going to Siberia? And go they must. That was the order from Moscow.

The sick. Most of them had not been away from their hot stoves for months. Many were beginning to stumble. On leaving a warm *isba*, one feels the ice cold air hit the face with the force of a sledgehammer. The weak. Those unprepared. It would bowl them over within a matter of minutes. The harsh Russian winter is not a respecter of age. None would last very long. Their bodies would line the road. But then in Russia, then as now, many roads lead to uncertain death.

Stooped old men. Hard men. Men who loved the little Mother Russia. Broad proud Mother Volga. The lifeblood of the great Motherland. Men with long memories. October Revolution. Many had actively taken part. Grasped it firmly. Salvation. Such a bright future was promised. A peasant's dream. A paradise upon earth that had never been known before. Years of toiling endlessly upon the land. They would share in its future wealth. Drudgery would go. No longer would they be virtual slaves. Suffer the indignities of tireless serfdom. Watch the children waste and starve away. For the first time in living memory they would be free men. Able to hold their heads high. Have no fear looking another man in the eye. Such a future—would it not make the Soviet Union the envy of the working classes of the world?

The heady excitement of the Revolution faded. Speeches from Moscow became monotonous. Work. Work. Work. Enforced collectivization. The famine of the thirties. Peasant rebellion. Short-lived. Brother Stalin proved more ruthless than any Czar. The dead piled high in the village streets. The gutters were full of those in the last dying throes of starvation. The dream. The idea it vanished forever. One wicked feudal system of slavery was replaced by another. Quotas had to be met. District commissars ruled with a hand of iron. Hours of labor became longer. The N.K.V.D. hunted down the so-called slackers. Each organ of the state knew no mercy in enforcing the new doctrine. Those late for work more than once could be rewarded with five years in a labor camp.

Women. Many of them were young and married. Their men had made the ultimate sacrifice, dying in defense of the great Motherland. Now they were branded for life. They had committed acts of treason with the invading fascists. Had they not billeted them in their *isbas?* Their children were taken from them. The wailing that rose from the mothers did not deter the N.K.V.D. They were to be brought up under the ever watchful eyes of the Komsomol. They would never see them again. Judged as criminals, they had no rights.

Within days they would all be in the cattle transports, heading for Siberia. There they would remain for the rest of their lives, in the new frontiers. The lead mines. Salt mines. Pulp and paper mills. Coal. Iron. Tin. There would be no chance of a final pardon.

The loathing and hatred burned within them. For Stalin. Police Minister Beria. The N.K.V.D. Unfeeling monsters. Devil serpents, who at the stroke of a pen in Moscow had condemned them to a life of utter misery.

Their village. Hovels of lice-ridden *isbas*. But home. Loved ones. Friends. Neighbors. Old folk. No longer would there be the long nights gathered about the hot stoves. Gossip. Fun. The happy squeal and laughter of the children at the Easter celebrations. Local marriages. The stomp of dancing feet. Old Vanov on the accordion. The colorful ceremony. It was finished. A heavy door that slammed shut. Never to reopen.

The Cossacks and Siberians stood about the large bonfires watching the sorrowful procession depart.

The hated N.K.V.D. guards lined the street. Heavily armed with automatic weapons. If anyone so much as stumbled, or fell, they were upon them beating them mercilessly with their whips. If they failed to rise to their feet, the crack of a nagan pistol ended their torment. There had to be order. And they were cruel and wicked enough to enforce it. What world of dictatorship ever changes? They go through a new cycle. The name of a new purge may change. But the end result means exactly the same. Repression. Unflinching and never ending.

"Leytenant Tsarurov. People of *kolkhos* go. Like fascists. N.K.V.D. put flaming torches to *isbas*."

To Sergi Vlasava, drunk as he was, it was the return of a haunting nightmare. Helpless, he had watched the fate of his own village in the forest. Now he felt no better. Still he was helpless watching the flames take hold upon the thatched roofs. What could he do against the armed might of the brutal N.K.V.D.? The order came straight from Generalissimo Stalin. Moscow was all powerful.

"Liberated by our Red Army. Now, as brothers, we watch the *kolkhos* burn."

At first it was muffled. A whisper. Then a cry of anger rose from the Cossacks.

"You must lead us against them, *gospodin* leytenant."

Other voices no longer afraid took up the call.

"You led us from Krasnaya Polyana. Ivanozero. Danskoie. We will follow you to the fiery gates of hell, little brother. As men we watch while little Mother Russia weeps," came from one of the Siberians.

"Say the word, *tovaritch* Tsarurov. We will die at your side."

A burly Cossack from across the Don drew his

curved saber, his colored robe swirling.

"Cossacks will join brother Siberians. Blood of the N.K.V.D. partisans shall stain our blades."

"*Nyet*," Anatoli Tsarurov raised his arms.

"Little brothers, this is not the way."

He had trouble restraining them. They had seen action at the front. Fought willingly for Mother Russia. Right and wrong had simple meanings for them. Farm boys from the steppes of two mighty rivers. Men from the forests. Those born to Siberia. The first to put Germanski on the run. Some had un-shouldered their weapons. Fingers were playing at the working parts.

"When you confront devil. You strike at heart. Suffering of people must stop," roared another Cossack.

"Cossack and brother Siberians fighting together. The glory is ours. Is it not the way? Way of ancestors. They rise in grave crying for revenge. . . ."

"*Nyet. Nyet.*"

A bearded Cossack had mounted up. Tsarurov made a grab for the other bridle. The stocky pony retreated a few feet, stomping impatiently, his hooves kicking up the snow.

See little brothers. See how the pony's nose bristles. He smells the evil ones."

Anatoli Tsarurov held the bridle more firmly with two hands.

The Cossack rose in his stirrups.

"It is written that my tribe die in war defending the great Motherland. Many in Red Army say Cossack no use against Germanski. We showed them. We . . ."

Other Cossack voices shouted in agreement.

"True, *tovaritch*. Partisans from Karachev. They

101

are not many. Your sabers would draw blood. It is the N.K.V.D. Many men they have. Mortars. Machine guns. They would overpower us."

"Strange are these words to a man with Cossack blood. Little brothers. Am I not the son of my father? When he took me out onto the steppe telling me of the tribe's legends. A boy astride his first pony. Old Ivan Nikoli Semyonov did not talk of defeat," he shook his clenched fist.

"A Cossack does not count enemy. Not when he smells blood of vengeance. Villagers go . . ."

Tears were rolling down his cheeks.

"Vengeance is ours."

"You will fight bravely as you always have. But when the sounds of battle are over. When men are dead upon the snow field with your ponies. N.K.V.D. men would move into the area. The victory would be short. Brothers I tell you, you would know the anger of the Kremlin. The commissars. They would bring your families back to your village. Our families would die because of our revenge."

A drunken soldier staggered to him.

"Gospodin leytenant. My village."

"*Da.*"

Another with a fierce beard looked up from nursing his vodka.

"Lichvin."

"Kaluga."

Another spat into the fire.

"My Venev."

"Your wives and children. The N.K.V.D. They are devils. Not like the brothers of our villages. Nothing would stop them."

"Wanda."

"Ewa."

"Halina."

"My laughing Hanna."

"My Witold and Lucjan."

Angry voices reeled off the names. The vodka made their worried thoughts all the more real. Some were wiping back the tears. Frustration. Hatred. They clung to their weapons. Checked magazines. Watched the N.K.V.D. as they laughed, driving the villagers on.

"Sergi has no village. No home. No family. I will fight. Fight to the death. Enemy has been replaced by other viper."

"Faithful Sergi Vlasava. Your Cossacks need you. Who will lead them against Germanski? Tell the new riders of the black deeds of fascists. No, it is I, Anatoli Tsarurov. I must take the revenge for the death of this village."

"Anatoli," a short Siberian pushed his way through to the warmth of the bonfire.

"Husband of my sister Tatyana. Father of her two boys. Who will light the victory fires when we return to Kultuk. As son of your father. *Staross* of Kultuk. Is it not your duty. . . ."

The words hit him with the fury of an enemy tearing at his throat. He thought of his two young boys playing on the frozen water of Lake Baikal. The dogs yapping, running at the sledges. Proud Tatyana. His Tatyana. Long dark hair flowing about her face. Tempting Tatyana. Their days of courting.

"You may see my tall Anatoli. But there will be no touching until after the ceremony."

Her laughter echoing out over the lake. Slapping her sides and throwing her head back. A defiant motion that he had seen in young stallions as a boy. Wild. Untamed. The pride. The flame of those born to Siberia.

Her gurgling deep-throated giggling.

"Come, little ones. I will show you how to fish like men of the far north. Come . . . you must learn. Siberian winters are hard. But there is food . . . for those who know how. Come, little ones."

He could sense the hard chips of ice plucking at his neck. The boys full of excitement trying to make their own holes. Childish laughter. Their breath hanging before their faces like a giant mist. One slip and the dogs were upon them. Together they would roll over and over on the ice. The dogs breaking free, teeth going for their fur caps. Had those days been so long ago?

"Death is not for you to face alone. Siberians have a rightful place by your side. It has always been the way with us."

"*Urah. Urah.*"

The loud shouting caused the N.K.V.D. to look in their direction. They raised their fists in salute. They thought the cries were yet another in praise of brother Stalin.

"Holy Mother Russia must be revenged."

"When the devil rests at his fire upon the steppes, you creep up and plunge your saber through his heart."

"*Nyet,*" he took a fresh bottle from a Siberian's hand.

His mind was made up.

"This I must do alone. That is an order. Never have I sent you into battle where I would not go. I will kill the executioners. Andri . . . and his partisans from Karachev. I swear by the Holy Mother of Kazan. They will die this very night."

"*Tovaritch.* They will cut you down like a dog."

He forced a laugh.

"I am Siberian. I will find a way."

The torches had been put to most of the *isbas*. The

104

Mongolians were running among them like demented children. The war against the fascists was much fun. Why stay at home in your *yurt* tending the herds of roaming goats. There was talk that soon they would come to the big cities. Such places where the skin of women was pure white. Many women there would be. Enough for every boy from Kazakstan.

Chapter 7
SIBERIAN SOLDIER

Ninety-eight repatriated Siberian soldiers marched into the burning village under a strong armed escort of N.K.V.D. guards. The enemy had crossed the Don River. They were captured on November 26th by the 167th German Infantry Division. They had fought at Ivanozero. Been surrounded and captured at Danskoie. In captivity they had been used for trench digging. The building of fortifications and bunkers. Chern fell to the advancing Red Army on December 24th. They had hugged the soldiers when they broke through at Chern. Sang and danced with them. Balalaikas strummed, and they stomped in dance circles in the snow. Once the front rolled forward, they were rounded up by the following N.K.V.D.

Stalin's order of November 25th was read out to them at the staging area east of Danskoie. Before the first shots of battle the Red Army commissar had lectured them. Each man had to stand and fight. Stand fast. Germanski had to be stopped once and for all on the road to Moscow. They swore to fight to the death. The fascists had to be wiped out. With four thousand others they were taken prisoner.

Freedom. Their release from captivity. Forward Russian infantry had fed them. Greeted them like long-lost brothers. The *machorka* was snatched away from them and trampled in the snow. More

N.K.V.D. arrived in motorcycles and side cars. Then followed the march out of the front-line area.

They had cursed the guards as only Siberians can. All they had wanted was to be re-equipped. Some *machorka* to smoke. They were ready. They argued aloud that they wanted to continue the fight against the invader. Begged for revenge that tore at their hearts. Many of their number had died in captivity.

An N.K.V.D. major had climbed into the back of an open truck.

"Brother Stalin's orders were to stand and fight at Danskoie."

"*Tovaritch*," they had openly laughed at him at first.

"With no ammunition."

"Barehanded against fascist panzers."

He had obviously not been in close contact with Germanski at the front.

"You had good Russian rifles and bayonets. You could have made a suicide charge."

More laughter sounded. Catcalls. Hooting. Here was a major who knew nothing of hand-to-hand fighting.

A Siberian captain forced his way through the men. He stood below the tailboard at the back of the truck.

"I saw no N.K.V.D at our positions at Danskoie. They pulled out before Germanski had us surrounded. Ran all the way back to the Kremlin. You talk to us. You dare talk to the Siberian of war. It was us . . . our men who put Germanski on the run."

The other Siberian soldiers roared with laughter.

"Why were those men of your uniform not arrested?"

The N.K.V.D. major was becoming uneasy. The

sea of faces before him was laughing. Laughing at him. The ranks of the N.K.V.D.

"They were withdrawn on orders from Moscow."

"*Tovaritch. Tovaritch,*" someone shouted at the back.

"N.K.V.D. ran for their lives. Like dogs with tails between their legs, when bears in the forest come out to hunt."

The renewed laughter welled up. One began to sing a convict song. A lament telling of the cruel long whips of the N.K.V.D. The long nights on the transports. The cursed forced trek over the steppes.

The Siberians began to rock the truck, lining it on each side.

"*Urah. Urah.*"

The major had to grip the side.

"Rearm us. The Siberian wants to fight."

"Death to the fascist invader."

"Enough political talk. Time is to fight for little Mother Russia."

A pistol shot rang out. The captain fell, his hands clutching at the truck. The N.K.V.D. major fired again. Half his face was shot away. Other Siberians fell, shot at point-blank range of only a few meters. Submachine gun fire crashed out, firing high over their heads. When the shouting stopped they were bludgeoned into tighter ranks.

"Siberians have pride. You are traitors. You collaborated with the fascists."

Angrily many of them protested their innocence. The guards moved in lunging with their rifle butts.

"You will be escorted out of the line until we get orders from Moscow."

The sealed orders arrived at the headquarters of N.K.V.D. Major Mikhail Kholminov. He turned to Lieutenant Alexandr Yershov, his second in command.

"Traitors. Incompetents. Stalin wants us to deal with them here."

"One out of ten, *gospodin* major. Moscow is indeed generous."

The ninety two remaining Siberians were shuffling forward in a long, wavering, single file. Their hopes of seeking revenge on repatriation were almost forgotten. Their joy and hope for the future had been dramatically shattered. They were back in the homeland. The rigid repression of the Stalin regime was still the same. The era of brotherly love that they had known when Moscow was threatened, gone.

Selection. The word that struck terror into the hearts of millions during the Second World War. It was not invented by the S.S. in the vile death camps of Poland. It had been used with devastating effect for countless generations in Russia. Under the dictatorship of Stalin millions of Russians entered the confines of his concentration camps. Many of the living dead are still there.

"Eight. Nine. You."

The savage thrust of a bayonet point into the small of the back. Tormenting guards laughing. The crack of a whip drawing blood.

"You. *Da*. You."

The terrified reaction on the face of the prisoner. Struggle and curse. Numb feeling flooding the body. The selected one. The suffocating realization.

"Him." That evil leering smile.

Another is pulled from the lineup. Head lowered, he tries to escape the flurry of blows.

"I have committed no crime, *gospodin*. . . ."

"*Davay!*" a rifle butt knocks him down.

Spitting broken teeth, bewildered, groggy, he stands to one side.

Selected one. By the authority of Moscow. You do not complain. You obey. Nagan pistols are near. Complain and a red smudge will appear behind the right ear. Do not the soulful songs of little Mother Russia explain? It is the land of suffering. Under the Czar it was that way. Under Stalin it became much worse. Has it not always been that way? Will it ever change?

Siberian soldier Victor Lazansky looked ahead at the group of sadistic N.K.V.D. guards. Other comrades were being beaten mercilessly forward. Two guards were grinning and poking at him. He stumbled. Righted himself. And when he looked up the selector's eyes met his. He was number ten.

"Him."

"*Davay. Davay.*"

He cowered under the reign of blows. Whips. Rifle butts. A bayonet just piercing his thick padded jacket. A boot. A stinging blow to the thigh. He fell sprawling into the snow and slush.

Vasilevich was there. Bruised face. Eye bleeding. Still he held his head well back. So proud. That defiant look gleaming in his eyes. Men like him were not easily broken. Hard as the Siberian winter. Even Germanski had not made him beg. Alexandrov. Koslov. Little Vladimir Matvienko. He was no Siberian, but from the rich farming lands of the Ukraine. He had kept their spirits high while in captivity. Pretended that he was a simple village idiot. Germanski infantry soldiers had taken pity on him.

"*Komm kleine Vladimir,*" they would laugh.

"Silver pheasants want their *scheisshaus* cleaned. *Los. Schnell.*"

"I come Herr Germanski *Soldat. . . .*"

He would come to attention, hat sweeping low in a gentlemanly bow. Do a little jig. As though he were a puppet from a visiting state circus. Arms bent, legs and arms jerking in time to a hidden string.

"Vladimir. I clean special outhouses for Stalin in Kremlin. Take much shit in Mother Russia. . . ."

The Landser gave him extra bread. At times whole sausages. Cigarettes. He shared his spoils with the other prisoners. He would dance for them. The high leaps of the Cossacks.

"I no *politruk*. No communist. Vladimir Ukrainian village boy. Silly boy . . . like song . . . village dance."

The Landser clapped in time to his antics. He would cavort and leap. Down on his haunches. To the left, to the right. His feet flying. All the time accompanied on the accordion played by Koslov. The more laughs he got, the more food was thrust into his Red Army cap. Food for comrades. Survival for another day. The regulation was one foul bowl of nettle soup between four men. His extras helped keep many of them alive.

A peasant idiot. Typical example of a mentally deranged subhuman. Something was lacking. How he delighted in fooling them. Clever Vladimir. To the war hungry Siberians he was something else. Vladimir the provider. In quieter moments. The dreamer. Of a Ukraine free from the communist yoke. No more tyranny. An end to the much hated collective. If Germanski gave him vodka, he would speak of his greatest wish. To escape. To go home to the plains of the Ukraine. Join the bands of *Organizatsiya Ukrainskikh Natsionalistov*. Partisans who fought both the Germans and Russians. Taking an active part in helping to create the new free Ukraine.

Little Vladimir Matvienko was no longer smiling.

Victor Lazansky watched the last of his comrades being selected.

"Stay clear of the political officers. The commissars," his father had warned before he left the *kolkhos*.

The elder Lazansky had spoken from bitter experience. Early in 1931, when Victor was but eight years old, his father had been branded as a *kulak*, a wealthy peasant. Stalin had decreed that in the communist state there was no place for those of wealth. He was the owner of a cow and a calf, and also two fine working horses. The *kulaks* were hunted down like animals and driven out from the villages.

On old horse-drawn farm carts, on sledges and on foot they were driven across the wide rolling steppes. The old and very young died off within the first few weeks. Cruel task masters, the escorting G.P.U. troops drove them on. Those that lagged behind through sheer exhaustion were shot on the spot. Men, women, children. The steppes and virgin forests of Siberia were littered with their dead and dying.

At the mighty towering forests they were turned loose, like cattle. The G.P.U. troops left them. They had to carve out a village in the wilderness or they would perish. The G.P.U. had promised to return in the spring to help set up lumber camps. In the bitter cold of the first winter, the surviving numbers from the long march were halved again. Victor's younger brothers and sisters died. His mother was already suffering from T.B. There was nothing they could do to save her.

With little remaining food, they tore the bark from the trees to eat. Twigs, pine needles, moss, it was made into a soup. Many others died. Others walked off into the snow, thoughts with their lost loved ones. Found a hollow. Lay down, never to rise again, at last finding the peace that would never come under Stalin.

The G.P.U. had left them only scanty tents as protection against the harsh winter, and the angry, growling incessant snowstorms. Starving men and boys hunted with the most rudimentary of weapons. A return to the Stone Age. For weeks on end they would starve until another deer or bear was killed. They killed their prey with rudely fashioned clubs. On the bear hunt it was not unusual to bury three or four of the hunters. To come within the reach of the tearing massive claws was to risk one's life. One swipe and another hunter was disemboweled.

Gradually, through the long winter months, the shape of a village appeared. For a while, once their hunting methods improved, they knew the joy of a newfound freedom. When the ice began to melt in the spring the G.P.U. troops returned. They came escorting another convoy of pathetic *kulaks*.

The village was formed into a *kolkhos*. A collective timber unit. Machines were brought in. Livestock. Cows. Chickens. Horses. Pigs. Work. Work. Work. There was timber to cut. Haul. Saw. They were granted only six hours sleep nightly. Moscow had set the timber quotas. They had to be met. They had also changed the contingent of G.P.U. guards. No longer were they White Russians. Now they were vicious Mongol guards. They knew only one law. That of brother Stalin in Moscow.

Some of those who had survived the winter rebelled. They had seen their families die off. To be exiled to Siberia was worse than any form of slavery. Far worse than working on their former collectives. The Mongol G.P.U. troops were far more brutal than their predecessors. The whip. The rifle. It was the Mongol answer to everything. A concentration camp without the walls of barbed wire. Slaves who

113

were only meant to toil with bent backs. Not daring to look up. The Mongols had sharp eyes. Work. Work. Work. For the state. Exiles had no rights.

The commissar lectured them.

"Kulaks. The party in all its wisdom has spared your wretched lives. You exploited the peasants in your old *kolkhos*. Your comrades. Your fellow brothers and sisters. You became rich. Czars in your own village. Had much livestock. Breaking the backs of those who worked for you. In your village shops. Blacksmiths. Mills. Upon your stolen patches of land. Moscow pardoned your wrongs. The great Soviet state transported you here to the new frontiers. Provided you with a glorious future in the pioneering lands. You will help build the new Mother Russia from the ashes of the old. You repay the state by refusing to go out to work. Did your beasts of the field ask how long they should labor? We are helping to build a strong nation. You are fortunate to be part of it. To create our Motherland's future everyone has to work hard. Fulfill the quotas set by those in Moscow. They are educated. They know what is needed in our land."

The Mongol's fiends in the arts of deceit and cunning went about their selections with renewed vigor. At the age of nine, young Victor Lazansky saw his first grotesque public hanging. The bodies were left to rot at the entrance of each village.

By 1941 Victor had become a man. The fascists had invaded the Motherland. From Moscow Stalin made impassioned speeches.

"Brothers. Sisters. Comrades in arms. Mother Russia is threatened. She needs you in these trying times. Our gallant Red Army must be strong. The Germanski terror must be stopped."

Many sons of Siberian exiles refused to join the

Red Army. Their haunting childhood memories of the long march were only too vivid in their minds. Watching as members of their families died. The G.P.U. troops casting the bodies away from the sledges, out into the snow-covered steppes. Seen many others die in that first awful Siberian winter. No one owed allegiance to the fat moustached pig in Moscow. To many of them Germanski was welcome. His new order could not be any more wicked than brother Stalin's.

Examples were made. The G.P.U. Mongol troops were only too willing. Selected ones were shot down in cold blood. Still the number of exiles' sons and daughters entering the Red Army remained at a trickle.

Moscow changed its tactics. The Germanski legions were flooding towards Moscow. Daily over the wireless came reports of atrocities committed by the invading fascists. Plundered villages. Half a million Russian soldiers had died fighting valiantly in the first few weeks of battle. Monsters they were gathering for the final push on Moscow. Soon all of little Mother Russia would be burning under the torch of the fascists.

Individual Red Army soldiers and peasant women told their stories over the air waves.

"We had lost communication to the rear. I was taking a message for the regimental commissar. He was calling for T.34s. More artillery."

Stirring patriotic music almost drowned out his voice in places.

"From my observation on the hill I saw it all. My regiment fought until the very last. They died gallantly with their rifles still in their hands. They fought Germanski panzers bare-handed. Only a Russian knows how to fight for his Motherland.

Wounded comrades. Sorokin . . . with only one leg . . . he charged Germanski . . . blowing himself up . . . but taking five fascist pigs with him. . . . I saw prisoners lined up. Laughing S.S. storm troopers cut them down with machine gun fire. They mutilated the wounded. Karpov . . . he had a head wound . . . the fascists made him dig his own grave. . . . then they beheaded him. Bandera . . . they crushed his legs and arms under the panzer tracks . . . then left him to die. . . ."

A peasant woman's story. The martial music changed to that of the village. Setting the mood for the making of the special Easter cakes. Dancing. The freshly sown fields. The wonder that is spring, coming with such a blast after the snows of winter. Creaking of the ploughs. The ploughman following the horses, smoking his pipe.

"I am Ludmilla Kornienko. My village is Litvinouka outside our beautiful splendid city of Kiev. The fascist invader came as we were out in the fields gathering the *kolkhos* harvest. Crop was a fine one. Older villagers said they had never seen such a potato yield. The blight had been cured. Our corn and wheat stood high. Germanski destroyed it with flamethrowers. He put the flame to all our fields. Took the young women and girls away to his brothels."

Here the music changed to the throbbing, pounding "Kalinka."

"Our babies . . . small children . . . he tore them from their mothers' breasts . . . threw them onto the bonfires . . . roasting them alive. No mercy did they show us. We . . . we were . . . only women . . . and old folk. Our brave menfolk . . . they were at the front. . . . All is quiet now. Not a dog . . . a cat or kittens. . . . My village is destroyed. My village is dead."

A ten-year-old boy.

"I am Feliks Leonid Dmitri. I am ten years. I come from Novogodek. My brothers have fallen for the Motherland at the battle of Volkovisk. My *papushka* fell at Slonim. My *mamushka* died in the bombing of Minsk. She was a T.34 driver. I help partisans of Mogilev. I beg for food from German-ski. Partisans give me hand grenades. I booby trap their back packs. At Orsha I killed three . . . and have wounded many others. My *mamushka* before she left for front . . . she said all must serve little Mother Russia. I am serving with the brave partisans. What are you doing, brother?"

The mood in the exiled villages changed. Not for the oppressive regime of communism. It was for Holy Mother Russia herself. They surged forward, running to the defense of the great Motherland. Trainload after trainload. Everyone was eager to join the ranks of the Red Army. The fascist invaders—none of them would leave little Mother Russia alive.

The Mongol G.P.U. troops looked on grinning. Not for long—they were soon back at their task of enforced slavery. With the young people leaving, those left at the *kolkhos* would have to work twice as hard. One whole day off every week would become a luxury of the past. Work. Work. Even the very old were driven into the forests. Everyone had to work harder for the final victory.

For Victor Lazansky and the other sons and daughters of the Siberian exiles there would be very little training with the Red Army. A few practice rounds of live ammunition. Then they were hurled into the raging inferno of the front line. There they would learn the art of war. What better way is there? They would learn on their first day under fire.

Their ranks were swelled by people of the Citizens' Militia. All the inhabitants of five nearby villages. The N.K.V.D rounded them up. Protesters were shot. They had no weapons or uniforms. They were expected to acquire them on the field of battle, to snatch them away from the wounded or dying, in the mass suicidal attacks.

The untrained Citizens' Militia died in their hundreds. Older men, in their sixties and seventies, froze with fear when Germanski stormed their positions. Unarmed, with not even a stick to defend themselves, they were bayoneted.

Some unarmed girls and boys reached the enemy positions. They ran down the trenches screaming for vengeance. They killed Germanskis with their bare hands. More often they died in the fierce hand-to-hand fighting. Many had their throats cut, their heads stoved in by the deadly entrenching tool. They were slaughtered with the ease of picking off sitting ducks.

"You others will be trekking to Novosibirst. To Marinsk. Kemero. For your collaboration with the fascists you have been sentenced to ten years' hard labor by Moscow."

N.K.V.D. Mikhail Kholminov watched the expressions on the Siberians' faces. He thought it had been unwise of Stalin to recruit the sons of exiles. Were they not proven reactionaries? Enemies of the people? Sons and daughters of proven Trotskyites? Kulaks did not deserve the honour of fighting in the ranks of the Red Army.

One swarthy Siberian proved braver than the rest.

"Are we all to be katorshniks? Convicts? What of the millions of our brothers and sisters, who are now in Germanski prisoner-of-war camps? When the Red Army advances, will they be treated in the same way?"

"*Da*. If they disobeyed Moscow's orders. Treatment will be same."

And us, thought Victor Lazanksy. What is to become of the selected ones? What will our fate be? Penal battalions. That was it. Worse than second-class citizens. Life in such a front-line mine-clearing unit was less than a couple of days.

Victor Lazansky and the selected ones were marched away.

"Son," how his father had constantly warned him, "In Russia never trust the politicals. They rule with fists of iron."

Four N.K.V.D. guards trailed behind them, laughing and smoking.

Penal battalions. A short life among the living dead. Battalions of the lost. Cattle of death. Half-rations. No mail. No vodka issue. Theirs would be a life far harder than any *katorshnik's*. His father had been right. There was no justice under the iron hand of communism. There never would be. Only further hardship and struggle. From one generation to the next. A cancer that would grow and smother all of society. The permanent bent back of cruel slavery. Speak out and it was ten years' hard labour. Or the short trip to the gallows.

The N.K.V.D. guards were dropping behind.

The selected ones kept up their fast pace.

"Run!" it was little Vladimir Matvienko.

"We must escape, little brothers. None of us will survive in the penal battalions."

Vasilevich was firm.

"We slow down. Attack the guards when they pass the *stolovayas*,"

"*Pliev*. Fire."

The sudden hail of machine gun fire hit them. Most were cut in two. No muffled cries came.

119

Curses. Cries for their homes in Siberia. They were dead within seconds. Shattered grisly hulks in the reddened snow.

"Sons of *kulaks*," Major Mikhail Kholminov spat into the snow. "They never make good Red Army soldiers."

Chapter 8
WHY DO YOU WEEP
LITTLE BROTHER?

Sergi Vlasava sat with his Cossacks about the bonfire. They had seen the Siberians shot down. Heard the hard labor sentences being imposed. The same fate could easily be theirs if they were captured. Slaves to the whims of Moscow. Fight to the death. No Russian soldier must allow himself to be captured. Fall for the Motherland. Or face a firing squad. For a cause which some of them were now beginning to question.

Seeing their sullen faces, the N.K.V.D. had issued extra vodka.

One of the Cossacks was weeping. A crumpled letter held in his right hand against his forehead.

Sergi Vlasava went over to him.

"Ivan Tuzhmanov. Why do you cry little brother?"

He looked up.

"My Stefan . . . Antoni . . . my sons. They died fighting for the village."

Another bearded Cossack burped aloud passing the vodka.

"*Tovaritch*. When we blast into Kiev, ride to Berlin, the fascist pigs will have much to answer for. They will pay for their misdeeds in blood. None shall escape our wrath."

"*Nyet*, Germanski," sobbed Ivan Tuzhmanov. "It was the partisans. Our Russian comrades."

The other Cosssacks drew closer.

"Came to village for cattle."

Sergi Vlasava took the crumpled letter.

"Partisans taxed us heavily. Like Stalin before Motherland war. We are simple Cossack folk. We have to eat. Raided our granaries. Stole our cattle. Horses. All in the name of Moscow. Partisan leader told us it was for the good of little Mother Russia. Stalin has ordered that we must support the partisans. But we too have to live. Stalin has said, only those who fight deserve to eat in the war against the fascists.

"Reprisals were many that they made against us. They come also for our young ones . . . our boys . . . our girls. They say they must go to the forests. Stalin gives little choice. To die for the Motherland. Die gallantly in battle against Germanski. Or like cowards before the doors of our *isbas* . . . if they refuse to take up arms.

"Germanski gave us arms to protect Cossack villages. Partisans stripped our larders bare. We formed bands of Citizens' Militia.

"I told the partisan leader you are serving at the front, dear Ivan. That boys and girls left in village are only fourteen and fifteen years old. Are needed in village to do work of men.

"A week later the partisan band returned. In the dark of the long night. Our boys helped defend the village. Partisans have mortars. Much was the damage done. Stefan and Antoni were wounded. Partisans hung them by feet and flogged them. Would not allow us to cut them down. They say no one has the right to die in peace, while Germanski is in our land.

"In the *isba* of their mother, *Khalauchuk* girls were raped. Partisans say . . . they need sport. It is lonely in forests without women. Older men protested. Old Anton Vlas Grigoryevich is no more. They tried to make him eat pony droppings. To lick the leader's high boots. All the time he shook his head. They killed him with saber.

"The partisans put the village to the torch.

"The Cossack Citizens' Militia from the next village drove them off. They found the *Khalauchuk* girls. Couldn't recognize them by their faces. They hung them inside the *stolovaya.*

"Dyada Dutov cut the boys down. Many of our villages have known the suffering. Stefan and Antoni rest at peace beside little Anna . . . who we lost in the great famine."

In grim silence the letter was passed from hand to hand.

Ivan Tuzhmanov wiped his eyes.

"I will not ride with the Cossacks to Berlin."

He began scraping a blackened burnt potato with his knife.

"I will return to my village."

"*Tovaritch.* Kiyasov and his sons will ride with you."

"Here. Platov will join you."

"And Krasnov. You will not ride alone, little brothers."

"Death to the partisans."

"Stalin purges start again in our villages. Cossack villages. None are safe. Must our people be forced to eat the hay of our cattle? Bark from the birch trees? Stalin made the Cossack promises and we rode to war. Now our families are threatened. It is time to make decisions, little brothers. Moscow is stabbing us in the back. . . ."

"Sharpen your sabers. Throw aside the shackles of Moscow. We are free Cossacks. Not old women of the village. The Cossack does not hide from the drums of war. He fights. He leads the battle charge. From the Don to the Volga, we are one."

"This night. Feed your ponies well, little brothers. The ride is long back to the home villages. We will return and put the partisans to the saber. No longer will he make our folk cower in their *isbas*. Time is for revenge. Germanski can wait. It is partisan blood we want."

"Hurrah! Hurrah!"

Drawn sabers glistened in the glow from the fire. Yermak took up his balalaika. Vodka bottles rose in a defiant Cossack salute to death. They spread out from the fire, the circle widening.

The horrifying scene became clearer in Sergi Vlasava's mind. The bodies strewn about the snow field. Dying mothers had reached out for their children. Very young children, babes in arms, had been left untouched. No bullets scarred their bodies. They died frozen in effigy, screaming, trying to wake their massacred mothers. His mind swam close to insanity. Now the dreaded S.S. had been replaced by their own partisans. The Motherland war had taken another turn.

Low at first, the Cossacks began to clap. The age-old pounding of Cossack hoofbeats. It became steady, threatening in its intensity. The full gallop. Dust rising in gigantic clouds over the rolling steppes. War cries. Cries that had chilled the hearts of many enemies.

Someone pushed Sergi Vlasava into the circle. He took a high leap. Two others joined him. Cartwheels. Down on their haunches. Leaning slightly back, hands and legs flying in a blur of speed. Still weeping, Ivan Tuzhmanov cartwheeled around the low dancing figures.

The hand-clapping was growing like distant thunder upon the steppes.

Their voices filled the cold night air. The lonely Cossack pining for the river of his homeland. That stand of birch trees. Dust rising from the flying hoofs as the village came into sight. The many-colored head scarves as the womenfolk came out to greet them.

"Play on, gypsy."

Laugh. Weep. Cry. Sacred blood flows in the veins. Blood crying for vengeance.

Lieutenant Anatoli Tsarurov caressed the keen edge of his *kandra* battle knife. At close quarters, when there was no time to reload magazines, it was the most ideal of weapons. Feared from one end of Russia to the other. With his men he had cleared whole trenches of Germanski with it. A swipe at the throat. The cross rip of the gut. No other close combat weapon was more deadly. No Siberian went into battle without it.

He thought of the sickly grinning bearded face of Andri Isakouski, the partisan leader. This long night he would know the fury of those born to Siberia. This night he would die. Kill all the partisans from Karachev. This long night their days of infamy would end. Vengeance would be his.

Monsters. They worked well with their cruel task masters the N.K.V.D. Two vile instruments of war, bound by no laws of man. Killing their own brothers and sisters. Comrades. Simple village peasants. Their men gone to the Motherland war. They had to be struck down.

Communism meant more to him than the religion

of his *mamushka* and *papushka*. As a youth he had laughed at their bent figures beneath the ikons. The bowed heads and clasped hands. Whispered prayers. Praise to the Holy Mother of Kazan.

Communism was the state. Since his days of youth in the Komsomol. It held Russia together. United her many and varied peoples. The savior of the masses. One day the whole world would see how right Russia was. When the days of capitalist greed came to an end. Then the world would be reborn.

He had studied at the Frunse Military Academy. A model communist. Troop leader of the Komsomol. The new breed of Mother Russia. He had such dreams. Hopes of his father. One day he would go far in his military career. To the heights of *Stavka*, the Russian high command. The war with the fascists: what young Red Army officer had not dreamed of rapid promotion? His came. After months of tough fighting he became a full lieutenant. That was at Danskoie. Danskoie—was it so very long ago?

The mock N.K.V.D. trial. Hostages, doomed to die of brutal torture. The fate of the repatriated Siberians. How many times at the front had he seen the N.K.V.D. shooting into the ranks of his own men, when for several moments they faltered under Germanski machine gun fire. They had stained the character of the Motherland.

In daily wireless bulletins, Stalin was calling for more heroic effort from the masses. While Moscow was laying to waste whole tracts of land. Villages, towns. Whole populations. The hangman's noose. Firing squads. Victims hastily covered in shallow graves. N.K.V.D. murder squads. Partisan units, making their own laws of the forest. Men who governed the country with a terror and brutality never known before.

He put the last of his vodka to his lips. How good it felt. An inner warmth that would make him strong this night. He had ordered his men not to help. When the N.K.V.D. found the bodies, they would assume it was a drunken fight. Rivalry between two bands of soldiers.

Throughout history many men had sacrificed their lives for the good of little Mother Russia. Thousands were dying at the front. His death would be but another casualty of war. A war which would also shape into a war of the people. Others would follow before the fascists were driven from the land. Revenge had to be taken for the death of the village, the treatment of the repatriated Siberians. He had to strike before the pages of history finally turned.

Chapter 9
PARTISAN FROM KARACHEV

The oil lanterns flickered in the interrogation *isba*. Shadows danced and played at the clay walls. One of the partisans was picking lice from under his armpits. Popping them with an oily splutter in the flame of a candle.

"*Nyet. Nyet*," Andrushka Koslova was crying hysterically.

"No fascist shared my bed. I am a married woman. My husband fell at the front. Have you no pity?"

Andri Isakouski was glaring at her. Picking his teeth with a small sliver of wood. He had joined the N.K.V.D. major in yet another feast of pork. It had been prepared by the major's Mongol mistress. She had the face of a Eurasian. Fine unblemished skin. Sixteen years of age, and already she was very skilled in the art of bedwarming.

"Germanski whore. All women of village were bedded by fascists. They stayed at your *isbas*. You kept house for them."

The lice-popping partisan looked up.

"You opened your legs to the fascist swine. Suckled them with your breasts."

Alina Akimenko had regained consciousness. Her eyes were swollen. Her face bruised by the beatings. Blood had congealed at the corners of her broken lips.

"Only the district commissar forced himself upon us. . . ."

A clenched fist smashed into her face.

"An official of our great Soviet state does not mix with village whores."

"He told of our men falling. . . ."

Again the fist lashed at her.

He ripped the front of her torn dress, tearing it away from the shoulders. The other partisans closed in. Her naked body was exposed from the waist. Her full breasts wobbled slightly as she struggled. The Mongol licked his lips.

"Fix now, Andri . . . like in Karachev." He could not take his eyes from the beautiful young breasts.

"Strip them," Andri Isakouski roared with drunken laughter.

"Now we see what Germanski took in the village."

They set upon the three women, tearing the rest of their clothes off. They screamed as the rough hands fondled their breasts. Fingers going low, brutally exploring further.

"Andri. This cow has milk."

While the others held her fast the Mongol cupped and squeezed Andrushka Koslova's breasts. The milk was yielded easily from the full breasts. He threw back his head, directing a steam of it towards his mouth.

"Better than sour milk from goat in Kazakstan," he giggled, the milk dribbling and running down his beard.

The Mongol got down upon his knees sucking hungrily, first upon the right, then upon the left breast.

Natasha Petrov screamed.

"Slant-eyed demon. You will rot in hell. May your mother . . ."

The partisan leader kicked her in the stomach.

"*Stoi*, Volga whore."

Igor Lutchenko had slowly regained consciousness. His face was a mass of dark bruises.

"Have you no shame?"

"October hero speaks," they laughed.

"Fine Red Guardsman."

Andri Isakouski spat a long stream of vodka at the old man.

"Hot your friend the iron," he ordered the leering Mongol.

"We see how brave you are when iron speaks." He doubled up laughing aloud. "You protect honor of women."

He leaned forward, savagely grabbing Natasha Petrov's breasts. He squeezed and twisted them until she cried out in agony.

"Iron takes eyes, old man. You beg for mercy like Germanski. Like those we take from Rollbahn blockhouse. Young boys with smooth faces of women."

Da, his mind went back to the battle on that mist-filled day. Under fire Germanski had showed white flag of surrender. Only four were left alive. Explosives and dumdum rifle bullets had done their job well. Fifty partisans had stormed the blockhouse after two hours of fighting. Ten of his comrades lay dead and dying in the snow. Revenge was theirs.

His partisans had stripped the young Wehrmacht soldiers. Bent them back over the broad logs. Spread their trembling legs wide apart. The filthy pigs. Excreta and urine had flowed down their legs. How they begged and cried. Those young men with faces smooth as women. Only days before he had found the bodies of seven of his own men. The S.S. had executed them.

Vasili the Mongol had taken their manhood from them. With stolen heavy duty Wehrmacht wire cutters. Burnt the eyes of the smooth-skinned ones with the hot irons. Screams had echoed out over frozen steppes. The old ones had been brought from a nearby village to watch. One of the *Soldats* had been fed to the old *babushka* from the village. She made him howl. She made the partisan H cut on his stomach. They shook his gut loose and turned the village dogs loose upon him. After twenty minutes there was nothing left but the bloodied cavity.

The fascist pig Hitler was sending schoolboys to the front. Boys with voices not yet broken. They fixed that. Made them sing. Voices lost woman's tone. Only croaking. Like the large frogs of the Pripet Marshes. Whining, screaming, through a torrent of blood and vomit.

Fair skinned Germanski *Soldats* would not die. Rolled around on all fours on the snow. Hands pressed to unseeing eyes. Calling for their *mamushkas*. Calling upon their fascist gods. Young men crying at the time of war. Fascist invaders who had swarmed over the great Motherland like a plague of summer lice.

Two cried vengeance. Never had they seen it before.

"Ihr verfluchten schweinhunde."

One of them got hold of an automatic rifle that had been propped against the log. He took the lives of two partisans and the *babushka*.

It was then that he gave the order to slice off their buttocks. Time for fun was short. A runner had reported another partisan ambush on the Rollbahn. Commissar was calling for him. Never could it be said that he did not heed the words of Moscow.

The steppe dogs had fought over the tasty flesh.

Barked aloud, growling and begging for more. Two came near to killing each other, fighting over the last bloodied piece. Germanski *Soldats* had scuttled about in the snow. Like old women looking for lost kopecks.

Strong birch saplings were bent back. No fascist would leave Mother Russia alive. Only partisans could teach the true meaning of revenge. They would seed the steppes and forests. Their remains left to feed the carrion. The wolves.

Arms were tied to one tree. Legs to another. Two fascist *Soldats* fainted. They were brought around. For true revenge to work, the body had to be wide awake. The pegged holding ropes were cut. The saplings sprang back to the vertical. Streams of spraying Germanski blood splattered out over the snow. With howling screams the bodies were torn apart. The shredded remains hung flapping in the trees.

Two days later the relief platoon found them. Not men of war these. They swarmed about the birch grove. Ran back to their tracked vehicles for strong axes. They cut the birches down. The explosive booby trap claimed more Germanski lives. Germanski was slow to learn. It did a stout Russian heart much good to watch the confusion. Afterwards the relief platoon buried the remains. They stood about the hole saying a prayer to their devil god. He let them finish. Then his men cut the last ten Germanski down with explosive bullets to the stomach. The lieutenant they saved for play. The Gross Deutschland pig. He cheated them. He took a small pistol from the top of his boot and blew his brains out.

Vasili the Mongol came into the *isba* with the hot glowing iron.

"Nyet. Nyet. Karachev devils. *Nyet . . ."*

Igor Lutchenko pulled at his wired bonds.

"Old man." Spittle and saliva were running from the Mongol's mouth.

"Da, October hero was brave Red Army Guardsman. He will take much pain." Andri Isakouski offered the vodka bottle.

"A toast to brother Stalin. Our great communist state . . . before you go."

The eyes of the old man flamed with hatred. He spat at the partisan leader, hitting him full in the face.

He wiped the spittle from his face with a grin.

"October hero has no stomach for war."

"Da, stomach," chuckled the Mongol.

"Make him sing like Germanski *Soldat."*

"Da, Vasili."

Igor Lutchenko cowered back into the corner of the *isba.* The Mongol followed him slowly, chuckling and clucking his tongue. The red-hot iron struck. Once. Twice. The flesh hissed, sizzling. He rocked back and forth, his eyes rolling. Still the iron found him. Striking again and again.

The women hostages fainted.

Long before the sadistic Mongol had finished the old man was dead.

"Traitor. No wish to defend the great Motherland. This is how all cowards should die."

"Da, Mongol way. Is sweet for traitors."

The *isba* reeked of burnt flesh. The old man's clothes were smoldering. A partisan stomped the grotesquely curled body. The red glow at his trousers was stamped out.

When the women came around they were gagged. He turned the Mongols loose upon them. His instructions were strict. Women were not normal. Not like the true women of Mother Russia. Was only one way to teach Germanski bedwarmers. Assault them from the back. Dogs of swine should be treated like bitches. Germanski whores, they deserved no better.

Later he called other Mongols to the *isba*. They came running, overjoyed at their good fortune. Boys, men from the dry wastes of Kazakstan. Their bestiality was well known in the Red Army. Years later they would blaze a trail to Berlin, which would take many generations to dull the horrid memory. Were these not the fruits they had been promised when they left their lonely *yurts?*

"Mongols different from Germanski," he cried sarcastically.

"Have fascists more passion than our little brothers?"

Chapter 10
VENGEANCE IS FOR THE COSSACK

He soon tired of watching the exhibition. He clapped his hands waving them aside.

"Home, little ones. Back to your posts." He chased the last ones out through the door.

When the last Mongols had left he turned to the other partisans.

"Cut hair off. All of it."

The knives glinted, the hair falling away.

"Moscow has declared that theirs must be slow death. We skin them alive. Breasts first. Show them what partisans do to Germanski bedwarmers."

The last of the hair was falling away. One of the women was foaming at the mouth. The howling that rose from her was like that of the devil himself.

"You opened legs to fascist. Gave him comfort. soon you will beg for death. It will not come easy."

"After breasts . . . we cut tongues out. . . ."

"Brand with sign of Germanski swastika," growled another.

The door shook on its hinges, falling to the floor. Anatoli Tsarurov stood in the doorway, his submachine gun raised.

"*Stoi*. Back off, *tovaritch*," he warned a partisan standing before Natasha Petrov, his knife inches from her breasts.

"Slowly . . . weapons to the floor."

The knives fell, the startled partisans backing off.

"So this is the new Moscow directive, Andri Isakouski."

"Anatoli . . . *tovaritch*."

Smiling he walked forward, his empty hands splayed wide.

"What are women to you? Peasant women. You want women. I will get women for you. Two. I'll give you young Mongol women. My men will fetch them. You like very young Mongol girls? They know gentle ways of the far east. You will like that, Anatoli, *tovaritch*. They will show you many ways. Ways a Siberian boy does not know. . . ."

"Drop the pistol belt."

"Anatoli . . . What is this? Partisans are under orders. N.K.V.D. orders. You sat at the village trial. You heard the testimonies. Moscow has decreed. You know. . . ."

"Drop the pistol."

Slowly his eyes became accustomed to the light. The stench of foul-smelling burnt flesh. Igor Lutchenko lay doubled up in a corner, in death his hands buried deep in his blackened mutilated stomach. The look in the eyes of the women. Two of them were already insane. One was talking, crooning to her hand with the soft voice of a child.

"Give me my children. I want my little ones." Her hand danced before her, thumb and forefinger opening like a mouth.

"The commissar said if I was nice he would take me to Orel. He has a fine house there made of brick. . . ."

Footsteps sounded in the crunching snow behind him. He swung around.

"Cossacks, *gospodin* leytenant. The Cossack lets

136

no man fight his battles alone."

Sergi Vlasava came forward into the light, four other Cossacks clustered about him.

Seizing their chance the partisans grabbed for their weapons. The Cossacks crowded into the *isba*.

Anatoli Tsarurov fired from the hip. The Mongol was thrown back against the wall with the violent impact, further rounds cutting his face away.

Then Andri Isakouski was upon him. With a high kick his weapon was knocked from his grasp. The first thrust of the partisan's long knife caught him across the cheek. Warm blood running. It trickled to his half-opened mouth. Grappling and fighting for a hold they fell to the floor. His right hand fumbled desperately for his *kandra*. The sweating bearded face butted him. He reeled, falling onto his haunches, falling amongst the women. They screamed, naked legs thrashing, trying to get away.

Natasha Petrov tore at the hated partisan leader's face. Her right clenched hand came away. Four deep gouge marks appeared under the eye on his right cheek, filling with blood. He kicked her low in the stomach, then came back at Anatoli Tsarurov.

Anatoli pulled his *kandra* free. He made a wide slash for the face. He felt it grind against the bone of the nose. The grin left the face. The nose hung on a sliver of bloody flesh. Again he struck out with the trusty *kandra*. The nose fell away, the partisan screaming aloud with tortured pain.

Natasha Petrov was on her feet again. None from across Mother Volga die easily. Her *papushka's* words came to her. Mother Volga watches over us, little daughter. We are the heartland of Mother Russia. Until the Volga is lost, there will always be a Mother Russia. She stood waiting with the cocked submachine gun. Waiting for an opening. A gap in the bloody whirling sabers. Partisans—they had drawn her blood. Blood of a Volga woman. Revenge must be hers. She emptied the remainder of the magazine into the stomach of a blood-spitting partisan.

Sergi Vlasava pricked a fallen partisan under the chin with his curved saber.

"Sergi was partisan over the Don. We helped the people of the *kolkhos*. You . . . you demons from Karachev . . ."

He changed his grip upon the saber, two hands now firmly grasping the hilt. With a well-practiced movement he decapitated the cringing partisan. The head fell away. The arms still moved, waving in the flow of blood. The body shot up. Headless it took several paces forward. Another two-handed blow and the body was cut in two at the waist.

A partisan rushed them, his right arm going high. A saber swished, sucking at the air. Arm and knife fell to the dirt floor. With startled eyes he could only watch as he was run through.

In amongst the sprawling struggling figures a nagan pistol cracked. A Cossack slumped against the wall. His jaw was torn away. Bloodied hands capped the jaw. Another shot. The bewildered look upon the Cossack's face. A neat red blotch appeared between the eyes.

They backed the remaining partisans against the wall. One tripped over the body of Igor Lutchenko. One burnt eye popped out upon his cheek. They cut them down. Again and again the sabers fell. Natasha Petrov was pounding the butt of the submachine gun into a screaming, crying face.

"Your devil comrades hung the Tuzhmanov boys. . . ."

Outside came the rattle and cough of automatic weapons. Rifles.

"For Stefan . . . Antoni . . ."

A full-throated Cossack war cry.

The begging. Whining of someone dying upon an impaled blade.

Anatoli Tsarurov's *kandra* was knocked from his grasp. He brought his knee up savagely into the partisan leader's groin. He winced with pain.

"Siberian traitor. I kill . . ."

"Die, Karachev pig."

The partisan's head thudded into his. Lights flashed, the bright colors seemed to make the *isba* shake and sway. He shook his head, trying to clear it. His fingers groped defensively. He could not find the hand clasping the knife. His fingers tightened around the repulsive bearded throat. Throttle the life out of him before he could use the blade. He tightened the pressure. His eyes cleared. Satisfaction welled over him. The eyes of the partisan were bulging. Standing out. The body began to tremble. Chest rising and falling, gasping for air. The windpipe was slowly giving. The body was off the floor. He could feel the legs kicking in spasms.

The cold steel of the knife went in under his ribs. Still he clung to the sickly throat. The windpipe was breaking. The face. It was clouding. Going dark. The foul mouth opened sucking its last breath. The knife twisted under his ribs. The grip slackened. He braced himself for the rip that he knew was sure to come.

He felt the rush of air as the bloody saber came down. The partisan's head was cleaved in two. Blood, sinews of brain blinded him. The body fell away.

He sank down the wall gasping for air. Pulled the knife out. The violent pain tugged at his stomach, shoulders, head. His fingers traced the wound. He watched, fascinated with horror, as the blood was pumped through his fingers.

Sabers were hacking at the partisan's body. Natasha Petrov was smashing at the face.

More shots sounded from outside. Nearer now. Others were joining in the fight. Cries of alarm. The high-pitched voices of the Mongols. Other Cossacks ran by the door. The chatter of a submachine gun. Explosive bullets thudding against the wall of the *isba*. Other rifle bullets sounding like a lonely sigh upon the wind.

He became aware of Sergi Vlasava straightening his legs. Had he passed out? Someone else was cutting away at his clothes. Deft searching fingers were applying the gauze to the wound. He knew it was too late. The partisan had known just where to stick his blade.

"Take you with us, *gospodin* leytenant. . . ."

"Wound is nothing . . . nothing. . . ."

"We go back to villages. . . ."

"Stalin is not our brother. . . ."

His mind was floating into a vast ocean of blackness, his vision was fading. From the door he could feel the cold wind. How many had he comforted before death? How many. All had groaned of the sudden cold. Cold even in the hottest of dugouts. His thighs were soggy with running blood. Gauze was not helping. Nothing would help.

His thoughts and eyes cleared.

Sergi Vlasava was crouching before him.

He tried to open his mouth. Tried to speak. The pain had taken a hold like a crushing iron casket. The casket of death.

"*Nyet*. No talk, little brother Anatoli."

Hand grenades exploded somewhere out in the village street. Shouting. Siberians. He had ordered them not to join the fight. He strained his ears. No. The trusty Cossacks. What had the commissar said at Ivanozero? Ill-disciplined. Unruly. At times with the Cossack you will need a hand of iron. But fighters, little brother. They are among Mother Russia's best. They will never let you down. A shrill command whistle. A motorcycle starting up. Heavy Maxim machine gun stuttering.

Sergi Vlasava's face swam before him. He felt his hot sticky fingers taking his.

The words seemed to be coming from a distance. From another world. Somewhere out there. As though they need not concern him.

"Gut wound . . ."

"Is much blood lost?" the words came out of the void.

He wanted to say so much. Now the weakness was pressing upon him. A heavy tiredness. Unseen force. Hammering him into the clay floor. Pushing. Pushing. The room swung momentarily.

Sergi. The brave Cossacks. Faithful till the end. *Nyet*, the words would not come. Something was welling up in his throat. The hand holding his squeezed gently. He could not see the face. He answered it, blood making his fingers clammy.

His vision became startlingly clear.

The Cossacks were leaning on their sabers looking down. Two of the naked women were sobbing. Another. *Da*, it was Natasha Petrov. She was wiping his forehead. Kissing his cheeks.

"Leytenant . . ."

"Natasha . . ."

He tried to force his back hard against the wall.

"Tatyana . . ."

The hand found his brow again. The lips brushing his cheeks.

"Tatyana . . ."

"Rest *gospodin*, leytenant. . . ."

Was it Tatyana? She was in Kultuk. With the boys. Could he hear the dogs barking? Runners of the troika racing over the hardened snow. The little bells she had fixed. The rush of wind biting against his face. The fast pace down through the trees. There was the frozen lake. Baikal. Sister of the forest. The first log cottages.

"*Heya. Heya. Davia.*"

This winter they would not be cold. The troika was packed with logs.

"*Heya* Anatoli . . ."

"*Piestre. Piestre.* Faster."

He heard the other whips crack in the cold air. They were on the track coming to the lake.

"*Piestre. Piestre.*"

The four troikas were in a broad line. Each driver bent forward. Tatyana was there, waiting beside the lake.

"*Piestre.*"

"Partisans all dead. We attacked the N.K.V.D."

The gentle hand gripped his firmly once again. The moist lips kissed his. His fingers relaxed. Blood gushed to his throat. He coughed, choking.

"Tatyana."

His body turned to one side. His legs kicked at the wall. Breath . . . then it was over. His head fell to one side.

Natasha Petrov closed the eyes.

Sergi Vlasava kissed him on both cheeks, tears flowing down his face.

"Dress women from dead. They come with us."

He ground his teeth, fighting hard to control himself.

"Death to the N.K.V.D.," shouted Ivan Tuzhmanov.

"Spare none," shouted another.

"Crush the devils."

They ran out into the village street.

Three terrified Mongolians collided with them.

"Germanski come. Germanski."

Cossack sabers ran them through. They cut and slashed. The Mongols raised their arms in an effort to save themselves. The sabers beat at them without mercy. One tried to slink away dragging his wounded leg. A saber pinned him to the snow.

"*Yob tvoymat*," they barked.

"Slant-eyed ones, meet your ancestors."

A heavy Maxim machine gun had been set up between two burnt-out *isbas*. The spitting blur of stabbing flames from the barrel. It lit up the machine gunner and his loader crouched low feeding the belt.

A grenade exploded. The Maxim was silenced. From the position came a high-pitched scream of terror.

They ran on.

They came to the Maxim, the air still stifling with cordite. A burly Cossack was astride a struggling Mongol.

"*Daavidanja, tovaritch*." He bent the head back.

"So long, comrade."

He tossed the severed head out into the street.

A group of riflemen fired from over the street. Ivan Tuzhmanov staggered. An explosive bullet had plucked his fur cap off. Another tore his forehead away. He tripped, falling headlong onto his own curved saber.

"*Pyos*."

They scattered about the ruins. Other explosive bullets whipped by above their heads. There was excited chatter. A sergeant was ordering them onto their feet. Threatening to shoot them if they did not move. They waited. Then four figures dashed into the road, guns blazing. They cut them down. Lobbed a grenade at the screaming tangle of arms and legs.

N.K.V.D. Major Mikhail Kholminov had thrown the naked sixteen-year-old Mongol girl from his bed. The first shots had been small arms fire. They were answered by a Maxim.

He fumbled getting into his padded trousers. Mongol whore. She had pleaded with him to take all his clothes off. The *isba* was very hot. He had kept the stove stoked high. She had wanted to show him the Oriental way of a thousand tongues. A gypsy had taught her in Alma Ata. There was more to Kazakstan than whirlwinds and blinding dust storms. The honey was still sticking to him. Fool. Idiot. Half-drunk he had listened to her bleating.

"Germanski. Germanski."

Frightened Mongols were running by his door. Germanski. The front was nowhere near. A raiding party. A foraging party searching for prisoners. It must be. By the sound of the shooting it was a very strong one.

He would get through to command. He grabbed the field telephone. Twisted and cranked the handle. Fool that he was. Why had he excused the N.K.V.D. from guard duty. It was all the fault of those damn Siberians. That Lieutenant Tsarurov. His men were guarding the outer limits. After this there would be another trial. A court martial conducted by the N.K.V.D. A firing squad. That was all those damn exiles understood. Examples always had to be made.

"Is Germanski," giggled the Mongol girl wiping honey from her lips.

"Dress, Mongol whore. If he finds you he will eat you alive."

She stared at him, wiping the honey from her lips

with her fingers.

"Is true, major. Germanski cook Russian babies. In Alma Ata people . . ."

He got through to command. Incompetent idiots. Pigs. They were all roaring drunk.

"Germanskis broken through the village line," he spluttered.

He heard the hollow laughter. Clink of glasses. Voices of women.

"Front is miles from you, *gospodin* major."

The Mongol girl came back from the door, a heavy Red Army blanket draped about her shoulders.

"Is Germanski. Some like Cossack."

"You hear that?" he shouted into the field telephone.

"I hear the voice of a woman, *tovaritch*. Good bedwarmer."

A fusilade of shots sounded from outside. Rifles. Submachine guns.

"Your party is wild, major," the voice laughed drunkenly.

Frustrated, Kholminov looked over at the Mongol girl. She had cupped her full breasts in her hands and was looking at her reflection in the long mirror. Her hands left the breasts and went to her plump thighs, caressing them. She struck a provocative pose and began to decorate her nipples with honey. Vixen. She knew the hold she had over him. She was wearing him out.

"Give me Colonel Arno Aleksei Babazhanyan."

A squeal of laughter came over the phone. A lilting Mongol woman's voice purred.

"Enough man for two women. Look how strong it grows. . . ."

A scuffling took place at the other end. The sound

of a strong hand slapping naked flesh.

"Colonel Babazhanyan. Kholminov. What's this about a party? Squandering party funds. You sly old dog. What have you got there, *tovaritch?* A detachment of searchlight girls?" he chuckled.

"Muscovites. Save a plump one for me, *tovaritch.*"

His drunken laughter echoed over the field telephone.

"Village is under attack. . . ."

"Kholminov. Take a holiday, little brother. The front is far from your position. Our great brother Stalin threw in a hundred divisions before Moscow. Germanski is on the run."

He heard the colonel slurping into his vodka and the cooing of a woman close by.

"I tell you, *gospodin* colonel . . . it grows again . . . are all white Russians so powerful? Like grass on the steppes after a summer storm. . . ."

He heard them go into a passionate embrace.

"An end to this nonesense, Kholminov. You need to be nearer the front attached to the Guards' Divisions. My pretties are calling me now. . . ."

"Alma Ata here," came a taunting teasing woman's voice.

He threw down the telephone in disgust.

"Again, Mikhail." The young Mongol girl was advancing upon him.

"The shooting is slowing down."

She thrust her large jutting breasts forward, her hands lightly clasping her rounded buttocks.

"I love you more, *liubimez*. Off with trousers. Come."

Her hands were at his trousers, fingers searching his swelling member. She took a playful bite at his pot belly.

"Once for Mongol girl is not enough. Second time. Drain blood," she giggled, her tongue tracing his belly button.

The door was kicked open. Four Cossacks burst in. They stood there grinning watching the frightened eyes. A submachine gun roared, deafening in the confined space.

The girl leaped over the bed, her dark long hair flying about her breasts. The Cossacks had a glimpse of her nakedness. The flat stomach. Smudge of pubic hair. Dancing breasts. The second volley of fire hit her at the waist, stitching up and smashing her face.

Kholminov fell, wounded in the head. He saw the lush thighs, the red gashes growing bigger at her waist and cheast. The full brests seeming to deflate, pouring blood.

Germanski. *Pyos.* The pigs. His mind lurched. Attacking wearing Cossack robes. He could taste the blood. The honey. Mongol vixen. Her buttocks were smudged with blood.

The hand found his throat.

"Yob tvoymat."

Confused, his mind spun away. Speaking Russian. Swearing like Russians. The pain. Head. Blood was running into his eyes. A gurgled cry came from his lips. Something was grasping and pulling at his brain.

For just one second he saw the knife. Felt the blade making its deep cut. Then he understood. The answer died upon his bloodied lips.

The high boots ground the face into the clay floor.

They stood above the whimpering Mongol girl. The eyes were looking at them like a sheep about to be slaughtered. With each fresh quiver of agony, her entrails spewed out onto the bed. One of them grabbed her by the hair and cut her throat.

"N.K.V.D. *allotjka*. Cunt," they laughed.

Hungrily they ate the fresh meats, wolfed down the honey that was left upon a tray on the table.

A hand grenade skidded over the dirt floor. It stopped by one of their boots. They tried to dive for cover. The red searing explosion hit them in the back. Red-hot steel fragments tore three of them apart. The fourth reached the door, arms outstretched. A shot from a nagan pistol tore into his head.

A hand torch glared into the darkness. Two N.K.V.D. troopers came into the *isba*. Quickly they went through the pockets of the dead.

"*Nyet* Germanski," one of them mumbled.

"It must be reported to Lieutenant Yershov."

They gathered up the telltale letters, running outside.

Two Mongols had changed their position on the heavy-wheeled Maxim machine gun. Germanski was everywhere. It was like the storm fire before Moscow. Coming out of the ground like evil spirits. Attack coming from all directions.

"Eee—hh!" The loader pulled at the machine gunner's shoulders.

He held his fire. Those brutal instructors on the plains of Kazakstan would have been proud of him. At eight meters he fired a cross burst. The two N.K.V.D. men literally flew apart with the impact.

Creeping along in the shadows they came to an N.K.V.D. *isba*. The noise of a party came from inside. Through the window they could see half-naked Mongol women soldiers dancing with N.K.V.D. troopers. An accordion blared its mournful notes. Yet another song of Siberia. A lament describing the horrors of the *Stoypin* cars, the railway cars that took prisoners to a *Minlag*, a mineral forced labor camp in the desolate wastes of Siberia.

"Ten N.K.V.D. for ten Siberians," roared Sergi Vlasava, kicking the door in.

The women screamed trying to cover themselves.

Ten chosen ones were manhandled outside. Made to stand against the wall. When the last was in place they bayoneted them in the back. One of the women ran out, crying hysterically, trying to comfort her dying lover. She met the same fate.

The remaining N.K.V.D. men were bludgeoned to death upon the dirt floor of the *isba*. Rifle butts. High boots. The hated faces disintegrated under the blows. A misshapen mass. Some loathsome voices of the Kremlin were silenced forever.

A Cossack wiped his forehead, smearing the sweat with blood.

"These women . . ."

Sergi Vlasava smiled.

"Turn the N.K.V.D. *allotjka* loose."

They finished stripping them, then drove them crying into the night. Bullets plucked at the snow about their feet. They began to run.

"Now Sergi," a Cossack raised his weapon.

"*Nyet*," he knocked the rifle aside.

"Have you no feeling for little Mother Russia? Would you save nothing for her? Drive them out onto the steppe."

Numb and confused with the biting cold, after several minutes they would stagger and fall. After ten it would be hard to rise. The cold would clutch at every vein and sinew. After twenty death would not be far away. After the throbbing pain, there comes an all-consuming numbness. A light-headedness when pain is no longer recognized. There is only the urge to sleep. To sink into the snow. To fight no more. At thirty minutes, already rigor mortis would be setting in.

They stormed the remaining *isbas*. Many N.K.V.D. were caught inside. Why should Beria's political troops brave the cold of the long Russian winter nights? Guard duty—that was only for the politically uneducated.

Sergi Vlasava threw himself down into the burnt-out remains of an *isba*. A small bundle of fur brushed against him. A kitten. He fondled it. Then thrust it into one of his deep warm pockets. Every peasant *isba* seemed to have its cats.

For me it is the songs. The haunting melodies. Accordion. Balalaika. A group of Russian peasants singing and dancing. On a train. Going back to Poland. Chickens squawking over the seated bodies. The vodka making its rounds.

"Drink, Germanski. Be happy, Germanski. For is it not tomorrow that history will be written? Today we drink. We dance. We have fun. Be Russian, Germanski. Drink." And that from a solid fat peasant woman.

And when her resounding slap hits the back, it is like the thundering fire from a Pak front.

The wide rolling expanse of the steppes. How dare other writers say the land is not beautiful? What of Kursk? The rolling hills. The fertile valleys. The patches of woodland. The waving cornfields. The lull before the biggest panzer battle known to man. You had time to look. Some of the Landser were in position two months before the battle got under way. Did you not look? And curse the high corn . . . knowing that ivan would soon be crawling through it. But more of that later.

The dark virgin forests. Finding peace there, when all around was horrific turmoil. Man and nature alone as one. A sky so big, so lonely it could become awesome. The days of youth. That other land. Mighty Mother Russia. Once you have experienced it, you will never forget.

And cats. They were so much a part of it all. Starving cats sniffing the Russian dead at Brest Litovsk. The three kittens the platoon saved at Baronowitschi, before Minsk. Cats eating the dead at Novosil. Muska of Plavskoie, that we got fitted with a leg splint. Starving lice-ridden teenage soldiers. Crying aloud with frostbite and the chill cold. The platoon loved cats. We ate horses, dogs and rats. Never cats. They reminded one of home. The lost youth one could never regain. March. March. The Eastern Front is waiting. Forward. Left, two, three, four. Forward. Russian Front comrades.

Moments later three other Cossacks joined Sergi Vlasava in the ruins.

"Have lost many, little brother. Ponies stand waiting."

He adjusted a new magazine, slamming it home.

"Kill the N.K.V.D. *djavolls*. Devils. Revenge for village. For fallen comrades."

"*Djavolls* will call reinforcements."

"Let them. We put many to the saber before we ride away, *tovaritch*. Would you forget Anatoli Tsarurov? Ivan Tuzhmanov?"

He knew he was breaking the first rule of Russian partisan warfare. Never continue the fight against a superior force. Strike first and hard. Run, fading into the countryside. The long night comes to an end. Other days will follow. Other actions. But no, the heavy scent of the hunt was upon him. The blind intoxicating rage of all-out revenge. Kill. Kill. For tomorrow you may die.

Overhead a starshell burst, crackling in the cold

night air. Bright yellow flares floated down. The village was bathed in a yellow eerie glow. To the left of their position the cemetery stood out. Not drab and gaunt like those of Western nations. Here was a place of much happiness. Full of color. Bright with gaiety. With names like "smiling Svetlana." "Happy Angelicka." A riot of color. Gold. Blues. White-painted picket fences.

Watch us, little brothers, the thought pulsed through Sergi Vlasava's mind. Revolt of the free Cossacks. No longer will we be slaves under the Kremlin. Stand and watch the destruction of our brothers' villages. Slaughter of our repatriated comrades. The slaves have risen. Moscow will hear us. Tremble when others join our cause.

Sniper fire exploded on the shattered walls above their heads. It was coming from over the wide village street. Two rifles. No more than a meter apart. Lying low, they watched the muzzle flashes.

Without waiting for an order one of the Cossacks crawled away to the side. They watched his progress through the mounds of rubble.

"Now, little brothers."

They stepped up their covering fire. A fur cap showed from the snipers' position, then hastily withdrew.

In the center of the street the Cossack moved. His arm went back. The hand grenade arced through the air.

Counting the seconds they thought it was a dud. It exploded. A brilliant vivid blue flash. Shrapnel tore through the air, whistling away. A low gurgling moan sounded. They saw their comrade run, bounding forward.

A shout. A strangulated sharp cry of fear. Two rifle shots. A loud laughing Russian curse. Then in the flickering shadows, thrown by the flares, he was waving them over.

Attacking the N.K.V.D. and the Mongols. It reminded him of the fighting at Krasnaya Polyana. The Germanski Second Panzer Division of the Fourth Army. It was the closest the fascists ever came to Moscow.

Cossacks had been moved down from Dmitrov. No further Stalin had ranted and screamed. One hundred fresh Red Army Divisions had been thrown into the crumbling front. The enemy tottered under the intense onslaught. Bent, buckled. Then the red hordes pushed and they began to run, many throwing away their weapons as the T.34s advanced.

Cossacks had dealt with the many pockets of isolated resistance. They overran Germanski taking a bloody terrible revenge.

Skirting the village they slithered down a low hill. The N.K.V.D. were regrouping. Five mortars had been set up. Constant fire was bombarding the village.

"Add fifty meters," shouted the observer.

The adjustment was made, the barrels winding up.

The dull plops came. Mortars roared away. Explosions tore the village street apart. The observer directed the fire forward, in a marching motion.

"Add—" he never finished.

His face flew apart, two explosive rifle bullets striking home.

The mortar teams ran. Not far. The Cossacks had carried a Maxim over the hill. It began to take its terrible toll. None survived. The wounded were killed on the spot by saber blows.

"If *djavolls* follow we cut them to pieces," laughed Sergi Vlasava.

With the thunder of hoofbeats they rode back into

the village. Fifty Cossacks left the village. They left behind thirty dead and seven missing. At a fast gallop they passed the empty granaries. The road forked in a curve up the hill.

A motorcycle headlight appeared in front of them. "Into the steppes," shouted Sergi Vlasava.

They surged to the right, ponies straining at the bridles, towards the dim outline of the forest. They found a track and their speed increased. Spurring their mounts they rode into the shelter of the snow-laden trees.

They bunched together as they left the track. Several voices rose upon the frost-laden air, calling for the villages of their loved ones upon the Don. For the mighty slow moving Volga. Lifeblood of little Mother Russia. The last excited riders trampled a board into the snow. A grim reminder of the earlier Germanski occupation. A white skull and crossbones were painted upon the black board. The words "Achtun Minen" were written underneath.

Only seven riders made it over the mined snow field. Five got back to their home villages with Natasha Petrov. Later in the war they joined the Vlasov Army, made up of captured Red Army men who fought alongside Germanski against the Red Army. They fought in the Cossack unit of Pyotr Nikolayevich Krasnov, fighting for what they hoped would one day be a free Russia. In 1946 the British military authorities handed them over to Stalin. They were hung alongside General Andrei Andrevevich Vlasov and Pyotr Nikolayevich Krasnov in Moscow, branded forever as traitors in the great Motherland war.

Over forty thousand other Cossacks were sentenced to long terms of imprisonment in the slave labor and death camps of Siberia. Don, Volga and Kalmak Cossacks. Their only links with the steppes of the homeland were their proud defiant Cossack songs.

Chapter 11
SOLDATEN KAMERADEN

Youth. A wasted youth. Snow. Ice. Hunger. The thoughts return with bitter regularity.

Heroes of the Third Reich. Russian Front Comrades. Through the murky haunting shadows of time. A column of Panzer Mark Threes heading for Moscow. Grenadiers cluster about the engine deck. Rain, sleet, icy howling snowstorms. Red Square before Christmas. Piss on the Tomb of Lenin. Ivans, they're run back beyond the Ural Mountains. And Grenadiers . . .

"Los. Los. Singen."

That grating voice. From far-off Berlin. Hypnotic tone. The wireless is turned up. Panzer manner. Landser and Grenadiers gather about the Steiner. A Hauptmann barks the command. The wireless crackles with static. You are of the master race. Proud youth of the glorious Third Reich. Nations have fallen before you. Holland, Belgium, France, Norway, Denmark and Poland. Bend your backs to the task. The Red scourge will be crushed before the gates of Moscow. On . . . On . . . ultimate victory is within our grasp.

"Sieg heil. Sieg heil. Sieg heil."

The lonely wastes echo with the roar coming from a thousand frozen throats. Hearts pound. Scent of victory. Youth do not desert me now. In Moscow you will be sheltered from the wind. Sanitation details. Deloused. Hot baths. An end to the gnawing hunger when supplies catch up. It's worth fighting for. Too many have died upon the snowy steppes.

"*Singen.*"

Forget the blinding snow. Raging wind. Gas gangrene. Frostbitten limbs. Fallen *Kameraden*. Through it all the glory of final victory sparkles.

"*Singen.*"

"*Was sollen die soldaten essen Kapitan und Leutnant.*

Gebraten Fisch mit Gressen das sollen die soldaten essen.

Kapitan. Leutnant, Fernerich Sergenant, nimm das Madel, nimm das Madel bei der Hand.

SOLDATEN, KAMERADEN, nimm das Madel . . . nimm Das madel bei der Hand."

"*Panzers, vorwaerts.*"

Steel tracks bite the hard frozen ground. Forward. Three hundred in the column. An armada of death. Panzer halt. Lorried ivan infantry. Ten o'clock. Soft targets. Fire. The ivans plunge to the ground. Lorries burn under a bombardment of high explosives. Spandaus rack the exposed bodies. Nothing remains. A black smudge upon the virgin snows.

A *kolkhos*. Forest to the left. Wooden huts. A Russian Pak opens up. Lead panzer belches black smoke. Crew and Grenadiers throw themselves to the ground. Many running, flaming, thrashing in the snow.

"Dismount."

Who needs to be told. Small arms fire crackles.

"Grenadiers, *vorwaerts.*"

Contact. Olive-brown uniforms wading through the snow. Deal with them. Panzers lurch away, left stick, right stick, into the steppe. An unbroken line of steel monsters advancing upon the huts. Commanders laughing, high in the turrets. Turkey shoot. Hatches close. Main armaments fire. The blue-black smoke is blinding. Machine guns splutter. Whirling racing tracks. First contact. The devils gallop to hell.

On . . . on. Heavy leaden feet. Half-crouch. Feet move of their own accord. Heads down. Hit the deck. A whole bunker full over there. Shrill Feldwebel whistles. Up. Russian fortifications become clearer. Fur caps bobbing about a wide cut in the snow.

"Heyer. Flamethrower. What are you waiting for."

"Got crabs, he has. Showed me last time he had a washdown."

"Hansen, shut up. *Feuer*."

"Lordy Lord. Six ivans on toast coming up. The Lord said I am a jealous God. I will come with the fires of hell."

"Feuer."

With a weird scream the flame licks forward. Russian heavy mortar crew and ammunition explode with a rushing roar of continuing explosions. Heads thrust into the snow, steel fragments whistle by, sickeningly close.

"Los. Schnell. Vorwaerts."

Dive for cover. None like ivan at camouflage. No one saw the trench. He melts into the ground. Near misses. Like a symphony. Each shot has its own tone. Steel against frozen earth. Another note. Join them together. Song on the road to Moscow. Phew.

Phew. Phew. Ice chips stinging the' face. They will sound different at Stalingrad. Bullet against brick. Higher note tone, Classical Russian there. Music from the heart of Mother Russia. She will scream at you there. The Volga is close. Phew. Phew. Phew. No fascist pig will leave my land alive.

Los. Los. Up again. On your feet. Schmidt you are a bastard. Iron Cross merchant searching for more tin. As long as I am in charge of this platoon you will move. *Schnell,* forward. Fire. Mausers. Spitting spandaus. Kameraden fall. You laughed and joked with him last night. Told you of his Russian girl friend. Still the lines of grey-green push forward. Those of the dark brown are only meters away.

Staring eyes meet theirs. Scream. Scream. Scream your lungs out. Into their trenches. Shoot. Fire from the hip. Point blank. Bayonet. Thrust, contact, rip. Butt. Kick. Kick. Rifle over the shoulder. Entrenching tool is better. Sharpened to a fine edge. He's dead. Leave it, Heyer. Swipe and slash. Like an axe to the neck. Face. Die, you ivan *moujik.* Die like a hero for your Motherland. Blood. Gore. Torn repulsive-looking guts. One with a stoved-in face is still breathing. A grenade-clutching ivan runs at a group of Landser. A giant yellow flash and deafening explosion. First concussion. Ringing head. Tangle of broken torsos and legs. Choking smoke. Roll the trench. Hearts pounding, pounding. Tunic alive. Sweat. Sweat. Insane laughter. Groans of dying. *Zigaretten.* Blood on the paper. Does not taste. Throw it away. Hands trembling. Heyer makes them. *Danke.*

Steggeman and Muller vomiting. Vodka. Long swig, it helps.

"On your feet. Lead out, Heyer."

Moans, curses. Hansen pissing against the trench wall.

"Freezing out there."

"Donna wetter, again."

Relieving singing Landser. First time at the front. Questions. Questions. Young boys without school bags. Is ivan tougher than the Poles? Does he fight to the death? Use sabers? Have you met Cossacks? Siberians? Shared black sausage. Farm boys from near Hanover. Mothers make good sausages. Spicy. Washed down with vodka. No time for seconds.

"SOLDATEN, KAMERADEN . . . nimm das Madel . . . nimm das Madel bei der Hand."

"It's like a brothel in here. Shall I order Ruski tit?"

"Ja, bitte. Full with nipples like . . ."

"Schnell. Move out. Follow me."

Where are the panzers? Too far ahead. Another bunker. They fight to the last man. None die like ivan. To the last breath. No ammunition. He attacks with swinging fists. That is a woman moving under that jacket. She swings her rifle. A young Landser falls. She crushes his skull. Don't kill her. My present for bringing the new order to ivan. Two other women soldiers are prodded out of the trench at bayonet point.

Whistles. Catcalls. Many lick their lips making lewd suggestions.

"Prisoners."

"Er, these runts. Heyer, we'll take them to the rear."

"Nice little bums."

"I'll go along, I suppose. Hansen—Adolf said, Look after the Bolshy women soldiers."

"No one touches them, and that's an order."

"It's my birthday."

"You lying swine."

One of the ivan women spits in Schultz's face.

"Hot bits. What a temper."

"Take them to the rear."

"Nein, no time."

A shrill command whistle.

"Mount panzers."

The ivan prisoners fall in a hail of fire. Defiant until death. The women cursing more than the men. An S.S. squad has cut them down. Have you not been told ivan takes no prisoners?

"I caught them. They were my prisoners. Shit, them S.S. runts."

"Shut up, Schultz."

"Unfair it is. I saw them first."

"Be quiet there's a war on."

"I thought we was on a picnic. Didn't you, Hansen?"

"Ja, going to the state circus we was, in Moscow."

"Shut up."

"Panzers, *Vorwaerts."*

Kill. Kill. Kill. Nothing can stop the mighty juggernaut of the advancing Wehrmacht. Forward. Four ivan planes attack the column. One Messerschmitt drives them away. He downs two then flies back low over the panzers waggling his wings. A roar goes up.

"Sieg heil der Luftwaffe!"

The pilot spins his plane in a victory roll, then heads back west for his breakfast of *frische Broetchen, Wurst und* steaming *Kaffee.* Lucky swine.

Forward. The wireless hums. At Beresa Karluska Grenadiers will dismount. Companies three, four and five will advance behind the panzer. Good hunting out.

Beresa Karluska. Name on the higher command

maps. Death. Fields of dead. Brewing panzers. A fire of sheer hell. Another marker will be moved.

Beresa Karluska. How many telegrams stood beside the clocks on mantelpieces over fires in the Fatherland? He fell for Greater Germany. A hero. A young boy screaming for ten hours on end, mortar fragments having punctured his guts.

All was quiet in the filthy musty atmosphere of the *stolavaya*. Live with the grotesque rotting dead stacked back against the walls. Sweet, putrid, the nauseating smell of death. In summer the sanitary detail picked them up. Or they were dragged out of smelling range. In captivity there was no escaping from it.

It clings to the nostrils. That tugging urge to vomit never leaves the throat. Gangrene. Face sores. Running pus, seeming green in the flickering lantern lights.

For some, those who have faced death, that nagging tormenting fear has gone. Hero, this you must face alone. The embracing. Waiting for final relief. Youthful horror-filled eyes, glassy and staring. That ashen terrified face. Last frantic catching of breath. They are also heroes, dying weeks after the fire storm of battle.

Earlier in the night, an older panzer gunner reservist had gone insane. His Panzer Mark Three had been hit before the wooden *isbas* of Verchoie. Generals can write their stories. Growing old and fat on large pensions. Guess and wonder. Move their colored map flags. Snug and warm in their fortified bunkers, far from the front. What do they know of the soldier's individual realities of war? Sip their drinks. Keeping war at arm's length. May they rot in hell, these armchair warriors.

Screams of the young driver as he was burnt alive.

Dead commander wedged in the turret hatch. Flames licking and playing about him. He pulled the body away. Gobs of blackened flesh came away in his fingers. At such times, terror, pain, agony, a red-hot knife twisting slowly in the skull. Unseen force welding the body against the breech of the main armament. Any minute the ammunition will blow. Gasoline. Raging fear drives the blistered body on. It gains unimaginable strength. Burnt alive. Horrifying nightmare of panzer manner. Loader writhing, screaming upon the floor of the fighting compartment. Burnt pork. He throws his body clear, rolling. Where once hands had been, only blackened bloody stumps remain.

He was quiet now, low animalistic whimpering shaking the body. Quick action could have saved him. Hysterics. The pinnacle before madness had passed. Crying. Haunting laughter. Now it came upon the same breath. Tortured minds can only take so much. See so much. In war raving insanity is never very far away.

Heyer was at the *stolovaya* door trying to force it. Feel of the needle-sharp *kandra* was comforting. Take out the guards. Escape. Away from the filth and daily brutal atrocities.

He was thinking of an incident near Orel. A collection of huts he had almost forgotten. The replacement Schmidt had made him responsible for. Going forward. Talk of the ivans becoming clearer. A youth of the Komsomol bragging what he would do with Germanski prisoners. A lieutenant arguing with him. The fight was against the fascists, not the Germanski people as a whole. A violent argument, others joining in.

Passing the knife to the wide-eyed youngster. Tapping his shoulder. Crawling away through the tangled clinging undergrowth. Soles of his boots, digging and pushing forward. Ivan humming a song, telling of two lonely old men talking of their youth.

The fight. Youngster lost his nerve. Deafening burst of automatic fire. Pitiful screams giving their position away.

"Hilfe, Kameraden."

How could such a mutilated wreck still talk?

You will knock out the forward popov positions using knives. Under no circumstances will shots be fired. Element of surprise.

Schmidt and Muller pinning him to the ground.

"Still."

In ten minutes the softening Wehrmacht barrage will come. All forward popov positions must be wiped out. Forced to listen as the ivans beat the life out of the replacement. Choking. Sobbing. Hideous laughter of the Komsomol.

"Mutti.. Hilfe mir."

Horizon glowing. Thundering rolls as the artillery fired. Falling short. Terror-stricken, bounding into ivan's slit trenches. It was either that, or instant death from their own artillery fire.

Slowly the *stolovaya* door was giving. Snow was banked high behind it. Four Mongols were curled up sleeping about the fire, weapons rolled up with them, only the black evil snub noses poking out.

"Schultzy take out the first one."

He had come up behind him breathing heavily.

"Nein, poxy door is stuck."

"Mongol shits. Stalin will be pleased. All asleep on the job," Schultz whispered.

The straw rustled, the others coming up behind them.

"Not a sound. One man each. Finish them. Take their weapons, then we move out."

Schmidt's hand tightened on Heyer's arm. An argument has broken out behind them in the shadows.

"Verflucht noch mal. Damn it. What are you up to?"

It was the lieutenant of a Rollbahn supply unit. Tsarurov had put him in charge of the *stolovaya.* They always made someone responsible for the other prisoners. Answerable with their own necks.

"Escaping, Herr Leutnant. Scenery here is too depressing," answered Hansen cheekily.

The Leutnant tried to stifle his hacking cough. His lungs could not last. The deep rasping. Younger men had died long before they reached his stage.

"My scalp," he spluttered, sucking loudly for air.

". . . rests with the discipline here." He bent over spitting and wheezing.

"We are going, Herr Leutnant," insisted Hansen. "It is the duty of every Wehrmacht *Soldat* to try and escape."

"Popovs find you missing . . . body count does not tally . . . They . . . they will punish me."

Schmidt went back to them.

"You are free to join us, Herr Leutnant."

"Schacrev noch mal." He was folk Deutsch from Anin, a suburb of Warsaw.

"Wouldn't last." He made an effort at trying to laugh. "How—how far do you think you will get? I . . . I forbid it." Some of the old barrack-square harshness came back into his voice.

"Unteroffizier. Wehrmacht discipline still applies here. The very strictest of military discipline. I have the authority. Your superior officer. My God-given right as sworn to the Fuehrer. *Nein, Nein.* You must stay. My final word. That is an order. Reprisals . . . "

"Filthy son of a bitch," Klima spat in English.

He pushed those standing close aside, kicking out with his right boot. Spitting and coughing the lieutenant buckled. With a sharp right he laid him out.

"Wants us to rot with him in a P.O.W. camp. Polack bastard."

Hansen and Steggeman dragged the unconscious body back against the wall.

"Folk Deutsch pig. Make bigger Nazis than Adolf and Heinrich," grumbled Steggeman.

"Remember his type and their National Socialist lectures. *Soldats* of the glorious Third Reich. Ours is a crusade in the East. Our fight against the pagan communists. Filling us full of crap. Now he wants to give up. Soon changed his tune."

"Heyer, Schultz, Klima. Now."

Schmidt leading the way, they leaped forward. With animal fury they threw themselves upon the sleeping Mongols. When you are beaten every day, watch friends die, starve—revenge had never tasted sweeter. Raped Blitzmadels. Horrific atrocities on the march. Decapitations. Two Hauptmanns burning at the stake. The days of the cowering *Gefangene* were over.

The Mongols were swathed in sheepskins. Extra skins wrapped about their bodies. Draped over their hooded heads.

Heyer straddled a Mongol. Ripped the face mask off through which only the eyes showed. The head appeared. Face. Shocked, bleary eyes, still in the throes of drunken sleep.

"Germanski!" he tried to free his pinned arms.

Heyer's *kandra* struck. Words of terror ended in bubbles of blood, foaming and bubbling at the mouth. A second savage thrust and the wound at the throat deepened. A stream of blood shot into the

166

fire, sending flames cracking and hissing. The body gave a final trembling shudder. Then it was over.

Schultz waited for his to come around. Slowly the pressure of his huge hands bit into the yellow flesh. He strangled him, then shook him like a dog with rabbit.

Klima was having trouble. He misjudged the bundle of furs. Chuckling, Schultz grabbed the Mongol sergeant from him. Right chop to the Adam's apple. Stunning him, light enough not to kill. He tossed the body up like a rag doll, catching it and bringing it down over his right knee. Still laughing he brought his full weight down across the chest and stomach. The spinal column splintered, breaking. Finally he killed him with a fisted blow of his right hand.

"Spit in my grub. Slant-eyed Oriental runt. Steal my S.S. man. Say hallo to Gabriel."

Schmidt strangled his Mongol. Clear eyes bulged almost leaving the sockets. The smooth-skinned face darkened. For only seconds there was the frantic struggle of arms and legs. The bowels exploded, a vile sickening rush of air. He threw himself away from the revolting wreck. Glance at the face. He could not shake off the idea. The apparition lying crumpled before him. It could not be more than thirteen or fourteen years of age. A kid. A mere child. Revulsion rose in his throat. Bile catching in his gullet.

The weapons were collected. Four submachine guns. Short type with circular magazines. Bags of spare mags. Four battle knives. Sack of grenades.

Schmidt waved to the others at the *stolovaya* door. Hansen and Steggeman were missing. Every second counted. The cries of the dying Mongols could have awakened the whole *kolkhos*.

"It's the Leutnant," snapped Muller.

"*Los*. Heyer. Schultz."

They ran back inside the *stolovaya*. Already Heyer began to visualize the hordes of screaming Siberians charging down the village street.

"With us, Herr Leutnant."

"*Dumkopf*. Popovs will catch you . . ."

"Kill the Polack swine."

Nein," protested Steggeman.

Too late. Heyer cut the lieutenant's throat.

"You inhuman . . ."

Schultz slapped Steggeman's face.

"Him or us. He'd raise the alarm. Four of their dead outside. How long do you think we would last if they caught us now?"

"Polacks like him slaughtered the Germans before the Wehrmacht moved in. Joined the Nazi party to save their own skins." Heyer wiped his *kandra* clean.

Steggeman was throwing up.

"One of our . . . "

Schultz slapped him again only harder.

"All right."

"J—jawohl."

"*Gut*. It had to be done. Forget it."

They rushed outside joining the others. Steggeman threw up again. Maybe Heyer was right. Law of the jungle. Pure animal reflex. No longer were they fighting for any glorified cause. It was a fight for the very right to survive. On the Eastern Front that was all that mattered. Too young. Buck up. Follow the veteran. Want to be human, cry later. Forward. Swallow. Head between the legs. Shut up. Or do you want another smack in the face? *Los*. Move it.

Approaching footsteps sent them scattering into a ruined *isba*. Automatic fire had them clawing the ground, seeking cover. Fur-capped ivans ran by only

168

meters away. Rifle shots echoed out down the whole length of the village street. Screams. Cries.

Heyer and Schultz were both at the low wall. Crouched low, bodies hunched, eyes trying to penetrate the darkness. Ready to return the fire. It becomes automatic. Months of harsh discipline. Months lining the trenches. If you were German and young you were almost born with a mauser in your hands. Muzzle flashes lighted up hurriedly fleeing figures. Target. Range 150 meters. *Nein,* 100.

"Hold it." Schmidt was behind them.

"Leave it. It's not for us."

They relax, muzzle flashes dancing a pattern down the street. A heavy-calibre Maxim machine gun begins its loathsome grinding purr. Once again their bodies react automatically. Crashing into one another. A burst from a Maxim can tear a man apart, dissecting the body as though it was on a surgeon's table.

"Cossacks!" Heyer could not hide the excitement in his voice.

"Shouting for vengeance against the N.K.V.D. Listen. It's a rebellion."

"Impossible. Bolsheviks don't rebel," cried Steggeman.

"Donna wetter. Nineteen-seventeen all over again."

Cossack cries of triumph. Who could forget. Ever. Thundering hoofbeats. Bear of a figure in the saddle. Slashing sabers sketched indelibly upon their minds. Arms of Grenadiers raised in surrender. Terrifying walk through the low ground-hugging mists. Hacking. Lunging. Swinging low in the saddle. Commissars driving them on.

"Germanski. He would eat your children. Rape their mothers."

169

Arms. So many arms. Heads. Mutilated writhing bodies littering the snow field. Bodies being pulled by ropes behind Cossack ponies and used for grisly target practice. Still the commissars roar.

"Remember Kiev! Orel! Little brothers, time is for revenge."

Pitiful lonesome whining screams. Four Cossacks standing above the body. The awesome fistful of bloodied flesh raised on high.

"Let them massacre one another. Leaves less runts for us to wipe out."

Hansen draws his breath, not fully believing his own eyes.

"Naked Ruski bits. Over there at the window. Orgy, that's what it is."

Schultz screwed his eyes up.

"Just what my front piece needs."

"Our rewards from the Gods after leading pigs' lives."

"Who said there was no St. Nicholas."

"Donna wetter, meine . . . "

A fight was going on in the *isba*. The naked women were waving their arms, breasts dancing sensually.

"Unteroffizier Schmidt," Hansen was giggling, smacking his heels together.

"Permission for a twenty-four hour leave pass. *Nein* make it half an hour. Been away from it for so long. Mine'll be like a repeater. Swear I'll get my concussion again when it goes off. Go right to my head, it will."

Schultz was busy scratching himself.

"My lice are doing a war dance. Right excited they are. Fresh ivan meat. Cruelty to animals it is, keeping them apart. Let's take them. Coming Heyer. Last chance we might get. What a cattery. Old Schultzy will make them purr."

Heyer got to his feet cocking his submachine gun.

"Had an *Ost Arbeiter* before. She was with the *Todt* Organization at Kromy. Real holy piece of goods. Blessed it before we got down to business. The Lord in his wisdom smiled and I went at it hammer and tongs."

Steggeman giggled, nudging Hansen, and whispered into song: "There's an old woman living on the hill, she won't do it but her sister will. The Wehrmacht's moving on, we're saying . . . "

Schmidt was holding Hansen back.

"Mein lieber Gott. Have you all gone mad? No one leaves here and that's an order."

"Always spoiling it," cursed Hansen.

"Not normal. Doctor didn't slap your arse when you came out. Twisted your front piece he did. Been bent ever since. Iron Cross gone to your head, has it. More to life than glory, you know. Go on, have a fit. One pass at her breakfast. *Nein,* wouldn't take long."

"Runter."

Another group of shouting Cossacks ran by. They sank back into the shadows.

"Easy, two handfuls. And that's not pulling the spare up from under the arms," whispered Steggeman.

"Will you two be quiet," hissed Muller.

"Like bitches in heat. You both need fixing."

The footsteps crunched away down the street.

"Ripe it is. Waiting for plucking. There's armed ivans in that *isba.* Anyone with me."

"Nein, Schultz."

"It's the duty of every Grenadier to go after the enemy wherever he finds them. I was all ears at my political lectures. Might even join the party if you let

171

me have a crack at them." He started to cluck his tongue.

"Schultzy always was a firm believer."

"*Nein.*"

"Liberate them. Take them back with us as hostages. I can see it all now. Our photos in *Ost Front*. Think how thankful Colonel Beckman would be."

"Hansen."

"Need more weapons. Said so yourself. Attack . . ."

"*Runter.*"

A volley of rifle shots rang out. Shouting in Russian. Unmistakable curses in Bavarian-accented German.

"*Schweinhund!*" Muller recoiled, gripping his weapon.

Ear-piercing screams. Someone was being bayoneted. Distinctive, the howling long and drawn out.

"There's your answer Schultz. Is that how you want to end up?"

"Nothing like dying happy. Crap, what else have I to look forward to?"

Cossacks left the *isba* over the street. Collided with running Mongolians. The fight was short, sharp and savage. After several moments the Cossacks ran off laughing up the street.

Heyer leaped over the wall. Breathless, he came back.

"Three rifles from uncle Stalin and ammunition pouches."

The Badowicker boys snatched them.

Four N.K.V.D. stopped at the Mongolian dead.

"*Da*, Germanski." An argument developed.

"Quiet," whispered Heyer, his head rising from the wall.

"Tovaritch . . . da, Germanski," he shouted.

The N.K.V.D. men turned weapons up facing the voice in the darkness. Hesitatingly, two of them took a few steps towards Heyer.

"Idisoder. Brat tovaritch. Come here, brother comrade."

Schultz felt Heyer move beside him. He could take it no longer.

"Hin legen. Lie down," he rasped.

He fired his submachine gun from the hip. They were knocked sprawling with the violent impact. One squirmed in the snow. He sprang forward, vaulting the wall. Brought his butt down upon the crying face. A kick to the face of another one and the trembling lips stopped moving. His cackling laughter sounded.

More automatic weapons were gathered up.

"About them Ivan bits. Do I get my free sample now?" he insisted when Schmidt joined him.

"Saved your lives, I did. Means you owe me in my book."

"Forget them," Schmidt snapped.

"Bloeder affe. You almost killed me," cursed Heyer.

"They were almost standing on my frontpiece. I had to do something."

"Wanted to tell them about old Ivan the terrible, he did," laughed Hansen.

"Or that Ruski princess with the wonky tit. Used to knock off that hunchback in St. Petersburg, she did. What was his name? Rumplestiltskin, that's it. Kept him on a chain, she did. Brought him up from the dungeons on Mondays and Fridays. I don't know whether you know, but Ruski royalty was right kinky. What with the right royal thigh boots, made out of Cossack hide . . . "

173

Schmidt grabbed him by the collar.

"Bleibt still. Hansen I swear your mouth will land you in a penal battalion. Everyone armed. *Los.* Move out."

Schultz gripped Hansen in a bear hug.

"Come little friend. We are not wanted here. There is a better life ahead."

Anyone goes near those women in that *isba.* I'll cut him down with this sprayer."

Flares went up, hovering high over the village. The steady crunch and flash of mortar fire. Hand grenades. Shouts of terror, triumph and shrieking fear. Sounds of close combat. Deadly. Worst kind. When friend is not recognized from foe. Any shape coming at you out of the dark must be cut down. No chances are taken. Death is at your elbow.

Muller caught up with Schmidt.

"How long to our lines?"

"Could do it in four days. Our best chance lies in the forest beyond the granaries. Have a better chance there than out on the steppes."

Schultz and Heyer covering, they bounded forward to the next cover.

Schmidt settled into the rubble. He pushed a corpse aside. A robed Cossack. Already it had begun to stiffen, like cold marble. Some of the others scrambled forward. Forest, it was the only answer. Like the Russian partisans. If they could survive there, then so could the platoon. Live off the land, surviving the best way they could.

"Heya. Heya."

A gentle sigh upon the wind. It became loud and frighteningly clear. Mounted Cossacks were charging down the street. The gut contracts and tightens. Gravel-dry throats refuse to swallow. A heavy hand is upon the heart. Hypnotic. Mesmerizing. Battle cries leaping from the bloody pages of medieval history.

"Bleibt still. No one moves," warned Heyer.

"Prime target. Slaughter them easily." Steggeman turned to face the Cossack horde.

Schultz rammed the snout of his weapon into his ribs.

"You heard, friend Heyer."

Schmidt looked over at Heyer's crouching figure. He meant what he said. He had grown very close to Sergi Vlasava. In such a killing mood only an utter fool would tempt him.

"Let the Cossacks pass," he ordered.

Sergi Vlasava was riding in the lead position. A Cossack with no family. Only haunting terrifying memories. Soon the war would become an obsession with him.

His last drunken words plucked at Heyer's mind.

"Tovaritch. Cossacks are the breath of Little Mother Russia. Through the long centuries we have been her spirit. Her conscience. It has always been so."

That last song under the lamp in the *stolovaya*. Sitting about in the straw, humming low. Tapping out the tattoo upon their saber hilts. The fall of hoofbeats that was so much a part of them. Tear-stained face. A lone voice singing.

"Cossacks ride bravely . . . horses through the steppes so lively."

Centuries of fierce Russian tradition.

"Dance Russian maiden . . . dance until the sun comes up to meet the sky."

Eyes clouding with tears.

"Volga and Cossack . . . that's what the romance of Russia means to me . . . open up your eyes and you will see."

175

Ponies snorted, shaking their heads in the bitter cold. The squeak and clink of harness as they galloped by. No one spoke. All thoughts were with the riders. After the first burst of revengeful atrocities, it was the Cossacks who had smuggled food to them. Vodka. Now they had openly defied Moscow. Hunted men for the rest of their lives. Theirs would be a tragic stand. But their voices would be heard.

Schmidt broke the silence.

"Fricke. Steggeman. Lead out."

The large granaries loomed into view. Fighting behind them in the village was growing more intense. Grouped mortar fire. Hell fire. Exploding at knee height it cuts a path. A devil-breathing violence of exploding light. Shrapnel rips and tears. Before such an onslaught nothing remains. Only burrowing into the earth like a rat will save you.

A Maxim fires. Spluttering dazzling flames. Meters away. From beside the granaries.

Feverishly they paw at the snow. A high-pitched scream.

"*Nein,*" someone falls rolling to the *isba* wall.

Schmidt and Muller go to the crying sounds.

"*Los. Heyer, Schultz. Vorvaerts.*"

"*Jawohl.*"

They roll, fanning out, inching forward. Tracers burn, roaring away above their heads. Markers, other bullets fall well below them. Face in the snow, they gasp for air. Minds race with the pounding pulsebeat. Me, *nein,* not here. *Ich nicht.* Not in this God-forsaken hole. *Nein.* Within seconds they answer the deafening chattering Maxim. Boots dig into the snow. Right leg pushes, getting a grip. Forward. Explosive rifle shots thud about them. Necks sink instinctively, deep into their shoulders. One hit

176

and half a face has gone. Shoulder mashed. A gut torn away.

The wounded one was dragged behind an *isba* wall. Young Fricke. Schmidt went to work on his tunic. The chest was a gooey cavity. Under his fingers he could feel his lungs, quivering, but still pumping.

"Hold on," muttered Muller.

A flare burst into life high above them.

"Home now. Badowick."

"*Ja*. You will make it."

"Two Badowickers left." The punctured lung wheezed, spitting boood.

"Fine . . . fine Badowicker bull I make."

Schmidt applied the gauze. Fricke stiffened. Eyes staring far into the night. He was seeing something for his eyes alone.

"Only pain in the back." He tried to straighten up.

"Lie still."

His eyes glistened with tears.

"Mutti," his head crooked to one side.

He coughed. Blood vomited through his teeth. He was dead.

There was no time to bury him. *Ich hatte einen Kamerade.* From Brest Livosk . . . Bobruisk . . . Orel . . . on to Moscow. How many times had they heard those words since the opening of Operation Barbarossa? Wehrmacht helmets, set upon sticks decorating the way. A highway of death. A youthful road into the infinity of hell.

Schmidt broke off the dog tags. Found his last letter home.

"Badowicker Bull."

"It's part of their village folklore. An attacking force was stopped outside their village. A bull

177

showed the way over the shallow water. Badowicker Bull. The name has stuck ever since."

"Klima, Suckau to me," Schmidt shouted.

"Heyer keep their heads down."

"Jawohl."

Suckau and Klima crawled to them behind the wall.

"Fricke . . . is he."

"Ja. We will be too if we don't silence that Maxim."

Out of the *isba.* Snaking through the snow. Schmidt led the way. It was becoming hopeless. The Maxim had to be rolled quick. One dead. There could be others.

"We attack from the rear."

To be caught now. He did not want to think of it. Persistent thoughts kept returning. No honorable *Soldat's* quick death. *Nein,* no firing squad for them. The N.K.V.D. had other ways. Lingering slow deaths. How many had they seen on the march. Victims screaming, pleading, begging for death. A shell case hammered into the back of the neck. Breaking every bone in the arms and legs. Only the S.S. could match them in brutal barbarity.

Dark and tall the granaries rose before them. The flares showed two figures hunched down against the wall. One had a bulky pack on his back.

"Mein Gott," whispered Klima.

A violent burst of orange flame spluttered into life. The tongue spewed out hungrily.

"Scheiss."

"Flamethrower."

The flame danced ten meters long in front of them. Hissing, probing. The sudden wafting heat seemed to engulf them.

"Feuer."

Rifles and submachine guns cracked out. Klima lobbed a hand grenade. The torrent of raging flame was moving like a searchlight. The grenade exploded. Hideous screams. The backpack tore apart in a billowing mass of licking flames gushing over the ground. Two flaming torches ran. Gobs, balls of flame falling away as they writhed about. Muller's submachine gun put them out of their misery.

"Schnell," shouted Schultz.

They ran to the granary. Two grenades hurtled into the snow mound. Held until the last possible moment, the explosions came seconds later.

"Los." It was Heyer.

Curses. Russian and German. Sickening crunch of rifle butts against skulls. Egg tapping. Two in the right place and it shatters. A rifle shot. Nagan pistol, shots whining away into the darkness. Blubbering. Death rattle from a cut throat.

Suckau sits trembling back against the wall, holding the rear. A door wrenches open behind him. He jumps to his feet, lunging his rifle butt at the squat yellow face. The grinning N.K.V.D. man parries the blow. His rifle falls away. Hands are clawing at his throat. Then the keen edge of a knife blade. He brings his knee up with all his force behind it. An answering groan comes. A brilliant explosion blinds him. He reels against the wall, hands at his eyes.

"Got the *Schweinhund.*"

It is Klima's voice. He staggers, falling to the ground. Dancing lights pound relentlessly at his brain. Part of his face is bloody. A burning, stinging sensation.

"Muzzle flash. Be all right in a minute."

Klima puts a cigarette to his lips. He draws it in deeply, head still reeling.

Heyer and Schultz were looting bodies.

"An ivan tart. Brown knickers," Schultz had lifted her thick skirt with his bloody battle knife.

"Long stockings. What a waste."

"Dirtied her knickers has she."

"Ja, look."

"You can have her then."

"Clean her up a bit. In my book . . ."

"Leave her alone, Schultzy. Or you won't be going anywhere," ranted Schmidt.

"Keep your tin on. I'm only looking. Feeling the merchandise. Don't mean I want to buy it."

Hansen found Schmidt.

"Two wounded. Steggeman and Griecebeck."

Both had been hit in the arm and back. First aid was applied. Stopping the blood flow with strips of uniform taken from the dead ivans.

"Can you walk Steggeman?"

"Ja, didn't feel a thing. Didn't know until I got up."

Everything happens so quickly. Slight wounds are not felt straight away. The adrenalin. Excitement. Only afterwards does the pain register. With others it is different.

"You will have to carry Griecebeck."

Griecebeck was moaning. In a coma. Sennelager came through a babble of words. A battle-training ground in the Fatherland. A place feared by generations of German soldiers. It has its own graveyard. Many youths died there, far away from the sound of enemy gunfire.

Mutti. With the married ones it was their wives' names. With the youths their mothers'. Pleading, begging for help. As though they were right there by their sides.

"Mutti, helf mir doch. Lass mich nicht allein."

The last remaining pockets of resistance were being cleared in the village. They could hear the sound of engines revving hard. Command whistles. Only scattered shots filled the night air. The N.K.V.D. farewell to the Cossack wounded.

"Heyer, Schultz. Vorwaerts. Into the forest."

SOLDATEN, KAMERADEN . . . Nimm das Madel . . . nimm das Madel bei der Hand.

The song sticks. Glowing village. Last shots. *Los. Los.* Forward. Schultz complaining.

"Bastard, he weighs a ton."

The quip was from Heyer.

"Be thankful the Lord did not call him."

"He can have him."

"Shut up Schultz."

"That tart you owe me."

"March."

No Wehrmacht helmet would mark young Fricke's grave. Where he died a Russian village no longer exists. That is war. Maybe one day a small Russian child will find a belt among the ruined *isbas*. Clean it up and read the inscription upon the buckle. *"Gott mit uns."*

"Germanski," the old tractor driver will spit into the dust.

"The great Motherland war. Time of much sadness in the land."

No more will he get from the old man. If he goes to the cemetery and the wind is just right. Little Mother Russia might whisper of the past. Breath of the land, blowing over the mighty steppes. She never forgets.

Chapter 12
SAMAHONKA WORKS WONDERS

Hard slogging. Only the Landser knows the true curse of putting one foot before the other. Trudging endlessly through the snows. Freezing backs hunched against the raging wind. It cuts and knifes mercilessly. Every bone aches. Each fresh footfall a superhuman effort, cries of stifled pain freezing upon their lips. The war is the icy blurred familiar backs of the *Kameraden* in front. What stories are written there. The triumph. The advances of the summer. Villages, towns, torn *isbas* open to the sky. Battle under the blazing sun.

None can deny, a cause was being fought for. Heady atmosphere. Storming legions of Germanic youth. It became sour on the plains of Russia. Brutality and atrocities. Villages wiped out. Not a child, horse or cow left alive. Constant reminder that the fight was against the subhumans of the East. When you ate and slept in the same *isba* as your so-called enemy, a transformation took place. Hate turned to friendship and understanding. How can you kill those that you have eaten, slept and drunk with? Danced until the vodka ran out. Girl friends, many relationships sprang up. The seeds of doubt were sown. Many youths reached their maturity under the watchful, smiling eyes of their generous hosts.

Time. Ice. Snow. Wind. Hunger. God-forsaken hole. Through the howling wind, a snarling cry of a wolf. If someone falls. Silently the pack will charge and rip him to bits. Swearing with the extra weight of the wounded. Like a burial detail in the hot summer.

"Take his legs. You his feet."

"Swine the shit is running down his legs."

"*Na, ja.* It's all gone over my hands."

"He was clean-shaven. He's grown a beard."

Spoken to them hours before. From talk you knew his Helga. His lovely Margreta. Their bike rides into the woods. To the family garden allotment outside Luneburg. Their idyllic love nest. Spoken not in man's jest of conquest. But in love, that strong love that blossoms in youth. Youth that knows death can be waiting over the next hill. The next group of *isbas.* Through the sights of a T.34. Or the bloodied bayonet of a rifleman from Siberia. Life was to be lived in minutes. For did not death beckon every waking call?

The excitement of the breakout has gone. Once again each man is alone, fighting the cruel elements of the harsh Russian winter. Corners of the eyes and mouth are beginning to smart and crack. Weapons sting and burn to the touch. Dream, *Kameraden.* Become lost in thought.

Relive that last meeting. *Mein Gott,* you can go insane on the long march. Ingrid. The walk through the waving waist-high corn. That trek to the patch of woods at Gifkendorf. That violent summer storm. Forebodings of the fire to come. Unwary. Tears freezing upon unshielded eyes. Hand returns to the mauser. Ungloved. The skin will peel. Haunting, dreaded fears of the foot-slogging Landser return. Lost in that land of endless white snows.

Shelter. Perhaps the warm inviting glow of a fire.

Chance to thaw out. To de-ice the bones. Aching with a fury far greater than rigor mortis. You would kill for the luxury. *Ja*. Kill without batting an eye. Kill and kill again. Smile in your cosy room. Seated in your favorite armchair. Do not judge unless you have known the wrath of mighty Mother Russia. Shivered in the long night when the temperature has plunged to forty-five below zero. Seen the blackened frostbitten fingers of *Kameraden*. Arms and legs that would have to be amputated.

N.K.V.D. Red Army patrol. If they follow well, that's it. A stand will have to be made. Fight. Who cares. The body craves warmth. How many frozen sentinels have been seen? An order is an order. Stay at your posts. Ivan could be here any minute. Crouching, stonelike figures, behind mortars and Spandaus. Boys, men, lieutenants, doubled up with the bitter inhuman cold.

What a different face was put out by the *Ost Front* magazine. No weeping pitiful *Kameraden* there. Only the very brave and dauntless. Intrepid heroes of the Third Reich. Fist-waving black uniformed panzer commanders, sitting high in the turrets. Long columns of *Landser* winding their way over the rolling steppes. All grinning. Youth on parade. Bathed in smiles. How many went to their deaths with that heroic Germanic smile frozen upon their young starved faces.

Schultz and Heyer tripped, falling headlong.

"He's heavy."

"How can he last in this filth."

Klima had also fallen and refused to get up. How welcome that blanket of snow can feel when you are exhausted. Utterly and completely exhausted. To melt into it. Mother earth. To become part of it. Never to rise again. Countless thousands died that way. Unsung. Left to die. If your *Kameraden* did not care for you, there was no one else.

"Los," Schmidt stood above him.

"Get up."

"I'm finished. Leave me here."

"Schnell. I said move it."

"Not my war. You fight it. I'm finished."

Schmidt kicks him hard. Kicks him brutally. It is the only thing that will move a man, if already in his own mind he has given up.

"Los. Schnell." He pummels him about the shoulders with his fists.

"To hell with your war," cries Klima in English. "I want no part of it."

"Do the Amis give up that easily? Did those *Blitzmadels?* Ivan finds you, you know what he will do."

Hansen grabs him, shaking him roughly. Pulling him up by his weapon strap.

"You can't stay here in the snow. What would we write and tell your parents in Seattle? He died heroically in battle. I'll tell them you refused to get up."

Schmidt helps him to his feet.

"Those *Blitzmadels.* They had no chance. And you want to throw your life away."

Klima's mind rebounded to the horrifying scene on the floor of the *stolovaya.* Naked, battered, frail bodies being dragged before him by the feet. One is still breathing. Bubble of blood bursting at her bruised nostrils. Her legs and thighs matted with congealed blood.

"Swine. They must pay for it."

Hansen slaps his face. Then he leads him away into the darkness like a stiff-legged zombie. And still his curses rend the cold air. The sound of another slap. Then all is quiet.

"Heyer, Schultz. On your feet."

Spitting defiance, they rise.

"Both of you would insist on taking those extra rifles and pouches of explosive bullets. Throw them away. You both have m.p.i.s."

Schultz positions Griecebeck upon the improvised stretcher. He screams and rolls off. Together they pick him up again. Take one handle each, and begin to pull him Indian-style.

"Every ivan I see gets an explosive bullet to the skull. He'll greet the Holy Mother of Kazan with half his thinking box missing. Throw them away, you must be wet behind the ears. I'm going to declare my own private war," growled Heyer.

"Goes for uncle Schultzy too."

"Catch up with the others. I've no time to argue with you two."

Schmidt doubled back to the head of the file. Captivity had made Heyer all the more bitter. Lost his whole family in a Tommy bombing raid. Since then he had become a dedicated killer. Now he was burning with hatred. A man without fear. The killing was becoming an obsession with him. Edging close to the final breaking point.

At times such men had been known to turn upon their own *Kameraden*. In future he would have to keep a close eye upon him.

"*Alles in ordnung?*" Asked Muller.

"*Ja.* Klima refused to get up."

"Everyone's tired."

"Hansen's looking after him."

"*Gut.*"

Into the forest. Solid sheets of icy snow lashed against them. Smashed cruelly into their exposed faces. At each fresh footfall the frost cracks, seeming to suck them down. As though something under the hard frost is trying to clutch at their boots. The vastness of Russia wanting to swallow them. Chuckling as the flurries of snow are whipped about their freezing feet. Nature fashioning minute frozen glaciers. The wind howls, laughing and whistling high in the trees. Eager, smiling at the intruders, wanting to claim yet another wretch in the endless white blinding space.

Light begins to filter through the low ground-hugging mists. Dismal, a maddening uncanny greyness. Monotony that seems devoid of life and normal human feeling. Dawn, heralding the very short day of the Russian winter. The temperature will rise slightly. It is noticeable. In summer it is all light, with very few hours of darkness. Winter, the dread of the Landser. Forlorn banks of soul-deadening cloud. A whole landscape seeming so unreal in the half-light. Torment. Soul-destroying. Speaking only new words of eventual death.

Before the early nightfall Schmidt calls a halt.

"*Verdammt noch mal*. Rest here. Make a snow house."

The house is made out of snow blocks against some thick fallen pine trees, out of the shelter of the wind. Just large enough to take them all huddled together. A small entrance tunnel, spare N.K.V.D. coats blocking out the wind. Crude Eskimo-like shelters, but they were to save many lives. After several hours the body heat builds up. At times they can become stifling.

Griecebeck became delirious. Once again he was drinking beer at the Loewenbrau or the Hotel Deutsches Haus in Luneburg. Finishing at the cosy *gasthaus* in Badowick. Jubilant adventurous spirit of youth. A *Soldaten* party before leaving on the long train bound for the Eastern Front. The parade march on the *Kaserne* square is over. Gruelling goosestep. Not so fast. Keep in line. Better. Heads high. Swing. Swing. Damn aching muscles. No longer were they members of the Hitler Jugend. Boys, faces shining in the bright summer sun. Chests out, proudly marching down the Bleckeder Landstrasse. Colored banners flying. Gauleiter Telschau taking the salute. Pavements full of cheering people. Now they were Grenadiers. Members of the rifle battalions attached to the panzer units. Men of war in field grey. Elite *Soldaten*. Like paratroopers. Storm units of the arrogant Waffen S.S. They would be in the very forefront, the fire hell, the nose of the blitzkrieg. Faces flushed and full of illegal drink. As always the very air vibrated with song.

His mumbled excitement became clear.

Pounding marching songs drummed in day after day. Through the sickly sweat of brutal training. From the shedding of youth to manhood there are eight weeks of repetitive training. Back-breaking. Later it would be only a matter of three weeks, sometimes even less. Oberfeldwebel commands. Day, night, day. Fat melts from the body. Eyes become gaunt and haggard-looking. A taut machine. Youthful automaton shouldering a mauser. *Abmarsch*. Forward. Left, two, three, four. *Singen*. *Singen*. Under such conditions a long-dead corpse will jump up and sing.

"*Auf der Luneburger Heide, in dem wunder schoenen Land.*

"*Ging ich auf und ging ich unter, allererei an Weg ich fand.*

"*Falderie . . . faldera . . . ha, ha, yoheirassa bester Schatz . . . bester Schatz.*"

The mound of N.K.V.D. coats were thrown aside.

"*Sieg heil dem Panzer Soldaten . . . Sieg heil dem Panzer Grenadiers.*"

Schultz fumbled in the darkness, adjusting the pile of coats.

"*Scheiss.* Our little friend will win the war against ivan all on his own. Half-dead, and still his mind won't let him rest."

Heyer laughed, taking a glowing *machorka* from Schmidt.

"Carried him for miles. He turns out to be a raving Hitler Nazi."

"He's no Nazi," shouted Suckau.

"Don't go putting him on your list. He's patriotic."

"Hitler Jugend wasn't he?"

"*Ja*, so are thousands of others. You forget we had to join."

"*Nah*, Russia cured you, hey Suckau."

"*Ja*. It opened my eyes."

"His subconscious," snapped Muller.

"He has no control over it. When you've been brought up on the diet of our youth. What else can you expect?"

Heyer continued, snickering. "With that kind of crap the Lord will send him straight down to the stoking rooms."

"We'll have to find shelter and operate on those two." Without realizing it, Schmidt voiced the thoughts that had been playing upon his mind.

"Klima."

"*Ja.*"

"You willing to do it."

"If . . . if I have to."

"It's gangrene that I'm worried about."

"At the aid station I helped hold a panzer man

189

down while the doctor operated. He cut away the wound until he found the shrapnel or bullet."

"*Donna wetter*. What other way is there."

"Muller's right."

Someone was struggling over the bodies, whimpering.

"No swine is going to operate on Steggeman. No drugs. Butchers, that's what you are."

"Stop him."

"He'll freeze out there."

Schultz grabbed him, pulling him back by the legs.

"Maniacs, the lot of you." He started to cry.

Schultz knocked him out.

"Why cut my leg off?" In the scuffling Griecebeck came around.

"No one is going to do anything to your leg. We will be back in our own lines soon. The doctors will see to you there."

A big sigh echoed in the darkness.

"Have I got gangrene? Tell me."

"*Nein*. Go back to sleep."

Heyer passed a vodka flask that he had taken from one of the dead N.K.V.D. Groping in the dark, Schmidt and Muller propped Griecebeck up between them.

"Here. It will make you feel better."

They emptied half the flask into him and he slumped back down again.

It was like the voice of a small child pleading.

"*Bitte*. You won't cut my leg off."

"*Nein*. There is nothing wrong with your leg."

"Unteroffizier Schmidt. That's a promise."

"*Ja*. You have my word."

"*Bitte*. I want to hear Muller say it."

"No one will touch your leg. Now settle down and go to sleep."

"*Danke.*"

"Don't let them steal it while I'm asleep."

"*Nein.*"

"I mean, one day I will be back home."

"*Ja.*"

"How could I help with haymaking with only one leg."

"You could hop about like a Schultz fart in a thunderstorm."

There was silence for several moments. Then Griecebeck spoke.

"Hansen. *Bitte.* Don't make me laugh. My back hurts."

"Sorry."

Muller put the coats back over him. Within moments he could feel the slight breathing against his ungloved hand. He had fallen asleep or lapsed back into a coma.

Cut his leg off. He was not yet eighteen. Muller shuddered at the thought. If gangrene did set in, he would have to lose a limb. It would be the only way to save him. Better the loss of a limb, than gangrene spreading throughout his whole body. If that did happen nothing would be able to save the both of them. They would become like the agonized dying hulks in the *stolovaya.* Doomed, rambling incoherently, going insane before life finally left their tortured bodies.

After first light Heyer and Schultz were detailed to scout ahead.

"Double back if you find a hut. Or any kind of shelter."

"*Jawohl.*"

Off through the trees. Occasionally they heard the lonesome drone of a searching Stormovich. It made

191

wide circles. Going far out over the steppes and returning low, sweeping over the forest.

The virgin forests of Russia go on for miles. Trees, trees and more trees. In places a low tangled mass of briar blocks the way. The snow seems to deaden the sound. A sudden shot sounds muffled. Each footfall cracks the hard frost, a sheet of snow moving meters away.

Fearful watch on the trees ahead. A forest that can only be hostile. In them were many partisan camps. Meters away from the tracks they waited like lice. The Russians had trained their partisans long before the outbreak of war. They knew the tracks and every inch of the vast forests. To them they were like a second home. Around Belgorod they were infested with them. Special units were detailed to hunt them down. Partisanjaeger. S.S. and Wehrmacht units. Hunting them down like rats in their own environment. Bitter fighting. Perhaps some of the most vicious ever fought in Russia. That I will have to leave for another time. When perhaps you have developed a much stronger stomach.

The sudden sound of a woodsman's axe sent them diving for cover. Heyer unshouldered his rifle, eased it forward, slamming home an explosive bullet into the breech.

"Put that away, you stupid runt."

"An ivan's an ivan."

"Leave it. He might have a hut."

Schultz made him lower the telescopic rifle.

"An old man."

"They've all got the disease."

"*Aschloch*."

"Kill and murder their own people."

"Join the clan. So do we."

Stealthily they advanced through the undergrowth,

weapons at the ready.

"*Sdrasvuite, tovaritch.* Good day comrade."

The old man looked up. The ruffled hairs upon the dogs' backs had warned him of their approach. He was smiling. He touched his fur cap in soldierly greeting.

"*Sdrasvuite, tovaritch. Germanski soldat.*" The uniform did not seem to bother him, although he still kept a firm grip upon his axe.

"*Da.*"

Schultz picked the ice crystals from his nose.

"Heyer. *Scheiss.* No long story."

"Patience, little brother."

Schultz struck out at him with the butt of his m.p.i.

"Don't go little brothering me. What do you think I am. A slant-eyed Oriental shit? A Stalin dog?"

Heyer took no notice, continuing to speak to the smiling old man.

"We have wounded comrades."

The old man pondered for a moment, still puffing on his ancient clay pipe.

"*Germanski* no take Moscow." The smile broadened knowingly.

"*Germanski* come back."

"*Da.* He will come back."

The old man walked over to his sledge, the dogs barking expectantly.

Schultz's weapon came up.

"Tell the old *moujik* no partisan tricks. I'll fill him so full with this sprayer, his *babushka* won't recognize the pieces."

"*Samahonka.* You like."

He produced an earthenware flask, holding it up. He pulled the cork with his teeth, offering it to Schultz.

Schultz smiled, grabbing the flask.

"*Spasibo*. That's more like it. Nothing like a bit of good old Russian hospitality." He put the flask to his lips.

"Could be poisoned."

Schultz gulped spitting the drink out.

"Now he tells me."

He made the old man take a mouthful. He swallowed, handing the flask over again.

"Is to drink slow. Keep chill from lungs."

The old man roared with laughter when Schultz came up gasping for air.

"*Fotz mit Plueschohrn*. Cunt with velvet ears. Witches' brew. Everything in it. Including *babushka's* regulation drawers from the first World War."

All the same his head went back, taking another long pull.

"That's better," chuckled Schultz.

"Stokes the fires of my 88, it does. Booze brings out the poetry in old Schultzy. Did I ever tell you of the time when I was a young lad straight off the farm. Seeing the bright lights of the *Reeperbahn*. Had this bit from Club 21. Drunk I was, couldn't stand. Happy though, I'd just belted two *Kriegsmarine* merchants. Lippy they was, because of my accent. She got me wedged in an alleyway near the Dammtor Bahnhof. Romantic it was. Early Sunday morning, all the church bells ringing out. Keen young lad. Went at it like a Stuka at Brest-Livosk. Nicked a pint of milk. Best breakfast I'd had in years."

He took another pull, his chest heaving.

"*Tittenlose Wuestensau*. Titless wonder. Friend, remind me to tell you of her one day."

Heyer continued his questioning in Russian.

194

"Village."

"Is no village."

"*Isba*."

"Is not far. Two hours. I am Alexi Leonid Bagaenko, watchman of the state forest."

"Soldiers. N.K.V.D."

The eyes of the old man hardened.

"All forest men gone of great Motherland war. N.K.V.D. come sometimes. I give *samahonka*. They drink much. Patrol forests."

"How often?"

He laughed.

"When vodka runs out. Get thirst for *samahonka*. Once . . . twice a month. Nothing in forest . . . only wolves. . . ."

"Partisans?"

"*Nyet*."

They all said that. Usually throwing their hands wide, and shaking their heads.

"Family."

"There is Tamara. Wife of my son Yuri. Her two little boys Roman and Mikhial. My daughter Aleni. Just a simple *isba*. Not like those of village. We have wooden floor." His eyes shone with obvious pride. "Make myself. When come to forest many years ago. Is dry, not damp like those of village."

They commandeered the old man and his sledge. Two hundred meters ahead of the others, Hansen and Klima waved to them from among the pines.

"Find a hut."

"Lost one of me prunes, I have," laughed Hansen.

"Better, little friend. He has a potato cellar full of booze. *Samahonka*. Good for the circulation. Have your prunes looking like fresh duck eggs before the night is out."

195

Hansen and Klima waded through the snow, coming to the sledge.

"Hate to mention it," Hansen was out of breath. "Gentleman. Being a respectable gentleman from the better slums of Hamburg. . . . But . . . er . . . talent."

"*Na, ja*. The usual. Daughter and son's wife living with him. Hairs on their top lips like Adolf. Backsides like a bogged-down Panzer Mark Three, I suppose."

Hansen began to pace up and down. Hands clasped firmly behind his back, look on his face like a lecturing professor.

"Na, you've got it all wrong, Schultzy. Get them long peasant dresses off. Many a curious Grenadier has been in for a surprise. Not saying that I go in for those thick-quilted Ruski drawers. Coming to just above their freckled knees."

"Getting ideas, Pushkin. With Schmidt with us."

"That's what happens to you when you become an Unteroffizier."

"Wasn't like it at the brothel in Kiev."

"Think he caught a dose before Moscow."

"That's as could be. Heard tell as some in the 45th Infantry got gas gangrene just pissing into the wind. Out here it's a killer, and no mistake."

"Nah. Don't do anything in the wind after Minsk and that fine Oberfeldwebel Brandt. How was I to know he'd come round to the back of the carrier, just as I was answering an urgent call from Mother nature."

"What did you get," laughed Klima.

"Went right against regulations he did. Walked right into my field of fire. Grenadier Hansen, he says. Had a mo, he did, just like Adolf's. When he was mad he used to pull on it. Prancing up and down

196

like a prize pimp in Frederichstrasse. Clean the road up. No slacking. Prussian swine. Took me hours, it did, with him strutting up and down watching me. You know how many horses it takes to drag an 88. You know what they are like after a rest and a good feed of oats. I ask you. Me . . ."

"*Los.*" Schmidt joined them.

"Load up Steggeman and Griecebeck. Ruskis might be behind us. You lot stand here gas-bagging. Move it."

Before dark they came to Alexi Bageanko's *isba.* Solid-looking, it was made out of hand-cut logs. Two small boys with shaven heads ran out to meet the old man. Carrying lanterns Tamara and Aleni came towards the sledge. They were dressed in long black dresses almost reaching to their ankles. Padded jackets and thick headscarves. High cheekbones make many Russian women outstandingly beautiful. Tamara possessed that kind of dark-haired beauty. Her eyes seemed to flash when she smiled. Like the women of Romny and Akhtyrka with their mixed gypsy blood. And yet there was a coyness there. She was unmistakably very shy. Like many Russian women are still, to this very day. In some places a woman tourist will be spat upon for showing naked shoulders. Or wearing shorts that are too small.

"In dead of winter he goes to collect firewood. Returns with guests," She wrung her hands.

Heyer bowed from the waist, greeting her. So did Schultz and Hansen. She blushed, her hands fussing nervously with her headscarf.

"Table is not prepared. In spring you come with pups of forest wolf." She clucked her tongue loudly.

"Alexi. Wanderer of the forest. What is woman to do with you."

Heyer translated.

The old Alexi roared with laughter.

"Is same in your country, Germanski. Women have much lip. Always they complain." He playfully boxed his grandson's ears.

Laughter came from their frozen lips.

Once again Schmidt saw it happening. The war in the East would be forgotten. All eyes were for the dark-haired Tamara. It had happened before. When the filthy lice-ridden *Soldat* from the front meets a woman. A very pretty woman. He is like a small boy lost. Stepping from the untold horrors of war, into a glade filled with sparkling sunlight. All manners, eager to please. A part of the world they had forgotten. The sensitive smile of a woman. The soft feminine rustle of her skirt. Meeting her eyes. Sometimes being offended if she blushed, and they were the cause of it. Make her laugh. The blackened toothless smile of Schultzy. Hansen, his eyes almost popping out of his head. Knowing that she was untouchable. Yet wishing, dreaming, hoping. Just small boys drowning in their lost wishful dreams of a lost youth.

The wounded were unloaded and taken into the *isba*, Tamara shouting with alarm each time Griecebeck moaned. Inside, the *isba* was larger than those of the villages. Lots of artistically homemade furniture. Even bunks set up at one end.

"Tamara, wife of my son. Already she rules me like the village *babushka*. Why do you stand there, woman. *Soldats* have bellies crying with hunger. Guests they have been, of our illustrious N.K.V.D."

Aleni left the wounded and began to prepare a meal.

Alexi continued.

"Our brave Cossacks attacked their N.K.V.D. masters."

"Always the way of the saber in little Mother Russia. Under the Czar times were better. Cloth I could buy cheaper. Pigs we had. A horse. The party took them away."

"*Kulaks* we never were, Tamara."

"The ruble went further."

"Times change. With the wind blowing from the gallant Cossacks, maybe this old man will see the day when we are all free men."

Aleni lighted another lamp, placing it above Klima's head on the wall.

"When the men come home to the villages, it is time for much rejoicing, Tamara."

Tamara smiled.

"*Da*, Aleni. When my Yuri returns to the forest, there will be much dancing. The Germanskis look at me with full eyes and long tongues."

She clucked her tongue, going over to the *samahonka* barrel.

Mess tins rattled. She began to fill them.

"Is for drinking slow, *Soldats*. Or *samahonka* goes straight to head." Her right hand went to Hansen's filthy hair, shaking gently.

She pointed her finger at him accusingly.

Heyer translated. She blushed, turning her face away, but they could see she was smiling.

Genuine old-world hospitality. Many Russian peasants gave food and shelter to lost roaming members of the Wehrmacht. Shared everything they had. Risked their lives helping *Soldats* in need. Traitors. *Nein*, they were human. An older woman's hand upon a young sweating *Soldat's* brow. Lost in the horror of total war. Bitter, sadistic. Such moments of memory stand out like jewels among the smoke, cries of fear and sickening stench of the dead and dying.

"Germanski invaders. What do they bring to the Motherland?" Old Alexi drew the two small boys to him, cradling their shaven heads against his waist.

"No harm will come to you," Heyer reassured him. "We will rest. Tend to our wounded. Then move on."

"Such are the times of war, *Soldat*. As guests you are safe under the Bageanko roof. No hand of strife will turn against you here. If son Yuri was home, you would not be welcome. Party member. From early youth in the forest. Always his head has looked to Moscow."

"What part of the front is he on?"

"His battery was at Dmitrovsk. At Suchinitchi was the last Tamara heard. With Katushkas. You heard of the Katushka, Herr *Soldat?*"

"*Da*. Stalin Organs."

Alexi smiled knowingly.

Stalin Organs. Multi-barreled rocket launchers. Mounted upon the backs of trucks, they were capable of firing sixteen rockets all at once. In the night their fiery trails could be seen lighting up the skies. In the daytime the smoke from their tails hung as though frozen upon the air. An archway of death and destruction. Their roar more fearsome than a Stuka in full dive. Each fresh volley echoing the death chant. Sound. Another note in the Russian symphony to haunt the memory.

"How's the old prunes, Hansen? Win a beauty competition would they? Smooth as ducks' eggs yet?"

"You was right, Schultzy. *Samahonka* irons the wrinkles out."

"Will you two cut out the filth," snapped Muller.

Hansen looked hurt.

"On me best manners, I am. Don't mean to say

200

I'm going to flash them, does it?"

Heyer sat down beside Schultz digging him playfully in the ribs.

"Feeling poetic. Tell us about the bit from Club 21 in the Reeperbahn."

Schultz's eyes lighted up as Aleni poured him more *samahonka*. He took a long swig, then leaned back against the wall.

"Now you all know that Schultzy likes a bit to specialize. I like a bit that knows what it's all about. No kiss, cuddle and get at it. Being a refined gentleman from Niedersachsen . . ."

"Schultz."

Schmidt came out from behind the draped blanket set up across the room so they could all take a bath.

"*Los*. You are next. You have five minutes. Wash all your things. Aleni will take your clothes and dry them over the stove." He came out, a blanket draped about him.

"My Club 21 bit."

"Another time, Schultz."

"Need a back-scrubber, I do. Any volunteers. Me granny used to do it in Bienebuttel. Needs a woman's touch, it does."

Happily drunk, Schultz rose to his feet. He lifted his right leg.

Muller threw a boot at him.

"Thought you was a gentleman," laughed Hansen.

The smile left Schultz's face.

"That includes bad air, little friend."

"*Ja*. When a gentleman wants to do it and he's in the company of women, he leaves the room."

"And freeze me nuts off out there?" He went behind the blanket.

"Schultzy, no letting off bad air. Can't tell me

Reeperbahn story. No one to scrub my back. *Himmel, Arsch, und Zwirn*. Heaven, arse and twine. Uncivilized, it is."

He began splashing about in the large wooden tub. A loud cackling laugh came from behind the blanket.

"Herr Unteroffizier Schmidt. Grenadier Schultz begs to report. Got a rash all over my body. Most of it around my tonsils and it itches."

Schmidt sat down, taking *samahonka* from Aleni.

"Shut up. Get on with it. The others want a bath too."

"And no one cares about my rash. Hansen, take a note. Reported it in the correct regulation manner. Looks like measles to me. Warsawitus. It might be flaming jumping syphilis. Shake the last drop, it could come off in my hand. Of course, no one cares about me."

Schmidt, Hansen, Heyer and Muller went to the blanket, pulling it aside.

"Where's this rash?"

He looked at them, a complete picture of suffering innocence.

"Look at them lice. Did you know Ruski lice don't swim?"

The water erupted. Foul air assaulted their nostrils. Schultz lay back in the bath, a satisfied smile upon his face. He gave a mock bow.

"Split that equally among you gentlemen. Compliments from the house of Schultz. Don't say I didn't give you anything for Christmas."

"You pig."

"*Sau*."

"Caught me old granny that way once. She always used to get the soap in my eyes. Not right, is it?"

"*Schnell*. Aleni's making something to eat."

"*Scheiss*. That should have cleared your lungs.

202

After me, *zwei, drei, vier.*"
He threw his mess tin away.

"Heute wollen wir ein Liedlein singen.
Trinken wollen wir den kuehlen Wein.
Unsere Glaeser sollen dazu klingen.
Denn es muss es muss gescheden sein."

After he washed his uniform he had to be dragged from the bath. On a piece of floating wood he had deposited all his rescued lice. After a rousing chorus of *"Wir fahren gegn England,"* he shouted for Hansen to attack with his paratrooper lice, his taking the part of the invading Wehrmacht. Schmidt broke it up. But it took four of them to drag him away.

"Someone should be on the lookout." He detailed Heyer to take the first turn.

"Singing like drunken idiots. Ivan could creep up. Then where would we be?"

Some form of sanity returned. The wounded were stripped and washed. The others contented themselves having lice races upon the floor. A sport that made the hours pass while waiting in the bunkers of the line. The boys Roman and Mikhial joined in. Even the cat and her kittens. It had to break up just when they had crowned a sixth-time winner with a rewarding shot of *samahonka*. The kittens insisted on eating all the new runners.

Later Aleni called them to the table. There were potatoes cooked in the red hot ash of the stove. Homemade bread. Honey from the forest that had been stored in earthenware jars. Pork the likes of which they had never tasted before. A royal feast. The aroma made their heads feel light. After weeks of starvation they ate slowly, savoring every morsel.

Heyer knocked a chunk of fatty pork from

203

Hansen's hand, nodding towards Aleni. She circled the ikon over their heads, mumbling a prayer in Russian.

"You said they were heathens."

"Pushkin."

"*Da*, Pushkin." Old Alexi roared with laughter.

"Bow your head like a Czarist gentleman," Schultz kicked Hansen under the table.

Aleni and Tamara glared at Alexi. He crossed himself and lowered his head.

The meal over, Schmidt and Klima carried Griecebeck to the table. He was still in a coma. The women prepared hot water. Heyer explained to them what they were going to do. They began to clean Griecebeck's wounds.

"Get Steggeman drunk—he's next," barked Schmidt.

"*Jawohl.*"

Most of them gathered about the table, looking at Griecebeck's prone figure.

"Hold him down; he might come around."

Each of them took his place.

Klima finished his *samahonka*. Cleaned the back wound. Fresh blood started to drain away. He had difficulty swallowing.

"Son of a bitch."

"Speak German."

"I . . . I can't do it."

All eyes turned towards him.

"You are the only one who has seen it done before."

Schmidt tested the sharp *kandra*, handing it to Klima.

"Too late to back out now."

Klima's head was spinning. The *samahonka* made it worse. He had felt the same way holding the panzer man down at the aid station. The full story had not been told. Torn bloody limbs in the bucket, covered with the yellow dust of the steppe. Arms, legs. Maggots, fat slimy things, crawling out of the infested wound. The doctor squeezing and picking them out with his long tweezers. Another operating table. Unearthly screaming. Harsh reprimanding words of the doctor.

"Hold him fast. How can I cut if he keeps moving."

The saw biting into the bone. Blood splashing as another smelly severed limb was flung upon the pile.

"Next. Gut wound."

The doctor's knife at the stomach. Hands deep in the stomach. Smell of excretion. Urine. Putrefying pus. Bloodied hands coming clear.

"Tie off. Give him a . . ."

Klima almost passed out.

"We—we've nothing to stitch up with. Infection . . ."

Heyer came to his side.

"Burn it with a hot knife. Cauterize the wound. That should stop the infection."

"Burn . . . burn Griecebeck. I . . . I—"

He lurched to the door, throwing up.

"You are their only hope."

"I—I'm sorry."

"Ami idiot," Heyer spat in contempt.

"Too much soft living in the U.S. I'll do it."

He took up the *kandra*, taking Klima's place.

Carefully he cut away at the wound low on the spine. With his left hand he gently moved the muscle tissue to one side. Blood gushed over the face of the wound. It oozed out, running around Griecebeck's waist. Tamara stood at his elbow dabbing, trying to stem the flow.

"Doctor," Hansen was at his elbow.

"Butcher. Thinks he's in a Hanover meat market."

"Do any better?" Heyer's fingers were probing the jagged wound.

Drunk, Hansen lurched to the other side, looking over.

"No better from here. Put him out of his misery like the S.S. do."

"*Aschloch.*" Schmidt pushed him roughly aside.

"I'll remember that next time you get a scratch. Carry on, Wolfgang. You are doing fine."

"*Bestimmt.*"

His fingers contacted a sharp piece of metal.

"Got it. Can't grip it. Get two spoons. *Schnell*, it's slipping."

Aleni returned with the spoons.

"Here, *gospodin.*"

Griecebeck stirred. His legs drummed the table. Frightened eyes wide, his head turned. His body convulsed in spasms, muscles trembling, trying desperately to break free. Sweating, they fought him, pressing him back onto the table. His dry, long, pitiful screams tore at their nerves.

Back at the table, holding down a leg, Klima vomited once again.

Muller wedged a cloth into Griecebeck's mouth.

"Grip with your teeth."

Eyes wide with terror. His body arched, thrashing from side to side.

"*Nein. Nein. Last mich in ruh.*"

"No gangrene."

"*Nein.*"

"*Gut.*"

"He'll make it."

"Schultz," shouted Schmidt.

"Forget the lookout. Help us hold him down."

He came to the table with a mess tin of *samahonka*.

"Sit him up. Get some of this down him."

His head was gripped hard, the drink forced into him. At one time he came close to choking. Schultz pounded his back. The head was pulled back and he swallowed.

Coma. The rough hands holding him. Faces that swayed and hovered. Griecebeck shook his head. His vision was frayed. Dream, nightmarish horror. It had happened. The train was stopped on the main line out of Warsaw. An explosion that shook and rocked the whole train. Four carriages were torn apart. Two more derailed lying overturned at the bottom of an embankment. *Soldaten* was running along the gravel at the side of the track.

"*Raus. Raus. Alles aussteigen.*"

Utter confusion. Grabbing mausers and backpacks. Carriages were burning. Wounded screaming. The sounds of rifle fire. Fifty young replacements were killed. Twenty more were gasping their last breaths. Head wounds. *Gut*. Two with no legs.

An S.S. Unterscharfuehrer took command. Through the snow. Into the woods. Fresh tracks of the partisans seeming like a herd of wild beasts on the rampage. Contact. Partisan rearguard. An S.S. Sturmann from Das Reich hits them with a flamethrower. Caught running, they were burnt alive. Griecebeck was one of the first into the trees. Two young girls were among the partisan dead. The S.S. Sturmann stomped the grisly remains. Kicking viciously with his jackboots.

"Polack pigs."

Forward. A farmhouse in a clearing. Tracks lead

straight to it. Machine gun fire. Small arms from the windows and outbuildings. A call for mortars.

"We'll teach the bastards."

Rifles and automatics keep the partisans engaged. The mortars arrive. The farm buildings disintegrate under a barrage of intense fire.

"*Schnell.*"

A penal unit sets off to cut off the rear. The S.S. Unterscharfuehrer stops the mortars. Griecebeck's group is briefed by the S.S. Sturmann. Left and right attack. Shrill whistle from the penal unit.

"*Los.* Forward."

The partisan fire is stepped up. A youth falls beside him. Dumdum. Small hole below the eye. Back of the head stoved in. A partisan charges, rifle and bayonet thrust out before him. Seven rifle shots cut him down.

Cover of a low wall. A storm of hand grenades. Lull. Excited nervous voices. Nervous laughter. The first battle for many. First wounded. Sight of their first dead. Like a battle game. Only the pulse is racing. Fever pitch. Excitement. Infectious. Breathtaking. Up on one knee. Waiting for the command. A white sheet appears at an upstairs window.

Stand down.

Twelve prisoners walk from the farmhouse, arms raised high. Among them there are three young women.

Griecebeck takes a cigarette, drawing deeply. His hands are shaking. But what he has feared most. First contact with the enemy. He has come through it. Without a scratch. The fever of the chase is still with them. Someone is talking about the outhouses.

"Took three with a grenade."

The S.S. are questioning the prisoners. Shouts. One is being pistol-whipped. Another is forced down upon his knees. A rifle cracks. The kneeling prisoner sways and falls.

"Long live Poland!" A cry of defiance.

From the lips of a young woman.

A Stabsgefreiter forms the replacements into column, ready for the march back to the train.

"Five for the firing squad."

The S.S. Sturmann grins. Griecebeck is among those detailed. The column marches off. Five prisoners are placed against the wall. The S.S. Unterscharfuehrer stands before the firing squad.

"You men are new to the front. You've seen what these bandits did to the train. To our *Kameraden*. We show them no mercy. Every partisan caught is always shot. You have been detailed to carry out the duty."

The lecture droned on. Among the prisoners was a young girl. She stood straight and erect. Her head high. Defiant until the last. No older than his sister back in the Fatherland. The S.S. man had his pistol under her chin, continuing his speech. She spat in his face. He drew back, wiping the spittle with a white handkerchief.

In a daze he heard the commands. Attention. Out of the corner of his eyes he saw the ashen face next to him. The youth's legs seemed to be giving way.

"Still gestanden."

In a daze he heard the harsh reprimand from the S.S. Sturmann.

The eyes of the young Polish girl were looking into his. Vaguely he heard her cries of "Long live Poland." And still those eyes bore into his. As though she was cursing him and his for all time.

"Take aim."

The mausers came up. None were steady. One youth fainted. The girl's features swam in his sights.

The soft face was smiling. Their voices rose in a Polish patriotic song. He aimed away from the body. It was hard to breath. War. But this. Women. His head felt light.

"Fire."

He fainted, his shot going wide.

When he came to all the prisoners were dead. On the snow beside him were two more youths. The S.S. Sturmann had had to shoot the prisoners himself. The S.S. Unterscharfuehrer finished those off who were still moving.

A car skidded through the snow towards them. An S.S. Obersturmbannfuehrer took the report, inspecting the dead bodies. He gave another lecture. Warned of the partisans in Poland and Russia. Told them they had to become hard. There could be no mercy in the war against the Slavic subhumans.

"We have to stamp them out. *Ja*, men, women, even children capable of carrying arms. We have to be ever vigilant. They try to sap our strength. Sabotage our supplies. Victory will only be ours when we have wiped the vipers out."

Helping to bury the dead back at the train Griecebeck found himself trembling once again. He had braved the first contact under fire. But the shooting of the partisans. The girl. Those eyes staring at him. They would haunt and accuse him always.

He struggled, screaming aloud. Broke free. The faces were clearer now. The hands trying to hold him down. The pains pounding at his body. Schultz hit him and he sagged unconscious into Klima's arms.

"Breed them tough in the Hitler Jugend," gasped Schultz.

Suckau took Griecebeck's arm.

"I told you, Schultzy. The training is hard."

"Hold him." Heyer's fingers went into the wound.

"No good. I need scissors. Can't grip it."

He spoke to Aleni in Russian. Within minutes she handed him a pair of scissors.

Spreading two fingers to hold the flesh back, he eased the scissors into the wound. They failed to grip.

He turned to Alexi, speaking in Russian.

"Blunt the ends."

Alexi went to the stove, tapping the points of the scissors with a hammer.

"Here, *gospodin*."

In deathly silence he probed, contacting the piece of spent bullet. He slid one finger into the wound slowly with the scissors. They slipped, jarring the bone. He motioned to Tamara. Blood was filling the hole. She dabbed with a cloth, soaking it up.

Hands shaking slightly, the scissors came clear. He dropped the twisted metal into a glass jar.

"More in there?" whispered Schmidt.

"*Nein.* That's all." His fingers were gently kneading the gooey mass.

He wiped his hands upon a cloth held by Aleni. Tamara kissed him upon the cheek.

"Two more to go."

Schultz passed him a mess tin of *samahonka.*

"Hidden talent, Heyer," he wanted to say more, but in his drunken state he was at a loss for words.

Griecebeck came around again. They had to fight to hold him down. Finally Klima got the cloth into his mouth. He came close to losing a finger.

"Ami, that's for losing your nerve."

"Get on with it. He's losing too much blood." Klima had recovered.

The struggling stopped. Griecebeck's body went slack.

Heyer's fingers traced the lower back wound. No need to cut. The skin was torn loose.

"Nothing in there."

"Flesh wound."

"*Ja. Nein.* Here it is."

A splinter of bullet was lying hard up against the spine. Alexi came lower with the lamp giving him more light.

"Two bits."

"Ricochet."

"*Ja.*"

It was partly embedded in the bone. He worked the scissors, prying it loose. The body moved, muscles quivering.

"If you can't get it, cut the wound more."

"I've got it."

The metal tinkled into the glass.

"Arm now."

He moved down the table.

The bone was intact. He pushed the bloody tissue aside.

"*Nichts.*"

"Straight through."

"Make sure."

He doubled-checked. The bullet had gone straight through the flesh of the muscle.

"Close up."

"Suckau, bring the hot knife."

He cauterized the wounds. Griecebeck was wide awake, body straining, sweating under their hands. At each touch of the hot knife he bucked, trying to twist out of their grasp. The screams were dry, as though there was no strength left in the sweating body.

"*Tovaritch,*" Tamara tugged at Heyer's arm.

"I stitch with silk thread."

The wounds were stitched and closed.

"Do that to me." Drunk Steggeman came to the table as they were dressing the last of the wounds.

"Mine are flesh wounds. Heal on their own."

"Gangrene. What chance will you have then?" chided Muller.

"Heyer. He'll cut me . . ."

Klima knocked him out. He was stripped and laid upon the table. Two wounds. One low in the buttocks. The other high up on his right arm. Neither of them had any fragments in them. Fully recovered, it was Klima who applied the hot knife. Tamara stitched them up. The wounds were dressed. It was all over before he finally came around. He was placed beside Griecebeck upon one of the bunks.

"Heyer, experiment with me," he shouted when he eventually came around.

Schmidt passed him some *samahonka*.

"It's all over," he laughed.

"We changed the dressings. You had nothing in there."

"See what he did to that Leutnant in the *stolovaya*. Cut his throat. One of our own officers."

"He did what?"

"From ear to ear. I saw him do it."

Heyer was cleaning his hands in fresh hot water.

"Should I have kissed him goodnight?"

"Bloodthirsty ghoul," Muller looked at Heyer threateningly.

"Runt of a Leutnant. Polack folk Deutsch pig. He would have run straight to the ivans."

"They were busy fighting the Cossacks."

"Was we to know that?" shouted Heyer.

"All that mattered was to get out of that place quick," added Schultz.

Muller moved towards Heyer.

"Killing our own. What are we coming to?"

Heyer waved the mainspring of his weapon at Muller.

"At times you make me sick with your high and mighty ways. What do you think we are in, the boy scouts? Total war. No holds barred. Only the strongest will survive. The weak will be left to rot in the snow."

"Cutting the throats of our own *Kameraden*."

"What about S.S. Hauptsturmfuehrer Sachs? Leutnant Lindenhof?"

"*Donner wetter*. That was different. *Schweinhund*."

"Runts had to die right," shouted Schultz.

"*Ja*."

Heyer finished putting his m.p.i. together.

"So did the Polack pig." He rushed at Muller. Schultz and Schmidt stopped him.

"Have you forgotten the 5th of September 1941? The town of Bromburg in Poland? Hundreds of German residents dying, butchered in the street. Retreating Polish Army did that. Get that in your book. Or are you only concerned with the atrocities committed by us Germans."

"The whole damn war. Each side is equally guilty. . . ."

"*Seid ruhig*." Schmidt pushed them roughly aside.

"It's done. Argument is over. Shut up. You are frightening the children."

Little Roman and Mikhial were clutching at Tamara's long skirts. Both were crying.

Schultz turned on the others, eyes flaming.

"Anyone frightens the *Kinder*, I'll help him meet his maker."

Hansen stirred, lying on the floor near the stove.

"Let's play hunt the Knickers." Bleary-eyed he

214

had just awakened from his drunken sleep.

They all roared with laughter.

"I mean hunt the Germanski."

Schultz went back to playing the bad Germanski bear that always hid in the darkness of the potato cellar. Soon the *isba* was once again full of joyous boyish laughter.

"*Stoi* Germanski. *Stoi!*" The *isba* walls echoed with the boys' giggling.

Little Steggeman cried himself to sleep. A child in the uniform of the Wehrmacht. He was always saying the wrong thing.

Chapter 13
TAMARA AND THE SOLDAT

Griecebeck woke up. Tamara was at his side. Roman and Mikhial were also standing there.

"*Da*, Germanski not sleep."

Their words came floating to him. A breath. A caress out of the threatening dark unknown. Tortured bouts of sharply vivid terrifying dreams. Young *Soldat* alone. Death waiting in the void. Grim reaper beckoning. Waiting, eager to snatch him from the hell he was reliving.

"*Trink, Herr Soldat*," she said in broken German, offering the hot honey.

"*Danke*."

Hazily he remembered Schmidt bending over him. He was to lead a patrol into the forest. Looking for the Moscow road. Or was it the road to the destroyed village of Livny? He left an m.p.i. upon the bunk. Spare magazine.

"*Soldats* no come. Two days." Tamara was worried, emphasizing the days with her fingers.

Two days ago. His mind began to clear. Had they deserted him? Gone back to the German lines without him? A wounded *Soldat* would only slow them down. *Nein*, Schmidt, Muller, Heyer, they would never do that. They would return. Two days. What had happened to them? Red Army patrol. Skirmish. Slaughtered bodies left to freeze in the forest snows. *Nein*, not the platoon. Veterans. They would survive.

"*Trink,*" Tamara was smiling holding the mess tin to his lips.

Each time he came around one of the women was there by his side. Once, deep in the night, he had awakened screaming. The smiling eyes of the partisan girl near Warsaw haunting him. Tamara had comforted him. Lantern in her hand. Soothing, wiping his feverish forehead. The constant throbbing pains of his wounds were unbearable. A suffocating blanket. Nauseous fear of death clutching at his throat. *Mutti. Mutti.* Incoherent cries screaming into the night.

"*Matj. Matj,*" she had crooned tenderly.

Tears in her eyes, she lay down with him, pressing his head to her breast. Sobbing quietly into the night. His sweating, exhausted body fell asleep in her arms.

It was the fourteenth day. The pain of the wounds was easing. He remembered the knife. The cut had not hurt. It was the fingers probing. The pull on his tender wounded flesh. The scissors scraping the bone. The burning. Being wide awake. Urine had flooded about his loins. No one cursed. For hours he had shouted in sheer agony. They were heavily sedated with *samahonka*. Steggeman was up and walking after ten days.

A continued cloud of drunkenness had settled over him. A hangover that wanted to burst his head. The others caught dysentery. He remembered Schultz loudly blaming the pork. Muller saying it was eating and drinking too much after the weeks of enforced starvation. Hansen and Klima were confined to the bunks next to him. The *isba* reeked of excreta for over ten days.

Tamara and Aleni changed his dressings regularly,

putting a stiff mixture of honey upon them. Heyer told him it was an old Russian folk remedy. Muller said villagers of the Heide used it for cuts and burns. It had a soothing effect upon his healing wounds. The stiffness was going from his shoulder. He could now flex the muscle. Earlier it would have had him howling with pain.

"Ruski Soldats!" Aleni came running into the *isba*.

He grabbed his weapon, checking the magazine. Terror, the fright of being caught. He would fight. They would not take him alive. Tamara. Aleni. Alexi. The boys. The patrol would severly punish them for hiding him. He looked at the two women helplessly. How could he tell them?

They made the decision.

"Davay. Davay." They helped him from the bunk.

Took him to the potato cellar. Roman lifted the trapdoor. Mikhial ran back to collect his m.p.i.

Sounds of shouting came from outside. Sledge dogs barking. Raised Russian voices cursing. None can curse like them. The devil. Demons. Ranting whore of the forest hiding in the darkness of the trees. Red Army or the dreaded N.K.V.D. He thought he heard old Alexi. Someone in authority shouting. Others joining in with loud boisterous laughter.

The women laid him upon the floor near the potato pile. Gave him his weapon. He cocked it. Covered him with old sacks. Shoveled potatoes onto him. The tramp of boots sounded upon the floorboards upstairs. Tamara was the last up the ladder, taking a pot of honey with her.

"Tovaritch Tamara," greeted N.K.V.D. Lieutenant Yershov. "We hunt the fascists. Have you seen

any Germanski pigs in the forest?"

She put the honey down upon the table.

"*Nyet, gospodin* leytenant. Why should Germanski come here?"

He stood with his back to the hot stove. Why should he answer her question, he thought. An inquiry would be conducted by Moscow. He would not be held to blame. That honor would go to his dead superior.

"Tamara, flower of the forest." He smiled cruelly.

"One day I will bed you, forest witch."

Revulsion shook her. An icy hand played at her spine.

"I am a married woman. My Yuri is a party member. He serves our great Motherland at the front. Would you take advantage of a defenseless woman?"

"*Da,*" he smiled scratching himself suggestively. "What do you see in your Yuri."

"He is the father of my sons. We are under the roof of his father."

"Mere foot soldier." He spat contemptuously upon the hot stove. "I am yours for the asking. An officer of the N.K.V.D. Much food I could bring to your *isba*. Sweets from the shops of Moscow for your boys." He reached out for Roman, who shied away.

"For Roman and Mikhial I make sweets from the forest honey."

"You steal the honey from the state forest, little flower."

"The peasants of the forest have always collected it."

"Have you no quota to fill for the forest soviet?"

"*Nyet.*"

219

"I must talk with the forest soviet. He is not doing his duty to the state."

Tamara hoped they would not get drunk. The last patrol, two of them had gone to the cellar to relieve themselves. Slant-eyed ones from Samarkand. If they discovered the *Soldat*—kill him. Take the family away. Brand them as traitors in the Motherland war. He reminded her of her Yuri. Their youth together wandering the forest. Courtship. Yuri the strong. Woodsman with the axe. But as gentle and tender as the spring breeze through the trees. Where they had whispered of their love, in the rays of the spring sunshine. Would he not help a bird of the forest with a broken wing?

"Come flower of the forest. Lavrov has his accordion. Would you not dance for an officer of little Mother Russia?"

As a young girl she had performed before the visiting Czar. Story of the forest. Breath from the winds rustling the tall pines. Hands held high trunk of the body slightly waving, she swayed before them. When the traditional dress is worn, long, almost touching the floor. Six young maidens of the forest perform, gliding majestically. No movement is seen of the legs, as they glide and twirl with breathtaking precision. Fragile dainty dolls. Telling the stories of old. Powdered faces set in toylike smiles.

Chin resting upon outstretched fingers, she bent to the left, then to the right. Yershov's lust-filled eyes were upon her. Always she had tried to avoid him when he was on patrol. His hands. Searching, clammy fingers. Always he tried to touch her. Treat her as though she was his woman. Yuri would kill him. Hot-tempered and very jealous. He would strike Yershov down. Once a couple were betrothed and married, they were life partners. The regime might change, but the traditions of peasant life in the Motherland remained the same.

Another Mongol trooper pulled Aleni away from the stove to dance. Her eyes went to her *papushka*, Alexi. His face was not smiling. He knew only too well the reputation of the N.K.V.D. Monsters, they were not like the men of the villages. Sinister. Implements of the restrictive harsh law. Taking, doing what ever they wanted. No man could stop them. Police Minister Beria's men. Hated like the Germanski S.S. Who would raise their hands against them. Would it not be like slapping the Kremlin in the face? Only a man brave in heart like Yuri would stand up to him. And some of the other men of the forest.

Later, Tamara felt Yershov's hand trying to paw her.

"*Nyet*." She drew away from him.

"Why not, little flower?"

"I am true to my Yuri."

He roared with drunken laughter, spittle hitting her face.

"Does your belly not ache for the thrust of a man? You have been long without it."

"*Nyet*. One day my Yuri will return."

"The day will come when you will crawl to my bed like a Mongol whore. Begging me to take you."

Tamara caught her breath. Her body stiffened. Fear gripped her heart. Two of the troopers had lifted the potato cellar trapdoor.

She shook Yershov.

"They ruin my potatoes."

Yershov grinned drunkenly.

"Flower, be nice to the N.K.V.D. A maid I will get to peel your potatoes," he laughed, already unsteady upon his feet.

"My Yuri would stop them."

Yershov grabbed her roughly, shaking her.

"His body might already be rotting upon the steppes. You could be alone. You would need a strong man to protect you."

"Aleni said a blessing over him before he left for the front. He will survive." Her eyes grew bitter and she wanted to strike out at his evil grinning face.

Griecebeck heard them coming. His sweaty grip tightened upon his weapon. He heard the sudden splashing. Satisfied swearing and grunts. One of them came within a meter of his prone body.

He smelt the body odor. Could almost feel the panting breath.

The other one was searching through the preserving jars. They clinked and rattled upon the shelf. He was stuffing his mouth, smacking his lips loudly. His comrade joined him. They chuckled in the darkness like children, enjoying themselves in their drunken revelry.

Sticky, he was bathed in sweat. The wounds on his back and arm were itching. If another of their comrades came into the cellar with a lantern, that would be it.

Kill them—Heyer. Schultz or Schmidt definitely would. Open fire. Get to the ladder and take on the others. He had not walked in weeks. Would he be able to make it? If they tossed a grenade down, it would be all over in a matter of seconds. A blinding light, his body torn to bits by the fragments.

Tamara and her family. If he did not succeed in shooting all the ivans, what would happen to them? His shattered remains would signify their guilt.

"*Yob tvoymat.*"

He began to shiver. Did they realize he was there? Had they heard his excited breathing? Slowly he eased his weapon up.

Another ivan came to the trapdoor shouting down. The two in the cellar went to the ladder.

He relaxed. Released the pressure off the trigger. *Ja*, if they came down again and found him he would fight. There was a good chance that he could make it to the ladder. Get a burst off in the room upstairs. That is what the veteran Heyer would do. Go down fighting. Only a weak *Soldat* would take the easy way out.

Captivity. He would not last. How could he hope to march? Fall. He visualized the laughing, bearded, mocking face. Bayonet. Death at the side of the road. The same fate that had fallen to countless other *Kameraden*. They would have no known graves. Only the sunflowers growing higher over their remains.

"I ask if you see any fascist pigs?" Yershov waved a Wehrmacht mess tin under Tamara's nose.

She snatched it from him.

"I found it in the forest, *gospodin* leytenant."

"Party is over," he roared drunkenly.

His hands were at her breasts. She closed her eyes, her body trembling. Holy Mother of Kazan. Forgive me. Yuri, you know not the men of Beria. His foul breath washed over her face.

"Time for dance is over, little forest flower." Eyes glaring at her he laughed lecherously, reaching out for her.

Griecebeck heard the first frightened animalistic scream. On his feet he leaned against the wall.

"*Nyet. Nyet!*" It was Tamara's voice.

He lurched towards the ladder.

Chapter 14
MASSACRE IN THE FOREST

Muller suggested the halt. Wearily they slumped down against the trees. Dysentery was still with Klima. Cramp, stomach pain, nausea. Vomiting became more frequent. Sweating with a high fever. Many times he collapsed. A pole stretcher was made for him. He rambled, past caring if anyone was listening. His whole life poured out. His nerves could not last much longer. One night in the snowhouse he begged them to kill him. Pitiful, beyond help. He had been with them since the beginning. It was like watching a caricature of themselves. They had seen too much. Been through too much. On the Eastern Front thousands broke under the awful strain.

They found the road. Huddled together at the top of a high bank watching as large Russian artillery units rolled by. Batteries of the awesome Stalin Organs. T.34s and other heavy monster panzers. Leather-hatted crewmen cheered shaking their fists in salute. Groups of partisans and helmeted infantry answered the call. The air shook with the deep-throated calls of "Urah Stalin." It rose with a roar above the snow-clad trees. A sea of voices crying for vengeance and death to the fascist invaders.

"High command thinks they're on their last legs." Heyer spat into the snow.

"Adolf should see this lot. He'd think twice about

calling them subhumans," added Hansen.

"Nazi fanatics. Heard a base bull giving a lecture in Kiev. He said it would all be over by Christmas 1941. After that we'd just have police duties to do. All the heroes of the glorious Third Reich would be granted a farm in the occupied lands."

"Muller. When did that shit ever see the Siberians?"

"Or get kissed by a T.34."

The last of Tamara's homemade bread was shared out. A frozen crust of bread can last a very long time. You have to know how to chew it properly. Over and over again. *Samahonka* from their small water bottles. May the golden pheasant who invented them in supply rest in peace. Preferably in the correct Prussian regulation manner, after retching and choking on a parched dry gullet. *Machorkas* rolled patiently, backs bracing against the icy chilling wind.

Schmidt rechecked the wrapping upon their weapons. He wanted none to jam if they came under attack. In the cold of the line they would frequently clear them by firing. Even a mauser can cause trouble if it is not looked after in the biting cold. A fire in the forest would only draw attention to themselves. The wrapping would have to do.

His thoughts returned to Griecebeck. They would collect him and be back in the German lines within days. Return to the front. Constant lack of sleep. Eating only when the Rollbahn supply units got through. Waiting. The endless hours in the bunkers. Gathered about the glow of a Hindenburg candle, playing skat. Popping lice. Reading and writing letters home. The quiet broken by the crying of full-grown battle-hardened veterans. A father or brother fallen for Greater Germany. Parents, girlfriends, relatives lost in a burning collapsed building during a bombing raid. Alert. Lining the trenches shivering. Falling flares. Signal for an ivan attack. Or a raiding party out in no man's land. Those in the listening posts would fall first. Meters ahead of the main defenses. Landser. Grenadier. It was not much to look forward to.

As usual Hansen was the first to break the silence, his face creased into a cheeky grin.

"When this lot's over. See it all I can. Me and uncle Schultzy with big cigars in our mouths. Marching up the good old Reeperbahn. Doing nicely, thank you, with our thriving brothel."

"Is that all you can think about? Brothels, exposed breasts. Heavy grunting. Cashing in on drunken slobs who don't know any better." Muller threw a chunk of ice at him.

"That reminds me. Did I ever tell you about granny grunt and f . . ."

"There will be silence on this part of the front. Let Schultz's little friend speak. There will be a big call for our services after the war. Everything will be rationed. I think you will only be able to get a bit of the other with little green stamps. We should clean up." He bowed from the waist, taking his hat off in a sweeping motion.

"The floor is yours. Carry on, Pushkin."

"Model it after them ones in Paris. Or the better ones of Brussels. Not like them ones in Hamburg where you bargain with the tarts at the open windows. No culture. Fancied a big ginger-haired one there, once I did. Red dress. What a cleavage. Could almost see the top of her boots."

"Had her name on them, did she?" laughed Steggeman.

"Runt." Schultz cracked his huge knuckles.

"Followed her up the stairs. Red panties winking.

Black seams in her stockings. Got a thing about stockings as well, I have."

"She carried a whip. A flick knife in her knickers," laughed Steggeman.

Schultz growled, looking frustrated.

"Long stockings, they was. Unhooked her bra."

Drooling, Schultz was leaning over almost panting.

"*Ja, und.*"

"Fell down they did. Like wet haddock at the fish market."

"Poke it."

"Nah. Turned me right off, it did. Lost me appetite."

Heyer threw his *machorka* away, grinding the butt into the snow.

"Hansen, you lying pig. If you met a nun at a bus stop you'd chat her up."

Hansen rubbed his hands at the thought.

"Why not. Nuns are choice bits. Imagine them being shut away for years. You'd need a can opener. Do you proud, they would. There used a be a nuns' place near us. This old priest used to always follow them about. Right randy he was. . . ."

"What about our knockshop?"

"Must be real class. No spitting on the floor. Have silver spitoons we would. Them sexy-four poster beds. Canopy over the top. Have a golden rule. No throwing old drawers up there like they do in Brussels. Puts the better-class customer off, it does. Nah, be real class. Leave your muddy combat boots down in the lobby."

Schultz's eyes gleamed relishing the thought.

"Uncle Schultzy would sit just·inside the front door, picking my feet with my *kandra*. Gently persuading all those who are too drunk to come back later. That way we'd get to charge them extra, saying they missed their first appointment. Can't wait for Adolf's little war to end. Shit, we'd give you all ten percent discount as an opening special."

"You won't be allowed to keep your *kandra* after the war."

A puzzled look crossed Schultz's face. He shook his fist under Steggeman's nose.

"No *kandra*. Listen to the Berlin idiot. I need my little persuader. Schultz's got to keep law and order. Can't trust the criminal *Polizei*. All on the take they are. Under the Gestapo. You know that lot, they'd want it for *nichts*."

"Gestapo. S.S. The lot of them would be finished."

Schultz looked as though he was going to strike Steggeman.

"Stupid Berlin crud. You think they will retire. There's good pickings in Hamburg. Have their fingers in everything, they do."

"You big ape. They will be interned."

Schultz jumped to his feet, red in the face.

"You are all witnesses. You heard him. Calling me names. Taking advantage he is because of my kind nature. Just because he's got a few scratches." His eyes caught Schmidt's.

"To keep the discipline I should be allowed to flatten him."

"Schultzy, forget it."

"Will you feed him to me later when he gets better?"

"*Nein*."

"There will be no Hamburg after the war." Klima had come back from another visit behind a tree.

"All the red light district. Everything will be in ruins. Tommy bombs it every night. Nothing but a

228

heap of smoking bricks and mortar. Only the rats left alive to feed upon the bloating bodies in the gutters. I've seen them on the hospital train. They come out when someone snuffs it. Big fat rats, fighting over the choice bits of the dead."

Hansen laughed nervously. A short, dry, snickering cackle.

"Be no dark Frenchy Creoles for you."

"Or a ten percent discount," chuckled Schultz.

"A Grenadier's got to have his dreams."

The smell coming away from Klima was vile. He seemed to be swimming in excrement.

"We are all doomed. Dreams. You are wearing field grey. The most hated uniform in the whole world. In field grey you cannot afford the luxury of dreams. This is no France, Holland or Poland. You all saw ivan before Moscow. Nothing stops him. He advances over acres of his own dead. It has no effect upon him." His voice rose higher.

"Shoot them down. Thousands rush forward to take his place. Ivan's cause is greater than ours. We promised them freedom. Nazi slavery. Reich commissars. Ivan will win. He'll grind the Wehrmacht into the snow and ice. Set up special concentration camps in Siberia. There is no escaping it. We will all end up there." He broke down sobbing, his shoulder shaking.

"Defeatism. It never won any war," spat Steggeman.

"Prize ponce." Schultz made a grab for him.

Schmidt stopped him. He laid a hand upon Klima's shoulder.

"We've got to keep going. This war won't last forever. We all made a mistake, our whole nation. We all helped the National Socialists to get in. Now we are paying the price of our political stupidity.

Once they got in there was nothing we could do. No system in this world is perfect, greedy politicians see to that. In future I will never trust any politician. In war or peace it does not matter. They are all out for what they can get. We have to make the best of it. We must survive. We have to. If it only means telling them that come after us just how truly barbaric war is. After this war, when the politicians tire of the peace, when they start rattling their sabers again, raise your voice. Let the whole world know. Tell them of the senseless fighting on the Eastern Front. Tell them of the men, women and children you've seen slaughtered. Tell them of the smell of death wafting over the steppes from the large holes in the ground. Shout it from the rooftops. Let the whole world know. We might be able to drive some sense into the politicians."

"*Ja*," Muller broke in.

"There is nothing romantic about war. Heroic unknown soldier fighting against all odds. Conquering hero grinning to his *Kameraden*, like in the war posters. We need you to fight the heathens in the East. Flushed with victory. It's the smell of blood, and spewed guts on a summer's day. Clouds of black flies disturbed at the dead bodies. Youth losing their limbs. Seventeen and eighteen-year-olds becoming useless cripples. And for a cause that none of us any longer believe in. Seeing *Kameraden* going insane under an artillery barrage. Waiting for a shell or bullet you know has your name up on it. Lunatics running screaming into the firestorm. Orphaned children before burning *isbas*, crying beside the mutilated bodies of their mothers. Shout aloud. Someone in the future will listen."

"You will be crying from a pit in a new Dachau or Auschwitz," sobbed Klima.

"Shout. Write about it. Those who raise their voices are silenced first. Under the Nazis or communism. It's all the same."

The dark, heavy hand of gloom settled over them once more. Complain. Man or youth in field grey. An order is an order, no matter what uniform the *Soldat* is wearing. *Nein*, I will not squeeze the trigger. This is wholesale slaughter. This action against hostages. Against all civilized laws of common decency.

Shoot over their heads. The hostages will still die. In every nation there are thugs eager to pull the trigger. *Nein*, raise your voice and your remains will join others in the deep death pit.

"*Los*. Heyer. Schultz. Move out."

Another track. Another clearing. Only wolf tracks break the monotony. Was there no end to the damn forest? Schmidt counted off the time. Once they were well ahead he motioned to the others. Two of them pulled Klima on a pole stretcher. That's what Russia means to me. The pitiful. The helpless. Two deep tracks in the snow. Cursing when it was your turn. *Ja*, it has to be admitted. Brother of my wife or not. Sometimes hoping they would croak. Fuck the war. Fuck the endless snow. And fuck Russia. Chapped frozen hands. Pine pole biting deep. Cracking of the tall trees when the mind wandered. Like some unseen voice calling your name. Insanity so close it breathed down your neck. You will die here, you fascist bastard. Little Mother Russia is ever patient. Do your feet feel heavy. Lie down *Germanski Soldat*. I speak with the voice of wisdom coming from centuries of human suffering. Lie in the snow and go to sleep. I will reward you. Lie down, *Soldat*. Soon it will be over. No more aching hands. No more to walk in my forests. Just sleep. Rest. Eternal peace at last.

231

"Klima, when we get back to our lines I'll go scrounging at our field kitchen. I'll make you *Bratwurst* and *Bratkartoffeln*. Melt in your mouth, it will. Or a hamburger like you talked of from Spokane."

"*Danke*, Hansen. If I make it to our lines."

"*Achtung*."

The dull plop of mortars in the tubes. Concentrated fire whined over their heads. Into the snow. Legs and arms shoveling. Like a chicken in a hen coop. The last down will have nothing to smile about. Down. Melt into the earth. The mortars fell into the trees behind them. Blinding yellow flashes cut at the eyes. The ground shook and trembled with the shuddering explosions. A rain of ice blocks, rocks, snow and torn trees cascaded about them. Choking dust and black smoke. Two machine guns stuttered through the haze. Slower bark of heavy Maxims. Shots whistled, whipping through the trees.

"*Donna wetter*. Where are they?"

"Ambush. The swine."

"Keep down."

Three more mortar shells home in. After the flashes sudden darkness enveloped them. The ground reared and bucked. Trees were felled like matchsticks.

"*Urah. Urah.*"

The Russian victory chant mocked. Like a tap it drains the body of all fluids no matter what the hero writers say. The urge is there and it has to be fulfilled. A warm glow. Comfort in the darkness as the smoke rolls away. Ivan voices can be heard distinctly. They roar aloud with their taunts of vengeance. Overconfident. Sure of the kill. None shouts like ivan. Such descriptive phrases. Short, sharp. Really to the point.

"I told you. Not a hope in hell."

Hansen slapped Klima's face.

"Kill us all."

Klima struggled to his feet, slipping on the ice.

"I—I can't take anymore."

"Head down." Steggeman lunged with his rifle butt, sending Klima sprawling.

"*Nein, nein.*" Whimpering, he put the barrel of his rifle to his mouth.

Hansen kicked the rifle away. Steggeman knocked him cold with a savage blow of his rifle butt.

"Low scrub three o'clock," shouted Schultz.

"Concentrated fire. Right of the tree."

The choking dust was settling. The smoke rising into the tree tops. Still the ivans roared.

"*Urah. Urah.*"

"Fire."

From the low scrub came the cries of the Russian wounded. One stood waist high shaking his long rifle. Renewed fire cut him down.

"Change position."

Scuttle away. On all fours dragging Klima.

"Keep his rifle."

"*Jawohl.*"

The Russians began their catcalls. Fritz. Heini. Promises of what would happen to them when they were captured. Nothing left to the imagination. Surrender or face the consequences. Chew on your manhood before the day is out. Eat the eyes of their *Kameraden*. Swallow raw cut-up tongue.

Heyer had seen them first. Two dog sledges. Mortars set up in the middle of the track. Laughing, joking, thumping one another upon the back. Two of them had thrown their hats into the air, firing automatic weapons high into the trees.

"Drunk," he hissed.

"Good," Schultz chuckled.

Only occasional haphazard rifle shots came their way.

"Shit, saving us for fun and games later."

Telescopic rifles were quickly unwrapped.

"Give them the kiss of the Lord."

"After you. Schultz's always the gentleman."

"*Danke*."

Heyer adjusted his sight. Eased an explosive bullet home. "I'm going to enjoy this."

"*Du alter Sack*. I know."

The Russians around the mortar became clear. Uniform of the N.K.V.D.. Heyer thought back to the brutal beating he had endured, trying to save the black uniformed panzer men. One of the Russians was shouting at his comrades, using typical obscene gestures. He lined him up. Slowly squeezed the trigger. The laughing face disintegrated before his eyes. The hands went up, only the nerves clawing at the bloody gory mess.

"One down." He worked the stiff bolt action.

Schultz put his eye to the telescopic sight. The sudden death had brought three ivans bending over their fallen comrade. Lying full length, he squeezed a shot away. Saw the startled Mongol stagger, both hands at his chest. Other ivans turned, arms waving.

"Calling us names, they are."

"Mortars first."

"*Ja*."

Machine gun fire sent them scuttling behind the shelter of a stout tree. Heyer felt the impact of the shots. The tree shook, as though it was trying to shake the bullets loose. Rapid fire ploughed at the snow, inches from his shoulder. Face flat to the ground, he watched with horror. Morbid fascination. Shot after shot. Tracers whining, digging the snow. Avenging angel of death, fire-hosing away. Abruptly the fire stopped. It started again, ranging in on Schmidt's group.

Slowly he raised his head. Eyes a part of the helmet, peering from under the brim, cautiously. Scrub. Dead ground. Stream in the summer. Cowering dogs. Sledges. Two mortars were still operating. White-capped Mongols on their knees passing the ammunition. He settled behind his rifle. Three rapid shots. Two ivans fell. Schultz fired twice. Three ivans lay twitching in the snow.

"Yershov," gasped Schultz.

"Where?"

"Behind the sledges shouting at them."

"Red knickers in a twist."

"*Ja*. Runt, he's mine."

Before they could fire the Maxim was back onto them. Schultz gave a cry of pain. Blood was streaming down his face.

"Lie still."

"*Sauhunde* . . . my ear . . ."

"Still."

"*Verflucht* . . . it's burning. . . ."

"Shoot the lot. . . ."

He roared with agony. From the Russians came the answering call.

"Down."

He had trouble holding him.

Machine gun fire hitting the tree pounded through their brains. They became a part of it. Screaming and tearing at their tunics as each fresh volley showered them with pine chips. Tracers howled with blinding frequency. Centimeters from oblivion. Helmet no protection, the thought flashed through Heyer's mind. Skull would crack and splinter like an eggshell. Get up and run. Away from the fire-storming hell. His pulse pounded as though he was but the audience, watching. The forest. Two Grenadiers' clothes and bodies ripped to shreds. Faces, the sickening deadly white. Gaping blood-filled mouths. Smashed teeth, broken and gleaming. Wolves sniffing at the grotesque shapes.

"Nein. Nein."

His cries of terror mingled with Schultz's. *Nein*, not this way. Not given a thought. It always happens to someone else. Vomit rose in his throat making him choke. Death. All over. No more struggle. Pain, then it's all over. That fear that comes when death is only seconds away tightened in his chest. But the legs had a life of their own. They kicked out trying to grip the snow.

Schultz held him fast.

The hammering machine gun fire slackened, swinging away. Heyer tried to focus his eyes. He was seeing double. His shaking hand went to his face, tracing nervously. Had he been hit? No, it was sweat. Sweat, the fear of impending death. The snow lashed at his eyes. They were smarting, filling with tears.

"Aschloch."

Schultz edged to the side of the tree, rifle stinging to the touch.

Mortar fire. Shell after shell was flung at them. Vision lost. A world dominated with violent stabbing color. Dancing tormenting sheets of searing light. Yellow. Blue. Red that seemed to burn their very souls. Ground leaping and ripping apart. Swimming in a channel of scorching explosions. Deafening. Something plucking at their sprawled bodies. Weight on the shoulders. arms and legs. Hammering, pounding them into the earth. Eyes. Mouth. Nose. Suffocating. Screaming, insanely unaware of their own cries. The mortars stopped. Their world still lifted, lunged and lurched. When the dust and smoke had settled they found themselves wrapped in each other's arms.

The brain will not clear straight away. Tortured nerves refuse to function. The whole body shakes in a riot of contortions. It is the time when death will come creeping.

"*Yob tvoymat.*"

The boots approached as though they were completely detached from the shouting bodies, the long bayoneted rifles.

"*Chort* Germanski."

Heyer fired with his m.p.i. at the taunting giggling laughter. Laughter seeming to come from the very tree tops. Two ivans groveled, rolling in the snow. Schultz hit them with another burst. Flaying legs, arms. Arching bodies. Piercing screams that meant nothing to them. Just the opened mouths and wide eyes. Snow splattered with dark striking color.

All about them trees were uprooted. Aslant. Leaning against one another in drunken support. Where there had been a continuous carpet of snow, there was now only brown earth. Pockmarked, blackened. Rocks and chunks of frozen earth were piled about their bodies in the hollow behind the tree.

Schultz broke into laughter. His face a bloody mess. Still alive. He laughed insanely, near to hysteria. Heyer slapped him. Schultz slapped him back. They fell against the base of the tree. Heyer threw his arms about it kissing the trunk. Uncontrollable laughter gushed from them.

"Lost your ear."

"Runt, ivan nicked it.'

"Nicked your ear."

"*Ja*, he collects them."

237

"*Schweinhund*."

"On a string for his *babushka*."

"*Ja, und . . .*"

"Makes Germanski licorice."

"*Ja*."

"Got a sweet tooth, he has."

"*Doch*. Who told you?"

"Pushkin."

Their faces grimaced into nervous laughter.

Rifle shots ricocheted about them. Mouths twitching, they pushed the chunks of frozen earth aside, returning the fire. Dead ivans were heaped about the mortars. Riflemen fired from over a sledge. One sledge pulled away, two dead dogs bumping along in the traces. It reached a bend in the track and was lost from view.

"Yershov."

"*Ja*."

"Doing a bunk."

The mortar fire slackened. Dust and smoke hung over Schmidt's position, a dense choking cloud. Stifling. There is an awareness of falling debris. Relief. Shattered nerves making the body tremble. That which was hugged in raging terror, moving in the blinding havoc, is but the leg of a nearby *Kamerade*. He had difficulty finding words. At times the voice is lost. Vocal cords refusing to answer after the deafening onslaught.

"Hansen, stay here with Klima."

"*Sicher*."

"Muller with Steggeman. Suckau . . . with me. Two hits. Left and rear. We'll take the rear. *Los*. Move out."

No hesitation. The training has not been in vain. To wait is to openly invite death. Schmidt scrambled away, Suckau following closely behind. Schultz and

238

Heyer once again were taking all the fire. Machine guns. Mortars. Occasional hand grenade.

There is gut grinding fear waiting for the smoke to clear. Waiting for pounding nerves to cool. From beside a fallen tree Hansen began to fire. The heavy Maxims answered. Horrified, he watched the pattern of hissing tracer spitting out of the low scrub. He made as if to pull Klima down. He was whimpering low like a frightened child, but he was firing his rifle.

"Those bushes."

"*Was?*"

"Five shots each."

Klima worked the sticky bolt on the Russian rifle. His trembling nerves stilled a little. His legs were running with filth. Up. Blurred hazy focus. Flashing, awesome, inspiring tracer. Fire. Again and again. In a frenzy of torn nerves.

Mortars whined in with a sickening crunch. Shells exploded in the trees. He thrust his face deeper into the frozen snow. Trembling body curling like in his mother's womb, knees almost to his chest. Each fresh roaring explosion had him gasping for air, body flinching and twitching. Debris hurtled down. He felt a hand gripped at his shoulder. The mortar fire stopped. Inky darkness. No air in the lungs. Sucked out. Only suffocating smoke.

"*Bitte . . . nicht mir. Lieber Gott. Nein . . .*"

His legs found traction. He tore loose the hand gripping his shoulder. Smoke. Dust. Killing ground. He had to get away. Away from the living hell. Man's prehistoric learning. He is equipped for flight. Run. Run. There is only the urgent need to get away. His world exploded in dazzling crashing lights. Luckily he had run into a tree, knocking himself out with the impact.

Schmidt plunged deeper into the forest.

Breathless, he lay with Suckau staring through the trees. The Maxims had stopped. Blockage, he thought. Two of them. Impossible.

"*Schnell*."

They bounded through the trees towards the rifle fire. A sledge came into view. Down. An ivan was cutting a dead dog loose from the traces. Suckau fired, the ivan fell. Schmidt brought his m.p.i. up. An ivan was breaking open an ammunition box. He squeezed the trigger. It gave an ominous click. He fumbled in his pocket. No mags left.

"Cover me. I'll go in with grenades."

The Russian fire was dying. Scattered rifle shots. Chatter of submachine gun bursts. Muller and Steggeman advanced stealthily from tree to tree. Steggeman entered the low scrub. Two hands with a grip of iron tugged at his legs. Mongol face. Hand with a long bayonet. With all his force he jabbed with his bayonet at the leering face. It missed going into the neck. The terror-filled eyes went wide. He wrenched his rifle free, kicking out at the face. Muller fired. The Mongol bucked, staining the snow.

"*Danke*."

One ivan was limping, holding his leg, running from tree to tree. The trail of splattered blood was easy to follow. Heyer went down upon one knee. One shot. The explosive bullet tore off half of his head.

Two ivans rose from behind the sledge, hands on their heads. Berserk, Klima cut them down. Hand grenades were lobbed in when two more ivans tried to make a last-minute stand. All was quiet except the crying of three sledge dogs. Muller put them out of their misery.

Schultz's torn stub, all that remained of his ear, was bandaged from N.K.V.D. medical supplies upon the sledge.

A very careful check of the ivan dead. No time for the squeamish. Even at his last breath a fanatic can still cause death, with a well-placed grenade, or burst from an automatic weapon. Shouts of victory can easily turn to the cries of terror, a *kamerade* fighting to hold in his mangled guts. When ivan was ordered to fight to the last man he did so with a vengeance that is hard for a Western *Soldat* to comprehend. Even a Wehrmacht veteran.

Cautiously Suckau turned over two bodies with his boots. Full blast from a hand grenade. Lower part of the body. Not a pretty sight, nothing but pulped bone and bloody flesh. The others were looting the sledges. Schultz shouting with joy. He had found several earthenware jars of *samahonka*. Klima, forgetting his dysentery, shouting aloud over his find of tins of Canadian sausages. Suckau looked at the bodies again. Civilians. One with an unmistakable brightly colored headscarf.

"Alexi and Aleni."

The laughter stopped. Everyone came closer, gathering about the bodies.

"Who threw the first grenades?" Heyer asked accusingly.

Schultz burped.

"Don't go blaming me."

"Steggeman."

"*Nein*, not me."

"Bury them," snapped Schmidt.

"No one saw them."

Muller forced Heyer's weapon aside.

"Do you think any of us would kill them on purpose?"

Hansen, Steggeman and Klima dragged the shattered remains into the trees, setting to work with stout Russian entrenching tools.

Something snapped in the snow-covered undergrowth. They threw themselves down. Several rifle bolts moved.

"No grenades."

"A wounded ivan."

Heyer jumped up, moving into the bushes, m.p.i.s at the ready.

"I thought so. *Mein lieber Gott*. Look what I've found."

He came out of the bushes, Tamara's boys, Roman and Mikhial, stumbling by his side.

"*Die arme Kinder*." Two leaps and Schultz had Roman in his huge arms.

The boys' eyes stared straight ahead. Deep shock. Heyer tried to question them.

"Slap their faces," suggested Steggeman.

"Both of them are in shock."

No one moved.

"Could have killed them." Tears were flowing freely from Schultz's cheek as he fussed over Roman.

"Anyone touches them I'll break his neck," he growled.

Klima gave them both Canadian sausages. The mouths moved. Not like children who were hungry. Just a slow rhythmical movement. Like little boys of the summer wandering from a heavily bombarded village. Zombies rising from the rubble. Stonelike. Faces set in the ghostly white mask of death.

"Griecebeck," mumbled Suckau.

"Tamara."

"He—he was armed," added Hansen.

"Against this mob of N.K.V.D. what chance would he have?" Heyer was dressing the boys in thick padded N.K.V.D. tunics.

Schmidt was checking the sledge.

"Take what supplies we can carry. Food. Spare ammunition."

At a distance through the trees they smelt the smoke of the still smoldering *isba*. Skeletonlike some of the main beams still remained. The rest was completely fire-gutted.

Heyer was the first into the ruins.

"Over here."

He found Griecebeck's shrivelled remains lying just inside the door. M.p.i. under him. It was empty. He was stretched out as though trying to reach the door. Schmidt broke off his blackened dog tag.

Carefully Heyer turned the body over.

"Chest wound. Swine burnt him alive."

Outside in the snow Suckau found two dead N.K.V.D. men. Schmidt shouted.

"Leave it . . . booby trap."

Heyer looked up. He had found Griecebeck's paybook. His chest had been pressed to the floor unburnt.

"Suckau . . ."

Suckau did not hear the shouting voices. He was thinking of his early youth. There had been four of them. Fricke, Schuman and now Griecebeck. The Badowicker boys, Heyer had nicknamed them. Now they were all dead. He was the lone survivor. What could he tell Brigitte, Griecebeck's sister. His mother. He had sworn in the gasthaus to keep him under his wing.

"Burnt him alive. Swine."

As youngsters on many Saturday afternoons they had played in the ruins of the Kalkberg, that oldenday fortress on the way to Meyers Garten. Storming it as youngsters will. Griecebeck had always been the first to the top. Mowing the others down as they came through the bushes. Childish play had so quickly turned to reality on the Eastern Front.

Youth the horror. Wasted. There is only the urgent need to cling to childish memories. Trips to the Ilmenau, roughhousing in the Anlagen park. Once again daring Hitler Jugend storming the Wasserturm. The discovery. Looking down on the Russian prisoners of war in the *"Am Alten Tor."* Watching them on a roll call. Strange-sounding names. Answered with guttural calls of, *da, da, da.* Stoning two of them. Were these creatures not the dreaded enemy? A smack in the ear from a railway worker going to work from Johannestrasse.

"If I catch you again throwing stones at the prisoners I will report you."

Another time having to watch as Robert was beaten by an S.S. man in the Anlagen park for stepping on the grass. Beaten brutally and kicked while he was down. Death's head grinning on the black uniform. If you live near there. Does that rekindle the memory?

Before they could stop him he had raised his rifle. Bayoneting. For Fricke . . . Schuman . . . Griecebeck. All his weight behind the rifle. Ripping. Tearing. Tears. Frustrated tears of hate pouring down his face. Death of his closest *Kameraden.*

"Idiot. Leave it." Heyer bounded forward.

"Runter," someone shouted.

Two explosions. Steel fragments whistled through the burnt timbers. The smoke palls drifted away from Suckau's body.

Heyer ran over to him. Cradled the torn body in his arms. Rocked to and fro.

"I told him. I always tell the young ones."

Chest, face. Unrecognizable. Oozing messy liquid buttoned up in a torn tunic. Legs missing. Deathly screams coming from the gooey apparition. Within

244

seconds he is dead.

Schmidt and the others came up behind him.

"Nothing you could do."

"Ivan booby traps everything. Bodies. Doors. Chairs. Tables. Drinking troughs. I'm always telling them."

"You did your best, Wolfgang." Schmidt and Muller lifted him away from the grisly remains.

Schultz found Tamara's body. Naked. Raped. Her hair had been shaved off. Breasts cut away. Shot in the back of the neck, downwards by a dum dum bullet. It came out at her waist, the hole the size of a large fist. She was draped over the sitting log in the outhouse. The Russian word for revenge was scrawled into her back by bayonet point.

The dead were buried in the same shallow grave.

"At least Griecebeck got two of them," said Steggeman as they covered the grave.

Hansen knocked him sprawling. Schmidt made no attempt to stop him.

After three days they came within hearing of the front. A wall of tracer marked it, arcing over from both sides. Heyer and Schultz silenced an ivan machine gun emplacement. Worming forward in the darkness, they crawled into no man's land, towards the Wehrmacht lines.

Heyer and Muller took the boys, shielding them with their own bodies. After a while the sporadic machine gun fire from both sides died down.

"I'll go in first," Schmidt whispered.

He disappeared. Tensing, all nerves, they lay full length clutching their weapons. If other flares went up they would breathe their last. No man's land knows no friends.

"*Wer ist da?*" came the accented German challenge.

Breathing became a little easier.

"*Nicht schiessen. Wir sind Deutsche Soldaten.*"

What sounded like the mechanism of a light Spandau was cocked. They could only wait in silence. It proved too much for Schultz.

"Runts. What's keeping them?"

"If ivan throws a flare—" a boot lashed out at Steggeman.

After ten very long minutes Schmidt was back with them.

"Austrians. One man with each of the boys. Sixty seconds apart. Then we follow. Careful . . . these Austrians are nervous."

Heyer moved off with Mikhial. Moments later Muller moved off into the darkness.

"What would I give for a good Lunenburger beer," whispered Hansen.

"*Sauerkraut und schweine Pfoetchen* . . . dripping with fat."

Hansen and Steggeman lowered themselves into the Austrian trenches.

"Son of a bitch," cursed Klima in English. He struggled trying to free himself from a barbed wire entanglement.

The light Spandau spat out a long burst. There was only one gasp. More like a sucking of air.

"He's one of ours."

Schultz and Hansen threw themselves upon the Austrian machine gunner. Two officers beat them with their riding crops. Schultz had his hands at the gunner's throat. Rifle butts struck them down savagely. Schultz was booted as he lay unconscious. A cocked submachine gun covered the others.

Later, when the renewed machine gun and mortar fire had died, a lieutenant allowed them to retrieve Klima's body. He was wrapped in a ground sheet. A full burst had caved in his chest.

"Welcome back to the filth." The voice came out of the darkness.

No one answered.

Chapter 15
ACHTUNG

Dawn came the ground-hugging mists whispering about the trenches. If you have survived the night, dear child. *Mein Gott*, there is much rejoicing. Smoke of the cooking fires gently wafting away to the forest beyond. A lone wolf stops, howling on a rise, then bounds off into the trees. It was time to collect the stiffened remains wrapped in a ground-sheet.

In the white hell of that hostile daylight Klima's eyes would not close. Defying that ancient ritual. Silent *Kameraden* standing about the snow mound. Tears that froze in that strange land. Accusing, as countless others of his generation had done before. A sobbing Russian prisoner of war covered the tragic face with a sprig of pine needles. Epitaph of the damned legions of youth. Eyes so blue. Face so familiar. Tales of Warsaw. The beautiful Polish nurse. Fallen *Kameraden*. No more to laugh, smile or joke. Burst into English, with that American accent of his. To be laughingly rebuked with, "*Aschloch*, speak German."

Stern faces passing the hole, throwing in that last handful of snow. Last gesture with bowed heads. Echoing military salute of raised mausers. Locked forever in the iron grip of that far-off land. A *Kamerade* never to be forgotten.

Bathing, such luxury. Delousing at the sanitation detail. Issued with new weapons. Grease to smear upon the hands and face. Vile stinking substance. Wehrmacht answer to combating frostbite. Wiped off hours later. Like walking around with your nostrils immersed in a perpetual sewer.

Hansen singing "Lily Marlene." Schultz happily drunk, scrubbing his back.

Arguments with the headhunter detail, their metal badges dancing ominously upon their impeccable chests. Even among those newly returned from the hell-storm, there must be Germanic law and order.

"*Still gestanden!*" More a bark than spoken words.

The venomous beady eyes stare.

"Where are your gas masks?"

The half-moon badges gleam. A sickening smile plays at the face. There is the power of life and death behind those cruel eyes.

"You were issued at great expense Wehrmacht ground sheets."

Damn things, they were never any good.

Again the beady eyes search like a viper eager to strike.

"Suckau? Where did he fall?"

Steggeman wetting his uniform, his brand new uniform under a shouting barrage of senseless questions.

Questions. Questions. Questions.

"*Los.* The name of that popov village."

May the military police of the Fatherland be forever cursed. Rot in your graves, you inhuman beasts. Where many of you lie upon the steppes of Mother Russia, surely not a blade of grass will grow.

The glorious Wehrmacht must have everything in triplicate. Files reliving the misery. Duly signed by bemedaled aristocratic Prussian generals. Retelling the contents in bed with their plump Ukrainian whores far behind the lines.

An official from *Ost Front Und Panzer Wolfram*. Jealously tight-lipped about Roman and Mikhial.

Afterwards back at the *isba*. A Russian couple have taken the boys in hand. A kitten is placed in each of their laps. They do not want to play.

"We owe it to Tamara to help the boys. She looked after the wounded. Cured the dysentery. Nah, *ja*. I'm not for handing them over to the Wehrmacht authorities." On that Heyer was firm.

Steggeman looked up from oiling the new weapons.

"Sometimes young children are adopted by families in the Reich."

A burst of cynical laughter filled the *isba*.

In actual fact it did happen, strange as it may seem. Many Polish and Russian children were brought up as Germans upon farms and in cities throughout the Third Reich.

"*Nein*. We could hand them over to the partisans," insisted Heyer.

Schultz jumped up, making a great play of inspecting his head. Grasping his face and looking deeply into his eyes.

"Sick in the head. Your lice got armor plating. Attacked the grey matter, have they."

"Wants to lose your nuts. Ivan does a good job. Remember that padre in the village," added Hansen.

"It's the only way. If they stay here at the front anything could happen to them. In the forest there are whole camps of partisans. Whole villages. The women there would look after them."

Muller and Schmidt agreed with them.

"It could be the answer. They would survive the

war. That much we owe to Tamara and her family,"
suggested Schmidt.

On the Eastern Front in the Wehrmacht occupied
areas there were signs everywhere. *Achtung*, near a
river in the summer, warning of cholera and malaria.
Achtung, mines. *Achtung*, uncleared buildings.
Achtung, isba's booby-trapped. *Achtung*, partisans,
a board nailed upon a tree. Proceed with the utmost
caution. You are entering a partisan zone. To say the
forests were like a jungle is oversimplifying matters.
Many were fortresses in depth. Pak fronts, artillery
units. Skirmishing patrols never far away. Most
tracks mined.

Heyer stopped the motorcycle and side car at the
edge of the forest. A sympathetic lieutenant had
loaned it to him, also bullying the field kitchen
Feldwebel to hand over extra rations.

Roman and Mikhial were still not talking. Shock,
the horror at the *isba*. Action in the forest. But at
other times they would answer with movement when
Heyer spoke to them.

He helped them out of the side car underneath the
first partisan warning sign. Another sign was tacked
to the tree under the Wehrmacht one, decorated with
the hammer and sickle. "Live you will
enter . . . dead you will depart! Signed by Little
Father Nikolai, the local partisan leader."

"*Tovaritch*. Go into the forest. You will be among
your own people."

They just stared at him with large uncomprehend-
ing eyes.

"The front is not the place for you," he gestured
with his hands.

"Too much boom . . . boom."

Their eyes reflected understanding and they began
to cry. Heyer bit upon his lips.

"You must go."

Roman was tugging at his greatcoat.

"Keep walking. The partisans will find you. Not on the track. Walk among the trees."

"*Matj*. Mother." Mikhial uttered his first words.

"You spoke. You spoke." Heyer squeezed them into his arms.

No longer could he fight the surging emotion. His tears mixed with theirs. If times had been different he would have kept them. Taken them home with him. Made them a part of his family. The Wehrmacht had no such provisions, not for Grenadiers. Since returning to the front he had been plagued with horrifying thoughts. Cattle car transports. Large doors slamming upon their crying faces. Camp names springing to mind, the inmates shuffling in striped clothing.

"Tamara would want you to go. Aleni. Your *papushka*."

Roman grasped his hand, staring up into his eyes. As though he was responsible for condemning them to an unspeakable fate.

"*Matj. Papushka*," his lips moved trembling, the whole terrifying scene at the *isba* becoming clear once again.

Shouts. Questions. The clothes ripped from their shrieking mother. Alexi trampled and kicked by vicious boots. Aleni attacking with flaying fists. *Matj*. Animal screams. Leering monsters holding her down.

Sick Germanski *Soldat*. First shots splattering the stove. *Isba* burning. Sparks leaping high into the air. Laughing, drunken N.K.V.D. shooting the cats. The screams of their mother from the outhouse. Her long hair in the fist of a Mongol, rubbed into the face of Alexi. And still she cried screaming to little Mother

252

Russia for vengeance. To their *papushka*. To the holy Mother of Kazan. The pistol shots. The groans of agony that lasted for minutes. A hate for the uniform with the Red Star. Hatred that was branded into their very souls. Never forget, *Matj*. Never. Always remember. Revenge. One day.

"Go now," Heyer pushed them into the fringe of the trees.

Ahead of them two dark figures ran across the track. Another was visible standing by a tree. A sharp command came in Russian. Several rifles cocked, their bolts rattling.

"*Tovaritch*. Don't shoot," he shouted in Russian.

"These boys are orphans!" he waved his arms.

Two other partisans left the shelter of the trees. One was a woman carrying a Wehrmacht submachine gun. Some of them went down upon one knee taking aim with their rifles.

"Their family was killed."

Those often heard words in Russia brought an immediate response. Two warning shots hit the snow at his feet. A weeping teenage girl had her rifle between her legs, fumbling fixing her long bayonet.

He raised his arms, weapon still gripped in his right hand. Slowly he began to back off.

An anti-tank rifle cracked out. The motorcycle and side car erupted into flames.

One of the women partisans reached the boys. She drew them to her. Taking them into her arms. Her words did not reach him. But her head kept nodding. He could feel her eyes upon him. Suddenly she stood up, screaming to the men by the trees. They threw themselves down into firing position.

Heyer gained the cover of the trees. Schultz's last words hit him once again.

"*Dummkopf*. Need your head tested."

Rifle shots whined into the trees. Five partisans were running alongside the track. Half-crouching, they advanced, the woman partisan leading them. The air was not filled with words glorifying Stalin. Some had lost their whole families. Blind hatred burned within them driving them on. Pure vengeance. Seemingly immune to danger. Nothing drives the human harder. Killing momentum. Revenge. Sated only by the sight of blood. An enemy's body lying mutilated and breathing its last at their feet.

A rifle shot creased Heyer's brow. His vision spun. Blood pounding. Trees. Figures. Flames spitting and crackling at the side car. Two small shapes swimming into view before him.

Mikhial and Roman threw their bodies across him. Helmet askew he felt the hand at his throat. At his hair pulling his head back. The eyes were those of a woman. Deep. Bitter. Tears of hatred freezing upon the cheeks.

"*Nyet! Nyet!*" he heard little Roman's voice.

Hear the angry working of a rifle bolt. He passed out.

Mikhial spoke to the woman partisan leader. Begging. Pleading. After several minutes she straightened up, turning to the glowering faces.

"Take his weapon. This Germanski we will not kill."

"Every Germanski *Soldat* must die," a teenage girl stepped forward, her long bayonet at Heyer's chest.

"Did they not kill my sister?"

"This Germanski saved two lives. Little Father Nikolai would want it this way. There is much suffering in our Motherland. He will take these two boys to his heart. Would you go against my brother

254

Papushka Nikolai?''

The partisans murmured angrily amongst themselves.

''Commissar. He will not like it.'' The teenage girl spat at Heyer's face.

''What the eyes of Moscow do not see they will not know.''

''Da,'' an older bearded man stepped forward. ''We control the forest little sister. Is it not right that we should make the decisions?''

Chapter 16
COMING OF THE GREEN LICE

Nikolai Pavel Izrailovich cocked his Red Army submachine gun in readiness. Always, waiting at the ambush, the racing blood had a cleansing effect. There was the breathless pride. The dry throat that vodka would not dispel. Jokingly they would raise their caps before the first shot was fired. Like they were forced to do whenever they met the fascists in the village street.

The new village his partisans were building in the deep forest was nearly ready. All the families of the old village would be moved there. No longer would they have to tolerate the strutting invader, elbowing men aside like cattle. Germanski would only be met then in the heat of battle. With the long bayonet at their throats. It was a satisfying thought.

They had surged across the Motherland like a plague of summer lice. Klin. Livny. Many villages would breathe no more. Their panzers. Their mighty iron-clad monsters knew no mercy. Cattle, pigs, chickens. Everything they took as though it was their own. In battle they slaughtered anything on legs. Men, women, children, the animals of the *kolkhos*. The lice. Nothing was sacred to them.

Slowly, very slowly the Wehrmacht trucks were climbing the forest incline. Out in front two motor-cycles and side cars, with mounted machine guns.

Eight big trucks loaded with supplies for the Austrians. The last truck, number nine, would contain the foot *Soldat* escorts.

Singing. Germanski *Soldats* were always singing. Voices echoing high above the trees. It would be their last song in the shadow of the mighty state forest. Soon they would be choking, blood vomiting at their mouths. Lips that had curled with youthful defiance, calling for their mothers in their far-off hateful land.

"Heimat deine Sterne.
Die Leuchten wie ein Diamant.
Tausand Sterne stehen in weiter Ferne."

Nikolai smiled grimly to himself. Lice. They would sing of the stars over their homeland. Were they not the same stars that shone down from the long night? Seeing the evil that had been done to Mother Russia and her children. Guttural song. When they sang the birds of the forest rose in protest, flying away.

When his daughter Marisha sang. Such a voice. Like a skylark rising into the blue clouds of summer. Gentle lilting notes. Her fragile body swaying. Even the hard eyes of the men of the forest did not remain dry for long. She was like a saint. A light in the times of gathering darkness. As though through her frail body the voice of the Motherland spoke. Giving hope. Hope for the future.

There was a movement beside him in the snow.

"Germanski pigs." Eighteen-year-old Svetlana Yuryevich wiped back her tears, both hands now firm upon the wooden grips of the wheeled Maxim machine gun.

He laid a hand upon her shoulder trying to calm her. Her loader, fourteen-year-old Lev Sheinin, had only eyes for the invader. His family had been taken away before he went into the forest. He visited the mound. That hump in the snow that would always scream the truth. Many times he had been there. Each time vowing that the fascists would pay a thousand times for killing the families of his faith.

"Little Father Nikolai. Today is the day of my revenge."

He steadied her sobbing shoulders.

"This day is yours, little sister."

She looked down at the Wehrmacht trucks. One had skidded off to the side of the road. The convoy came to a halt. An officer walked up and down shouting and cursing. A tow rope was attached and slowly the trucks moved off, coming nearer.

"In Klin they raped my sister."

"*Da*," he stroked her long blonde hair back.

"Today the green lice will pay."

For a man who would listen, a multitude of voices were crying out over the Motherland. Most families had been touched by the suffering.

Her sister Wanda had been a student. Studying at an academy in the fine city of Kiev. After the invaders had had their way with her, she was made to stand naked at the well. Many *soldats* took pictures of her. A Feldwebel held her head high with a short, cruel-looking riding crop.

The assembled villagers were told of the new order. Germanic culture, as the laughing Wehrmacht officer called it. She died reciting Pushkin well into the cold bitter hours of the long night. At dawn she was stiff like a marble ikon. Her right armed raised slightly over her right frozen breast. The mouth apart. Teeth gaping. Lips chilled with the blue of the frost. As though even in death she was still mouthing the words of her beloved Alexsander Sergeyvich Pushkin.

The motorcycle outriders missed the mines. Nikolai felt his sister Anna tug at his arm.

"Nikolai. Order to fire."

"Fire!" he roared.

One hundred and fifty partisans touched their caps.

The first truck hit a mine. It disintegrated. Yellow flame showed through the smoke. The explosion rolled back through the trees. The piercing screams of the wounded sounded. Gasoline drums spilled out of the smoke. Lines of crackling flame rushed to them. The drums ignited, exploding, sending up a shower of roaring flames. The second truck was engulfed. Like madmen burning soldiers ran blind, covered in fire. Small arms fire sent them kicking into the snow.

A Pak opened fire. A dry cough. The last truck covered in flames crashed into the trees. The escorts ran clear, throwing themselves down in the ditch.

One motorcyclist was trying to get away. The sudden revving made it slip and slide. Svetlana's Maxim fire caught it, throwing the two soldiers aside as though they had been suddenly snatched by an unseen hand.

Shrill command whistles blew. Here and there the soldiers returned the fire. The partisans had been trained well by their Red Army instructors. Choosing of the high ground for the ambush had paid off. No matter where they crawled, the murderous concentrated fire followed them.

One group covered by heavy automatic fire from near one of the trucks tried to charge Svetlana's chattering Maxim. Lev Sheinin held the ammunition belt steady. Weeping and laughing hysterically, Svetlana shot them to pieces. And still racked their bodies as they groveled screaming in the snow.

Within minutes it was all over. Only Svetlana was still firing, Lev directing her to new targets. Nikolai dragged her away from the Maxim.

"It is enough," he chided her.

"They show the white flag."

Eyes blazing she turned upon him.

"For my Wanda it's not enough," she cursed.

The prisoners were rounded up. Hatless young soldiers with short blond hair. Some were made to kneel in the snow. And before Nikolai could stop them six were shot in the face.

Again Svetlana struggled to free the Maxim grips from him.

"All Germanskis must die."

Shaking, she was becoming hysterical.

"*Nyet*." He slapped her face.

Trembling she looked up at him, hatred twisting her young face, saliva flecking and freezing upon her lips.

"Naked, my Wanda knew no white flag."

Lev Sheinin eyed the prisoners being brought into the trees. They were no older than his brothers Vasily and Gleb. So they must have gone to their graves. Hands on the back of their necks. Eyes wide with terror. He turned away, no longer able to look. For his people there was the final humiliation before death. Stripping in front of the pits. Their legs back against the wooden pole that ensured that they fell when shot into the pit.

"Svetlana," again Nikolai was trying to calm her. "I give the orders here. I say we take the prisoners with us to the forest. The new village. We have more huts to build. Our people must be taken out of the clutches of Germanski."

Later upon a forest track Svetlana was leading one of the stocky ponies. Climbing a bank, she slipped.

260

Horst Lupert, a young Landser, stopped to help her to her feet.

"Germanski filth. You dare to put your hand upon me, like they did with my sister!" Her fingernails tore at his face drawing blood.

She knocked him to the snow with the short butt of her automatic. Hit him under the chin with the stub barrel. Then thrust it at his throat, forcing his eyes to meet hers.

"Germanski *pyos*," she spat into his face.

"Herr *Soldat* I want to hear you beg. As my Wanda did in the long night."

A shaggy-bearded partisan translated.

Nikolai came behind her and took her weapon away.

"You are a soldier of the forest, little sister. A partisan. I have given the order. There will be no more killing. We have much work to do. A landing strip to clear. Would you go against the wish of the Motherland? Today is one battle. From the depths of the forest the war must be continued."

Svetlana was crying with rage, her chest heaving.

"I say kill. Keep killing. Nikolai, you are a man. You have not known what the fascists do to our women. It is only for a woman. The giver of life. Only a woman knows the pain when a precious life of a loved one is taken away."

The bearded partisan kicked Horst Lupert, his weapon at the small of his back, making him get to his feet.

Nikolai took Svetlana in his right arm, leading her away.

Far behind them the smoke was still rising away from the ambushed Wehrmacht convoy. The dead had been stripped. Already they were frozen rock hard.

Two hours later a lone Stuka swept in low. Then made another pass. The radio message from the nineteen-year-old pilot passed through command to Orel. From there it went to S.S. headquarters. Once there a well-rehearsed action was taken. Another message went out to a Ukrainian S.S. unit in the field. Hilfswillige. Ukrainians who had volunteered for service with the S.S. The unit was commanded by S.S. Hauptscharfuehrer Ziegler, a German who had served first with S.S. Das Reich.

A Flintenweiber telegraphist wrote down the message. She was a captured woman of the Red Army who had volunteered for the Wehrmacht.

She walked out of the farmhouse going around to where the armored cars were parked.

"Convoy attack."

S.S. Hauptscharfuehrer Ziegler smiled, taking the slip of paper. His right hand cupped her breast.

"Village," he snapped.

Her fingers traced over the field map.

"Here," she giggled, as his hand continued to squeeze at her breast.

"Near forest. Is here," she stabbed her finger at the map. "Maybe you find me a nice Jewish fur coat. For that I could give you much pleasure at the bedwarming."

S.S. Hauptscharfuéhrer Ziegler had not heard her. He turned to his S.S. Sturmann.

"*Meine Herren*," he said in his thick accent. "In thirty minutes we mount up. Take the flamethrowers. We might be needing them."

"Any my coat. You get my coat," pleaded the Flintenweiber.

He only smiled. Why bargain with a slut of a Flintenweiber. On a reprisal raid there were many women to pick from. Young ones who had never

262

known the breath of a man upon their faces.

In the village Nikolai's daughter Marisha was walking the milking cows. So happy she was. Soon everyone would be moving to the forest. Deep into the forest where no fascist would ever find them.

There would be a new school hut. Teacher Boris Anastas Pisarev would teach again. Tall Viktor with the dark eyes, the blacksmith's son, would not have to keep watch anymore with his handbell near the white *isba* of the Kurochkins. Warning of the coming of the green lice.

When her *papushka* and the other men had left for the forest, she helped with the animals of the *kolkhos* as much as she could. Old man Dyakov said the milking cows needed their walk even in the snow of winter. He lived in a hut near where the village soviet once lived. The brick house with the fine tall chimney. Many villagers called him the wise one.

"Does your woman sit and stay by the hot stove?" he had argued at the meeting of the men. "When her belly is swollen with child? *Nyet*. Like the other women she still goes to the well to collect water."

And so Marisha had helped to walk the cows. When the wise one spoke the other peasants listened. Had he not worked on the boats of the swift-flowing Volga? Lifeblood of the Motherland. Great cities he had seen. So far had he traveled. Kiev. Smolensk. Cracow, in the land of the Poles. The jewel of Moscow of which he sang many songs.

Happy were the times when her *mamushka* Zofia wet his lips with the home brew, *samahonka*. So many songs he taught her. How the children would gather about him in the late summer sun. Waiting for him to relight his old clay pipe and tell stories of the olden days. And the songs. Of the days when the

263

brave Cossacks fought the White Army. Songs of the gypsy folk of Romny and Achtyrka. They were so far beyond Kharhov. Why it would take the best troika weeks to reach them over the snows.

When Germanski was driven from Mother Russia, there were some in the *kolkhos* who said she should go to a fine school in Moscow. Such a fine, strong voice of the people, that spoke with the strength of the wind over the forest. Training it needed. Then she could visit other villages with a choir. And the songs of the mighty land would never be forgotten.

On this day she was walking with her comrade. Such a small boy Niki Akimenko was. He had arrived weeks earlier. Dogs barking out of a howling snow storm. Dyada Rzoko driving the sledge, his younger brothers wrapped in blankets.

He said he came from a village that was over three days away by horse. A very fast horse. With all the riding at the gallop. Marisha found that hard to believe. How could a horse keep running for three days. Even the prancing stallions of the gallant Cossacks. But then she was all of twelve years old. And dark-haired Niki was only nine. The boy still had much growing to do.

When she danced with her *papushka* Nikolai holding her hands, did he not say that one day she would blossom into a fine woman? With the woodcutter's sons riding in from the forest, knocking upon the *isba* door? A bunch of flowers they would have in their hands. The blue ones that grew in clusters under the trees. Fear showing in their eyes from the barking dogs. Bowing to her *papushka* and asking for her hand. The spring walk. Dancing near the well at the Easter celebrations. When the old women stayed up all night to prepare the making of the cakes. Such a life she had to look forward to.

Da, one spring morning she would awake and already she would be a grown woman. Why should she listen to the prattle of this young boy. All the same, when he told his story at the stove all those long weeks ago, was it not the eyes of the men from the forest that grew hard? Did they not spit at the stove and curse? Talking with voices of anger well into the long night. And was not the voice of her *papushka* the loudest of them all? Anna of the long hair wept into her tea. She was a woman born of the land, with no time for the tears of old women. A partisan who fought Germanski.

Niki said it was soldiers with the slant eyes who took his mother away. They put the torch to his village.

Dyada Rzoko had driven the dogs tirelessly. He died of the frostbite. Dead hands blackened like claws.

Mushka, their cat, stayed with the cows. He would not come near the *isba*. Even when the best place at the hot stove was offered to him. He would bite and scratch if anyone brought him near to the door. Cats, they were such strange creatures. She had heard some old folk saying that sometimes in the depths of winter the spirit passed from the body of the dead into a cat. That is why they lay upon the steps in the summer just watching. Keeping their eyes on their former loved ones. To see no harm came to them.

When they had taken the cows back to their stalls the wise one fed them their hay. Marisha took Niki by the hand. She knew her *mamushka* would have the hot honey drink waiting. He was making her mad. Forever talking of the fascist Germanskis.

"Germanskis were our friends," he insisted. "At our village they fed us."

Marisha drew herself up to her full height. She thought as a partisan's daughter she had to put the silly little boy right. He did indeed have much growing to do. In his body. And in the dark shaven head of his.

"*Papushka* Nikolai's partisans slaughter the green lice," she said smugly.

Niki pouted, pulling a face. How dare this girl who was much taller than he talk of the Motherland war. Her village had been safe. They had the partisans to protect them. He and his brothers had seen the war. The steel monsters of Germanski with their long evil-looking gun barrels. Had they not eaten their dogs bred from the bitch of a forest wolf? Not seen the singing and dancing in the *isbas* when the fascists came. Sweets and chocolates from the soldiers. Their mothers and sisters who had forgotten how to smile. Seen them smiling and laughing once again. Could these men from the other land be so bad as Marisha said they were?

"The slant-eyed ones set fire to our *isbas*," he shouted at her.

"Soldiers of the N.K.V.D."

"It is the fascist green lice who are our enemies," she screamed at him.

Marisha smacked him in the face. The boy could grow up to be a village fool. Children running after him at haymaking, pulling faces.

Later her *mamushka* made her make it up to Niki. He crawled out from under the bunks with his brothers. After sweet cakes the smiles returned. She stood before the stove singing.

"I sing for you Niki," she laughed.

She sang of the birch trees, those sentinels of the steppe swaying gracefully in the wind. Of spring that returned the life to the land after the harshness of the long winter. A ploughman treading his way. Steppe flowers bursting into life. A field of yellow going to the horizon. And how the peasants of the villages were happy once again when all about them was growing green.

As she sang she watched the eyes of the old ones. Semyon and his grey-haired Izabela. Her *papushka*'s parents were weeping. What would a young maiden, soon to be a woman, know of their grief? Like Niki, she thought. Just perhaps. Well, maybe even a young maiden of twelve still has a lot to learn.

Others, hearing her singing, came to the *isba* of her mother. Many came to the door. Even Dyakov the wise one bringing his accordion.

Over the tree tops her voice floated. Vibrant, like a fresh bubbling spring.

"It's Little Father Nikolai's Marisha," people told one another, stopping at their work.

"Voice of Mother Russia speaking in the child." And they would cross themselves going about their work.

"As long as our Marisha sings, no harm will come to our village. The Holy Mother will look after us."

Viktor the blacksmith's son stood in the *isba* door panting.

"The green lice. The green lice are coming."

A black-uniformed Ukrainian policeman knocked Viktor aside. He stood grinning, waving his pistol in the air.

"Everyone at the well in five minutes. *Schnell. Schnell.* Or we burn village to ground."

"I am singing our favorite song," Marisha said boldly as the policeman threw her through the door out into the snow.

"It's a song you will be singing from hell if you don't hurry," he cackled, kicking out at the old ones.

S.S. Hauptscharfuehrer Ziegler looked at the shuffling villagers. Down to the smallest child they were wearing the unsightly caps. Peasants. High cheekboned. Illiterate. When they grinned it was like the smiles of demented imbeciles. Many were almost Oriental in facial features. The farther East one traveled the more Mongol-like they became. That look was always there in their eyes. Animal in them coming near to the surface.

Tear-stained eyes were upon him. Even those with hands clasped in prayer. His hand strayed to his tunic collar. It was the Teutonic S.S. runes that did it. A power never before known to man. Such immense power. Holder of life or death. He smiled to himself. Later the young girls would make good sport pickings. Being the Hauptschar he would of course have first choice.

His experienced eyes were quick to notice the absence of many men. In any roundup all subhuman peasants stayed together in their family groups. The Juden had been the same. No doubt the men were skulking in the forest with little father Nikolai. The bandits. They could have lived the war out in peace. Why take up arms? Germanski always made reprisals.

"May the Holy Mother of Russia look over us. Spare us Herr officer!"

He spat at the old man hugging and kissing his boots.

Always the inferior races did that. It would seem that boots had a special attraction to them. At the ravines in Kiev some mothers had offered their daughters in return for saving the lives of the whole family. One gypsy mother had beaten her daughter until she was standing naked before him. He did not take advantage of the situation. At all times a show

268

of discipline had to be preserved.

Janina Gering had been different. Volksdeutsche, she claimed. Caught up in the roundup by mistake. Keen Ukrainian Police. The element of doubt was there. His S.S. Rottenfuehrer had pulled her from the lineup. He was most careful in letting her witness some of the executions. It always broke down their last resistance.

She joined him at his cottage billet at the edge of the ravines later that night. Twenty years of age, she was unused by man. The three hours with her had been well occupied. There was no trick that she was not eager to learn. Before first light he gave permission for his whole section to go with her. Drunk on vodka, she had not complained. He kept his word. She was spared. Her papers were stamped, making her a Wehrmacht field whore.

She spent one day at Gestapo Headquarters at 33 Vladimirskaya Street. They stamped her papers once again, officially making her a Ukrainian volunteer. The rest of her short life was pledged to serving the whims of the glorious Third Reich. A Steiner delivered her to the Wehrmacht brothel at 72 Saxaganskaya Street. Later many of these women were transferred to Ravensbruck concentration camp. Once there they were used as guinea pigs in vile infamous medical experiments. Hardly any survived the war.

He had first become associated with roundups in Warsaw. There he had been attached to the S.S. Reiter Regiment, at their Podchorazch Street barracks. August 12th 1940, a day all Warsaw would always remember. S.S. units had swarmed all over the city, going to their prearranged positions. To their shame many Wehrmacht units were brought in to help.

The Poles, of course, had to be given credit. With the Juden problem they had been most helpful. Even coming to the barracks and reporting cases of hiding Juden. Their priests had taught them wisely that the Juden were nothing but scum, to be despised. Some children were rooted out hiding in Catholic orphanges. *Ja*, much credit had to go to Polish cooperation.

He had been stationed with his men at Marzelkowska Street. Their victims were the sixteen-to twenty-five-year-old males needed for slave labor. Polish Police had stopped the trams. All those in the suspected age groups were lined up against the walls. Ever diligent, the Polish Police even rounded up newspaper and delivery boys.

How well he remembered the futile efforts of those who tried to escape. The pavements of the city ran red with blood. Women and children in the streets tried to warn the youths in advance. His men bundled two escapees behind a tram and neck shot them. In full view of the women and children. For an operation to work, one had to be thorough.

A vast throng of youth was gathered together in the city-wide round up. Doctors, lawyers, army officers, priests, town hall employees, taxi drivers, laborers, railway workers. They were beaten and herded through the streets to the S.S. barracks. They remained there without food or water for two whole days. All 1,153 of them.

At the end of the second day they were herded into the streets once again. This time to Towarowa Street. Once there all restraint was cast aside. Brutal beatings were the orders of the day. They were locked aboard the cattle car transports bound for Auschwitz. On August 15th they were tattooed with the numbers from 1,513 to 3,179.

It was the first successful transport from Warsaw to Auschwitz. Duly toasted in the mess that evening as a job well done. He was commended for his zeal to duty. Within days his promotion came through to S.S. Hauptscharfuehrer.

In Russia his unit came under direct control of Reich Fuehrer S.S. Heinrich Himmler. There was no need to use kid gloves. As in the case of the forest village. Father Nikolai's bandits had attacked a Wehrmacht convoy. All action had to be swift and decisive. It was the only way the peasant subhumans understood.

He nodded towards his S.S. Sturmann. One had to be doubly hard when handling the Bolsheviks.

"The old man will do."

He was dragged towards the village well. No announcement. None was needed. Everyone in the village was watching. The crowd became silent. Children snuggled closer to their mothers.

"*Los.*" He nodded his head.

A shot rang out. Luger pistol at point-blank range. The old man slumped, hands clutching at the well as he keeled over. The right leg twitched. Another shot behind the ear killed him outright. Blood oozed away from him.

Fear. The binding factor in man since prehistoric times. Fear of nonacceptance. Failure. His ultimate fear of death. It worked with all classes. Even wide-eyed uncivilized peasants.

The S.S. Sturmann straightened up, blood running upon his boots.

"Tell the swine we want the family of the bandit Nikolai Pavel Izrailovich. Their so-called little father. The family will take one pace forward march," S.S. Hauptscharfuehrer Ziegler ordered.

The smiling Ukrainian Police interpreter translated.

Marisha felt her mother's hand tighten upon hers. Someone behind them cursed in Russian.

"Another, Herr Hauptscharfuehrer." The S.S. Sturman finished wiping his boots.

"*Ja*. This time one of the older women. It always works better if we choose a female."

"*Jawohl,* Herr Hauptscharfuehrer."

A peasant woman was pulled out of the crowd. Two children were clinging to her coat. They were shoved roughly aside. Again the question was asked of the silent villagers.

"The family of the bandit Nikolai Pavel Izrailovich is to take one pace forward march. At each refusal another villager is to be shot. The next one will be a child of under ten years of age."

"Long live our *Papushka* Nikolai," shouted the woman.

A rifle butt struck her down. Angry cursing came from the villagers.

Seeming bored the S.S. Hauptscharfuehrer signaled with his arm.

Two quick shots rang out. The crowd swayed. The woman's children ran to her. Other mothers wrung their hands in prayer.

Marisha's mother stepped forward. Close behind her were the old ones, Semyon and his grey-haired Izabela.

"I am Zofia Izrailovich." Her voice was low in the hushed silence, broken only by the weeping of the executed woman's children.

Her voice rose with impassioned pride.

"I am the woman of Little Father Nikolai, hero of the people."

Marisha stepped forward joining her mother.

"I am Marisha. Daughter of the brave Nikolai."

Viktor the blacksmith's son clenched his fists. An

S.S. man was only a meter away from him. Grinning in the way of the green lice. Other men moved out from the crowd. Women spat at the S.S. men.

"When *papushka* Nikolai hears, the days of the green lice will be numbered."

"It is for you to take a pony, Viktor, and ride to the partisan forest camp."

Two submachine guns fired warning shots over their heads.

Ziegler waited until he had the villagers' full attention.

"Interpreter," he barked. "Tell them if the bandits do not give themselves up within twenty-four hours," he paused to let it sink in, "The whole family of Nikolai Izrailovich will be executed."

He jumped down from the armored troop carrier. Overeager, some of his men were already moving among the weeping villagers, selecting the evening's entertainment. Young girls under the age of twenty. Full-breasted and long-legged. Always he insisted upon it. As near to Germanic perfection as possible.

"The family under guard to the school hut," he rasped.

"My headquarters will be the brick house of the village soviet." He smiled with the irony of it.

Once before they had taken note of the authority coming from that brick house. Now with the new Germanic order he would make them more than tremble. They would be given reason to remember the Waffen S.S. In their lifetime the survivors would never forget.

Chapter 17
DEATH CAME DANCING

After the 5 o'clock evening soup, a Leutnant Schuster came to the *isba*. Brand new well-brushed uniform, a Hitler Jugend badge sitting proudly upon his chest. Submachine gun set at a rakish angle, blond, twenty years old, a Teutonic product from the parade square of an officers' training school on the outskirts of Berlin. Officer eagerly screaming for tin. Destined for the pages of the *Ost Front* magazine, and no mistake.

A strong blast of cold air scattered those nearest to the door.

"*Gott noch mal.* Not house trained. *Mutti* needs to wipe his arse."

The brothel and women chatter that always ebbed and flowed died down. What seventeen- or eighteen-year-old would talk of the merits of Brahms or Chopin? There were some. But mostly it was the talk of what they were missing. Many units were represented. Artillery, Engineers, Landser and Grenadiers. Scratch troops. Hastily formed after the rout of the retreat from Moscow.

As usual, the old Russian couple Pyotr and his wife Kadatskaya were seated upon the logs near the open fire, puffing at their coarse *machorka*-filled pipes. Jabbering as older Russians will. Arms waving and punctuating their sentences. Sipping vodka from earthenware jugs in their hands.

Schmidt brought the *isba* to attention.

"Twenty men detailed for listening post duty, Herr Leutnant." He clicked his heels aloud, knowing the eager young Leutnant would appreciate it.

"At ease," he answered with a flourish of his gloved hand, knowing that envious eyes were upon him as he unbuttoned his thick sheepskin-lined coat.

"*Dreck*. Dirt." He kicked old Pyotr aside with his jackboot and stood smiling with his back to the fire.

"Third Reich hero," someone mumbled angrily.

Kadatskaya moved, her dark eyes alive and speaking. One day, Herr *Soldat*, they seemed to be saying. Boots that kick village old folk will be running over the snow fields. Our tall forest will speak. Little Father Nikolai and his gallant partisans. Trumpets will herald their coming. Snow will run red with the blood of the invader. Little Mother Russia will curtsey and smile. Our mighty Volga will sigh as the land is cleansed of Germanski.

Schultz and Hansen helped Pyotr to his feet.

"Make a note," Schultz whispered.

"Consider it done."

Still smiling, Lieutenant Schuster kicked out at Schultz.

Those watching gasped in disbelief. Once an officer was hated in the line, officer or noncommissioned officer, their days were numbered and no mistake.

"Leave the filthy scum alone. A Deutscher does not dirty his hands with the popov swine. Such pigs are only fit to grovel in the dirt. It is the duty of every National Socialist to behave in the correct regulation manner. Any *Soldat* who tries to help these subhumans are traitors to the Third Reich in my eyes."

Angry muttering rose from the assembled men. Veterans, they were thoroughly sick of the typical Nazi behavior. Such arrogance went right on until the very end of the war, even spilling over into P.O.W. camps. A festering cancerous disease that even defeat failed to stop.

Schultz straightened up, his face bleeding.

"You lout. Don't just stand there. Name, you uncouth imbecile. Have you no manners in front of your superior officer?"

The Prussian officer training schools were very explicit. There was one place for those born to be gentlemen officers. And quite another for the peasant *Soldaten*.

Schultz made his report, still smarting from the stinging blow.

"So," the Lieutenant stood with his hands poised upon his youthful hips.

"You do not have the honor of belonging to my company."

Lieutenant Schuster glanced over the men with obvious distaste.

"Scratch unit."

"*Jawohl*, Herr Leutnant. We were taken prisoner. . . ."

His eyebrows rose.

"You let the popovs capture you?"

"Ivans were everywhere, Herr Leutnant," Schultz shouted with great effect.

"Came out of the ground like worms. Right lot of subhumans they were. I told Pushkin. He's my little friend, Herr Leutnant. Pushkin, I said. Old ivan will be in Luneburg before we can stop him. Pushkin didn't like it, see. He thinks they will head straight for the brewery, nicking our beer. Partial to good Luneburger beer, he is."

Low laughter came from some of the men.

Lieutenant Schuster's face was becoming more puffed, and decidedly red in color. Unthinkable. Here was a *Niedersaschsen* country clod admitting that he had let the popovs capture him. Flagrant violation of the Fuehrer's orders. Every *Soldat* was expected to remain at his post and fight to the last breath for the glory of Greater Germany. His honor. It was expected of him. His Germanic birthright.

Schmidt watched the expression upon Schultz's face. Officer-baiting. It was Schultz's greatest pastime. He said the bright young ones were like young virgins. On the Eastern Front they had to be broken in gently. And he was a specialist.

"We were taken after the fall of Livny, Herr Leutnant. After a . . ."

Full of fury, Lieutenant Schuster turned on Schmidt.

"Unteroffizier. Did I give you permission to speak?"

Schmidt brought his heels together with a loud crack.

"*Nein,* Herr Leutnant. I thought . . ."

Two older artillerymen were trying to suppress their laughter.

"Unteroffiziern do not do the thinking in the Wehrmacht. That solemn and sacred duty is left to the commissioned officers. Officers with culture and learning. It takes years of breeding. Selective Germanic breeding."

"With swine," whispered another blowing wind.

"*Jawohl*, Herr Leutnant."

"*Gut*. So be it. Always remember," he turned, facing Schultz, who still stood straight as a ramrod, fingers pressed down the seams of his trousers.

"I will deal with you in the morning Grenadier

Schultz. Is that understood?"

"*Doch*, Herr Leutnant." He clicked his heels in his best parade ground manner.

He had difficulty in containing himself.

"Begging the Herr Leutnant's permission to speak."

"Out with it man. What is on your mind?"

"I know I've got bad breath, Pushkin told me. Jumping lice, and an anus a foot long that causes atmospheric disturbances. But what is this innocent, blushing Grenadier to be put on report for? Surely it can't be me crabs, my C.O. Colonel Beckman knows I got rid of them. Remedy from my old granny, it was. If the Herr Leutnant is interested I'll pass on the ingredients."

Lieutenant Schuster's mouth opened. The words would not come. His throat had suddenly gone parched dry. In his few days at the front, no one had dared to answer him such a manner. He was at a complete loss for words. Utterly speechless. No manual at the officer school had dealt with such a mutinous situation. An officer of the Fuehrer was the unquestionable master. There was no room for argument. Not under the strict discipline of the Wehrmacht. His undisputable right. Like his fathers had been in the muddy trenches of the first World War. Sending hundreds of his regiment to their deaths. His brothers fighting the partisans in Norway.

Schmidt tried to stop Schultz. Laughing quietly, others were egging him on.

"Shovel it, Schultzy."

"Prize pup."

"Dying to be a hero, he is."

"Insubordination!" At long last he found the words.

Schultz grinned, chest out, still standing stiffly to attention. He liked to see them when they were fighting for words.

"Begging the Herr Leutnant's permission. Could I help being captured and taken by ivan? I was carrying out orders as is my duty. Old Adolf," his hand came up smartly coughing, which brought more chuckles from the back of the room, "the Fuehrer, our grand and noble leader. Pointed us all towards Moscow. Take it boys, he said. We didn't mind freezing our nuts off. Had a bit of experience, see. Veterans. Seen a bit, we had."

Growled agreement came from the others.

Hansen's voice piped up from the back of the crowd, doing one of his well-known impersonations.

"I said to Heinrich, while Martin Bormann was standing there picking at his nose, Eva's keeping her hand on it until the victory parade in Red Square. And you know just how that will affect my sinuses."

The uncontrolled laughter burst out.

Schultz leant forward, staring down into the startled lieutenant's face.

"Saw the towers of Moscow, we did. Standing out like big onions they were. You must have still been at the officer's school Herr Leutnant. . . ."

Lieutenant Schuster found his voice again. He shrieked in a high, almost effeminate tone.

"Unteroffizier. This creature is under close arrest."

"*Jawohl,* Herr Leutnant." Schmidt had to look away, there were so many laughing faces.

Schultz rubbed his hands.

"Means I don't get to go out and freeze in the listening posts, does it. Seven days out of the line. Hot soup in the *Kallabusch.* Thank you, Herr Leutnant." He bowed from the waist.

"I'll get my granny to send you some flowers, I will."

"Take fourteen," someone suggested.

"Hitler's war might be over by then."

Lieutenant Schuster hit Schultz in the face with his gloves.

"You will go out on listening post duty. You . . . You will come before me in the morning. Full pack, combat gear as for punishment detail. Insubordination. Willful defiance towards authority. Court martial in the field. It's a penal battalion for you and no mistake."

The snickering still continued.

"Unteroffizier."

Schmidt sprang to attention. It only brought renewed laughter.

"Every man in this detail will report to me in the morning. Slovenly lot. I will show you discipline. You will all regret the day you met me and no mistake. Few weeks in the line and you think you are heroes. I'll show you."

Under the threat of further repercussions they were turned out into the village street.

"Shoulder arms."

The bitter cold struck with its full blast. Like opening a turret hatch when a panzer is at full speed. It seems to peel the skin from the bone. As the English say. That brass monkey is inclined to lose some parts of his lower anatomy.

"By the right . . . right turn . . . forward march."

Boots crunched in the hard-packed snow as they marched away towards the trenches.

Frost paints the landscape with a cruel heavy hand. Cold knives like a crushing vise of steel. Dreaded long night. Temperature has plummeted. Stout pine trees sigh and crack. From deep within the

280

very bowels of Mother Russia, age-old demons seem to rise up chuckling, muttering upon the harsh wind. Metal snaps with ease. Men and youths slip into oblivion, protesting cries mocking in the darkness. Death haunts with its crackling, insane mantle of frost, skipping, kissing the many limbs of frozen black.

A fat general, safe and warm in his headquarters, has endorsed this form of horrific death. After the failure to take Moscow. Even at the wireless truck, the static coughs and wheezes. From a fortified bunker in Berlin comes another heroic speech. Retreat no further. My Wehrmacht will stand and fight. The screaming Bolshevik hordes must be stopped. Fight to the death. Soon the advance to the East will begin again. Be patient lining the trenches. Great victories in the East will soon be ours.

The icy finger of death takes no notice and continues stalking in the trenches. Fastens at the gaunt figures with its lacework of sparkling frost. Patterns weapons with its stinging works of art. The mind is only conscious of two numb, aching feet. Skull encased in a heavy helmet, radiating the intense crying cold.

Fire, warmth. Tormented bodies craving heat. When the agony of the lingering pain has gone, there is only the certain knowledge that frostbite has set in. And its depraved soulmate, gangrene.

Midwinter in Russia. Teeth-chattering hell. No more does the very thought of death hold any mystery. At times in the soul-destroying long night it is welcomed. Hand grenade clasped to the chest. Mauser barrel in the mouth. Taunting fear that dawn will never come. Insane, lunatic terror. Long night without end. Infinity etched with pain. For many standing watch in the trenches, it is more than the confused human mind can take. Sudden tragic flash at the snow mound. Crack of a mauser. Release from the man-created torments of sheer hell.

The dull crunch of boots through the snow. For several moments the moon hangs clear of the low clouds. Sharp and clear. Tipped with fiery red. Bad omen. Killer's moon.

"Zigaretten aus," the whispered command works its way down the column.

They skirt the massive bomb craters. A visit from the coffee grinders, old biplanes flown by women. Most nights they come over in pairs. Chugging in low over the line, dropping bombs and leaflets. Why continue fighting for the fascist imperialists? Come over to the Russian lines. Bring your weapons. Warm thighs and breasts of a woman skilled in the ways of love await you. All you can eat including many cuts of pork. Why freeze and rot in your trenches? Come over . . . paradise awaits you. The leaflets end up folded between the pages of many Wehrmacht paybooks.

The front is quiet. A frozen nightmare. Snow mounds reeking of death.

"Boy scout won't last the night," someone promises.

"Could tread on a mine," another laughs low.

"Ivan might get him."

Stifled laughter comes from the middle of the column. It could only be Schultz.

"Friend, the honourable gentleman is mine."

Lieutenant Schuster kicks out at the shapes around him. He cocks his m.p.i.

"Next man that opens his mouth—" he leaves the threat hanging upon the cold night air.

The shuffling figures come to a halt. Metal strikes an entrenching tool. Curses as another slips.

"Forward. One at a time."

The first man goes forward. At spaced intervals others follow. The listening posts are set ten meters apart. Well forward from the main trenches and bunkers.

It is the time when the new relief can easily be killed. Eyes that have stared out into the darkness. Raw nerves highly strung. Each mound or shadow takes on a menacing shape. Death awaits those who are not too careful.

Three of those about to be relieved are missing. A fourth is found in his hole, his throat cut. Body badly mutilated. Ears and nose cut off. The Siberian way of showing that the war is still going according to plan. Eye for an eye. Murder for murder. There is no let-up, even in the long night.

From every third hole a wire runs back to the command bunker. One pull and the whole front will come alive. The Siberians are quick to learn. Two man commando teams. Many times they will cut the wire first. Then finish their chosen victim in their own time.

Quickly the Russians have adapted to Wehrmacht techniques. No longer are they like those captured in the summer dust of '41. The brutal Red Army commissars have seen to that. Now it's forward or be mown down by the sadistic thugs of the N.K.V.D..

Egg grenades at the lip of the trench. Sharpened entrenching tool within easy reach. Mauser resting upon the edge. Waiting. Forever waiting. Shivering. Trembling. Each man frightened, lonely, completly upon his own. The mindless fear creates havoc.

Nervous tug at the *kandra* in the top of the boot. Fright, it might stick when it is most needed. Entrenching tool. Mauser. Grenades. The hands flick and check. Nerves tying a knot at the throat.

Is that something moving out there? The hiss of

skis. Muffled cough. Quiet chuckle of a Siberian. Something slithering through the snow. Eyes watching, waiting to pounce. Each slight sound is magnified.

An artillery man runs screaming from his hole. He cannot take the cold any longer. Weeping and crying like a lunatic he calls for his mother in far-off Bielefeld.

From the Russian positions a flare bursts high overhead. The artillery man runs in a confused circle, his arms raised, trying to ward off the invading light. A Maxim stutters. Automatic weapons. He staggers, falling. He will never see his home in Bielefeld again.

Spandaus answer the chatter. The air is alive with tracer. Then suddenly it stops. Darkness closes in once more. Someone is crying softly. Minds go out to him, trying to communicate. Stay down. Not much longer. Hang on. But the intense cold is insistent.

Gibbering, he can be heard crawling to the next listening post. A *Kamerade* drags him down. The low voices come—barely audible. Everyone knows what is happening. Will he last. Only an idiot would get up and run. Never stand a chance. Flare. Maxim. Over within seconds. The whimpering continues. The cold bites deeper.

Siberians. No time to fire a shot. They swarm over the listening posts. Hardly anyone has seen them. Rising from the ground in their long white snowcapes. Six youths die in the first savage onslaught. Two were caught half-asleep. They have waited to strike before the new relief arrives. When man and youth are at their lowest frozen ebb.

Shock of sudden attack. Frantic, horror-filled realization. Vengeful shouts of the attackers. Short stocky figures bellowing like enraged bears. The high-pitched terror-stricken screams of alarm.

"Ivan!" A young *Soldat* falls, throat gurgling, to rise no more.

Knives. Entrenching tools. Boots. Bare fists.

"*Hilfe!*" Siberian teeth tearing at the bloodied throat.

Each snarling, blurred shape a threat to survival. Fear. Near drunken breathless exhilaration takes its place. Fight and kill. As old as man himself. From the time of the caves. Fight or die.

Smell of blood distinct upon the cold air. Ripped torn stomachs. Foul steaming intestines. Ghastly mess quivering in the snow. Vile, repulsive. Sweating wolves of prey. To vomit. Pause in the battle. Death lurks grinning only seconds away, eagerly claiming victims of those who linger.

Humanity lost, in a spitting maelstrom of sadistic brutal fury.

Schultz grabs a white-coated figure, running at him, entrenching tool held high. The flat of the blade hits him in the shoulder. No pain registers. Only the blinding urge to kill. He kicks out at the shape low in the stomach. His opponent loses his balance. His *kandra* flicks out, slashing at the throat. The body gasps, sucking for air in midflight.

"*Mein Gott.*"

Killed a *Kamerade*. It always happens. Close combat. Fighting hand-to-hand in the dark. Tell friend from foe. Sweating, raging momentum. Nearly impossible. Happens to both sides. Kill and maim. Survive. Breathe, to live another day.

A Wehrmacht youth cries at the rim of his hole. Blubbering insanely. His first contact with action. No time to break them in in a quiet part of the front. It is all ablaze. A laughing Siberian with slant eyes kicks viciously at the helmeted head. With shaking hands he fires his mauser. The first kill takes courage, when the eyes are only centimeters away. The cry of stabbing pain. Inflicting death to another breathing human. War at its most bestial. The soul rebels with disgust. The nausea. That sickening feeling wells in the throat. That age-old urge tugs at the gullet.

The Siberian falls. His unscrewed hand grenade rolls into the hole. Both are blown apart in the blinding flash of the explosion.

The Siberian's comrade is crawling upon his hands and knees.

"Mishka!" His wife's name rings out from bloody lips.

Beseeching from eyes that can no longer see.

His fingers bite deep into the frozen snow.

His arms and back are full of minute grenade fragments. A Wehrmacht bayonet stabs him between the shoulders. He calls for his children. Again the blood-greased bayonet finds him. A field boot stomping his face. Suddenly all is quiet. There are no screams and cries of terror. The snow field is still. Only the breath of the Motherland. That timeless wind. And from afar he can hear the voices. From that other land. The smoke rising lazily from the village stoves.

"Taras, come down. It is for us to see that you are hiding in the hay."

His blood stains the snow. Body sobbing. The tears are like fire. His fingers dig deeper.

"Taras, it is time to wash. Mishka from Igarka is waiting by the water trough."

Gay laughter as she enters the new *stolovaya*. She is wearing a bright new headscarf. A roll of thunder sounds from the mountains in the East. A fierce summer storm. The mighty devil Gods at play.

"Holy Mother of Kazan. Light of . . ." the prayer dies upon his lips.

The bayonet goes in again, a chuckle of triumph filling the air.

"Ivan's got me!" Someone is being dragged bodily back to the Russian lines.

Two Landser rush to the rescue.

"*Yob tvoymat.*"

Ghostly shapes rise from the snow. Siberian knives cut them down.

Utter confusion. Tangled bodies fighting. Grunts. Groans. Breathless fighting for a new hold. German and Russian curses. Death rattles. Hideous whimpering from those with stomach wounds. Some die quickly. Others will scream for hours.

There is no God. If he exists why does he allow such slaughter? Why does he not answer the many prayers. Why does he watch with dry eyes. And still the lips move, mumbling.

Schmidt ran from the main trenches with reinforcements.

"Use your combat knives."

Two Siberians charge. He blinds the first with a cross swipe of his double edged *kandra*. He falls and a mauser butt crushes his skull. The youth stays on the fallen Siberian, pounding him with his fists. Strong hands pull him away. The other one runs off screaming into the night.

Two *Soldats* come across a Siberian straddling a body. They stab the life out of him. Killing him again and again. One of them is crying uncontrollably. The body screams pitifully, writhing in the snow. Blood gushes from the mouth. He curses them with his last dying breath.

"Pushkin."

287

"Over here."

Hansen and Schultz fight back to back, swinging sharpened Russian entrenching tools. Aiming for the necks. Only sure killing place. Thick padded jackets deaden the blows. Two ivans are dead at their feet. Another, gashed in the neck, has succeeded in crawling away.

Roaring like a devil from Russia's past, another white-caped figure wields a Cossack saber. Decapitates a Wehrmacht youth upon his knees, fumbling frozen hands trying to hold his stomach in.

"Urah Stalin!" He bounds off, the grisly dripping trophy hanging from his left hand.

"Germanski *kaputt!"* He waves it at an old Engineer reservist.

A Luger cracks, firing twice. The giant lunges with his saber. Together they fall. Within minutes they both die. Hands clasping at one another in the last twitching death struggle.

Lieutenant Schuster ran out of the command bunker with two Obergefreiters. Ten meters into no man's land they trip over the mass of cursing fighting men in the snow.

"For the Fatherland and our glorious Fuehrer!" His short bayonet rips a Siberian gut.

"Fuehrer, balls. Get the swine off me!" snarls a veteran, blood streaming down his face from a gaping head wound.

"Victory is ours. The Bolshevik subhumans . . ."

A nagan pistol coughed. Lieutenant Schuster fell, the bullet shattering his hip.

"Get him off," croaks the familiar voice once again.

"Nein," the steel hands tighten at his throat.

Brest, Livosk, Minsk. The long march before Moscow. Scratch troops. His leave was due in seven days. Train to Kiev. Change at Warsaw. The leave trains were always slow. He would make it this time. His lucky charm. The medallion in his paybook.

Brunhilde would be waiting beyond the head-hunter barrier at the Schlesischer Bahnhof in Berlin. It was there that she had waited when he had returned from France. Her *mutti* would be looking after young Heinz and Heidi.

Heidi the spitting image of her mother. Blonde hair and blue eyes. The same dimples when she smiled. Always giggling. Never a sour face.

Heinz was having trouble with his teeth the last time he was home. The doctor fitted him with a brace. Brunhilde said in her last letter that it would soon be off. Brave little fellow. Soldiering on. Never a complaint.

He missed Brunhilde so much. To have her sitting upon his lap whispering in his ear, as she always did on the first day of his leave. The children at his right knee. Little Heinz playing with his chest collection. Damn war. The Wehrmacht should never have gone into Russia.

"*Verdammt*," the pressure was released from his throat.

He gouged his thumb into the Siberian's eyes.

The knife went in under his ribs. Hot stabbing pain. He butted with his steel helmet. Then the knife cut an arc under his rib cage. And it was as though he was floating. Leaving his body. Swimming. And there were the faces. That one face over the barrier. The handkerchief waving. The head hunters growling.

"Gerhard," Brunhilde was smiling.

And then the pain. He was on fire. The lights. And suddenly the cold and darkness closed in.

"Brunhilde!" He died in a seventeen-year-old's arms.

Stiff with fright, at first Steggeman had cowered in his hole.

"Every man for himself!" The sharp command brought him back to reality.

He gripped the edge of the hole to climb out. A fur-capped figure jumped out of the darkness. Spat in his face.

"Germanski pig!" The knife cut at his arm drawing blood.

A flurry of arms. Legs. Positioning for a hold. His hand found the knife arm, bringing his knee up. An answering grunt confirmed contact. He jabbed with his *kandra*. Felt the thick hair as he fought to cut the throat. Firm body of a young woman. Screaming in agony she slipped from his hold.

"*Pyos!*" blood sprayed over him.

She clawed at his trousers. Tried to pull herself up. He found his mauser. Her knife went deep into his thigh. Shaking violently he brought the mauser up. One bullet shattered the skull. The grip at his leg slipped. He slumped to his knees in the gore and blood. Near choking upon his own vomit.

A shoulder blow sent Muller sprawling. The little Siberian came back at him shouting, sure of the kill. Stunned, head reeling, he braced his rifle between his legs. The Siberian ran onto his bayonet with his full weight. A shot crashed out. Someone had shot him from behind. The hot sticky blood poured down the length of his rifle.

"All right?"

"*Ja.*"

"Sure?"

"*Ja, danke.*"

290

Several crouched figures in flowing snow capes ran by.

"Where?" Undecided, a youth was standing near a pile cursing figures.

"Here. *Schnell*," came a muffled reply.

He went in two-handed, swinging his entrenching tool. Metal crunched against flesh. A dull sickening thud. Once, twice, the Siberian died without a sound. Head cleaved in two.

"*Hilfe*." A lonely voice sounded over the snow field.

Too late. A blood-gurgling cry. Vocal cords choking with blood.

"*Mein lieber Gott*," someone gasped.

A line of white-caped figures could be seen looming out of no man's land. Weapons at the ready, advancing in a steady half-crouch.

Amid the cries of dying screams, that often heard concerto of the Russian long night, someone pulled on the alert wire. A rattling of tins sounded in the command bunker. Heavy Spandaus spluttered into life.

"Back to the holes," shouted Schmidt.

Survivors and wounded scurried, crawling through the snow.

Beams of red-hot tracer tore away into the night. Cross-sweeping motions. Back and forth. Mortar fire, adjusting the range after every few shells. Beyond those trembling in the advance listening posts, death went dancing. Quick-stepping to the Russian positions and waltzing back again. Awe-inspiring. Majestic music of hell. Military precision. Wehrmacht knowhow. Steel fragmentations ripping the night apart. Devils scythe-reaping. Predetermined, cutting everything down before it.

"Teach them naughty little Siberians," laughed Schultz.

Hansen slammed the door of the *isba*.

"Diced Siberian for breakfast."

Someone laughed nervously. Another swore as they trod upon him lying in the straw.

They washed the blood from their arms and faces. Bleary-eyed, Kadaskaya and Pyotr made the sign of the cross over them.

Dawn swept in over the trenches. Patterns of frost glistened in the early morning light. No relief, only the stark reality of war in the East. Two moaning Landser with severe frostbite were being moved. A medic swore as he slipped upon the frozen intestines of a bayoneted Siberian. They had infiltrated back beyond the main trenches. And then were beaten back again.

A machine gunner cleared his weapon. The Spandau loader was smoking behind cupped hands. One shot from an ivan sniper hit him just below the helmet ring. He slumped back, the still smoking Juno between his lips.

Barked commands could be heard coming from the village. The dull metallic clank of noise about the field kitchen.

From somewhere in the ivan positions came the neighing of a horse. Shrill and protesting. Laughter from an outpost, tossed upon the wind.

A young lieutenant, new to the front, stepped back from his lowered periscope. His hands fumbled at his greatcoat.

"Slaughter. Sheer slaughter."

An Unteroffizier standing close to him slowly raised the periscope. No man's land was dotted with holed helmets, torn uniforms and snowcapes flapping in the wind. Gruesome remains littered the

292

snowfield. Chunks of human limbs and bones pointing to the early morning sky.

"Against our mortar barrage, Herr Leutnant, they never had a chance."

In that horrifying long night death went dancing. Victims, thirty Landser of a returning Wehrmacht patrol. But then, that was war on the Eastern Front.

Chapter 17
MARISHA, LITTLE DOVE

That early-afternoon winter's darkness settled upon the village at the edge of the forest. A fierce wind from the depths of Siberia lashed the main street. The cutting chill snap of fresh severe frost about the snow-laden thatched roofs. The muffled steady tramp and coughing as the S.S. guards take up their positions.

Grumbling of the S.S. Sturmann with the detail.

"Scheiss, dies verdammte Wetter!" Frozen breath hanging about his face.

Lantern light gleamed from the heavily sacked windows of the *isbas*. Then the sound that many of the villagers had been dreading. Germanski sport. Cries from the chosen ones. The young maidens with long plaited hair. Mixed with the sound of an accordion. It echoed to the tall pine trees and back again. Like a warning demon from the voices of the long dead. A lament that always followed the green lice in Mother Russia. Coarse bestial laughter. Taunting and mocking, from throats that had taken too much vodka. One after the other, from the white painted *isba* of the Bochkovs, the thin *kolkhos* dogs joined in the unearthly wailing.

Women in the *isbas*. Those who had known the pangs and pains of childbirth. The first suckling, through tears, the young infant child at their breast.

The proud amazed stare of the father looking down upon them both. They could only huddle together, wringing their hands, swaying to and fro. The curse of the green lice was upon the village. Clutching the treasured ikons they muttered their prayers. Holy Mother of Kazan. Do not desert us. The Motherland had known much suffering. Now it was their *kolkhos*. Their village. Their family. Their young loved ones.

After loud prompting and much giggling S.S. Hauptscharfuehrer Ziegler's drunken voice rose in slurred song.

"Schwarz braun ist die Haselnuss.
Schwarz braun bin auch ich, bin auch ich.
Schwarz braun soll mein Madel sein . . . gerade so wie ich."

All under the age of sixteen years. Vodka was forced into the young maidens. At gun point, laughing Ukrainian Hilfeswillige S.S. bullied them into stripping their clothes off. Like a scene from a large *kolkhos* cattle market the auction followed, with Ziegler pocketing the Deutsche marks.

Screaming hysterically and struggling the young maidens were dragged bodily into the deep straw, pinned down and raped. Always the couplings like the beasts of the field.

One maiden escaped. She was caught by two laughing S.S. men in the village street. Viktor the blacksmith's son could only stand watching from the shadows. Her naked body gleamed in the light coming from the red brick house of the village soviet. His well-oiled pistol felt heavy in his overcoat pocket. It was Tanya, eldest daughter of the couple Kurochkin. His promised one. Long flaxen hair like a stand of corn under the summer sun. Eyes that had known the laughter of their youth together. That first touching of hands together down by the river. The wonder of that first kiss. When Viktor had jumped into the air, throwing his cap to the trees. And they had fallen to the bed of pine needles, alive, so alive in that first spring of their pledged love.

He bit deeply upon his lips, drawing blood. Dyakov, the wise one, had given him the pistol and his orders. He was to shoot the hated black beetles in the schoolhouse and escape with Marisha and her family to the forest. If he failed, the men of the village would never welcome him again in their *isbas*. Was he not the runner for the partisans? A guardian of the village while they were away? Had he not warned of the coming of the green lice many times? As much a soldier as a Guard in the ranks of the Red Army.

Tanya screamed as one of the S.S. men grabbed her brutally by her full breasts. The other was slapping and squeezing her buttocks, hands searching low, chuckling drunkenly.

"Soon it is a woman you will be, little flower."

She tried to fight them off. They pulled her back to the door of the village soviet by the legs.

For several moments Viktor wanted to charge with his pistol blazing. Kill the two evil ones. Kill and kill again. But he remembered the solemn oath that he had taken by the logged-in village well. *Papushka* Nikolai's words came back to him once again.

"Never forget, *tovaritch*. It is for Mother Russia that we fight. Our families, our loved ones will be threatened. Little Mother Russia must survive."

Tanya's screaming taunted him. He turned sobbing, pressing himself against the wall of the *isba*. Germanski would pay. Pay a thousandfold for deflowering his beautiful Tanya. And the other gentle young maidens. They would be pegged out upon the floor of the forest. Death would not come easy for them. Their remains would be left for the carrion of the forest. No partisan would stay his hand.

Unable to stop himself he crept closer to the red brick house of the village soviet. Two giggling S.S. men were forcing the head of the Leibovich girl down. One had her head in his right hand, pulling her closer, his face leering and dribbling with spittle. Senses reeling, Viktor staggered away, vomiting into the snowdrift.

From the *isbas* that had known the sorrow of losing their daughters, men gathered under the lanterns at the hot stoves. The bitter, deep, angry eyes of the women were upon them. Attack the village soviet. The invaders were drunk. Most of the men remaining in the village were old. Was it not the younger stronger men who had taken to the forest? They armed themselves with axes, the hooks that were used in the making of the hay. It was the wise one who crept from *isba* to *isba*, talking them out of attacking. There were too many guards for the older men to attack. Nothing could be done against the armed might of the Hilfeswillige S.S. Only shudder and suffer as each new cry of childish pain tore at the cold night air.

Tanya? Was it little Marushka? Or Anna, who would soon join hands with the woodcutter's son from Klin. They had only their fists against quick-firing automatic weapons. It would be a fascist bloodbath that would be left in the *kolkhos*. Only a very faint glimmer of hope remained. The partisans would return. The blood of the ones with long plaited hair would be avenged.

Standing by the stove in the schoolhouse, two

297

drunken black beetles stood guard. Black-uniformed Ukrainian Policemen. Feared as much as the hated Germanski S.S. Was it not whispered in the village that they drank the blood of slaughtered Russian children? Evil monsters who had turned upon their own people. Marisha had seen Germanski foot *Soldats* spitting upon them and calling them *Hiwis*. The folk of the *kolkhos* had a much better name for the turncoat Western Ukrainians. Eagerly changing sides in the great Motherland war. It was with much fear in their hearts that they walked.

Matvey Vyacheslav Radishev, the political commissar with the partisans, had announced the special Stalin order from Moscow. A price was upon all their heads. Every black beetle would be hunted down. It was their eyes that would be put out first. Theirs would be a slow, cruel death. Black beetles—they were all living on borrowed time.

From the tiny window in the schoolhouse, between the sheets of *Pravda* that were plastered to the glass, Marisha had watched the Yugoslav slave workers of the *Todt* Organization erecting the gallows. They had used explosives to blast holes for the posts. Standing erect, a French slave worker had refused to help. One of the captured Free French pilots serving in fighter planes with the Red Airforce. He was beaten mercilessly with riding crops. Still he stood proudly to attention, refusing to take part. For the first time in the village the folk heard that strange defiant language of his. He sang a song, telling of meeting upon a bridge in his homeland, once the world was free of the green lice. It was a simple song, the song of a strange proud man that none of the survivors would ever forget. A hail of savage machine gun fire cut him down. His shouting filled the air as they had forced him to kneel in the snow.

"Vive de Gaulle!"

Once again Marisha shuddered, thinking of the smiling S.S. Hauptscharfuehrer's ultimatum. Death by hanging if Papushka Nikolai did not give himself up to the S.S. Grey-haired Izabela had taken old Semyan's hand in hers. One day the fascist invaders would pay for their many crimes. And her brave son Nikolai would be the man holding the long bayonet at their throats.

"The family of a partisan leader does not shed tears." Her mother Zofia had shivered beside Marisha, whispering. "We must have a straight back like the men of the forests. In the great Motherland war, we are all soldiers of Mother Russia."

"Da," Marisha took her mother's hand in hers.

She was thinking of the poor frozen kitten. Had not Roman and Mikhial also had tears in their eyes? And Niki, when he placed the small wooden cross over the snowdrift. Why was there so much weeping in Mother Russia? Had it always been so?

Semyan gathered Marisha to him, trying to share the warmth of his body.

"When Nikolai hears of the green lice," he winked in that knowing way of his. "Our forest will shudder with the might of his anger."

"Da, his wrath will be a terrible thing to see," Izabela nodded, tightening her headscarf.

"Marisha my child," Semyan continued, "my Nikolai stood high in the saddle, when . . ."

The smaller of the black beetles struck him in the mouth with his Luger pistol.

"Talking again, old one. It will not be the morning mists that you will be seeing," he smiled cruelly, the half-empty vodka bottle going to his mouth.

He cursed aloud.

"Scharcrev noch mal. Here we stay guarding

299

hostages while our brothers in the brick house are having much sport." He eyed Zofia, clucking his tongue.

"Here in the schoolhouse we need no auction. The bandit's woman is ours to take."

The other black beetle restrained him.

"*Da*. You would take her. But the Hauptschar would punish us."

"He would know nothing." The first black beetle spat against the red-hot stove in disgust.

"Her neck will stretch at dawn, if we bed her or not."

Marisha felt her mother's hand tighten upon her arm. Little Niki said the green lice were his friends. Even the children new to the *kolkhos*, Roman and Mikhial. Had they not also said that the green lice had played with them in the *isba* of their mother? Playing the part of a forest bear on the hunt. When the black beetles led the family away from the well, was it not Niki who she had seen turning his tear-stained face into Dyakov's overcoat? Now all the children new to the village knew who the real enemy was. Long would Niki remember her harsh words. Daughter of a partisan leader, she had to speak up. For a small boy there was much growing that he had to do.

First light. She thought of those other chill winter dawns. Going to the cow stalls. Dyakov there. Sleep still in his wise old eyes. Taking the milk buckets out to the women. She had been the chosen one to lead the milking cows to the new forest village. And there would be much singing and rejoicing. Viktor on his handbell. The wise one walking beside them playing his accordion. How beautiful it would sound upon the forest track. And the older women of the village would nudge one another and giggle, as was their way.

First light. Her frail young body began to shake. Sensing her fear, her mother squeezed her closer. There would be the short walk. None of the folk would greet her as upon other mornings. Many of the heads would be bowed. She would see the treasured ikons. Her *mamushka* had said that the head must be held high. No tears. No signs of tears must the green lice see. All the folk of the *kolkhos* would be there watching.

No more would she sing to those happy smiling faces. Women taking their washing down to the large rocks at the riverbed. Or hold hands and romp and dance with the other young maidens. There would be no trip over the snows to far-off Kharkov. No fine academy for a young maiden, soon to be a woman. No training of the voice. She would never see all the fine Russian old cities.

Her hand went to her throat. Tears were biting at the corners of her eyes. Her teeth clamped upon her lower lip. A daughter of a brave forest partisan does not cry. She fought back the tears. In her heart she knew that she was still a child. Many times she had cried over the dead kitten. Tried to heat it by the hot stove to bring it back to life once again.

Her *mamushka* was right. No demon of a black beetle would ever see her cry. She was Marisha. *Papushka* Nikolai's little dove. Never would she cry in front of the helpers of the green lice. Never. If death struck her down before she blossomed into a woman. Out of the depths of winter, Mother Russia would call her. The Holy Mother would take her to her breast. Was it not always that way, as the old folk said. She was a child of the forest. Did the mighty pines bend easily from the gales of Siberia? *Nyet*. They were strong like the great Motherland.

She knew that no partisan would give himself up

to the S.S. Had they not sworn and taken the oath before the commissar and an officer of the Red Army? Standing in line, watched by the women. Before the coming of the winter frosts, it was. Right clenched fists raised. One hundred and seventy men of the *kolkhos*. The fight for Mother Russia was a fight until death. They would have fire in their bellies. Revenge in their hearts. When they heard of the green lice they would return.

Other days would dawn. Days when no fear would come with the mists from the river. No more would the black beetles terrify the old ones. Commissar had ordered that the old village would be burnt to the ground. No Germanski hunting party would find shelter. He would be left with the cold and howling winds. The partisans would hunt them down like wolves.

Viktor heard the scuffling in the schoolhouse. Zofia's cries of protest. Semyan being beaten when he tried to protect her. Marisha's screams of anger. Izabela cursing them.

"Leave my *mamushka* alone. *Papushka* Nikolai will burn you in oil."

Her cry of pain as one of the black beetles threw her against the wall.

He crept closer to the potato cellar entrance, lifting the wooden door.

The black beetles pulled the struggling Zofia to the storeroom, where teacher Boris Anastas Pisarev kept the school texts.

Within minutes Viktor was up the ladder and into the schoolhouse. Izabela had Semyan in her arms.

"Where?" He went to them, his hand sweating upon the pistol.

"*Nyet*," Semyan rose to his feet.

"Viktor you cannot save us. . . ."

"I have bullets for the beetles. . . ."

"*Nyet.*" Semyan took him by the shoulders as Zofia began sobbing behind the closed storeroom door.

"Take Marisha with you. If you shoot the black beetles no one will escape."

"Nikolai's woman . . ."

"It is too late." Semyan shook him by the shoulders.

"We two are old. We would be shot down in the forest."

Izabela grasped his hand.

"Go. Go. We will not leave Zofia. Go quickly. Bring the men back."

"I have been ordered by the wise one. . . ."

"*Nyet.* We would not survive. Go now, Viktor. Go with Marisha. You both must be saved. Tell Nikolai of this long night. Never forget, my child."

As the renewed cries of Zofia filled the schoolhouse, Marisha would not leave. Semyan struck her in the face with his open hand.

"Viktor. You are a soldier of the forest. Take Marisha with you."

Semyan and Izabela were sobbing. Never had one of them laid a hand upon their favorite golden-voiced child. Marisha. Her voice. She meant so much to them in the time of much suffering.

"Take Marisha and go." Semyan pushed her towards Viktor.

Together they left the schoolhouse. Behind them the old ones were knelt in prayer before the stove.

Marisha staggered along with Viktor leading the way. Her *mamushka* had been beaten by the black beetles. They had taken her coat off and ripped her blouse from her body. She would tell her *papushka* when she returned with the partisans. He would have

303

their tongues for this evil deed. Dawn would bring revenge to the village.

Viktor turned towards her, choking upon his words.

"My stallion is near the Korochkins' wood pile."

"*Da*." Marisha took his hand more firmly.

Viktor was a soldier of the forest. He would get them quickly to the new forest village. *Papushka* Nikolai. Him. Suddenly she knew that she could not leave. Her *mamushka* had always told her how proud she must be. Hold the head high. Even when she knew that death would come with the dawn. The folk of the village. Were they not also frightened in this cold long night? Only she, Marisha could bring them warmth. They must know. The lanterns were still shining from the *isbas*. They would want to hear her voice.

She stared down at the village. The roofs that she knew so well. Viktor was leading his stallion behind her. It snorted in the darkness. Eager to be off. It too could smell Germanski.

And it was as though she could hear the voices at the village well once again. Those many faces turned towards her as she stood upon the logs. The wise one strumming a balalaika. They were all there. Niki and his younger brothers. Roman and Mikhial. All the new children of the village. And the bright faces were shining. It was spring. And the young maidens like her, soon to be women, were chattering.

"Sing Marisha, little dove."

She would smile and raise her hand like in the forest dance.

"Such a voice the girl has. Singing the wonders of our land."

"Sing, Marisha, sing. Holy Mother Russia will look after us. Sing, child."

The blacksmith's son Viktor gaily laughing. He had curls at the nape of his neck. Her *mamushka* said that he was soon to become a man. One bright spring day he would be looking for a woman. Some said his eyes were for Tanya of the long blond hair. Daughter of the Kurochkins. Had he not been seen holding Tanya's hand when he warned of the coming of the green lice? A handsome couple they would make. Spring flowers in Tanya's hair.

Her hand went to her headscarf.

"For the folk of the *kolkhos* I will sing my favorite song."

"*Nyet*," Viktor was working his way through the deep snow.

"Marisha . . . come. . . ."

She did not hear him. The folk of the village would be gathered about their stoves, the old ones with fear in their hearts. It was her voice that they would want to hear. She sang of the birch trees. Of the time when the young maidens sang and danced in the circle, waving their birch sprigs. That was not a time of sadness for the village. It was a time of gaiety. When the men drank *samahonka*. And everyone was happy.

O, mighty Mother Russia hear me now. Your daughter. The brave Viktor has saved me. Now I sing my favorite song for my beloved *kolkhos*.

Many *isba* doors were thrown open.

"Marisha. Marisha," came the cry from hundreds of choked throats.

And it was not as though it was the voice of a young frail maiden. One with laughing eyes who would soon be a woman. Daughter of their little Father Nikolai. *Nyet*. It was the strong vibrant voice of centuries old Mother Russia. High notes held upon the chill night air.

Many of the village folk crossed themselves.

Had they not seen her go into the schoolhouse with the demon black beetles?

She sang of the Motherland bathed in glory. Of the days when the brave soldiers would return and free the land. Men of other villages. Once again there would be the sound of laughter. Such a gathering of folk at the well. Green lice. They would be no more.

A drunken dry cackle of discovery rang out in the forest.

"*Stoi.*"

Still Marisha sang. It was for the folk of the village. They must hear her voice. Know of the hope of the land. Soon the partisans would return. Horses pounding through the snows. Singing the songs of victory. Like the soldiers of the Red Army.

A flash of blinding light. A lone shot. Another shot. Another spat death upon the cold night air.

There were those of the village who said they could still hear her sweet voice singing. It was of the Cossack that she always sang so well. Was it not the wise one who had taught her?

A multitude of village voices joined in the singing. None could stop them. No longer were they afraid. Little Marisha had shown the way. The Hilfeswillige S.S. stood back in awe. Some were seen to hurriedly cross themselves. They swore later that the old ones put the evil eye upon them.

"On the road where Cossacks run.

Across the plains from mountains to the sea.

To the Cossack his world is free."

Sobbing, the villagers clapped their hands. The S.S. Sturmann fired a full magazine from his machine pistol into the thatch of an *isba* roof. They would not stop.

Within seconds Viktor was upon the black beetle.

Papushka Nikolai had always said the bullet must be sure. They had none to waste upon the green lice. With his long bayonet he stabbed him. Again and again he slashed at the vodka-soaked throat. For Tanya, his promised one. For Nikolai's woman. For Semyan and grey-haired Izabela. For little Marisha of the golden voice.

The beetle writhed in the snow, breathing his last. Still Viktor cut at the body.

With one last look at the *kolkhos* he mounted his stallion. The folk in the village were still singing. He strapped Marisha to his stallion.

"*Heya. Heya. Davia.*"

The stallion set off at a gallop. He knew the way. But already Marisha, little dove, was dead.

Chapter 19
ATTACK AT FIRST LIGHT

Ninety minutes to zero hour.

Soon the faint light of dawn will roll in over the snow-laden trees. That mist seeming to cling to the ground. Too late for some standing guard in the freezing trenches. Their names will go in the Feldwebel's death tally book. Mere numbers. Names. That inevitable telegram from the Third Reich. The announcement in the local paper. He fell bravely fighting for Greater Germany.

Inside the *isba* the air is stifling. Another pungent sickly smell to add to the nightmare. Rustling in the straw. Half-awake, with bated breath, thinking it is the rats. A strong hand shaking the shoulder.

Schmidt is making the rounds.

"*Los*. Wake up. We move out in ninety minutes. Wake the others up."

"*Donna wetter*. Not again. Don't we ever get any rest?"

"No breakfast. That's not right. I'm going to write to my granny and complain. She'll tell our runt of a Gauleiter. I need my wind first thing in the morning. Otherwise I'll get stomach cramps."

Schultz pulls Hansen away from the fire by his feet.

"Wake up, little one. Adolf says we move again. Out of that fart sack."

Hansen sits up, picking the lice from his chest and popping them in the fire.

"I saw it all clear, I did. Smelt it. Had cologne under her arms. Silky pants on her bum. Me hands being rough they kept snagging in them. And silk stockings. Smiling she was. Then *Los! Los!* comes. Not right, it isn't. This war isn't for Hamburgers like me. I'm for going back to sleep. I might catch her before she goes to work in the sausage factory."

"I said move it, Hansen."

"Come, the Lord is waiting. A new dawn, a new fight. Take a deep breath, and greet it like your Germanic soldier ancestors."

Heyer is the first up, as usual, using the old razor blade in the light of a Hindenburg candle.

"Why shave? We have no inspections here," from Steggeman.

"I shave, dear child. Because have you ever seen the way a beard grows when you are dead? A Deutscher *Soldat* must go in the correct regulation manner. Legs at attention. The right hand holding his mauser. The left neatly folded under his head. And shaved down to the last bristle."

Steggeman scratches and makes a face.

"Never thought of it that way."

"You have much to learn if you want to be a success in the Wehrmacht. Even in death everything must be done by numbers."

"Cut the crap and let's have some action. I said move it."

While the *kolkhos* slept, storm units have crept forward through no man's land. Their task to silence the first ivan defenses prior to the attack. Only battle knives will be used. They go in minutes before zero hour.

A new general has arrived from the Afrika Korp.

He does not believe in spending the winter sitting idly in defense. The legions of the Wehrmacht were created for attack. Mobility in warfare, as Guderian said more than once. The very essence of battle. Surprise. Advance. Conquer.

Each soldier is issued 120 rounds of mauser ammunition and five hand grenades. Spare magazines for submachine guns. Heyer becomes the owner of a brand new flamethrower. The incident with the motorcycle and side car is long forgotten. Suffering from mild concussion, he was picked up by a Rollbahn supply unit.

Panzers have bombed up back from the line. A symphony of panting, impatient engines. Shielded hand torches. Truly Germanic curses as the ammo is stowed aboard. They will follow through the first Landser assault. Amazing how far the smell of gasoline fumes will carry. It gives comfort to the Grenadier, though. To go into the attack without mother. It's like running naked. There is comfort in these prehistoric hulks.

Lieutenant Schuster did not make it to the aid station. In war you only look after your immediate friends. Those in the platoon. Someone did report him missing. It was expected. Truth is he froze to death, lying in white waste alone. No one held his hand. His remains joined others in a shell hole. May his bones rest in peace.

Sixty minutes to zero hour.

Muller is number one on a heavy Spandau. Steggeman his loader. His trip to the aid station came near to ending in disaster. The chief *Arzt* wanting to do his patriotic duty, with talk of slapping a report on him for self-inflicted wounds. Anti-tetanus shot. Two strips of plaster. A stern-faced head hunter escorted him back to Schmidt.

"Next time we will only accept a shot in the head. Cowardice in the field. The *Arzt* will make an example of him. Too many of you are running crying to the aid station with minor wounds. What do you think the front is? A carnival holiday camp?"

Schultz and Heyer chased him out. Heyer's knife flew past his head into the hard clay wall.

"Swine. You did that on purpose," he whined.

Schultz chuckled, cracking his huge knuckles.

"Impossible, friend. He never misses. Ask friend ivan."

Eyes wild the NCO backed out of the *isba*, fingers close to the trigger of his submachine gun. Lice-ridden front scum. Illiterate louts. If they had not been so squeamish Moscow would have been in the Wehrmacht's hands.

"If the popovs don't do the job, you . . . you will all be in my book. Your day of reckoning is not far away."

Bolts worked on mausers. He left the door open as he ran off up the village street.

In the smoke-filled *isba* the minutes tick by. Extra schnapps had been issued. Within minutes it is gone. No thought of tomorrow. For some it might never come.

"None of your common vodka today. *Nein*, this time Adolf wants an extra effort. After the fifth mile you all qualify for a crack at Eva."

"What if we only make three?" comes from Steggeman.

Hansen smiled, prancing up and down.

"That leaves only Martin Bormann as a consolation prize."

The urge to urinate is constant.

"Ruski cold it goes right through me," Steggeman says.

No one argues. Many make the trip to the door.

Schmidt's platoon is made up to strength with other scratch troops. There are even several from a sanitation detail.

"Glad to have you with us." Hansen shakes them in turn by the hand.

"Your specialist training might come in handy. Good at scraping legs down, are you. Now I have a friend here who is always doing it on the trot. A bug in the bowels, the *Artz* calls it."

"Drop it Hansen," barks Schmidt.

And for once Hansen remains silent.

Forty-five minutes to zero hour.

Hurried writing of the last letters home help pass the waiting. They will rest in the right-hand tunic pocket, between the pages of the *Soldats Buch*. Strange how the mind can think of something new to write. Schmidt hands out the Wehrmacht field letter paper. It makes poets from the slums of Hamburg and Berlin, makes hard men gentle, thinking it could be the last time.

"*Und Mutti*. In my next parcel I'd like *Bockwurst* bought from that stand in the Markt Platz. The boys loved the last lot and thank you for the liverwurst. And all those pairs of heavy socks. It took eight days to reach us. We are moving up now so I will bring this to a close. *Hals und Beinbruch*. Your Werner."

"In this winter that knows not the warmth of the sun. I sit in the peasant cottage with my *Kameraden*. There is Wolfgang over there. Tough in battle. A model *Soldat*. But he has a heart of gold. Always cleaning his submachine gun. It must be the cleanest in the whole Wehrmacht.

"Heinrich is reading a book from his mother. She is out of the bombing living somewhere on the

Heide. Gerhardt and Werner are squabbling. Always talking of Hamburg and what they are going to do after the war is over. It's either tears or laughter. But they always make it up again.

"Dieter, our leader, is talking to me. Being the youngest I am the baby of the platoon. It was not always that way. The other young ones got transferred. He says we have nothing to fear. Ivan is as afraid as we are. To us, being a bit older he is like a father. Scolds us when we need it. Especially when Werner gets lippy. Patting us upon the back if he thinks we have been brave. We would follow him anywhere. Through hell and back. And just sometimes I think we have been there already.

"So you can see I am in good hands. So stop worrying, *Mutti*.
Herzliche Grusse, Jurden."

"Searching a wrecked peasant hut for food, Wolfgang found these two poor little kittens. Near frozen and starved they were. Adolf and Heinrich we called them. Werner said they were half-dead and we should drown them. Me, I'm soft and I always have been. Like runts they were. You know like when a sow has too many in her litter. Chilled little piglets they were.

"I brought them around in the warmth of the *isba* fire. They loved a slug of schnapps. The cook gave me some horse flesh. You know this persuading way I have. Volunteered with the meat he did. They came right in two days. A Russian peasant family is looking after them now. Cheeky like a young boar in heat they are.

"*Los, Los* is getting the men ready. Ivan's throwing a party. I don't want to miss it. Owe him one I do.

Your sweety pie . . . Gerhardt."

"Our original platoon is down to six now. Your son, our good *Kamerade*, fell the other day. There was no pain. He died instantly. He told us so much about your new adopted land. His trips into the Rocky Mountains with his father. We seem to know so much about Spokane. The hills and valleys of British Columbia that he loved so well. Long will we remember his tales of Skookumchuck, Kicking Horse Pass and Ta Ta Creek. The Columbia River. We will never forget him. He was one of our very fine *Kameraden* whom we will always miss.

"It is my duty to ready the men now. We are going in again. The field post office will send along his last effects.
Dieter . . . one of your son's *Kameraden*."

"I have no one to write my last letter to. Hein said you would not mind if I wrote to you. I am always arguing about the war with him. But I do respect him. Because many times he is right.

"It seems that all I have known is war. France. Poland. And now Russia. The loss of my parents. My little sisters. I have a hate that is hard to control. Sometimes I think I am going insane with all the killing. The groans and cries of dying men upon the field.

"My dismal life in the slums. A father disabled who could not work. Going to bed hungry as a child. And then the Wehrmacht. This is my family now. The others think that I am a loner. But I care about every man in the platoon as though he was my brother. I would destroy thousands of ivans without batting an eye, if it meant saving just one of their lives.

"The Fatherland has turned into a monster. I kill

314

with such ease, like others would tie up a bootlace. There is only the killing. Day after day. We have to survive. Some of us must return. I hope one day the Lord will forgive me.

Mit recht herzlichen Grussen, Wolfgang.

"As each day dims into night I seem to stand apart from this war. No longer does the pulse race as we go into the attack. It becomes harder to laugh when someone makes an obscene joke about the *Untermensch*. I see only the children. Tugging at their mother's skirts for nonexistent bread. We give them what we can. A half-baked potato. Flesh from our many horses that die in this bitter cold. In their last throes they scream like the voices of women.

"My body reacts to the commands. I will fight with all the wrath of a cornered stag. Yet, inside this uniform of grey green, I know the cause is wrong, *Mutti*.

"Names that will be a curse upon our nation for years to come haunt me. Concentration camps. Death camps where the Reich herds Jews and other politicals. And even people in the occupied lands who do not know what wrong they have done. They were born in the wrong country. Mounds upon the steppes. Trenches in the forest. Villages where the hatred for the Germanic race will last for centuries. None can put it right in our time. It is a cross that even our children's children will have to bear.

"I long for a peaceful sunlit glade upon the Heide. Where only the gentle hand of nature reigns supreme. Migrating birds know no barbed wire, or fortified national boundaries to hold them in. If I survive the war the Heide will no longer be my home. I will travel the ends of the earth seeking a peace that I know must survive somewhere out there. Where a uniform will no longer herald such a cry as, '*hande hock*. Or *raus . . . raus.*'

"Lonely I will wait until the world has forgotten these infamous crimes. And politicians are thinking once again of war. Then I will rise like a falcon upon the wind, recalling the horrors of total war out here in the East. Man's utter inhumanity to man. Some might listen and take heed.

"Destroy this letter after you have read it. Even your cottage upon the Heide can have ears.
Alles liebe immer, dein Heinrich."

A final half-hearted game of skat. Schultz's cards are found to be marked. Hiding behind Heyer he protests his innocence. To make his point clear he threatens to take on his accusers. An Engineer puts his name down. Heyer gets old Pyotr to make the sign of the cross over him with an ikon. If he comes out of the fighting alive he will need it.

Hansen and Steggeman and a few others are shoving copies of *Isvestia* into their boots. Someone has told them it will save them from frostbite and gangrene.

Thirty minutes to zero hour.

A new lieutenant introduces himself. Hatched on a short officers' course. He is taking over the scratch company.

"The name is Kurt Harpe. I came up the hard way through the ranks. I won't be behind you shouting you on. I'll be up front leading. Any questions."

Schultz burps loudly. All eyes turn towards him.
"Gesundheit."
Smiling the lieutenant takes two paces forward.
"Schultz."

"Your fame has traveled far," giggles Hansen.

"Come to greet you like a long-lost brother, he has."

316

Schultz comes to attention clicking his heels.

"Herr Leutnant."

"I hear you are musically inclined, Schultz."

"Grenadier Schultz begs the Herr Leutnant's . . ."

"Cut the crap. At ease. What's this I hear about you playing 'Lily Marlene' upon your wind section?"

Schultz straightened up once again, proud of his fame.

"Begging the Herr Leutnant's kind permission. Schultzy never does it before an attack. Bad for platoon nerves, it is. Save it for ivan, I do."

He leans forward slightly. His way of taking young lieutenants who show promise into his confidence.

"If the Herr Leutnant could see his way clear in stoking me up on half a bottle of vodka. Dortmunder beer. Or better still the good old Lunenburger brew. Well, like the fine Berlin Symphony Orchestra, I have not been idle. Been practicing, I have. How about the opening lines of 'Annemarie' for starters? A few bars from 'Soldaten Kameraden.' Or a rendition from that immortal classic, close to a soldier's heart, 'There's an old Ruski living on the hill. She won't do it but her sister will. Four times a day. Four times a day.' "

Leutnant Harpe cut the laughter with a wave of his hand.

"Later Schultz. I'll take you up on that offer."

Twenty-five minutes.

The *isba* is empty. Pyotr and Kadatskaya held the ikons, blessing each of them as they left. They shuffle through the village climbing aboard the waiting half-tracks. Panzer Mark Threes edge forward slowly. Here and there are Mark Twos, idiot boxes on tracks. The bright supply spark who invented them must have been pissed to the eyeballs, as the Americans say. Or maybe the Fuehrer was having that recurring trouble with his piles, as Hansen would say.

Twenty minutes.

Steam rises from beside the half-tracks. Nature calls at the oddest of times. Black-uniformed panzer men are doing the same.

Ten minutes.

Pushkin's voice comes from the silent nervous throng.

"*Verdammt noch mal!*" he cups his hands so that all can hear.

"I'll take the last call for the *Scheisshaus*, gentlemen, please. Adolf, our leader, says it's strictly *verboten* doing it on the march. You are out here to educate the masses. Out here in the East you must learn to behave. That goes for you naughty panzer men as well."

The laughter is drowned out by the noisy throb of racing engines. Panzer men did it in empty shell cases. Throwing them out through the hatches. Pity the Grenadiers huddling upon the back, Russian wind being as harsh as it was.

Five minutes.

The outline of the tall trees is becoming visible through the swirling mist. *Isbas* with their high-pitched thatched roofs. Outhouses made out of woven sunflower stalks. Smoke from the hot stoves going straight up. A dog howls. Or is it a wolf? A lament greeting the new dawn.

No speech. Perhaps telling of the might of the Wehrmacht about to be unleashed. But then maybe a scratch unit does not warrant such heroics. Or more to the point, who needs it? Those lectures have been heard so many times before.

A lone flare soars high into the crisp cold air.

Headsets crackle with static.

"Panzer leader. Forward."

The Mark Threes gather speed. One slews to the right, crashing into an *isba*. First of the casualties scream, silencing the excited chatter. Head-hunter post. They won't be missed. Mark Twos slip, regain traction, then speed out, following. Half-tracks swing in behind.

The wind's a killer. Rushing icy air. Thanks go out to Mutti for that extra scarf. Those socks. Those long johns that everyone laughs at. They come in handy now.

A Wehrmacht artillery barrage opens up far to the West. A diversionary shoot. The early morning sky throbs and glows. Bright reds and yellows dance, painting the clouds. Pulsing as though alive. A monster breathing with a breath of fire.

Storm units inch forward. Past Siberian guards with gaping cut throats. Maxim machine gun nests that are now manned by youths of the Wehrmacht. Surprising one bunker, drunken sleepers deep in fresh-smelling straw. Incompetent fools. They have slept with their boots off. Automatic weapons stutter. The straw comes alive with bloody writhing bodies. A Mongol reaches the door, saber slashing. He wounds two before a Schmeiser machine pistol stitches him across the chest.

Small arms fire. Hastily set up Spandaus. Bright tracer etched against the background of trees. Detonations of hand grenades sounding hollow in the deep snow.

Dawn peels the landscape. Trenches. In one place the front is less than thirty meters apart. Charging Wehrmacht troops. Knots of men fighting hand to hand. Rifles. Bayonets. Butts. The shouting becomes clearer.

Turret hatches are closed. Drivers brace themselves. Gunners hang on, gluing their eyes to the sighting mechanisms. Loaders stand ready. The ammo lockers are open. The panzers leap forward. Like '41. Only no dust. Storm unit tracer leads the way.

Ivan infantry have been beaten back from a high ridge. Their dead and dying cover the snow. They held the high ground to the last man and last bullet. Its importance must be in their manuals. In many places they had to be burnt out.

"Stick close to me when we go in," shouts Schmidt.

He places a reassuring hand upon Steggeman's shoulder.

"First off get that Spandau set up."

"Can I go home? I don't like the look of this," screams Hansen above the noise.

"It looks too easy—ivan's holding something back."

"Today the Lord has decreed that death will greet you. *Sieg heil* and kiss my . . ."

Heyer's words are drowned out by screaming panzer engines.

Schultz's blackened teeth show through the grin upon his face. He takes his last swig of vodka and passes the bottle to Schmidt.

The lead panzers wheel into line. Halt. Gloved loaders ram the shells into the breech. Commanders shout the range. All seems confusion to the gunner. So many live targets. Olive brown. Khaki. The storming grey green. All is excitement. Near insanity. Waiting to smite with the death wand.

"Edge of trees. Moving to right."

The gunner acknowledges, with a voice that no longer seems his own. Turret motor purrs. The landscape races. Ants, nothing but ants. A white, seemingly endless sheet. Then the trees. Mighty trees of Russia. An open-tracked carrier. Fur-capped heads are visible in the back. All seem to be sitting neatly to attention. Sometimes in war the details are startlingly clear and will haunt.

Kick in the back.

"Fire."

Sighting mechanism blacks out. Empty shell case rattles to the floor smoking. Ears are popping. Choking smoke curls away from the breech. It assaults the eyes and mouth. The sight clears. Target. Dead on. One troop carrier on its side blazing furiously. Blackening smudge in the snow. There are arms moving out there. Legs thrashing. Spandau chatters. Puffs of snow rise like dust. Bodies are ripped apart. Arms and legs move no more. The snow takes on a new color.

Kick in the back.

"Left. Left."

No longer is it a training session at Sennelager or Munster. Where the targets popped up and were cut down with ease. Where the first detonation of the main armament tightened the guts. Out here it is move, *schnell*. Or no longer will you live to tell the tale. Speed. Speed. Out there, there are Paks just waiting to zero in.

"T.34."

That first sight tears at the bowels. So many tales you have heard. The Wehrmacht has nothing to touch it. Only later will the Tigers and Panthers equal it in the field. Beautiful monsters. Answer to a panzer man's dream. A gunner's delight. Such fire power. The gunner like a *Gott* in an iron casket. Only sheer weight of numbers beat them in the end.

The turret spins. Never quick enough. The loader rams an armor piercing shell home. T.34 shows in the sight. The shot will have to be perfect. Heavy sloping armor could cause a ricochet. Shell roaring off harmlessly into the trees.

Turret ring. Turret ring. Weakest point. Hands sweat. It's urine running down the legs. Hot. Warm. Comforting. Have no fear, it happens to the best of them. The lines in the sighting mechanism meet.

"Fire."

Blackness envelops the sight. Ears ring as though burning. In those few seconds the panzer is most vulnerable. He could get a shot away. That's all he needs, those few split seconds. Then all is at an end. Nothing but screams in the white-hot inferno.

Shout of the driver. It's holed. Loader slams another shell in. Fire. Away it goes again. Pause. Blood throbbing at the ears and temple. Cheers from the others in the crew. Sight clears. Flames belch from the T.34's turret. Two of the leather-helmeted crewmen are running. Spandau marks the snow behind them. No race from death can outpace it. It catches them crawling up an embankment. Pounds them into the snow. Never again will they see their home village.

Gunter spit into the Elbe at Bleckede. You and I know that only eight per cent of the panzer men came back. Daydream of the times you bailed out. Flames roasting your *Aschloch*. Laugh with that dry cackle of yours when I come to visit. But do not forget. Never again must the youth of the nation go to war. Let politicians rant and shout. They have not known the sweat of a fighting compartment. The thunder of T.34 tracks as they race over the snow, eagerly crushing the burning panzer survivors.

The Panzer Mark Twos come into their own. Machine guns hammer relentlessly.

Ivan Landser are among the bravest infantry to

walk the earth. Fighting upon the soil of the Motherland. Soaked in vodka before the fight. Thoughts of Mother Russia throb in their heads. The peasant soldier becomes a fighting maniac. To sacrifice their life. It is a tradition. There are no thoughts of self. There is only little Mother Russia weeping. A village. Yellow flames coloring the billowing smoke. Children and mothers knelt in prayer. It is his village. His folk. His Motherland. Only sheer bloody slaughter will stop him. The all-consuming rage in his breast will burn until the very last moment.

Ten ivans attack the line of Mark Twos with mines. At the very last moment they rise from the snow in their long white snow capes. Only three make it. Landser Mausers cut the others down. Two Mark Twos go up in smoke. The crew escape from one. The other crew is burnt alive. Landser tries to free them. The heat is too intense. Above the noise of battle there are the screams. Fire sucks and plays at the turret. From the white-hot hell the screams go on, never ending. Such is the fate of the black-uniformed panzer men.

If you have known the fight, battle in all its sickening ferocity, part of the very soul dies out there upon that steppe. Never again will you willingly seek the company of man. He is a vile and loathsome creature. Something to be shunned for the rest of your life. You will crave only the birds and animals of the glade. The solace of the forest. Nature. Where the creatures of *Gott* do not hunt and stalk for the pleasure of it. A never-ending search for peace and harmony.

High-explosive shells pound away at the ivan bunkers. Some Siberians, wiry, stocky little men, make it to the trees. Once there they dig themselves in within seconds and continue the fight. Russian Maxims cut into the lines of grey green. The field is seeded with crying, whimpering, dying youth.

Panzer headsets crackle. The war like a forest fire storms ahead. There is no time to count the cost of the carnage. The fight must go on.

"Panzer leader. Large group of T.34s sighted at next village. Use the forest track," comes from the air radio link.

"I say disengage. Advance to new position."

Most of the panzers break contact. Like heavy cavalry monsters they wheel about throwing up clouds of snow. Going back to the road. Several mounted Grenadiers fall to small arms fire. Unable to avoid them the Mark Twos run them down. Boots, arms and legs redden the tracks. One Grenadier sits trying to hug his crushed legs. A thrashing track chews, spewing out the grisly remains. The helmeted head bobs away grinning, staining the snow.

An older Landser stops awestricken. An explosive bullet tears his face away. A *Kamerade* bends down to assist. Two explosive bullets hit him in the back. He dies with the lost look of youth painting his young face. Eyes staring into that grey foreboding sky.

Some Siberians have thrown their weapons away. They stand in small isolated groups, hands up resting on the backs of their necks. Landser collect them, prodding them to the rear.

"Dismount!" Schmidt's voice is hardly heard above the sound of battle.

The half-tracks have swung into the shelter of the tall pines. Most jump clear. Three fall to Maxim machine gun fire. Medics go to them. Two die propped against the tracks. Blood freezes. Later they will be hard to move.

Already the third Grenadier is rambling on about his hills in Bavaria. Thick-accented speech. The hand of his dead *Kamerade* is clasped in his. Morphine helps. Blood pulses from his mouth. The face is ashen.

He sobs gently. Thirsty. He wants to drink.

"Just a drop," he begs.

His left hand is at his stomach. Blood oozes between the fingers. It seems black against the snow.

"*Wasser, bitte.* I'm burning up."

"*Los.* Move."

The eyes have lingered before they bound off. Two medics cut his trousers away. The red of the entrails against the white of the flesh.

Four log bunkers upon a small rise. Flames spit from the apertures. They squirm forward through the deep snow. Like swimming. Hard frost on top. Bullets hiss and plop. Whine away into the trees.

Lieutenant Harpe taps Heyer upon the shoulder.

"*Los.*"

Heyer fires. The flame from his flamethrower snakes out blackening the snow. Blobs of flame hiss cascading about the bunker. Answering screams. It is not a pleasant way to go. Heat shrinks the human form. A head becomes like a burnt apple. The revolting smell assails the nostrils.

"Next," Schmidt barks.

Heyer adjusts the flame. It licks forward with a deadly whooshing sound. A hellish cry. Finger of death.

Four ivans run berserk. Flaming, they run blind, hands clawing at their faces. Mauser fire hits them. They tumble. Flames seem blue covering their faces. Arms move, digging at the snow. Always on the Eastern Front there was the urge to dig. To become part of the earth. Only way of escape from the torment. Even a tortured brain will remember. Renewed fire stills the twitching.

At the third bunker none run clear. They fight unto death. Only the unearthly wailing echoes out over the snow wastes. Mortar ammunition explodes. The whole emplacement goes up. Bulging before their eyes. The displacement of air rolls over them sucking at their lungs.

Schmidt charges ahead spraying a trench from the hip. He pauses at a half-crouch, changing the magazine on his submachine gun. Schultz and Hansen work their way down the trench, Steggeman and Muller close behind. Small arms fire crashes out. Unmistakably ivan. Heyer is waved forward. The heat from the flamethrower is unbearable. For several moments he is lost from view. Then six burning torches run decorating the parapet. A burst of submachine gun fire finishes them off.

The trench is secured. *Zigaretten* are passed around. Vodka from Schultz's water bottle.

Again the steam rises from Steggeman.

"Don't give him any. Vodka's only for them who know how to hold it," laughs Hansen.

Steggeman snatches the bottle and tilts it back. He almost chokes himself.

"That's not vodka. What is it?"

Schultz looks on innocently.

"Virgin's piss from the streets of Moscow. Ninety-eight percent proof."

From the snow field come strangulated screams. A group of Siberian prisoners have throttled their two Landser escorts. They make a run for the tree line. The command Panzer Mark Three gives chase, its tracks churning up the snow. A Hauptman is shouting orders from the open turret.

Some of the Siberians give up, hands held high. The panzer ploughs them down. Two kneel in the snow wringing their hands in prayer. Smoke coming from its exhaust, the panzer wheels about. For them there is no escape. The tracks hit them. Snow turns to blood-red slush.

From the pine trees a Russian Pak opens up. A dull cough on the cold morning air. A pall of smoke drifts lazily away from the trees. The command Mark Three blows up. The impact of the shot seems to lift it from the snow. Smoke gushing from every rivet. Like the shaking of summer steppe dust. Another shot seals its fate. Only the driver is seen to escape.

"Over there." Steggeman is feeding the Spandau. Muller directs a deadly fire into the trees.

Supporting ivan infantry return the fire. Almost invisible in the blanket of snow. A half-track with the wounded is hit. Screaming they crawl away from the blazing wreck. Explosive rifle bullets pick them off. Only two make it to a nearby trench, life leaking away from them, leaving a trail of red over the snow.

"Cover!" Lieutenant Harpe is out of the trench and running at the tree line.

Mausers aided by Muller's Spandau keep the ivan heads down. Yards away from the trees he throws himself down. He lobs stick grenades. The deafening explosions strip the trees. Blue-black smoke stands out against the white of the snow. Hansen, Schultz and Heyer charge. Not a whimper greets them. Ivan dead like so many spent rags. Not a movement. All faces are mashed and pulped. Only several pairs of eyes are seen to stare accusingly from what have obviously been young faces.

Muller and Steggeman bound into the trees. Schultz and Heyer are sitting upon some bodies rolling *Zigaretten*. Muller and Steggeman vomit. After a while some get used to it. Others never do.

Schultz's doctored vodka makes the rounds. Hansen lingers too long. Schultz grabs at him roughly, shaking him by the shoulders.

"Runt. I said take a swig. Not kill the whole bottle."

"*Danke*. Sweat's pouring off me," gasps Hansen.

Steggeman wipes his mouth, taking the bottle.

"Join the clan."

Shrill Feldwebel whistles sound from over the snow field.

The panzers have moved on. Four were knocked out. They soon became blazing-white hot hulks. A fifth has a blown track. Suicide attack. A Siberian with bunched grenades. Despite the mauser fire directed at him, he made the shelter of the trees.

"Back to the carriers. Mount up."

"No times to finish our smokes. What a way to run a war."

"Move it, Hansen. That goes for you as well, Schultz."

There is still the sound of battle. Isolated pockets of ivans still refusing to give up. The following Landser will make a clean sweep. Shouts of command. Stray shots still finding victims.

Schmidt pulls Hansen aboard the carrier.

Muller and Schultz help Heyer off with the flamethrower. Lieutenant Harpe had noticed that it was leaking. First time it has happened. It is thrown in a trench. Automatic fire rips it apart. The pack explodes with a rushing roar.

"Had your number on it, did it," laughs Hansen.

"Cheap shit. Made in Poland, it was," Schultz playfully jabbed Heyer in the ribs.

"Was close," added Muller.

"It was that Lord of yours calling you. He saw that you was all cleanly shaved and ready to go." Heyer clipped Steggeman, knocking his helmet off.

"Forward."

The half-tracks circled back to the road.

The radio crackled, seeming to fight the heavy frost. The panzers had run into more ivan infantry dug in at a *kolkhos*.

Lieutenant Harpe grabbed the hand mike.

"We hear you, Panzer leader. Am proceeding as instructed."

A wing of Stukas flew over at tree-top level.

"Flyboys. That's the way to go," shouted Steggeman.

"Drop your load, then back to the billet for breakfast."

"And their Ukrainian bits," Hansen made the well-known gesture with his right arm.

"In an hour they'll be snug and warm, a Ruski tart's legs wrapped around them."

The Stukas climbed away to the right. One after another they peeled off, their sirens blaring. They came up again far beyond the trees, like graceful birds with their bent wings, then turned, soaring in again for a low-level attack.

A group of black dots appeared upon the tracks. Bunched, like a herd of animals.

The air radio link came to life.

"You have partisans to your immediate front. Intercept."

Twin-mounted Spandaus began firing. The black dots broke up, making for the trees. Some were hit. Their comrades dragged their wounded with them.

Twenty half-tracks slewed to a halt.

"Dismount."

Platoons tumbled out of the carriers, some running at the double down the side of the track, others going into the forest. Running through the snow soon bathes the body in sweat.

Schmidt threw himself down beside Muller. Steggeman was busy loading the Spandau. Shots from the partisans were going wide.

"Amateurs." Heyer spat with disgust.

"Keep your heads down," shouted Lieutenant Harpe.

"Might be some Ruski tarts out there," said Hansen hopefully. "My front piece is getting nervous. It's a good sign. Raring to go, it is."

Heavy Maxim machine gun fire sent them sprawling and hugging the snow.

Schmidt was looking through his binoculars. He passed them to Muller.

"Some of them look twelve or thirteen years old."

Heyer cackled, staying low in the snow.

"Getting cold feet, are we?"

"Watch your tongue. Some of us here don't enjoy killing."

"Getting fussy, are we Muller? A twelve-year-old can kill you as good as any Siberian."

Lieutenant Harpe turned on his side, looking back at them.

"Will you two shut up? That's an order."

A Feldwebel's whistle blew. From all around them Grenadiers rose, running forward. Steggeman went to move, gathering his belt of Spandau ammunition together.

"Not us!" Schmidt lunged out at him. "We move on the next whistle. We move through them."

Hansen grinned at the others.

"It's like I said. Adolf's running this war from the top floor of a brothel in Frederichstrasse. Got right frisky, he has, since his last piles operation. Too much for poor Eva. Had to farm him out, she did."

"Too much for her, was he?" asked Schultz.

"Nah, *ja*. Wanting it all the time he was. You know them little cuckoo clocks they make in Bavaria. Had an alarm fixed on one he did. Had it every other hour on the hour."

"Right Prussian gentleman. Does that as well by numbers, does he?" Steggeman wanted to know.

"*Ja*. It's *los, eins, zwei, drei. . . .*"

A shrill command whistle sounded.

Lieutenant Harpe looked over at Hansen.

"With your kind permission, Grenadier Hansen. May we continue the war?"

Hansen grinned.

"Might as well, Herr Leutnant. Me old prunes are sagging a bit. If we lay about here much longer they might drop off."

"Right. *Los*. Move out."

They surged forward into the trees. Partisan rifle fire whipped about them. Several fell groaning, clutching chests and stomachs.

Chapter 19
NIKOLAI, WOLF OF THE FOREST

Once again I have partaken of too much vodka. A habit, dear child, acquired in youth, upon the cruel steppes of Russia. Trick is to sip yourself slowly into insensibility. War. Smoke. Feldwebel's whistles. Cries of terror that will not fade. A music pulsing from that far-off land. Songs from drunken lips. *Soldats* who are no longer here. Screams that once again sound, in the still of this night. Here it is four in the morning. Milk trucks are rolling in the streets. You sleep so warm and snug. I must remember.

The Russian Front. To you nothing but words. Empty words with little meaning. To others they kindle a nightmare constantly relived. Eyes that will haunt with the passing of time. A lonely track full of puddles and spring mud. Children. Cheeks that were once rosy with health. Ragged flotsam of war. Where are they now? It was the time when teenagers in field grey knew the madness.

A plane bound for London, Hamburg, Paris or New York. It is enough to awaken the light sleeper from his sweat-soaked sleep. Peace will only come with death. One day the glands will refuse to function. Rest will be eternal.

Stray cats my constant companions. Through them the living memory of mighty Mother Russia breathes once again. Novosil. Plavaskoi. She will never forget. Ravisher of the land. *Soldat* of the field-grey legions. There will be no peace in this life. Only those cursed memories.

When the wind howls and blows I shut my eyes. It is familiar voices I can hear. *Kameraden* that no longer smile and joke. Leaving me haunted and alone to face these endless nights.

"*Bitte melden*. Panzer *Gruppe* will advance."

And how the sounds of those thrashing tracks still manage to fascinate.

Bedrolls are being stowed aboard. All are bombed up. There is H.E. in the breech. Spandau loaders he reports, are cocked and ready. Huts. Poverty-stricken abodes come into view. Another village the yellow dust billowing up. Choking smoke biting at the eyes. You are nearly eighteen and already a seasoned infamous killer. Ivan infantry. More ants clustered in the telescopic sights. Scythe them down. Rest Spandaus. H.E. Singing in the turret. Drunken songs to wash away the dreadful monontony of continuing death. Humanity torn apart. More blue black smoke. Target clears. Again. Machine gun bullets cut them down. Will it never end? Can man ever be forgiven?

Old man with your scarred hands. Death and destruction once at your fingertips. Eastern Front where you became of age. Starved. Froze. Cried like a child with the insanity of it all. You are a fool. Vodka-soaked idiot. Weep. No man will listen. They are too busy talking of the new war. Already the eager shining faces of youth are lined up.

Why do the ragged children of the villages constantly come to mind? Through those eons of time. Refugees. That sorrowful cry that causes the heart to jump, when sleep will not come. She will never forget. No land can blanket one from the torment.

"*Khleb. Khleb*."

Only vodka helps. The Cossacks knew that.

Villages where now there are only monuments. Stone effigies. Where in the summer you will stop with your young Intourist guide, and place the flowers. That quiet place with the son in his father's arms. S.S. reprisal action. All the villagers herded into the barn. Set afire with gasoline. The partisan father returning. His young son dying in his arms. That large statue stands there for all to see. Tall. Gaunt. Pointing to the sky. Never to be forgotten.

Place the flowers for the young ones. The sprigs of birch. Anna. Murushka. Niki. Marisha. Others whose eyes once knew laughter. Place them for me. That other brutal reminder will come from the October factory in Stalingrad. Volgagrad. Who knows what *Kameradens'* bones will soon be bared to the late summer sun. Blackened teeth that take thousands of years to disintegrate. Once again they will smile as the *kolkhos* fields are ploughed. War. Total all-out war. Man's ultimate stupidity. To have known it. To have glimpsed the madness.

Besoffen. Old fool that I am. All my tears are spent. Thousands have been forgotten.

Photos. I look at all the old photos that were secreted away in the P.O.W. camps. Manheim, that clearing house where the Americans chewed their gum. Stern-faced youth with full cheeks. Faces of *Kameraden* become clear. Some had survived. Where are they now?

Besoffen. The story it will have to wait. I am going to hit the sack.

Viktor rode his sweating stallion into the partisan forest village. The outer guards of a Siberian rifle company awakened the partisans.

Big-bearded Grigori took Marisha's already stiffened body to Nikolai at the nurses' hut.

He broke down under the harsh glare from the oil lanterns. Tears flowing down his cheeks, he pressed her marblelike face against his.

"Marisha. Marisha. My little dove."

The young nurses from Moscow tried to comfort him. He shrugged their hands aside. For long minutes none dared to touch him. He brushed the snow from her hair.

Behind him the partisan camp had come alive. Maxim machine guns were broken apart. Barrels strapped to one pony. Wheels to another. The mortars that would bring cringing terror, wherever their shells fell.

He felt Anna's, his sister's, hand upon his shoulder. Her slight body was shaking with rage.

"Green lice must pay, Nikolai."

"*Da*," his lips went to Marisha's cheek.

The commissar came into the hut protesting.

"Nikolai I forbid it. We are not ready for attack. Orders from Moscow. They state. . . ."

With a hefty clenched fist Grigori sent him sprawling.

"Is that what they teach in Moscow? The state first. Home village no matter? It is *our* village that you talk of. The people who suffer are of *our* blood. They know not the rules of the leaders safe in Moscow. A stout Russian heart bleeds for revenge."

He turned towards a fur-coated Siberian Red Army lieutenant. "Are you with us, *gospodin* leytenant? Or would you listen to the talk of our political commissar?"

The lieutenant grinned, scratching his head.

"My place is with the partisans. My men will join you."

Nikolai's mind swam dizzily. His little dove Marisha was dead. The face. Wind from the door ruffled her hair. Her shoulder and chest were matted with congealed blood. Her voice had held such promise. How she had babbled so excitedly of going to the fine academy in the city. Such a voice. Now it was stilled forever. No longer would it echo through the quiet glades of the forest. Or in the pastures where the cows grazed.

Zofia. His woman Zofia still under guard with the black beetles in the schoolhouse. When Viktor's heaving chest was stilled, after the vodka, he had spoken of the gallows. He would not let it end this way. A fast ride through the forest would save the rest of the family. A partisan attack before dawn.

Two Free French Airmen who had flown ammunition and supplies into the new landing strip refused to fly out again.

"*Mon ami. Nyet. Cherie Marisha.* She reminded us of *la belle France.*" They struggled with their broken Russian.

"Monsieur. We come with you to the old village."

The commissar exploded once again, smashing his fist down hard upon the table.

"You fly with the Red Airforce. You are under strict orders from Moscow." He turned glaring at them.

"We are Frenchmen first, *mon ami,*" one of them growled threateningly. "The war in the air can wait."

Nikolai laid Marisha's body upon one of the bunks. A nurse covered her eyes. Nikolai ripped the blanket away.

"Do not cover the eyes of my little dove," he cursed.

The nurse jumped back in alarm.

"She must know of the vengeance that will soon be ours."

The Siberian lieutenant spread his field map out over the table.

"My Siberians will cut the road out of the village," he smiled, jabbing his pencil at the map.

"No Germanski will get by the Siberians, Nikolai."

Nikolai straightened up wiping his eyes.

"No prisoner will be shot." His eyes narrowed.

Svetlana pushed her way through the crowd.

"Little Father Nikolai. Would you save the necks of the green lice?" she spat.

336

"*Nyet*, little sister. All will be kept at the old village. They will be put to death at the scene of their crimes."

Germanic cries of terror came from the prisoners' hut. Haughty rage-filled taunting laughter. Death rattles as the throats were cut. Many times Nikolai had stopped the brutality before. Now he did not stop it.

Grigori came back into the nurses' hut.

"Lice," he was grinning.

"They died slowly."

He wiped his bloody long knife.

"Pigs," he spat at the stove.

"They were planning to escape. I, big Grigori, understand their thoughts. Was I not a prisoner of theirs at Darnitsa, where the fascist made us beg for food like dogs?"

On the trail in the forest the Siberians rode ahead of the partisans. Soon dawn would come. They would spring the trap as only Siberian woodsmen could. No Hilfeswillige S.S. or black Ukrainian beetle would escape. For the black beetles there would be a special ending. Had Moscow not decreed it so?

Viktor rode beside Nikolai. He could only think of his beloved Tanya. How the two S.S. had dragged her by her feet. Nikolai had promised that the two turncoats would be his. First there would be the cutting out of their tongues, the vile instruments that had spread terror throughout the great Motherland. Then he would take their eyes out with his father's blacksmiths irons. Nikolai had promised.

Always Nikolai had feared the sudden coming of the green lice before the new forest village was ready. The commissar had insisted. The landing strip had to be finished. Orders from Moscow. From the lips of Stalin himself. Only then could the villagers move. Supply lines had to be established. In their plush state apartments in Moscow they had forgotten the ways of the villages. What did they care. Their families were safe. The Motherland war to them was but marks upon the maps.

Slowly the trees were becoming visible. Dawn was but minutes away. He spurred his mount faster.

"Heya. Heya. Davia."

The call went down the column of fast-moving riders.

At dawn, the boy Viktor had said. Maybe the green lice would not be so punctual after their drunken orgy with the young maidens. Germanski efficiency. Was it not their byword? Did they not pride themselves on it?

Marisha would be buried beside the new hut in the forest. Made of stout logs, it would keep the winter out. Zofia would hang the old lace curtains. Izabella would find a place for the ikons. Semyan, the broad steps had been made for him. When spring came he would sit there smoking his clay pipe. All would be well once again. But Marisha, she . . .

As they came upon the frozen river bed, they heard, carried upon the wind, the wailing of the village women. He knew it was too late. Grigori, Anna, Svetlana and some of the other partisans began to fire from the saddle. They thought the shooting might stay Germanski's hand.

Wheeling in under the trees they dismounted. Maxims and mortars were set up. Shells whining away within minutes as the Siberians had so expertly taught them. Over the rooftops they could see the village. All the people were drawn up in front of the logged-in well. An S.S. had been talking to them from a tracked troop carrier. Always they had to make their speeches. Their new Germanic law for the occupied lands.

Partisan fire sent the villagers and S.S. scurrying for cover.

"Tovaritch."

338

Grigori tapped him upon the shoulder, passing the field glasses. The scowling look upon the bearded face. He knew what he was about to see. Forever it would remain imprinted upon his mind. Three bodies hanging from the gallows. Semyan's legs were still treading air. Izabela's head twitched grotesquely to one side. Zofia. His woman. The eyes were staring. Up the hillside to the forest. She knew they would come. His Zofia. Blue, her tongue hung from her mouth.

In blind frenzied rage he ran down the hill, firing from the hip. Two S.S. keeled over. He fired again at the kicking limbs and animal screaming.

Other partisans broke cover. The limp figures upon the gallows. All thoughts of danger were lost. Only Russian revenge beat at their chests. Some fell to Spandau machine gun fire. The rest came on shouting like maddened bulls. The first *isbas* were gained. Mortar and Maxim machine gun fire moved ahead of them, like a brush sweeping the wide village street.

Two tracked troop carriers sped away, mortar fire leaping after them. One black beetle fell over the side. Maxim fire ground his screaming hulk to pieces, staining the snow.

Under the onslaught the main body of S.S. retreated to the red brick house of the village soviet. Grigori and Viktor by his side, Nikolai ran to the gallows. Holy Mother of Kazan. Let there be life. The thought locked in his brain. The bodies were cut down. Zofia and Izabela were dead. Semyan died within seconds of rescue, without recognizing the partisans.

Nikolai fell across Zofia's body. Fresh S.S. rifle fire pounded at the wood of the gallows. Grigori ran back to the *isbas*, taking charge of the attack.

"Green lice helpers. Alive I want them," Nikolai hissed through his tears.

"Marisha as well," he spoke to the dead Zofia, sobbing aloud.

A black beetle had been captured. Two of his comrades were taken with him. One was battered to death with rifle butts. The other they tied to an *isba* fence. Anna unscrewed the cap from a hand grenade, shoving it into the front of his tunic. He screamed until the explosion ripped him apart.

Lev Sheinin and Svetlana led the last remaining black beetle away. They took him around to the side of the Kurochkins' *isba*. Out of the line of S.S. rifle fire. Someone had stripped him of his trousers.

Svetlana took the *machorka* from Lev with a shaking hand. She drew deeply upon the foul-smelling rolled cigarette.

"Naked they made my little Wanda dance in the snow. Beg, black beetle." She prodded him in the stomach with her long bayonet.

He fell to his knees, fear-crazed eyes rolling.

"Little sister. Have pity. Germanski forced us to fight," he begged cupping his hands together in prayer.

"Forest. You could run away," shouted Lev.

"He would kill us all. You know the way of Germanski. Wives. Children. He spares no one."

Svetlana walked up to the cringing figure. She brought her rifle butt down hard into his face. Sobbing she kept lunging at his face.

"Tell me of the works of our beloved Pushkin," she rasped. "Speak to me of our steppes in summer. Children laughing and picking the yellow flowers. Say the words pig. Like my Wanda did far into the hours of that cold long night."

The black beetle drew his legs up, crouching together in a tight ball.

"*Millosti,*" he begged of the other watching stern partisan faces. "I know nothing of them. I drove a tram in Kiev. What do I know of the man Pushkin."

Taking his rifle in both hands Lev struck at the hated face.

"Tell me how Jewish children cried when you threw them in the big trucks. When you lined them up before the logs at the shooting pits."

"I want to hear you beg, black beetle." Svetlana jabbed her bayonet into his stomach.

Blood oozed over the groping hands.

He tried to twist the rifle from her grasp. Another older partisan kicked him. The rifle went off. A dum-dum bullet gouged at his stomach. He curled up pawing at the snow. His legs kicking.

"*Millosti.* I have a wife and children in Kiev. I kill no Jews. *Nyet.* No Russian girls."

Lev and Svetlana fired together. The body bucked, the legs still thrashing. Another partisan made as if to shoot him in the back of the neck with a pistol. Svetlana knocked him roughly aside.

"Did you not see the body of little Marisha? And Nikolai's family upon the gallows? Would you not want him to suffer, for the deaths you have seen this day?"

Looking guilty the partisan backed off. The eyes of those around him followed him.

"All green lice helpers must die slow. Pain in the belly that will take them to their devil's hell."

"*Da,*" Lev worked the bolt on his rifle.

"Come Sveta. There are more lice at the village soviet."

"*Da,*" she spat at the face twisted in pain.

"Tie the pig to the fence and turn the village dogs upon him."

"It shall be done little sister," two old *babushkas* began to pull the screaming body towards an *isba* fence.

Only scattered sporadic shots were coming from the house of the village soviet. Not hearing the shooting,

341

Nikolai was rocking to and fro, Zofia in his arms. First it was their Marisha, little dove. Now his woman Zofia. The old ones, Izabela and Semyan. His parents. Life was at an end. Now there was only the war. The fight against the Germanski hordes. A battle that would take him to the very gates of Berlin.

"Come." The wise one Dyakov was kneeling by his side. "Siberians. They come back with prisoners, Nikolai."

The words had no meaning to him. He was thinking of the days long before the great Motherland war. Of Zofia. That bright blue headscarf from the market at Kharkov. Courting. The shy Zofia. Eyes that turned a strong forest man to water. Walking in the forest. The first touching of the hands. How as a young man he would run ahead, finding the flowers under the trees for her. His gentle Zofia. Now she breathed no more. Already the face was blue.

Marisha. Even at an early age all the villagers were struck by the lilting beauty of her voice. They longed to hear the child sing. At weddings. At the Easter festivities. Nights before the stove in the depths of winter. Voice of a frail young child. Such a special child. His little dove. Those eyes were the eyes of her mother. Though her songs could bring tears, a fire glowed there, the same as in Zofia's eyes.

She had wanted so much to see the city of Kharkov. The wise one had told her so much about it. One day, he had told her, we will go there by troika. Her eyes had glowed. He could see her so clearly—the way she had the habit of tossing her head. She gave so much to life. Expected so little in return. A true young maiden of the forest.

"*Mamushka* will plait my hair. We will take the heavy blankets. Dyakov says it is a great distance from here. But they will hear us coming. Viktor's father the blacksmith has made me some little bells. I will fix them to the troika. *Da*, they will hear us from afar over the snows. . . ."

He had ruffled her hair.

"They will say it is Marisha. The child with the voice."

He choked upon his sobbing.

A partisan shook him by the arm.

"Little Father Nikolai."

How Marisha had taken the new children of the village to her heart. Niki and his brothers. Roman and Mikhial. Such a sensitive child she was. Even the tragic death of the stray kitten had left its mark upon her for days.

When she sang the fury of war seemed to stop. For just moments there were only thoughts of peace. Sunlit meadows. A smiling Mother Russia. The land would be free. Young ones walking hand in hand. Spring, the time of the pairing. Like the birds of the forest. Now it was over.

"Six prisoners we have, Nikolai. Many tried to run away. My men shot them down like dogs," the Siberian lieutenant grinned.

"One troop carrier with S.S. got away. But have no fear, there will be other days."

The villagers were coming forward paying their respects to the dead. Crossing themselves and mumbling their prayers.

"S.S. are Western Ukrainians," the Siberian lieutenant spat at them with disgust.

"Volunteers for Germanski."

Nikolai rose from the dead bodies. His family had perished. Much more suffering would come from the great Motherland war. The S.S. men were beaten and bruised.

Viktor came to him with the blond-haired Tanya and

the small Borochkin girl. They told him what had happened to the young maidens with plaited hair, in the village soviet's house.

He signaled to Grigori and Dyakov the wise one. In spite of his tragic grief, once again he was Nikolai, the little father. The forest partisan leader. The war must continue to be waged.

"Lead the villagers to the new huts in the forest," he barked.

"Father Nikolai," little Niki edged closer taking his hand.

Roman and Mikhial were also with him.

"Our Marisha, *papushka* Nikolai."

He felt the rage once again welling within him. He shrugged the boys off, nodding to the wise one.

"The new children will lead the milk cows." He turned away from the boys, the tears flowing down his cheeks.

"*Davia. Davia,*" he shouted at an old couple taking one last look at the *kolkhos*.

"Green lice. They will return."

"These monsters." Svetlana stood beside young Lev, her bloody long bayonet in her right hand dripping blood into the snow.

"Viktor's promised one says they were the demons in the red brick house."

His sister Anna's hand tightened upon his shoulder.

He looked into the terrified young Ukrainian youths' faces. They were not much older than the blacksmith's son Viktor. Two were crying like children. One was upon his knees. Another took Tanya's hand in his, kissing it. Viktor struck at him brutally with his rifle butt.

The winter sun broke through the clouds.

"Would our *papushka* Nikolai spare them?" Svetlana cried. "It is for the men to give them to the women."

Another of the S.S. men fell to his knees gibbering insanely.

"The givers of life should deal with them."

Other partisans were packing the dead bodies of his family upon pack ponies. Gently they moved them as though they were made of fragile china.

"*Da*," Nikolai waved his arm.

"Are these the devils who forced themselves upon the young maidens?"

Tanya nodded, clawing at the nearest S.S. face.

"Peg them out," Nikolai snapped.

Viktor forgot Nikolai's earlier promise. He passed Tanya his long bayonet.

"When the women have finished the bodies will be left here to rot."

Svetlana, the Borochkin girl and Tanya moved towards the S.S. men.

"Fire the village. Nothing will be left for Germanski."

"*Nyet. Nyet.*"

Foaming at the mouth one of the Ukrainian S.S. men broke free from the watching crowd. He was caught by young Lev. Grigori and Viktor stripped him. Others fastened them spread-eagled to the pegs in the snow.

The strains of the wise one's accordion floated over the horrifying scene.

As the screams echoed down the length of the valley, again the sun broke free from the clouds. It touched the chimney of the red brick house of the village soviet. And the watching blackbirds of the forest flew away. They always did that when Germanski or the helpers of the green lice began to sing.

Chapter 20
LOS. UP ON YOUR FEET

Sharp angry chatter of automatic weapons. Blinding white tracer from Spandau machine guns. Head-splitting cannonades from continuous field artillery. Trees in the forest stripped of all growth, scorched, swaying like burnt matchsticks. At times an unholy heat that rolls over the line, coming near to suffocating.

Many *Soldaten* lie screaming dotting the snow, twigs, dirt, snow. They cram it crazily into their mouths. Bundles of bloody rags. Madness stalks that shattered landscape.

A lull. A quiet when the ears and eyes will still throb. Smoke will drift away. One. Two. Four Landser run insane, mausers firing high into the air. They stagger towards ivan's lines. Reason is lost. Their tortured minds push them on. Forward. Forward. They fall under a devastating salvo from ivan's grenade launchers.

It was a day when no clouds could be seen. Both sides threw everything they had at a few square kilometers of that hateful soil. Thousands died in the hell. Nightmare of choking, flaming smoke and endless dust.

The Wehrmacht advance of three days had been blunted. Only ammunition and replacements got through. Recruits, their training only a matter of weeks near Romny. How proudly they marched up through the fire-gutted, smoldering villages. Voices of youth raised in a chorus of *Sieg Heils*. Song before the storm.

Those first barrages of Stalin Organs had them whimpering like sick deranged animals. No fire devised by nature could compare. They pawed and clawed at the frozen snow until their fingers ran red with blood. No time for breaking them in gently. The Eastern Front would devour them. Licking its lips as that cruel harsh wind howled in over the steppe. Chuckling as massive trees splintered. Ancient devils of Mother Russia dancing with glee. Your days are numbered, Germanski. The land must be cleansed. And the new cannon fodder died in evenly spaced rows of grey green.

"*Los*. Odd numbers. Up on your feet. Forward. *Schnell*."

Feldwebel command whistles rend the air. The shouting of Lieutenants. That fateful step. That leap into often dreamt of Germanic manhood. No glory there like in the books. Brave smiling blond heroes. Only the flow of hot urine, dear child. Vile, watery excretion. Smell that would linger for days. Lice still bite. And such a tightness in the throat, it came near to throttling.

As one they surge forward. A mass of charging unbroken grey green. Order is an order. This is the reward taught back home in the Fatherland. Fear. Horror. There is no time to fully comprehend. This is what you sang about in the ranks of the Hitler Jugend. Those summer days. In that other far-off land. Where there always seemed to be sunshine. *Soldaten*. *Kameraden*. This is the Eastern Front firestorm. The days for singing and the goose step of the parade march are over. This is the life in the line. Hell on earth. War as it has always been. Death. Mutilated bodies. Heads smashed to pulp. A terror-stricken insane *Kamerade* scuttling away on all fours. If this is glory, dear brother, you can have it.

Into the very mouth of murderous Maxim machine

gun fire. How slow it sounds to the fast Spandau. *Da. Da.* How it seems to talk. *Da. Da. Da.* Come, Germanski. Another few steps. Come fascist pig. Come. *Da. Da. Da.* Here.

Death does not come instantly for some, as was so often written in the field letters back home. In Mother Russia there is always the suffering. Has it not always been so? Each invader has known that. Wounded fall. Groveling, wincing with pain. Leg. Arm. Eye. Gut.

On their own. So alone. From the snowdrifts they whine. Trying to call above the sound of raging battle. Last resting place. *Mein Gott*, how that realization pounds home. If you have lain with the whimpering wounded and dying you know what I mean. Names hang mocking in the cold air. Margreta. Brunhilde. Ingrid. Helga.

Arms now weak paw at the bloody snow. Names so familiar, sounding strangely out of place upon the hostile killing ground. Who listens? Many have heard those calls before. So many times. No longer is the ear so keen to listen. No longer does it want to. Each platoon. Each section lives in a world of its own, part of it all, yet so isolated. Confined to their own space. Trench. Snowdrift. Panzer fighting compartment.

Commanding panzer general standing so high in his Steiner. Shabby sheepskin coat flapping in the wind. Fresh from the sands of desert warfare. He has much to learn. Ivan does not give up so easily. He will not run before the might of the panzers like the Aussie and Kiwi in Greece. He fights for every minute inch of his native soil. Fights with a bitterness never before known in any previous enemy.

Dead *Soldaten* litter the steppe and fringes of the forest. Glassy eyes stare. Flurries of snow waft about them. Wind whips at their torn overcoats. Still those stony ashen faces stare. What red-hot steel fragments failed to do, the severe cold of the Russian winter will finish. Only death walks upon that steppe. Searching. Forever sniffing, finding its own.

Respite. *Zigaretten*. Remaining vodka makes the rounds.

"Maybe our number will not be called."

Wishful thinking. There is still the wait. Manhood beckoning youth. Feldwebel whistles herald the feared christening.

"*Macht schon*. Even numbers. Up on your feet. Forward. *Los. Los. Schnell*."

Shaky, jellied legs push the weary body. Deep snow grips like glue. Unseen something in that accursed soil seems to fasten onto the jackboots. Holding for just that instant longer. Ivan bullet. Dumdum. Grenade. Long bayonet. The end upon that savage steppe is still the same. Only the very brave. Those with lips trembling with insanity die with a smile and chuckle.

To come through the terrifying inferno. All is breathless. Pain-filled lights before the eyes. Sweat. Sickly. Body odors so distinct upon the chill air. Throats gasping for moisture. Cracked lips that feel as though they are peeling back from the teeth.

Waiting for the next command. There is no talk. Chest heaving. How truly wonderful the snow feels. A miracle. The act of being alive. Snow has a taste. That filling has come out. Bloody mouth. Otherwise not a scratch. Jangled nerves tug at the jaw. First smiles. Eyes do function. A grin. Others. That slap upon the back. Sanity returns.

"*Mein lieber Gott*. We . . . we made it."

Sometimes ivan was slow to react. They did not encourage individual thinking in the lower ranks. When his mind was made up there was no stopping him. He could be heard growling in the forest, like a gang of enraged bears, only a hundred meters away. Skulking, vodka-soaked devil, just marking time waiting to be unleashed.

Huddled together. Forced to spend the night out in the open upon that snow field. Waiting. Curse of all *Soldaten*. Waiting is the hardest to bear. Some become raving maniacs lost in their own horrifying thoughts.

"Panzers," a whispered cry of terror would pass from man to man.

Listening. Helmeted heads cocked against the wind.

Again it comes, the revving of panzer engines.

"Ivan. T.34s."

"Building up for a big push."

The very ground vibrates with a dull throbbing echo. It shudders, as though it has a life of its own deep within its bowels.

Fear can be heard in the hissing breath of *Kameraden*.

"Two hundred meters."

"No one moves." It is a voice full of authority.

Panic. A sudden cry of terror would send them fleeing into the snow. Someone sighs deeply. The cold air knifes at the lungs.

"Stukas will deal with them at dawn," comes from Steggemann.

Schultz breaks wind, that knowing dry laugh of his sounding. "And in the meantime? Maybe you believe in the fairy tales of the brothers Grimm as well."

The whispered talk stops. Shouting can be heard. Loud commands in Russian from their lines. The T.34s are milling around. Gradually they move away. Taunting upon the wind. They know there is not much opposition waiting for them. Most of the Wehrmacht's panzers were blown up the day before.

Full of vodka ivan would bellow over the snowy

wastes. Voices thundering into the night.

"*Germanski*. You awake. It's your balls we will be having for breakfast."

It never failed to draw an immediate response from Schultz.

"Come over here you, Bolsehvik runt. I'll show you what Schultzy from Bienebuttel can do."

It looked as though some of the ivans had built log fires.

"Fritz. Come. Warm your ass."

"Promise me a crack at one of your plump women commissars and I'll be over in two seconds," shouted Hansen.

Loud drunken cheering came from ivans' positions.

"Germanski *pyos*," mocked another gruff voice. "My trusty long bayonet has your name upon it. I'll cut out your manhood, fascist pig."

Knocking another Grenadier aside, Schultz struggled to his feet.

"Threaten my friend Pushkin, would you? Make yo-yos out of your nuts, I will. Send them to uncle Stalin through the field post. Any of you shits fancy your chances, let him come over and front up to Schultzy."

Schmidt came down the line with two older reservists from a Rollbahn supply unit, handing out grenades and ammunition.

"Quiet, Schultz. I can't leave you alone for a minute. How many more times have I got to tell you. You will draw their mortar fire," he snapped.

Schultz danced up and down in the snow, swinging his apelike arms.

"You heard the Bolshy swine. Shouting at me, he was. Think I'm afraid of a few drunken ivans?"

"Stop the shouting and that's an order."

351

Schmidt moved on with the Rollbahn supply men.

Hansen's snickering laugh came out of the darkness.

"You tell him, Schultzy. Burning all the *isbas*. Scorched earth. That brother ivan is no gentleman."

"Raping. Pillaging their land. Just what do you expect from ivan? A band on parade and bunches of red roses?" grumbled Muller.

Shivering, backs against the biting wind. Several murmured in agreement.

"See them gallows. *Mensch*. The ropes had been cut. Something was hanging there before we went into that village."

"Those pegged-out Hiwi S.S. got no red roses."

"*Ja. Bestimmt*. Deserved pegging out, they did. Never could stand traitors. All S.S. are swine no matter what country they come from."

"I agree with that," growled someone else.

Other footsteps crunched over from a nearby hole. Lungs could be heard wheezing heavily. The approaching man coughed.

"My eldest son has the honor of serving with the S.S. Das Reich. Watch your tongues or I will be putting all of you on report. I am a Feldwebel. I demand respect even if you cannot see me."

An angry muttering rose from those who had seen the approach of that first bitter winter, those who knew at first hand the deeds of the S.S. Einsatzgruppens.

The Feldwebel crouched down upon his haunches.

"If we had more heroes like those in my son's elite regiment, this war in the East could have been over within the first year."

"Pardon me while I fart. I must clear the air." It was undoubtedly Schultz's voice.

Heyer spat in the direction of the bragging Feldwebel.

"Another disciple strayed into our midst. The Lord Almighty is indeed a generous *Gott*."

"I would like to know. Do you suffer from splitting headaches when you roll out of your fart sack first thing in the morning?" Schultz asked.

"Something loose in your skull, is there?"

Knuckles were heard cracking.

"Pushkin. Where are my instruments? Fat head of a Feldwebel here. He wants his skull examined."

In spite of Schmidt's earlier warning, he cupped his hands to his mouth shouting over to the ivan positions.

"Ivan. Little brother. *Tovaritch*. Got a right Hitler ponce here for you, I have. Soften him up first I will. Then you can come over and get him. One fathead for a full bottle of vodka. Can't be fairer than that, can I?"

He swung his fist blindly. It hit the Feldwebel upon the shoulder, making him stagger.

"Who did that? Who did that? Own up? Who was it? Name, rank and number. Striking a superior officer in the course of his duty. In the line that can be punishable by death."

"Threatens like an Oberschar, he does."

"You take his soldiers' book. Break off his tag. He won't last the night."

"Who said that? Give me your rank and name." He fell into the snow hole grabbing the nearest shoulder straps.

Hansen laughed quietly.

There was competition in the breaking of wind.

"How can our beloved Fuehrer . . . your beloved Furhrer—" Hansen moved out of the way of the flaying arms and continued his Goebbels' impersonation. "How can he achieve his aims in the Eastern lands? The aims of all true Deutsches folk? The officers are hanging and shooting my trusty Grenadiers. I ask you in the name of the folk. All that is sacred and Holy to us. From the brothels of the Reeperbahn. Tanta Anna's in Luneburg. I beseech you . . ."

Grunts and groans came from nearby. The solid contact of balled rock-hard fist upon flesh. A heavy body fell into the snow hole.

"Gentlemen. St. Nikolaus," laughed Schultz.

"Needs the rest. Head case, he is."

Lieutenant Harpe came back trudging through the snow from a section commanders' meeting.

"Pass the word. In thirty minutes we move."

It was met with the usual curses and protests.

"Retreating, are we?" replied Heyer.

"Wehrmacht coming to its senses at last."

"If I did not know you better, Heyer, I would say that is a defeatist attitude to adopt."

"*Kamerade* Adolf, is it?" whispered Hansen.

"Piles all fixed up, are they? Wants us to have a crack at his new knockshop on the Reeperbahn, does he? My legions of youth. My Grenadiers to the fore. Hold your heads high. All those who saw the spires of Moscow. We qualify for a crack at the new shipment of Oriental tarts."

Schultz roared with laughter. The ivans began catcalling. No one bothered answering.

"Schultzy wants an Oriental bit. My front piece needs action. A master at her craft."

Hansen took the vodka bottle from Heyer. Took a long slug, then passed it to Steggeman.

"Mongol bits from Alma Ata. They can really perform. Did I ever tell you about friend Manheim from four platoon? Swears he'd give his right arm for another crack. Bums all rosy and pink. Last one laid him out for four days, she did."

"Lord, I'm coming," laughed Heyer.

"Quick, put me on the bus."

"Manheim reckons they draw blood, they do. Something to do with their eyes not being able to see the target properly. Poor shit, he walked with a limp for ten days. *Arzt* had him on glucose and honey water to bring him right. In good old Alma Ata they start them off at the age of fourteen sitting on the alum pot."

"Hansen, be quiet. *Halt die Schnautze*," rasped Lieutenant Harpe.

"There is going to be no retreat for us. What do you think we are, Rumanians? We go in to report on ivan's build-up. Take prisoners."

"Nah, *ja*. Not again, Herr Leutnant. What about my corns and blisters."

"Shut your mouth and form up."

"Hansen," Steggeman rose with the others, arms swinging trying to restore the circulation. "I would recommend two days on Schultz's special nose salts. Keep you going for a week, they will. On the trot, trying to run from the smell."

Nervous laughter came from the darkness.

Schultz poked him playfully in the chest.

"The house of Schultz never advertises its wares in the line. Strictly *verboten*, it is. Direct orders from the chief Arzt. He gets the wounded in, not a mark on them. When he shouts you can hear him back in Orel. First thing he does is call for yours truly. I get my ten days full battle order on bread and water. Now I ask you, is that fair to this gallant hero of the Third Reich?"

The laughter came to an end. Two Landser could not be moved. Like ice blocks. Hours on the snowy wastes. Frostbite had taken its toll. Some went quietly like that. More often it was with screaming that refused to stop.

The Feldwebel was coming around. He mumbled incoherently. Schultz hit him again. He crumpled into the snow.

"What was that?" hissed Lieutenant Harpe.

Schultz's best soldierly voice came out of the inky void.

"Beg to report, Herr Leutnant. A Landser it is. Keeps getting fits of hysterics. Grenadier Schultz had to knock him cold."

"Only way to treat them, Herr Leutnant," confirmed Heyer.

"Point him towards ivan when he comes around. Soldier's soldier, this one is. Had thoughts of going over to the Das Reich. Failed the medical. Turned him down. Circumsized. You know how Heinrich Himmler feels about that."

Lieutenant Harpe tried to disguise the laughter in his voice.

"Heyer. Schultz. Forward. Don't forget we need live prisoners."

Schultz was heard to mumble as he pushed off through the deep snow.

"No one trusts me. You hit them too hard, uncle Schultzy. Can I help it if the crud ivans have thin skulls. Never do anything right."

"And quiet. Our attack is supposed to come as a surprise."

The mood Schultz was in, everyone was straining their ears. They did not have long to wait.

Out of the darkness came the sound of metal upon metal. Heyer had obviously bumped into him.

"*Himmel, Arsch und Zwirn.* Think you are marching to Tanta Anna's. Frightened about being the last in the queue. . . ."

Lieutenant Harpe took off his helmet and pounded the snow.

"*Mein Gott*, he thinks the war is a Hitler Jugend Sunday outing."

A kilometer behind the Russian lines their bonfires became clear.

"Cheeky. Can I go and warm my hands?" giggled Schultz.

"Tarts there with red knickers and regulation Stalin suspenders," whispered Hansen.

Then all hell broke loose. Siberians. Within seconds they were upon them.

A Landser replacement fell, breath sucking, blood gargling at his torn throat. His arms flayed at the struggling legs. They moved back and forth fighting desperately. Three times he was brutally stabbed. Siberian. Grenadier. Hand-to-hand combat. Any searching hand is surely the enemy's. It is struck down. Death beckons at the elbow. Only the fastest survive. Kill. Kill. Kill.

Cries of terror fill the night. Ghastly gurgling death rattles. Russian voices. Deutsche. Always the boots fighting for a hold in the snow. Slipping. Sliding. And off to one side it seems as though the shawled figure of old Mother Russia is grinning, standing back in the trees ever watchful. Come *Germanski*, come. The long knives of my little brothers await you. Prepare yourself, fascist invader. This is the long night I have chosen. Come rot in the sacred belly of my forest.

Unteroffizier Schmidt lunged through the snow. Some of the patrol were drunk. On the Eastern Front, who remained sober for long? There were new replacements. The veterans would be all right, he had no fear of that. The others. Some would cower in the snow incapable of moving. Their training was too short. No time for hardening. Romny was nothing but a transit camp. A passport to death.

"Knives . . . *nicht schiessen.*"

Blood spurted at him from a cleaved neck. Warm. Sickly. Quickly freezing. Something grotesque and soggy slid past his boot. He heard and felt the swish of a double-edged *kandra*. Siberian butchering knife. One swipe would decapitate. A rifle butt smashed into his shoulder.

"*Pyos,*" the white snow-shirted Siberian grunted.

He found the arm of the padded jacket. Gripped it, twisted his body and brought it down with all his force across his knee. The Siberian howled. Bone splintered. Shaggy-bearded face. He jerked the head back savagely. His knife slashed at the throat. A stifled whisper sounded. He let the dead body slide away.

"*Nein Nein. Hilfe.*"

Fighting for their very lives, they could only listen as another youngster was put to death. A laugh of triumph rent at the air.

"*Daavidanja* Germanski."

They could hear the dull metallic crunch of a saber against flesh. Again came the bone-chilling laugh. Giggling of an obvious Mongol. Imagine him as he danced with childish glee. Like in the time of captivity.

"*Kameraden*. Here. *Schnell.*"

Hansen ran towards the whimpering voice. Steggeman was caught in a bear hug by a stocky Siberian. Hansen stabbed him low, putting all his pressure behind it. The giant turned and began to throttle him. His legs trod air. Steggeman gouged at the Siberian's eyes. Heyer crawled to them and cut his throat.

"Don't rely on your strength. Use your spades."

"*Ja.*"

"*Los.* Another one."

Heyer kicked out with his right foot. The Siberian

stumbled, cursing. Then he hit him with the sharp edge of the spade. Hardly a sound came. He wiped the blood from his face.

Two Mongols jumped the Feldwebel with the son in the Das Reich. He threw one into the scrub where he crashed against a thin pine. The other he grabbed from behind and strangled.

Schultz was fighting with his fists. A Grenadier came close, just recovering from a death struggle of which he had been the victor. He buckled, spitting teeth. Two Siberians caught Schultz by the arms, throwing him to the ground.

"Fascist pig," vodka-soaked spittle spat over him.

On his back, he instinctively threw his head to one side. A rifle butt hit the packed snow, sending his helmet flying. Giggling, sitting astride him, one of the Siberians was going through his pockets. As though the victim already was dead.

Double-handed, Schultz brought his *kandra* up with all his strength. It plunged into the Siberian's stomach. He ripped with an upwards jerk. He pushed the squealing Siberian aside.

A bayoneted rifle pinned him to a log. Pierced his greatcoat to the right of his waist. Both hands upon the rifle stock, he threw the heavy-breathing Siberian off balance. He hit him with his sturdy Russian entrenching tool. Bone splattered. A second blow ended the screaming.

Lieutenant Harpe was one of the first wounded. *Kandra* slash to the face, taking half of his ear. With his Luger pistol, again and again he struck at the face only inches away. The Luger went off with a blinding flash. He saw the startled face. Bulged slant eyes. Then the apparition fell forward, covering him in blood.

Taking Heyer's advice Hansen and Steggeman

were fighting back to back, mauser and entrenching tool swinging.

"Germanski *kaputt*."

An ivan burp gun went off close by. Hansen brought his entrenching tool down. A cry came. He beat the life out of it. Other hands climbed his legs. He kicked out. Steggeman turned and fired.

"*Scheiss*."

Muller was squirming in the snow. Fingers were tightening at his throat. Slowly the sound of fighting was fading. He strained to keep his senses. He could not unlock the hands. There was no breath. His lungs heaved. Nothing. And the blackness came from the back of his eyes. Sheets of light dancing. Sparks. He brought his knee into position. Brought it up with all the strength he could gather.

A tortured grunt came.

A searchlight was switched on.

"*Dummkopf*."

He had been fighting a Landser Gefreiter. They looked at one another sheepishly.

For just seconds in the dazzling gleam of light the fighting stopped. Most were momentarily blinded. Only seconds. Then it came.

"*Urah! Urah!*"

Siberians in their long snow shirts surged around the searchlight position, bayonets glinting in the eerie light.

"Each *Soldat* . . ." Lieutenant Harpe had no time to finish.

Two blood-dripping bayonets were coming at him. He fired. Twice. As though it had been struck with a sledgehammer the face flew apart. At three paces Muller cut the other one down with a burst from the hip.

How ivan loves his searchlights. They were used

upon the River Oder prior to the Berlin onslaught, with great effect. But that is the last story.

Schultz, Heyer and Steggeman were down low in the snow firing point-blank at the massed Siberians.

"Urah! Urah Stalin."

Every shot found its target. It was not enough. They charged on over their own wounded and dead.

A hand grenade sailed over from the searchlight position. The explosion killed four Grenadiers, wounding others. The Siberians poured over them, hacking and cutting.

"Zuruck. Los. Back," roared Lieutenant Harpe.

"Hilfe, Kameraden."

Two burly Siberians had disarmed a Landser. They were dragging him back towards the searchlight. Heyer shot them. The Landser scuttled away. Other Siberians caught him. They forced him onto his knees in the snow. Two automatic rifles went off. He collapsed into a bloody heap.

"Los. Move," rasps Schmidt.

To turn and run is fatal. Cut down within seconds. There are too many Siberians. A stand is made in clusters. Others fall back through them, then reform, firing once again.

The heavy smell of blood pulls at the nostrils. Ruptured guts. Hands implore, reaching out. Some would not last.

Schmidt lobbed a stick grenade. It explodes with a roar. Another follows. The searchlight snaps off.

Cries of the wounded searchlight girls ring out.

Hansen and Muller fire at the Siberian muzzle flashes.

"Pomoshch. Medics."

Grenade explosions bite at the low scrub claiming more Wehrmacht lives. Shadows dance. Steel fragments knife into the trees.

"Pushkin."

"Here."

"Run."

"Muller."

"*In ordnung.*"

"Heyer."

"*Bistimmt.* Here, Lord."

"*Los. Los.*"

"*Schnell.* Run for it."

"Stegge."

"*Hilfe.*"

Muller and Heyer went to him.

"Splinters. Grenade. Right leg."

They take him by the arms pulling him through the snow.

Hansen, Schmidt and Schultz bring up the rear.

The first Siberians have swarmed over the wounded. They beat at the faces. Plunge their bayonets into the wriggling bodies. Fire from several replacements hits them. They crumple over their intended victims. Their howling joins the nightmare.

Lathered in sweat, someone ran headlong into an ivan trip wire. Five large land mines go off in quick succession. Two Landser lose their legs. Another is blown apart. Yet another turns, running blind, back into the arms of the Siberians.

Heyer applied a tourniquet to Steggeman's leg. He was shaking his head and mumbling. Muller gave him morphine from his field pack.

"Bleeding like a chicken."

"Chest ticket."

"Nah, *ja.* Orel more like it."

Ivan star shells went up. Under the canopy of light mortars shells screech in. Others fall wounded. Their pitiful cries hang accusingly upon the night air. Pursuit. Ivan at the heels. No time to stop. They have only a few precious seconds to live. Laughing Siberians soon find them.

A flare ahead and to the right. Wehrmacht. It hovers, smoke trailing away. White tracer laces the night. Skidding, bouncing over the broken ground. The whole Wehrmacht front seethes with life. Heavy stuff. 88s tear into the trees. Some idiot has rung command. No man's land is a hostile sea of exploding light. Red-hot steel fragmentation flashes away. Once again that dreadful sowing takes place. Seeds are youthful Landser and Grenadiers.

Eleven out of thirty make it back. Another gets his in the final few meters. Chin must stroke the snow. Ivan has missed. But the raw Romny replacements are closer. They fire by instinct. They have been told that there is only death before them. Another green seventeen-year-old is blooded. *Sieg Heil* and become a hero.

The front becomes quiet. Only the cold can be heard. Frost cracks the trees. Rest of the night promises to be easy. Some have dared to fall asleep. Then the Hauptmann arrives.

"I said take prisoners, Herr Leutnant."

"But Herr Hauptmann. We were ambushed. The popovs slaughtered us. I came back with only a third of my men."

"It is your duty as an officer in the Wehrmacht to obey orders. And to see that they are carried out. Do I make myself clear, Leutnant Harpe?"

A clicking of heels sounds down the trench.

"You will wait two hours and go in with four platoon, Herr Leutnant."

"*Jawohl*, Herr Hauptmann."

From somewhere in the ivan lines someone is singing. A full baritone voice. A song of a lonely love-starved Cossack.

363

Not to be outdone Schultz and Hansen break into song. Schmidt tries but fails to stop them. Muller and Heyer join in.

"Wenn die soldaten, durch die Stadt marschieren.
Oeffnen die Madchens die Fenster und die Tueren.
Heidirum . . . Heidarum . . ."

"And the vodka is warming.
When the soldiers march through the town.
All the girls open the windows and the doors."

Lieutenant Harpe comes back to have a last drink.

"Eine Flasche Rotwein und ein stueckchen Braten . . .
Schenken die Madchen ihren Soldaten.
Heidirum . . . Heidarum . . .

Halfway through the chorus Lieutenant Harpe leaves.

"A bottle of red wine and a piece of roast.
The girls give to their soldiers."

And four platoon rise from the icy snow mounds. Lieutenant Harpe gives Schmidt his men's last letters. The field blue post stamps are stiff. They do not return. Mother Russia just swallows them up.

Chapter 22
GRENADIER, FOR YOU
THE WAR IS OVER

Far behind the front line Steggeman came to. He was lying in deep fresh straw with other wounded. The farmhouse room was large. At one end there was a large bricked-in stove. The heat was welcome after the white wastes.

Near him in the straw someone was crying. Another moaned and groaned with pain. A maniac was laughing, thumping at the clay walls. And from it all came a throat-catching sickly smell.

He remembered being stretched out full length upon a table. Hindenburg candles were spluttering. There was the horrid overpowering smell of gangrene. Sweating hands held him down.

Two tables were operating. The words came from out there somewhere. As though they did not concern him. Almost as if he was listening in. Eavesdropping. To another world. A time in another ivan village. A time that had filled him with fear and torment.

"If you come in here again with a scratch, I will make an example of you, Grenadier. A court martial will be called in the field. I won't have youths cluttering up my post with simple scratches."

And then those earlier frightening words had lost their meaning. There was only the pain. It was there all the time.

He thought of the ivan hand grenade. Those warning shouts in the darkness. Confusion. Bodies pushing. Explosion. Youths falling. Screams. The sharp pain. Hands sticky with blood. It would not stop.

Muller and Heyer. Among the shouting and screaming he thought he had been left for ivan. He heard the Siberians coming. Heard them fall upon the other wounded. They were not killed quickly. From some there came no screams. Only that faint horrifying humming. Other dead he had seen with short blackened stubs of tongues. Siberians. Partisans. Both practiced cruelty to the extreme.

"How can I stitch this up? Crushed thigh. Caved-in thorax."

A figure near him moved.

"He still breathes, Herr Doktor."

He caught the smell of blood-stained bandages being removed.

"Not for long. *Sicher*. Put him to one side. Morphine. I can do no more."

The razor-sharp scalpel cut at his thigh. The hands at his shoulders and feet tightened. His mouth opened. Eyes went wide. He screamed and screamed, until the pain at his throat threatened to choke him. The pain pulsated. It seemed to beat time with the candles. Thump. Thump. Thump. The pain entered his head. Hammered at his skull.

"Stay still, Grenadier. We have only anaesthetic for really bad cases."

The scalpel. Going in it felt like a massive *kandra*. Blunt, scraping the bone. He twisted and turned throwing his head about. The sweat-lined hands held him firm. Candles. Clay walls. They were of a dirty yellow. Blurred faces. They whirled and whirled. Faster. Like a childish roundabout on the Heide. Roll up. Roll up. Twenty cents a ride. Who is game? Who has the money? Come along, don't be scared. It stopped suddenly.

Giddiness made his mind reel. He had to vomit. It was there building up in his throat. If it was not one end it was the other. Would they laugh like Schultzy? The thought struck home. In spite of the pain. He tried to hold it down. *Nein. Nein. Nein.* Schultzy was only joking. Joking. Joking. Like Pushkin. Friend Hansen. Joking. He swallowed hard. He would fight it.

That first voice came back.

"Torn left ventricle."

Someone was tugging the flesh from his thigh. It was like a large pair of pliers. Gripped. Pulling. He felt the tear. Walls. Candles. They danced and spun. He arched his body, screaming. A hand went over his mouth. He bit down upon it hard.

And that voice came again. The same quiet drone.

"Swab."

His mind wanted to leave his pain-racked body. Shudder. Come loose. Glide away. The body can only take so much. He was still seeing. Still hearing. Still feeling. Pain, it was in both legs. Creeping. Moving down his arms. It clutched at his throat. Burnt with fingers of ice. Stabbing. Stabbing. Thumping.

"Blood—too much loss. Why keep giving me cadavers? Herr Feldwebel, this is a hospital post. Not a morgue."

"It came back with the others from patrol, Herr Doktor."

"They should have left it for the Popovs. They were carrying a dead *Kamerade. Los. Schnell.* Get another one. We still might be able to save some of them."

Mercifully Steggeman passed out.

Two days later he joined the other wounded upon the straw in the *kolkhos* farmhouse. His body lice were active. Under the armpits. Between his legs. He could not find the strength to scratch.

The air was thick, heavy, stifling. Foul. The youth in the far corner was sobbing. Blinded by ivan mortar fire. He was talking to his sister Monica in Munster.

He shouted aloud. He wanted her to take him to the park. He had to see the daffodils. There were lots there. In flower beds. Wild under the trees. He must see them. *Nein*. He would only feel them. Smell them. Hold them. He longed for flowers. All those hours in the trenches. Advancing over the snows. Ivan's land was all dead. Only dead and unfeeling. He had to be there. In the Fatherland in the spring.

They were not daffodils. He tossed about in the straw. She had cheated him. As she had always done when they were children. They were colored paper. Unfeeling dead. Like the steppes. Stems like blackened frostbitten fingers of *Kameraden*. Icy cold. Cracked. And Monica was leaning against a tree, laughing.

The wheelchair rolled. Down the path. The jerk of the curb.

It was going towards a T.34. The engines revved. The right track spun. The ivans on the back laughed. They were beckoning him. Come, Germanski. One bearded face twisted in an evil leer. They had him by the throat. He threw himself hard against the clay wall of the farmhouse. The screams died away to childish sobbing.

"Monica. Where are my daffodils?" he cried.

A panzer Obergefreiter was laughing. He looked like a zombie. Bandages covered most of his chest, arms and face. Only his eyes and mouth showed. The laughter coming from him was hideous. A laugh that can only come from those who have passed over. Forsaken the world. A world where there were once smiling, sharing *Kameraden*. Now there were only the vivid memories of the horror. Killing. Greedy yellow flames. A blackened body writhing upon the floor of the panzer fighting compartment. He lobbed his head at the clay wall, then fell forward whimpering to the straw.

"Awake are we?" a young smiling *Arzt* high-stepped his way through the straw.

"Transports will be here soon. Nothing to worry about. You have all had your operations. You will feel light-headed. It is the drugs. It will pass. Wear off."

He paused at each patient, checking. With a flourish of his pen he scribbled upon the labels, pinning one to each chest as he passed. He stopped at a youth with badly lacerated lungs.

"No more coughing today. *Gut*. That's the spirit."

Those youthful yet almost lifeless eyes stared up at him.

"Grenadier," he beamed. "You are lucky. For you the war is over," he pinned the label to his chest.

"It's the Fatherland for you. Plenty of rest. That's all you need."

It was only after the young *Arzt* had left that his words had any effect. Slowly the Grenadier's hand went to his chest. He tilted his neck, straining. Bewilderment flooded the ghostly white ashen face.

"Home. I am going home," he croaked.

"Fire. Fire," shouted the mad panzer Obergefreiter.

"Idiot. Short burst. You waste ammunition."

He sat feet braced against the wall. Feet and hands moving.

The blinded youth was tearing at his bandages.

"Monica. These are not daffodils. Do you hear me?"

He was cramming straw into his mouth. Sobbing. His legs kicking.

The panzer Obergefreiter now had his back to the wall.

"That's it. Give ivan a taste. Pour it on!" His body shook with laughter.

"Flamethrower. Beautiful. Crisp. Don't let them get away."

"*Aschloch.*" His mood changed suddenly. "Who stole my *samahonka?*"

Then he just stared up at the roof. He was smiling. Now and again his tongue flicked out between the bandages on his face.

The Grenadier announced his news to everyone.

"*Die heimat.*"

He played with his life-saving chest ticket.

Other wounded struggled to sit up. Faces covered with grin, many of them grinned. Some swore under their breath.

"*Scheiss.* Damn war."

Most would be on the transports to Orel. A large Russian town a little to the West. A few were destined for Kiev. Out of the firing line for a while. Like others before them, they would return. Anyone with a *Garnisonverwendung* was to be envied. Fit only for the lightest of base depot duties. They would outlive the war.

The mound moved in the straw. The Grenadier hissed and strained. He rested his weight upon one elbow. His eyes flooded with tears. At seventeen he knew the hellfire. He had fought at Demyansk near Lake Ilmen, alongside tough Waffen S.S. units. The fighting S.S. Week after week, each ivan assault had been repelled. That killing ground stank of blood. *Ja*, he had tasted more than enough of the brutal fighting on the Eastern Front. Now it was over.

"Home to Uelzen."

Another Grenadier with a broken arm straightened up. A *Kamerade* wounded in the same barrage from the deadly Stalin Organs.

"Gunter. Lie still. No upsetting yourself."

The Grenadier began to laugh.

"*Kameraden.* For me there is no more war. *Kein Krieg mehr.*"

A Landser recovering from frostbite started to hum. Voices, low at first, strengthened, then joined in.

If they could not go home they could at least share in the joy of the Grenadier's return. Always it was the Heide. Heather heavy with the scent of blossom. Quaint thatched cottages. Old men sitting on the benches lazily smoking their pipes. Where they had marched so very long ago. That very first time.

"Auf der Heide, blueht ein kleines Bluemelein.
Und das heist Erika.
Wird umschwaermt von tausend kleinen Bienelein."

The young *Arzt* returned. He looked quickly about. The first days after the operations. They were very crucial. Smiling, satisfied, he too began to sing. They were coming along fine. Just fine. Once that will returned, the battle was as good as won. He checked the panzer Obergefreiter, then left.

"*Heimat.* Eight days . . . *Gott.* I will be there."

"Gunter, be still."

Laughter exploded. Steggeman as well. It sounded just like Schultzy telling Hansen off. The front was miles away. Occasionally it growled and thundered. Russian artillery. It would not reach them. In laughter there was sanity.

The Grenadier was crying and laughing at the same time. Infectious. The laughter of youth who have known the fury of total war, is very hard to control.

"Stop him," shouted his *Kameraden.*

"*Bitti. Hilfe.* His lungs."

The mad panzer Obergefreiter crawled to the wall once again.

"It's spreading." He rolled, pressing the straw to his body, beating at it with both hands.

"You won't get the turret hatch open. *Los.* Through the escape panel."

He pulled at his hair. And he was back there in that white-hot hell. The driver was dead. Flames were licking at Jochen. His face was lost. Skin was peeling. Peeling and spitting. Bones were frying.

He threw bundles of straw high over his head.

"Fresh air. Uelzen." The Grenadier doubled, coughing.

"Three cheers for the Grenadier," someone said, voice cracking with emotion.

The cheers echoed into the village street.

"Ammunition," screamed the panzer Obergefreiter. "Throw Jochen out. Move. *Schnell.* It's going."

Stumbling, he got to his feet. Head down he hit the clay wall. The wall shook. Fell back. Charged it again. Then sat smashing his head again and again into the wall.

"Stop him."

"*Mein lieber Got.*"

"Someone do something."

Steggeman was first to reach him, the stitching at his thigh breaking open more with every step. Two artillery men helped to hold the panzer man down.

"Sister. Sister," everyone was trying to shout.

Two Ukrainian nurses came in at the double. The panzerman's buttocks were bared. A nurse lanced him with a hypodermic needle. He relaxed, head to one side. Through the froth at his mouth she at last found his tongue. The danger was over. He would not choke.

"*Tovaritch.*"

A nurse knelt by the youthful Grenadier. Steggeman and the others hobbled over. He saw it in the eyes. Utter disbelief. Waxlike face. Thick blood pumped through his fingers at his mouth.

For the Grenadier the war on the Eastern Front was indeed over. Youthful laughter had ripped open his torn lungs. He would not see the Heide at Uelzen. He lies buried with others east of Orel. Where there are still only a few scattered *isbas*. A lonely water tower. And where in spring the River Oka gushes not far away.

Chapter 23
ROLLBAHN ESCORT

The relief have arrived. They are cursed for taking their time. They are thirty minutes late. It could spell death for some. Those who are beyond caring are moved in the groundsheets. Some need to be shoveled in. Like Reinhardt.

He was checking a telephone line. Some Siberians with a saber must have caught him. No one heard his cries. His remains were found lining the rim of his hole. Seven pieces. Siberians are butchers. They even stole his porno books.

Dogs can be heard barking back in the village. The dawn is like many others. Wind howls, whipping faces, knifing at the nose and ears.

Nineteen-year-old Lieutenant Streich runs over to Schmidt.

"Four platoon. No one in their trenches. Only gas mask cases."

Schmidt shrugs his shoulders. Two days in the line and already the boy lieutenant is losing some of his brashness. Others never do. Their aristocratic class have always supplied the officers. Hitler's war has given them the chance to strut before their men. They do so like prize parrots. The eyes of a Prussian officer are cold. Like those of their fathers in 1915. There is no mercy there. Only chest decorations. Iron Crosses. Ritter Crosses. How many men died for the gold decorating their chest collection? How many never came back?

The tramp of feet silenced forever in Russia. A wind

that might bring the wisp of a marching song. The name of a *Madel* once known. Now her long blonde hair has turned to grey. Erich never came back. And still the prize pheasants stomp and perform at social functions. In Bonn. Stuttgardt. Munich. Those legions of youth are silenced forever. None can call them back. They never got to taste the schnapps of a revitalized fatherland. Their bones lie rotting. Who can now recall their names.

The scratch platoon forms up.

"Forward."

They tramp off into the packed snow. There will be soup. Maybe field post. Rest. If it was not for Hansen and Schultz no one would talk. A night watch has a deadening effect. Bones ache. Something presses at the back of the eyes. The mind craves only sleep. Sleep of the dead. And vodka, it always helps.

Near the field kitchen Hauptmann Schiller is sitting high astride his horse. He always has a gallop first thing in the morning. Shows the men that he is up and about.

"Unteroffizier Schmidt. Get the men together. Look at them. Like ivan prisoners. I want them to march. March. March. They should be proud of themselves. Heads high. Legs and arms swinging. A song in their hearts. The Fatherland is marching to conquer the world. Sing."

"Old mouth and trousers," laughs Hansen.

"Give me a song, gentlemen. I want to hear you sing."

"Permission to speak, Herr Hauptmann mouth and trousers," giggles Schultz.

"Go ahead, Grenadier," giggles Hansen.

"Make it brief. I have a war to fight."

"*Eins, zwei drei*, after me.

There's some Grenadiers who die in bed, die in bed.

All on account of what the Hauptmann said, Hauptmann said.

Ordered him to the front, to the front.

Laughing Grenadier more interested in c . . ."

"Stop this column. Take that man's name!" Hauptmann Schiller was prancing about on his mount.

Someone had thrown a clod of ice. The horse was nervous. It started to back away sidewards. Ever the gentleman Hauptmann Schiller still sat erect in the saddle.

The column was ordered to halt.

The Hauptmann rode about them. The horse seemed to be having trouble with its pampered nose. It neighed shrilly, backing up once again.

"That imbecile there," Schiller pointed with his crop at Schultz.

"On report, Herr Unteroffizier. I'll teach him to giggle in the ranks. Discipline. It is a quality that I demand in all the men under my command. Discipline. Nerves of steel. That's what makes a good Deutscher *Soldat*."

He gained control of his horse, nuzzling it behind the ears.

"Four platoon under Lieutenant Harpe were men. Men the Fatherland can be proud of. They went out again into the chill night. Duty. Duty. That's what they were made of. Heads high. Chests out. Their families will be proud of them. It is an honor to die for the Third Reich. Die like a *Soldat* upon the field of glory. There is no finer way to go."

Another piece of ice sailed through the air. It hit the horse upon the rump. It took off down the village street. Not wishing to lose face, Hauptmann Schiller rode it out. Gentleman to the very last.

"March and sing. March and sing," he roared.

"Chests out. Heads . . ." the horse swerved in behind some *isbas*, almost unseating him.

When the laughter died out they set off once again. "Annemarie" had never been sung with such gusto.

Curious ivan threw over some mortar fire. They exploded harmlessly out in the steppe.

Stabsfeldwebel Thoma was pacing up and down before a line of armored troop carriers and trucks. Smiles appeared upon the grimy marching faces. Somehow that hostile landscape became a little friendlier. Surely the wind had dropped. The column was halted. Schmidt made his report.

Stabsfeldwebel Thoma continued to pace. "There is nothing to laugh about. You are all detailed to escort the convoy of wounded to Orel."

Orel. Civilization. A Russian town. Who had not dreamt of it? Daydreamed? Lying frozen in the dugouts. Cursing among the snow mounds. There was more to Mother Russia than the snowy wastes. Not as large as Kiev. Or as beautiful. But a real live town. Where people walked without the fear of being cut down by Maxim fire. Mortars. There would be no ivan flares. No diving into the snow. And. And women could be smelt from ten meters away. How sharp the senses do become at the front. But there were times, times in Russia, when they paid good dividends.

"You must be ever vigilant. Partisans. Bandits, they are everywhere. Last week they attacked a convoy. All the *Soldaten* were butchered. No one survived. Trust no one. Stop for no one. It could be an ivan ambush."

Hands firmly behind his back he paced along the front rank. Boys. Nothing but boys, he thought. It needed a professional *Soldat* like him to whip them into shape. In the Wehrmacht since the start. He was only sorry that his officer posting to the training school had not come through. Schiller said it would. He marveled at the way he kept everything in order at company headquarters. So much paperwork. Replacements. Leaves. Wounded. Ammunition sheets. It needed a good methodical head to keep everything straight.

Thoma put on his special face. The solemn look. That look he preferred for occasions such as this. Fatherly. Stern. And yet still the face of a fellow *Kamerade*. Someone who had suffered. Why the other day one of the village stray dogs had run off with a ham of his. He knew what it was like to suffer at the front. Of course the men did not miss its being stolen from the field kitchen. It was no good being kind to them. Feeding them with fancy goods. It made them weak. Hard-tack was good enough for them. They had to be hard to face ivan. And by *Gott*, he was just the one to toughen them up.

"Some of you will never make it. That is war. That is the way of the gallant Deutscher *Soldat* out there in the East. Some die. Some survive. That is our destiny."

His voice droned on and on.

"You go that way, Stabs. Might have to dig two holes for you, though. Be hard to get that beer sack of yours in. What a gut," chuckled Hansen quietly.

"Now, Hansen here."

He paused, mentally licking his lips.

Already his mind was walking the streets of Orel. Seeing the trams. Those eyes of the young women. Those full Russian blouses.

When he spoke in a whispered voice, like those times in the trenches, all ears listened intently. Even a loose milk cow walking down a village street. He could with just a few words turn it into an object of breathtaking passion.

"Not far from your River Oka in Orel there are brothels. Palaces of pleasure. Pink Ruski tit just sweating slightly. Legs in warm sheer silk stockings.

Pussies waiting. Pussies purring for the coming of the Grenadiers and Landser."

Schultz scratched himself. And he was heard to hiss through his blackened teeth, "I want a choice Mongol bit like our friend Manheim."

"What is wrong with a nice plump Ukrainian bit? They love front dirt. Something that has been away from a pair of knickers for months. The Lord in all his infinite wisdom will have to order blood transfusions. Me, I like them big. Big hips. Big bums. Big breasts. Bigger the better. Something real firm. Something you can really get your hands into."

"Heyer, you are all animal."

Schultz scratches under his belt trying to clear the lice. He babbles low, almost like a child. "When uncle Schultzy goes to Orel, clean myself up, I will. No smell. Got a tin of powder in my pack, I have. No one can catch me on the hop. Been saving it for special occasions since Kiev."

"How much is the fare?" someone snickered.

"Two ivans and a lock of hair from Schiller's horse."

"Do my hair I will. Clean my nails. Brush my teeth."

"Teeth," laughed Muller.

"*Mein lieber Gott*. All three of them. Each one is black."

Schultz pulled a hurt face.

"Can I help it if I got bad teeth from my Granny's side? Don't get snotty with me. You've forgotten what I look like in a well-brushed uniform. There were some girls in Hamburg who said I am a fine figure of a man. Crud, Muller. You know I can look real sharp."

"Them thighs will be waiting," continued Hansen.

"Have no lice, they won't. It's the head hunters,

see. Inspect them every Friday, they do. Smelling of Eau de Cologne and rosewater. None of your cheap Brussels scent. The real stuff. High heels and all. Black seams in their stockings. Waiting upon sofas with blue frilly cushions. One or two of them might be scratching themselves when a Grenadier is not looking. They do say there is a new breed of lice in Orel. Came over from Poland, it did. Of course the Wehrmacht is blamed for introducing it. Goes for the warm parts of the body it does."

Schultz kicked some snow at him.

"You pimp's doorkeeper. You said they were all clean. No lice."

Hansen seemed genuinely puzzled by the interruption.

"There's some lice in Russia that have been accused of belonging to ivan's fifth column. Get by all the roadblocks they do. Only one way to get rid of them. Spray them lightly with schnapps. That makes them scatter."

"Ungrateful shits!" Schultz waved a clenched fist behind his back.

"Trying to spoil a Grenadier's hard-earned fun. I'll pulverize every one of them."

"There is another way. You can try singing to them softly. Cossack songs are best."

"*Bestimmt*. Who would have thought of that."

"Nah, *ja*. When they get intoxicated and start to dance you just flick them away."

Low laughter ebbed about them.

"Making fun of Schultzy, little friend. Want your arse kicked?"

"*Nein*. Would I dare? See them red knickers, I can. It was brother Stalin's idea, you know. All women over the age of fourteen wear them. Bolshy color see. Encourage patriotism, so he thought. . . ."

380

Lost in his ever widening dreamland Hansen did not see the Stabs creeping up behind him. He came within inches of his right ear.

"Name, you miserable creature. Stand and report."

Hansen's slumped shoulders straightened. His position was always behind the huge shoulders of Schultz.

"Grenadier Pushkin, Herr Stabsfeldwebel."

A ripple of laughter came from the ranks.

"So. *Gott noch mal.* We have a joker amongst us. String on your greatcoat for buttons. If the Fuehrer could see you now he would have you shot."

Hansen straightened up, pulling his mauser in to his side.

"*Still gestanden.* Report, you numbskull. In the way the Wehrmacht taught you."

"I beg to report. Grenadier Hansen, Herr Stabsfeldwebel."

"Unit."

"Scratch unit number five, Herr Stabsfeldwebel."

He peered down into Hansen's eyes. So this was one of the creatures that had buckled before Moscow. No backbone. They had run before ivan like the wind. There was only one way to deal with these gutless types.

"One of the heroes that ran before Moscow. Siberians too much for you, were they? Did you throw your rifle away like the others?"

Those standing in the ranks moved, just slightly. It is easy to criticize once an event has passed. For others the Siberian onslaught would remain a living and bloody memory.

Schultz shifted his large hulk uneasily. He half turned, looking straight into the Stab's eyes.

"I looked after him, Herr Stabsfeldwebel. Carried

him I did. Didn't weigh much. Just threw him over my shoulder. Schmidt and good old Muller helped Steggeman. Heyer covered us from the rear.''

The Stabs turned upon Schultz. With each sentence he poked him roughly in the chest.

"Who gave you permission to talk. Mother him, did you? You *Niedersachsen Aschloch*. Changed him, did you, when his trousers were full.''

Schultz looked at him with those pure innocent eyes of his.

"You've got it all wrong Stabs. That happened to Steggeman. . . .''

In the doorway of an *isba* two young women were laughing behind raised hands. A small boy before them was throwing out his chest and pulling faces. An older peasant was smiling knowingly. He had served in the ranks. Even in the Red Army there were the bullies. Men who thought it was their duty to pick upon others.

The Stabs sniffed around Schultz, walking around him with a stiff-legged motion. His nose bristled like a bloodhound's. When he came to the front of him again, he stood back a pace, bracing himself.

"You smell, as well. Both from the same dung heap. I've seen everything in this war in the East.''

He made a big show of sniffing once again, then backed off, his face masked with disgust.

"Even dogs would run from a smelly individual like you. You are not fit to be in the ranks of the glorious Wehrmacht. You should be locked away in a mental institution.''

Schultz shifted his feet. They always picked upon him. Big build, it was. If they had a rank upon their shoulders. And if they were small. They made straight for him. Muller had told him more than once that it was his Beinebuttel charm. Young officers were the worst offenders. Smelling of mothballs. In their brand new uniforms. But more than once he had fixed them.

"Just out of the line, Herr Stabsfeldwebel. No rest. Just friend ivan. Now you know in the line we have no showers or baths. A Grenadier has trouble finding food, never mind washing."

Murmured agreement went through the ranks.

"Front scum. Filth. In all my time in the Wehrmacht I have never seen such a slovenly lot. Coming on parade in this condition. Each one of you needs a good shave. I should do my duty and put you all on report."

Out came his notebook. Even in the line there had to be the very strictest of discipline. More so under ivan fire.

"What did you do before being called to serve the Third Reich?"

"Farm laborer, Herr Stabsfeldwebel. I looked after pigs."

The Stabs smiled cruelly. He could not believe his luck. The big illiterate oaf. Heide peasant. The uncouth imbecile looked the part. He threw back his head and roared with laughter.

"Swinekeeper. You *smell* like a pig. Repeat it after me. I am a filthy swine. I smell like a pig."

Chuckling came from the ranks.

"He confesses. Take his name."

Again Schultz looked innocently into the staring eyes.

"Pigs don't smell, Herr Stabsfeldwebel. They are clean animals."

Again the Stabs shook with laughter.

"He looks like a swine. He dresses like a swine. He smells like a swine."

The hurt expression upon Schultz's face changed. He began to smile. The smile of a veteran. A man who could not be pushed any further. The real fireworks were about to begin.

A shrill whistle sounded down the column of trucks. Schmidt came running over.

He put himself between the Stabs and Schultz. One more poke in the chest. That was all that was needed. It would take four strong men to pull Schultz off. Officer. Stabs, it did not matter. It had happened more than once before.

Schmidt fought hard to keep a straight face. Both Muller and Heyer were looking straight ahead. Hansen had trouble standing still. Some were openly laughing.

"Wounded are loaded up, Herr Stabsfeldwebel. Hauptmann Schiller requests that the escorts should mount up. The convoy moves off in two minutes."

"Front filth," the Stabs were staring hard at Schultz.

He would not forget that smiling face. Insolence of the peasant.

"When you come back here I will be dealing with you. I will have you doubling through the village until your stinking feet drop off. I broke bigger men than you at Bielefeld. I was the recruiter there for the penal regiments. Yours is a face I will not forget, Grenadier."

Schmidt took command. They were fallen out. A mad scramble was made for the best places upon the trucks and armored troop carriers.

"That runt has signed his name for a transfer. You with me, Heyer?"

"*Ja*. Do you have to ask? Orel is waiting. We can think up a booby trap for him later."

The carriers edged by the line of trucks. Hauptmann Schiller took the salute, still astride his horse. Schmidt and Muller took up their positions behind a mounted Spandau, Schultz and Hansen behind another at the door.

"That Stabs was right. Pigs do smell," spoke up a bright-eyed replacement, not long out of the Hitler Youth.

Schultz got to his feet.

"I must do my duty."

He hit the youth with a hefty backhand blow. He was sent sprawling. Other youths looked wide-eyed at Schultz, fearing the worst. He grabbed the youth, shaking him by his overcoat collar.

"You will say after me, so that everyone can hear. Uncle Schultz's pigs never smelt. He had the cleanest sties upon the whole of the Heide. Schultzy was also very attentive to his stock. Loved them he did like a brother."

Wiping his mouth, the youth looked up.

"Pigs are only pigs."

Muller and Schmidt restrained Schultz.

"Stabs arselicker. You have a debt to pay. For bringing down shame upon my name, that is one full bottle of vodka you owe me. It must be delivered to me in the correct regulation manner after the wounded are unloaded in Orel. You will make a survey of all the brothels. You will report back to me when you have found a Mongol tart to satisfy my gentlemanly desires. Is that understood?"

The rest of the convoy duty passed in peace. Even the partisans failed to show themselves. Maybe the bitter cold got to them as well. It was so different over that same pure black earth in 1941.

Early October and fourth panzer had fought their way into Kromny. There was a windmill out there. Heavy Maxim emplacement. Ivan snipers who fought to the death. The metalled road was reached leading to Orel. It was an important road and rail center, having many factories.

Metalled road helped. Panzers and Grenadier sped

ahead. Landser dealt with the stubborn pockets of resistance. Orel had to be secured at all costs. Nothing stopped the raging advance. Everything crumpled before it. In Orel ivan was taken completely and utterly by surprise. People were queueing at the shops. Grenadiers upon the backs of the leading panzers looked at through the tram windows by the startled passengers. It was like a mock war. Crated machines were still being loaded aboard freight trains at the railway station, for shipment to beyond the Urals.

Winter came in one night. Snow. By morning there was knee-deep mud everywhere. A black foul-smelling liquid. Nowhere else is there mud like Russian mud. That was the night of October 6th. In places panzers ground to a halt. It was a short, sharp, gentle taste of what was to come.

Reforming. The headlong push to Mzensk. Swarming T.34s in force seemed to come out of nowhere. Massed ivan infantry. Again and again they threw themselves at the Wehrmacht positions. It became a massive slaughtering ground.

The lot of the panzer gunner was a real horrific nightmare. The only place to hit the T.34s was above the grating to the rear, just over the engine. The driver had to whip the panzer around fast to get into the best position. Go like hell to stay there. Hope the gunner's nerves would last. He could not afford to miss. There was only one chance. Most times one single shot. Stop. Fire. Get away quick.

Orel airfield came into view. Heinkels and Stukas were fueling up. A head-hunter roadblock flagged the convoy down. They patrolled their territory like vultures. At times, especially during a retreat, they were more feared than ivan. Theirs is not a proud record. Many swung from the bough of a tree after being stopped by the Field Police.

Papers and movement orders were checked. All escorts had to stand down, lining up in front of their vehicles. A young, smooth-faced lieutenant came down the line, a guard on either side of him carrying submachine guns.

He stopped near the drawn-up escorts.

"The wounded will go to the base hospital. After that, Unteroffiziers and Feldwebels will report with their men to the sanitation detail. I will not have them roaming the streets of Orel in such unkempt condition. Look at yourselves. You look more like ivan prisoners than Deutscher *Soldaten*".

He gave Schmidt a sharp look of distaste. Tugged at his padded Siberian jacket with elegantly gloved hands.

"What are your men doing wearing those stupid fur caps? That is not regulation Wehrmacht dress. Where are their helmets? Those fur hats. You were not issued with them. Where did they come from?"

He was obviously new to the East.

"From ivan, Herr Leutnant."

"They will be thrown away. In future while on active service you will wear your helmets. In Orel we go about our duty properly dressed. Slack, unsoldierly behavior is not tolerated here. Do your officers never lecture you? Ours is a cause out here in the East. These men look like *Untermensch* from the Todt Organization. Mount up and be on your way."

Slowly the convoy moved off. The head-hunter motorcycles and side cars disappeared from view.

"Toy soldier," laughed Heyer.

"Did you see his white lace handkerchief?"

"Had a family crest on it, it did. Either that or the brothel laundry mark from Frederichstrasse."

Schultz was busy unloading one of the mounted Spandaus.

"*Los*. Coming up on the right. Women. Real live

387

stuff with legs." He stopped breathless, his mouth hanging open.

Four laughing Ukrainian girls with headscarves, high boots and heavy overcoats drew near. They were walking along, arms linked. They waved.

"Drop me, Hansen and Heyer off right here. We'll get a tram and catch up with you common lot later."

He was halfway out of the carrier. Schmidt pulled him back by the scruff of the neck.

"Schultzy, how many more times? We unload the wounded first."

"You saw how that Stabs picked on me. No gentleman, was he? Them girls waved. Brought my confidence back, it did."

"Driver advance," bawled Schmidt.

"Schultz, I've never known anyone like you for stopping the war."

"My front piece needs action."

"So does mine," shouted Hansen.

"And for me the Lord had decreed a fat Ruski Jezebel."

Schmidt kicked the driver in the back. On the pavement a crowd of ivans had gathered, all talking at once, pointing and laughing. Heyer fell among some replacements, as the carrier leaped forward once again.

Schmidt and Muller supervised the unloading of the wounded at the Wehrmacht hospital. Ivan P.O.W.s helped. Some of the gangrene cases had died on the trip. And two cases of tetanus. They looked yellow. Stiff as rock. The eyes are the last thing to go. It is one of the most horrifying forms of death. All that can be done is to hold their hands. Those eyes try to talk. And slowly the seizure grips the whole body.

The ivans were always as gentle as lambs. None took more care with the wounded. It was forbidden to speak to them. Heyer once got ten days for it. He handed them cigarettes. They snatched at them greedily.

"Look after our friend, little Steggeman here," he told them in fluent Russian.

"He is too young for women. You can show him your porno photos. I'm sure the Holy Mother won't mind that. Only twice a week, mind you. With his body temperature going up any more than that, his wounds won't heal properly."

"I take much care, *tovaritch*."

A bearded giant hugged Heyer, knocking the breath out of him.

"I am Igor Konstantin Shalomov. I was in the Red Army Guard battalion. I fought at Bolchov. I know the front. I will look after the little brother. You like he should have vodka, sometimes."

Heyer consulted the others. They nodded. More cigarettes went to the big prisoner of war.

"Get him fixed up with a bit," suggested Hansen.

"*Aschloch*," cried Schultz, cuffing him in the ear. "You want him overactive so his stitches come out? Get gangrene or something. He can have some when his wounds heal. His bowels come right. And not before."

He bent over and soothingly stroked Steggeman's hair into place.

A Wehrmacht orderly finished writing upon his stiff board, then came walking over to them.

"Last one?" he asked Schmidt.

"*Ja.*"

"*Gut.* You can go now. The popovs will take over."

Muller shook hands with Steggeman. Schmidt ruffled his hair. Heyer winked, patting him playfully upon the shoulder. Hansen pressed his hand. Schultz shoved some chocolate bars into his tunic.

"Look after yourself, little friend. Before you know it you will be back with us."

Steggeman pulled a face. He hoped his thigh would at least give him a couple of months in Orel.

The orderly laid a hand upon Schultz's shoulder.

"*Los.* We have work to do here."

Schultz's eyes clouded with tears. He pinched Steggeman under the chin.

"I'm sorry about calling you a shithead," he sobbed.

"Schultzy didn't mean it."

His shoulders were trembling.

"Just you get better. You hear. I will miss you and so will the others."

Steggeman tried to look away. But Schultz's face was too near. He had seen him cry once before, in Kiev. It was not a pretty sight. Knowing tough Schultzy it was still moving, nevertheless.

"I will. I promise."

Rubbing his eyes, Schultz pushed the hand of the orderly away.

"Forgive me for pinching that apple cake from you. The one your mother sent from Berlin in her parcel."

"So, that's where it went," gasped Muller.

Heyer looked at him, shaking his head.

They had thought that the rats had got it. But then Schultz had lost the game of skat and sulked off out of the bunker. No one had given it much more thought.

"I forgive you for pinching my mother's cake, as well.

"You big pig."

Steggeman corrected himself.

"You are bigger than the rest of us. Your body needs more food."

Muller put his arm around Schultz's shoulders.

"If I am unkind to you when you come back,"

Schultz looked hard at Heyer, "I'll stand with my hands behind my back. Heyer can tie them up. And you can beat me, right."

The others had difficulty keeping straight faces.

"I'll look forward to that," answered Steggeman easily.

Schultz looked all the more hurt.

"I only said if I was rotten to you."

"Don't cry, Schultzy. You big lump. I feel better already."

Schultz swung around, lifting the hospital orderly bodily off of his feet.

"My little friend here gets number one treatment, right? If he brings me back bad reports. I'll come looking for you."

Muller and Schmidt led Schultz away. He was crying like a small child.

"Did you hear that Steggeman?" he sobbed. "He's looking forward to giving me a crack in the mouth. Me. After the way I owned up about his mother's cake."

Delousing and showers were quickly dispensed with. There was even a giggling *babushka* giving out the soap.

"Quick dip. One for the road," Schultz suggested lewdly.

"Tonight is the night. Orel has seen nothing yet."

With the large towel wrapped about his waist she chased him with a big flat wooden ladle. He lost the towel out near the dressing hut, in the deep snow. A group of uniformed Blitzmadels whistled, as his bare cheeks rounded the corner into the hut.

"Hung like a bull," shouted one of them.

"Seen better on a butcher's table," laughed another.

Later they wandered into the Wehrmacht canteen.

It was a long low wooden hut not far from the hospital. Near a large brick factory.

Inside, it was full of black-uniformed panzer men on rest leave. Men from the XXIV Panzer Corp. They were stamping their feet, in tune with some mouth organs. Beer glasses thumped upon the tables. Drunken voices were singing.

> *"Muss ich denn, muss ich denn, zum Staedtele hinaus.*
> *Staedtele hinaus, und de mein Schatz bleibst hier."*

The canteen shook with the vibrations. Stamping feet. Pounding beer glasses. The air was thick with cigarette smoke. The three bare light bulbs swung as though keeping in time with the music.

After several beers Muller was the first to speak.

"I wonder if Roman and Mikhial are safe."

"*Ja*. Stop worrying," added Schmidt.

"The partisans will take care of them."

"*Mein lieber Gott*. I can't help thinking about them. Sometimes I dream about them."

Hansen took a long swig at his beer and hit the table with his near-empty glass.

"Only things I dream about are places like Kiev and Orel. Drink up, I'll get another round. Then it's off to the Oka with trousers at half-mast to the nearest brothel. It's back in the line for us tomorrow."

Heyer emptied his glass handing around cigarettes.

"Hein. You are too sensitive for this war."

Muller took the cigarette.

"Is there something wrong with that? All this killing. Some of us cannot shut their eyes like you."

"Did I start this damn war? Am I to blame?"

"For *Gott's* sake," Schmidt chided them. "We have a few hours off. Let's enjoy ourselves. Who knows what tomorrow might bring."

Schultz hit the table with his glass. He burped, nodding at Hansen.

"More beer, slave. Uncle Schultz is thirsty. This time I'll get a Mongol tart like Manheim's. Go at it slow. Really take my time. I can't wait to get to that whore's paradise."

Muller looked disgusted, pulling a face.

"That's what is wrong with the both of you. Guts. Beer and sex. Have you nothing else upon your mind."

"Ukrainian bits," laughed Heyer.

"A real plump bit that nearly flattens me. Just nice so that I have to fight for me breath. Nothing like it."

Hansen came back, spilling beer all over the table.

"Of course, friend Hein here don't want no woman. In one of his prim and proper moods he is. You can come along and just look. We won't charge you for it. Maybe that's how you get your kicks."

"*Arschloch.*"

Schultz rose slightly off his chair, breaking wind.

"Must clean the tubes before I go into action."

A panzer man at the next table called him a swine.

"Fancy having a filthy pig like you in turret."

Schultz shook his fist jokingly under his nose.

"No getting lippy, funny man. On my best behavior, I am. First time out of the line for weeks. Who wants to fight?"

He leaned over, chuckling confidentially. "I've got a date with a Mongol bit."

Slowly and deliberately the panzer man rose to his feet.

"If the foot *Soldat* had as much guts as the panzer

393

men, this war would have been over long ago."

Other black-uniformed men around his table shouted in agreement.

"Yellow-bellied shits," cursed one of them.

"First sign of a T.34 exhaust and they go for cover."

"What about Mzensk?"

Muller got to his feet.

"What about it? If you lot had been more active. Had more go in you. . . ."

The fight began. Schultz grabbed one of the panzer men and threw him bodily against the wall.

"Make it quick. My front piece needs the workout, not my knuckles."

Hansen was standing on the table. He took another slug at his beer. Someone hit the table. He lost his balance.

"Who wants to fight. Remember we've only got two hours."

Beer was thrown in Muller's face. He was kicked low in the gut. A panzer man moved in with flying fists. Heyer lashed out at a grinning face with the butt of his Schmeisser. Schmidt was knocked cold before he had time to get to his feet, by a half-empty bottle of vodka.

"The tarts. Don't forget the tarts."

A chair hit Hansen across the head and shoulders.

No one really took much notice of the scruffy young Russian boy in the simple cloth hat. He took no notice of the rough-housing. Who would ever understand Germanski? He continued going from table to table selling his wares. He had Germanski and Italian cigarettes.

In his pocket there were the two hard shapes of the hand grenades. Frequent the same places of Germanski relaxation for weeks on end. That is what they had told him. After not many days the *Soldats* would make jokes. Familiarity. It always worked.

"Ruski. Your cigarettes are too expensive. Got any new porno photos?" laughed a drunken medical orderly in Russian.

"Them Oriental ones," he winked, beer flowing from the corner of his mouth.

"Them ones where they play dipping into the honey pots. You know."

The boy tried to slip by the groping hands. The canteen was full. Many *Soldats*. Lots in black uniforms. Others. Fighting *Soldats*. His two hand grenades would do much damage.

"*Nyet. Nein, Nein,* Herr *Soldat*. No photos today. All sold. Only *Zigaretten*. Germanski. Iti . . . you like."

He tried to smile, but it was hard. His hands were sweating.

The medical orderly insisted.

"I know you've got photos."

He made a grab at the boy's arm.

"Manfred says you have them in your inside pocket. Here . . ." He lunged at him, taking a hold of his shoulder.

The boy tried to shake him loose. Those drunken eyes peered into his.

"*Komm, kind. Los.* Honey nights. I want to see."

The boy's hands went to his pockets. It was for his promised one. Such long beautiful long hair. It had to be this very night. Lice. They had abused her. His flower. Nurses were taking care of her. The disease had gone to her head. Nurses said she was insane. It sometimes happened that way. There were not enough medical supplies to treat her in time. All she did was stroke the little new kitten. Stare into the hot stove.

"*Nyet*. Photos all finished, Herr *Soldat*."

Last night of the black-uniformed *Soldats'* rest days. Killing many would leave the steel monsters without crews. On one part of the front it would slow Germanski down.

"*Komm*. The photos."

How he had argued with the older men. Day after day.

"I must go to Orel. I must avenge my loved one."

At first they would not listen.

"Stay here. We will strike at their supply lines. There will be more than enough revenge for all."

"*Nyet. Nyet.*"

He had kicked the table over. Beat at the broad chest with his fists. Beat at it. And cried with the tears of a child.

"You talk to me in this way. I am soon to become a man. You have not sat the long hours with the maiden. Looked into those eyes. They are dead. The nurses fed her. There is nothing there. She touches the kitten. When I come near she slinks away. I am my father's son. This I must do alone. I must take many with one blow. No man of the forest has the right to share in my revenge."

He turned away from the medical orderly, unscrewing the caps upon the hand grenades. He would tell his loved one. Tell her that the revenge had been taken in her name. Maybe her mouth would open. The words would come. Once he had struck. Struck at the hated lice.

"*Das kind.*"

The orderly had seen the grenades.

"*Kind*. He's armed."

Other drunken eyes saw the grenades.

"*Runter!* Down!"

Those at the nearest two tables dived for cover.

The boy in the simple cloth cap ran for the door. He tossed the hand grenades at the milling crowd of fighting *Soldats*. It was good. He felt his body glow. He sighed, still looking, eyes full of hate. They would do much damage. Many would never see their homeland again. He ran out into the night.

Now he was a boy soldier no longer. No more would they call him Viktor, son of the blacksmith. Revenge was his. Tanya. Tanya. It is done. He ran crying into the cold night air.

The two hand grenades went off in quick succession. Twin blinding explosions. Sounding like the roar of artillery in the confined space. Chatter. Fighting. Swaying bodies. The boisterous singing was cut as though with a sharp knife. Choking smoke filled the canteen. The nightmarish screaming. Shattered glass ripping through the air. Bodies crashing into one another. Then came the cries of alarm.

"Alert. Alert."

Front-weary Feldwebels took command. They quickly put a cordon around the area of the canteen. Others were detailed off setting up roadblocks.

Wounded were tended to. Eight were dead. Seven beyond help. They were lying among the overturned tables and broken glass. Many had torn stomachs.

"*Hilfe. Hilfe.*"

Blinded one lurched out into the darkness of the night. He leant against the wall, blood streaming down his face.

"*Halt. Wer ist da?*"

He tried to mumble. His eyes were full of blood. It welled in his throat.

A submachine gun chattered, short violent flame stabbing the air.

"Over here. I've got one of the swine. Here. *Schnell.*"

Two drunken panzer men urinated against the brick wall of the factory.

"Fireworks. Come to Orel for a rest. See what happens." His *Kamerade* laughed.

"Old ivan never gives up."

He buttoned up his fly.

"*Tovaritch. Nix ponemayu*. Comrade, don't understand."

They broke into a fit of laughter.

Another Landser Schmeisser spat death.

"Over here. Think I winged one."

Running footsteps sounded in the snow.

"You dumb shit." An Obergefreiter straightened up after over the bodies.

"You've killed two of ours."

"They were talking Russian."

"I'll have your name and number," shouted a voice full of authority.

"Never fire until the target is properly identified."

"Not where I come from, *Kamerade*. Wait that long in my company lines and you are one dead shit."

Not far away, within view of the steep banks of the River Oka, staff officers of General Von Paulas's 6th Army were going over their maps.

"Gentlemen. June 28th is the Fuehrer's decision. Fourth Panzer Army will attack with over eight hundred panzers and assault guns."

There were smiles of approval all round.

"The popovs expect us to go for Moscow again. We will attack between Kursk and Kharkov. Aim for Voronezh. Swing right. . . ."

There were gasps of approval from the assembled red-braided officers.

"The 6th Army will have the honor of going for Stalingrad."

Glasses were raised once again in toasts.

All was quie in ward 1A on the second floor of the military hospital. A nurse arrived pushing a trolley.

"Come, children. Bare your souls."

She advanced towards Schultz's bed, throwing back the bedclothes.

"Not again, sister. I'm no pin cushion."

"Turn over and show me what you are made of."

She slapped his gleaming white rear end.

Hansen sat up in bed laughing.

"Treat him real rough, sister. The rougher the better. He likes it that way."

She turned, putting the syringe to the light.

"You are all very lucky to be alive." She looked over at Hansen's grinning face.

"You have nothing to laugh about, young man. You are the next."

"Me too." Heyer hid the vodka bottle under his mattress.

The sister smiled.

"All of you. That goes for you too, Grenadier Muller. And you Unteroffizier Schmidt."

Schultz feigned a scream as the needle went home.

Hansen's bedclothes were pulled back. A resounding slap of flesh against flesh.

"Anyone ever tell you you had cold hands, sister?"

She rubbed low on his buttocks.

"Nice. Nice. Don't stop now. My trip to Orel was not for nothing."

Then the needle went in.

FIRST-RATE ADVENTURES FOR MEN